THE FLAME KING'S CAPTIVE

FIRE AND DESIRE BOOK ONE

CHLOE CHASTAINE

LILITH VINCENT

He snatched me from the jaws of death for one reason—to be his.

I was a dead king's sacrificial bride, until his murderer claimed me as his. Zabriel invaded my country of Maledin on the back of a monstrous, fire-breathing dragon and took me prisoner.

The lethal Zabriel towers over me in steel plate armor, and he could easily crush the life out of me—but the Flame King isn't interested in harming me. Instead, he destroys everyone who has hurt me in a storm of fire and vengeance.

There's malignant rot deep within my country. My family has vanished along with whole villages of people. As I desperately try to find those who are missing, my body and heart awaken under a powerful and alarming force.

Zabriel sets my soul ablaze every time he growls, "*Mine.*" He calls me Omega. The rarest. The most precious. The one he craves to possess and protect.

When evil forces in Maledin threaten everyone I know and love, there's only one person who is strong enough to help me defeat them, and the only place where I'm safe from an ancient foe is in the arms of the Flame King.

Author's note: The Flame King's Captive is a slow-burn non-shifter MF omegaverse romance set in a fantasy world of magic and dragonriders. Zabriel is a jealous and possessive Alpha, and

Isavelle is a sweet but strong virgin Omega heroine. This is the first book in the Fire and Desire trilogy. It contains steamy content that increases with each subsequent book and ends on a cliffhanger.

THE FLAME KING'S CAPTIVE by CHLOE CHASTAINE

Cover design by The Book Brander
Editing by Fox Proof Editing
Proofreading by Rumi Khan

Created with Vellum

I am indebted to the glorious fitness reels posted by Christian Koutny. I never made it to the gym, but he did inspire me to show up to this Word document day after day, so thank you for the motivation, Christian. You make a lovely Flame King.

AUTHOR'S NOTE

Dear readers, I've been dying to escape into a lush fantasy world filled with magic, peril, and a dangerously sexy hero. Lilith Vincent and Chloe Chastaine are the same person, and if you've read my Lilith books, you'll be familiar with my medium-burn style and obsessed and dangerous heroes. The burn in this book is slower, but the chemistry and attraction are high, and the hero is triple-shot obsessed with his girl. That's what I love best about fated mates and omegaverse romances, the connection between the two main characters that makes them blind to everyone else, even when one of them is fighting it.

This book has a size difference, knotting, slicks, nesting, and scenting (but no shifting). Zabriel is a batshit obsessed hero, and Isavelle is innocent and sweet but clever enough to wrangle this king. On a serious note, this book has swearing, blood, violence, death, and detailed sex scenes on page. It is not suitable for those under eighteen.

If we've never met before, thank you so much for being here and picking up this book. I hope you love the jealous type as much as I do. Even his dragon is obsessed with her.

1

Isavelle

Freezing winds from the northern mountains whip across the clearing, driving flurries of snow and ash into the air. Two Brethren Guard have a merciless grip on my upper arms as they drag me toward the towering funeral pyre. Heat scorches my face, and my bare feet stumble over the frozen, rocky ground. My hands are bound and my mouth is gagged.

I can't run.

I can't scream.

My body is covered in bruises and cuts, and I've been deprived of food and sleep for three days. From behind my long veil, I glimpse dozens of Brethren in their robes, hands buried in their sleeves, and Brethren Guard in battle-scarred armor. The air is thick with the acrid scent of burning flesh and incense.

The Brethren drone on, chanting their hymns as the guards drag me through the watching, silent crowd. The mood is more like a funeral than a wedding, which is fitting considering my bridegroom is ashes and charred bone atop a burning pyre. There will be no vows spoken today. I'll be joined forever with my husband, King Alaster, when they throw me atop the burning pyre, my fiery death the last hope the Brethren have to turn this war around.

What a great privilege it was that I was chosen above all others for this sacred duty.

I spat in the High Priest's face when he told me that, which earned me a fresh coating of whip marks. I know why, of all the Veiled Virgins, they chose me to wed King Alaster. Because of my disobedience. My impiety. My insolence. The High Priest is so fragile, so paranoid, that he couldn't bear my contemptuous glances and small acts of rebellion, like mouthing the words of my prayers instead of saying them.

He's watching me now with a gloating smile twisting his lips. His gray eyes bore into me as firelight glimmers on his short, silver-flecked beard. With my hands bound and my mouth gagged, I'm finally what he's always wanted me to be. Willing. Silent.

Defeated.

At the last harvest equinox over a year ago, I was wrenched from my home and family as part of the tithe that the Brethren demand from every village in Maledin. One-tenth of the harvest and livestock. If there is not enough food to sustain everyone that coming winter, they take daughters of the village instead. The harvest failed, and the animals were sickly, so I knew they'd be coming. I hid my sister, two other girls, and myself, but I didn't hide well enough. I was dragged onto a cart and sent to live in the monasteries where I became a Veiled Virgin and was forced to serve the men I hate most in the world.

The Brethren rule over the people of Maledin with a bruising fist as they preach the word of God. We're taught that death is a gift and suffering is a privilege. If we're not suffering, then we're probably sinning. The Brethren's decrees are enforced by the Brethren Guard, armed soldiers who force the people of Maledin to attend church if they will not go, flog families, and execute those convicted of blasphemy. They are our absolute overlords, and our kings are their puppets, though it's rumored that the Brethren serve another, known only as the Shadow King, and he is crueler and more merciless even than his devoted servants.

But all that changed a week ago when the dragons came.

They erupted out of the north, breathing fire and filling the skies. Improbable creatures. *Impossible* creatures. Churches are on fire, hundreds of dead Brethren Guard litter the roads, and Brethren priests have run screaming into the forests.

All my life, we told each other tales of dragons and dragonriders on long winter nights, but that's all they were. Stories. The Brethren hated us telling those tales, and anyone caught would be beaten and tortured. My favorite tale was called 'The Mountain Prisoner,' about a fierce dragonrider and the rightful ruler of Maledin who was betrayed by a wicked mage and trapped beneath the Bodan Mountains hundreds of years ago. The Brethren preached that there was nothing in the Bodan Mountains to the north except for bloodthirsty wolves, bears, and snow. Dragons and dragonriders belong to immoral tales not befitting the pious followers of the one true God.

Now the Brethren being slaughtered by the creatures they claimed do not exist.

I've heard their leader rides an enormous black dragon and has burning coals for eyes. Some of the Veiled Virgins were whispering that he comes from the depths of the underworld. A creature from hell walking among us.

King Alaster was slain in battle yesterday, supposedly bravely defending the capital. Seeing as his body is here, hundreds of miles from Lenhale where he was meant to have fallen, I suspect that he was really fleeing south for his life.

His spirit must be appeased with a bride to follow him into the next world, or Maledin will never rise up and defeat the invaders.

The funeral pyre roars greedily. I can feel the heat through my veil. When I dig my heels in and whimper, the soldiers pulling me along resort to dragging me across the ground. A few more feet and they will toss me into the flames. Heat scorches my legs. A log rolls off the pyre and showers my feet in sparks, and I'd scream if it wasn't for the gag.

Despair and rage flare in my heart.

I hope the dragons burn them all.

Every single Brethren and Brethren Guard, and they're all sent screaming to hell.

The soldiers grasp my underarms and lift me as the Brethren's chanting reaches a crescendo.

Overhead, there's a mind-shredding roar. The sky darkens as an enormous shape eclipses the pale winter sun. I glance up through my gauzy veil and make out an enormous scaled and clawed foreleg the size of a house descending right on top of me. The soldiers holding me release my arms and run, but I haven't got time to do anything except fling myself away from the pyre and fall on my stomach.

There's a crunch, and the earth shudders beneath me. When the dust and ash settle, an enormous black dragon is visible. It's landed on top of the funeral pyre, stomping the flames, and what was left of my bridegroom, out of existence.

A *dragon.*

And I'm lying on the ground between its scaled forelegs.

I've seen their likeness carved into rocks that line the road up into the Bodan Mountains; warnings not to go that way, for the monstrous creatures slumber, awaiting the day their riders will return to summon them to battle. I would touch those carvings and *wish*. What a foolish child I was, for now I'm about to be trampled to death by the ravenous black beast on top of me.

There are half a dozen *whomp* sounds that I suspect are more dragons landing in the clearing, and snarling roars erupt all around us.

The High Priest shrieks, "Demon! How dare you desecrate King Alaster's funeral? His bride was about to join him on the pyre."

Demon?

There's a sliding sound from atop the black dragon, and two armored feet hit the ground an arm's length from where I lay. I crane my head up, and I can tell I'm looking at the biggest man I've ever seen. This giant stands head and shoulders taller than the guards and Brethren, plate armor gleaming on his broad body and a cloak swirling around his shoulders. A curtain of black hair cascades down his back.

His left hand lazily holds the hilt of his sheathed sword, and he glances toward the High Priest and inquires, "Bride?"

The High Priest points to me lying beneath the dragon.

The invader glances over his shoulder, and if he's surprised to see me there, I can't tell because of my veil. He hunkers down on his heels, one hand braced against the dragon's flank, and there's a smirk in his voice as he says, "Hello, little queen. I apologize. What's left of your bridegroom has been ground into dust."

He's not sorry at all. The man's deep baritone is tinged with amusement. I can't make out much of his face, but there are dark smudges on his jaw that look like blood or mud. The inside of his black cloak is lined with crimson.

"You can be burned alive another day if you wish it. Come out from beneath Scourge." He holds out a gauntleted hand that's bigger than my head, but I can't take it with my arms tied behind my back.

When I don't reach for his hand, he growls, "I haven't got time for this," before grasping me under the arm and pulling me to my feet. I stumble and he grabs me, and when he feels my bound arms beneath the veil, his impatience changes to surprise. "Blood and dragon piss. You're tied up?"

Did he think I was eager to be flung atop a burning pyre?

I've always been short, but next to this giant of a man and his hulking black dragon, I feel like an ant. The top of my head just clears the invader's elbows.

Whatever the stranger was about to say is drowned out by a battle cry and shouts of "*Kill the demon!*" The Brethren Guard are attacking the invaders, and the clash of steel rings out across the clearing. Plumes of fire and smoke erupt left and right, and men scream in pain.

The invader draws an enormous broadsword and parries a blow from one of the attacking guards. He raises his armored foot and shoves the man toward the black dragon's snout. The monster opens its jaws and bites the guard in two with a sickening crunch of bones.

The High Priest appears at my side and tries to grab hold of me, snarling, "You're coming with me."

I've had enough of men pulling me around, and I dash in the other direction, past the dragon's foreleg, and toward the cloaked invader. I'm not running to him for protection. I'm trying to get past him and flee the clearing, but just then the wind changes. The edge of my veil whips into the air and brushes his armor. His long, dark hair dances in the gust.

The invader turns toward me, his sword lowering as if he's in a trance. I can't make out the expression on his face, but the nape of my neck prickles.

"*Sha'len*," he says in a husky, intense voice.

He steps toward me. The gag is so tight around my lips that I can't make one peep of protest, but I shake my head emphatically, and I twist my bound wrists back and forth as I back away from him.

Don't pay attention to me.

I'm not important.

I'm no one.

A guard runs toward him with his sword raised, but the invader is staring at me and doesn't turn to defend himself. The black dragon snatches the attacker up with its jaws and tosses him out of the clearing like he's a rag doll, and his scream fades on the wind.

I keep backing away, but the invader follows me, breathing hard and walking like he's in a dream. Fire erupts to my right, lighting his face, and I can make out the slash of his dark brows and eyes that seem to burn like red coals, though that must be a trick of the firelight.

Does he mean to kill me? Have I angered him somehow?

Behind him, the massive dragon is watching the battle, its teeth snapping left and right as it defends its master.

A scream comes from atop a nearby hill. "*Kill the invaders. Kill the demon.*" Reinforcements have arrived, and Brethren Guard race down the hill toward us, hollering their battle cries. The black dragon snarls, and the invader's attention is finally drawn away from me.

I turn and run, but I'm not fast enough. The invader reaches out and grasps my wrist through the veil. I squeal in the back of my throat, wrenching against his grip.

"Fuck," the invader growls, and looks left and right as if trying to decide something. A moment later, the invader loops an arm around my waist and pulls me against him. Every ridge of his steel plate armor digs into my scored flesh. He lifts me off the ground and carries us upward until he swings his leg over something and settles me in front of him. There's a lot more light up here without the enormous black dragon blocking out the sun. Then I realize why.

We're sitting *on* the enormous black dragon.

Two huge wings rise up on either side, and the ground lurches beneath us. I squeal again, and the invader's arms tighten around me. I twist back and forth in his embrace, trying to wriggle free, and exclaim urgently, "*Mmph—*"

The man holding on to me murmurs soothingly in my ear, "Don't be frightened. I've got you."

That's exactly what I'm afraid of. The black monster's

wings beat the air, and we lurch into the sky. My eyes go wide and I scream, thin and high in the back of my throat.

I'm trapped in the invader's iron embrace. What I can see of the ground drops away with alarming speed, as if the earth is collapsing into hell and we're on the brink of plunging after it.

2

Isavelle

Demon.

That's what the Brethren called the invader, and as he effortlessly sits astride a fire-breathing dragon as it soars through the air, I'm inclined to believe them.

The ground spirals beneath us. Wind whips past us, growing colder and colder. Perhaps he's going to fling me from dragonback, and I'll be smashed to pieces on the ground, punishment for being about to wed the enemy king. I didn't even have the chance to tell him I wasn't a willing bride.

The stranger pushes his hands beneath my veil, and I shake my head frantically from side to side as he gropes around. Strong hands. Searching hands.

"Relax. I'm not going to hurt you," he rumbles in my ear.

There's a *schhk* of a knife, and the rope falls away from my wrists. The burning pain in my shoulders suddenly dissipates, and my eyes close in relief.

The invader holds out the cut ropes, and the wind snatches them from his fingers, whipping them away behind us.

I reach up beneath my veil to yank the gag from between my teeth and moisten my parched lips. I hold on to the gag, taking deep lungfuls of air. I'm not free, but I'm a little freer than I was a few moments ago, though there's still a huge, armored man holding me tight against him.

When the dragon beats its wings, the horizon pitches and falls with the undulations of its body. A pang of queasiness sweeps through my belly and my head spins.

I don't think I like flying.

"What is your name?" the stranger says into my ear so I can hear him over the wind.

As I open my mouth to answer, a wave of nausea ripples up from my stomach, and I clamp both hands over my mouth.

"What's wrong?" he asks urgently, his arms tightening around my waist.

I clutch his wrist, wishing he wouldn't squeeze me like that. There's no food in my stomach, but I can feel acid creeping up the back of my throat.

"You're sick?" The stranger hooks an arm under my knees and rearranges me so that I'm curled against him. He speaks in a low, soothing voice as he wraps his cloak around the both of us. "It's all right, *sha'len*. The journey is short and you will soon be on the ground."

The world goes dark as he presses my face into his neck.

My cheek is pillowed on the thick fur around his shoulders. I feel slightly less sick now I can't see the horizon moving, but the dragon is still rising and falling beneath us.

"I'll help you," he murmurs.

I wait, wondering what he's about to do.

Nothing whatsoever happens.

The wind continues to whistle past us, and the dragon beats its wings. I take a deep breath, and the stranger seems...relieved. Though I don't know how I know that. Or perhaps I'm the one who's relieved because all my aches and pains begin to fade away. My fingers and toes feel warm. The burning behind my tired eyelids diminishes. I want to *sleep*.

I recall the story of the king under the mountain, and I wonder if he felt as comfortable as this as he drifted off to sleep for hundreds of years.

We pitch forward and into a turn, but I'm only mildly interested in what's happening now. The stranger. He's so *warm*. Even his armor feels comfortable where it's pressing into my side. One of his large hands is wrapped around my upper thigh, and I snuggle into his touch. He gives a low chuckle and squeezes my flesh. I've always had plump thighs, and he seems to like what he feels.

It feels like we're gliding peacefully through the skies. If dragonflight were always like this, it wouldn't be so bad after all.

We hit the ground with an almighty jolt, and my eyes snap open. One of my arms is wrapped around the stranger's waist. My other hand is playing with a silky tress of his long, dark hair, twirling it around and around my finger like a lovesick maid.

He smirks down at me cuddled against him. "As much as I'm enjoying this, *sha'len*, I have a battle to return to."

I rip myself away from him with a gasp. What the hell was I thinking?

With an arm around me, he swings his leg over the saddle, holds on to something, and we slither to the ground. His booted feet hit first to absorb the impact, and then he sets me gently on the grass.

"Godric," he bellows in the loudest voice I've ever heard. "Godric, where the *fuck*—"

"Commander?" calls a voice from the other side of the dragon.

"Ah, there you are. Godric, come here and show this woman to my tent. Don't let anyone else enter, and guard her like you would guard me."

His tent. *His tent*. I don't want to go anywhere near this man's tent. I want to go home. To hell with the Brethren and being a Veiled Virgin, and to hell with this invader. I want my family. Ma and Dad. My brother and sister. For all of us to be together again.

The stranger turns back to me, and his tone is filled with warmth and velvet. "I will say goodbye, though it makes me ache to leave you." He reaches for the hem of my veil. He even takes it in his fingers and starts to pull it up over my head but changes his mind.

"No. That will be my reward for killing everyone who tried to harm you." He bows his head and brings the edge of the veil to his lips and kisses it. "I won't be long. This is the safest place in Maledin, and no one will harm what belongs to me."

I wish the stranger could see me scowling at him behind

this veil. What belongs to him? I won't be a tithe, or a sacrifice, or whatever this man wants me to be. I bring my hands up to shove him away from me. My palms land on his chest plate, but before I can push him, he wraps his hands lovingly around my wrists, and the delighted note in his voice tells me he thought I was reaching out for him.

"I don't want to go either, because if you are who I think you are..."

To my horror, he leans his huge body down and buries his face in my throat, inhaling deeply. Then he groans, a delicious sound like melted butter dripping from a hot scone that caresses me from the tips of my toes to the roots of my hair. It takes a full minute for the vibrations to dissipate, and by then, he's letting me go and climbing up the dragon's flank.

I swipe my throat and then stare at my hand. Did I get coated in something that smells good to enemy invaders? Or is he a lunatic?

"I wasn't trying to make you..." I start to say, but it's too late. "...stay."

The dragon's enormous wings unfurl and darken the sky, and a powerful gust of wind knocks me on my ass.

There's a frantic shout on the other side of the camp. I look up and see a soldier in armor drawing his sword and running away from me, heading for an entrance gate. Fighting has broken out, swords are clashing, and soldiers all around me are rushing over to defend it. So much for this being the safest place in Maledin.

I'm not waiting here to be dragged into that barbarian's bed. I scramble to my feet and duck into a nearby tent after checking that it's empty. With my eye to the tent flap, I watch as invader soldiers clash swords with Brethren Guard.

There's a silvery blur in the sky, and something darts over the battle. It disappears from view, and two Brethren Guard crumple to the ground.

What was that? A dragon?

The dragon I flew on and the ones I glimpsed at the funeral were enormous creatures and couldn't possibly move that fast. Three more times something very fast appears out of nowhere and takes out Brethren Guard. Whatever they are, they're vicious, and they'll quickly kill all the guards at the gate.

I draw back from the tent flap, thinking quickly. If I stay here, I'll be in the hands of the enemy, and stars and skies know what will happen to me when that black-haired invader returns. I could return to the monasteries and seek shelter among the Brethren, but the monasteries and churches are burning, and the Brethren just tried to sacrifice me to the dead king. The invaders and the Brethren are not my people. My people are at home, in Amriste.

With a pang, I think longingly of the home I was torn away from a year ago. Amriste was where I grew up. Amriste is where my family will be, and with this invasion going on, I'm worried for their safety. Ma and Dad have never been farther than the nearest market town in all their lives. Anise is fourteen and was probably up a tree two miles from home when the invasion began, eating stolen apples. Waylen is twelve and afraid of storms, so the dragons in the sky must be paralyzing him with terror.

What if they're all dead? A dragon might have burned the whole village. A dragon might have landed on our cottage and trampled them to death. Invader soldiers could have razed the village, and those silver blurs attacked them in the fields when they ran for their lives. They could be shivering and starving in the cold right now. Dad's lungs were never strong. They could all be lost. They could all be dead.

I press my hand over my heart and find it racing dangerously fast. If I panic now, I'll be no help at all to my family. With Maledin being torn apart from the inside out, the safest thing for us to do is flee over the border to the west into Grendu. I have heard dark rumors about that land, that it's full of evil magic, but at least it's peaceful. I'll return home, gather my family, and we'll start walking toward the border. Maybe I can even persuade the whole village to come with us.

Now that I have a plan, I start to feel calmer, and I take a look around the tent. There are half a dozen sleeping pallets on the ground, an open chest of weaponry, and another filled with foot soldiers' clothing. Shirts, breeches, jackets, simple helms, with muddy boots in a row nearby.

I'll be conspicuous wherever I go if I keep wearing this clothing. I haul the heavy veil from my head, tip up my chin, and take a deep breath of fresh air. The stench of smoke from the funeral pyre finally dissipates, and I ball up the veil and shove it under a sleeping pallet, where hopefully no one will find it until I'm long gone.

The soldiers who own this clothing seem to be tall and narrow. I'm on the short side, and I'm rounded as well, so I have to wriggle a pair of breeches over my bottom, roll the hems up about ten times, and then stuff the bulging cuffs into too-big boots. These clothes were made for someone with no bottom and enormous feet, so everything feels too tight *and* too loose. The shirt is a little easier to deal with since I'm able to stuff most of the length into the breeches and rip off the cuffs. There's an old jacket at the very bottom of the chest that seems to have shrunk in the wash, though it still swamps my shoulders. I bundle up my long, dirty blonde hair beneath a helm and squash it down.

I probably look ridiculous and not at all like one of the soldiers currently defending the camp, but at least I'll draw less attention this way than in a white dress and veil.

With every soldier still fighting at the gates, I'm able to sneak out of the tent and over to a damaged section of fence. It's been hit hard by something, and I wiggle through a small gap and out the other side. From there, it's a short dash across some open ground and then I'm surrounded by scrubby trees.

Freedom. For the first time in over a year.

I alternately run and walk through the woods. I have no idea where I am or how far I'm going to have to walk to reach my village, but right now I'm flushed with excitement and relief.

I don't know what the invader will do when he comes back from battle to find I'm not in his tent or at the camp, but I have no doubt he'll soon forget all about me.

3

Isavelle

I've seen Maledin in spring and summer when fields and meadows are bursting with blades of green grass and wildflowers in a hundred delicate shades. I've seen fall sweep across the land, turning everything gold and crimson while berries grow fat and sweet on thorny vines. I've witnessed dry winters like this one where only a few snowflakes are blown over bare ground, as well as winters when the drifts stand as tall as houses and we have to dig ourselves out of our own front doors.

But I've never seen Maledin like this before.

I stand at the crest of a hill, gazing into the valley below. Smoke belches from a burned-out monastery and guard barracks. I can guess which creatures left those long, blackened streaks on the earth.

There's a roar above me, and I shrink back into the bushes as three of them fly overhead.

Dragons.

I study the enormous creatures closely, wondering if one of them belongs to the commander, but the dragons in the sky aren't black, and they're not quite so large. The biggest dragon is snow white with shades of sky blue at the tips of its claws and tail. It's flanked by two smaller dragons, one a bright apricot, and the other dove gray. The graceful movements of their wings and undulating bodies captivate me. These monsters are beautiful but deadly. As they bank to the left, I catch sight of the riders perched between the dragons' wings. They hold no reins and don't call out commands, but they sit in saddles and gaze ahead as if they're the ones in charge.

A few moments later, the dragons and their riders disappear beyond the hills, and I can breathe once again.

As the smoke clears, I see something on the horizon. A jagged cliff that juts over a distant valley, which has been a familiar sight every market day all my life, though I always saw it from the other side. If I follow the way that cliff is pointing, I'll find my village.

Desperately, I scan the skies. Will I be able to make it all that way without being seen? It will take me more than a day of walking, and probably closer to two.

Whatever happens, I'm not any closer to home just by standing here, so I set off.

I don't want to walk along the road that's being used by Brethren Guard, so I follow the stream instead, knowing it will eventually join the river that flows beneath that jagged cliff. I stay beneath the canopies of the leafless trees as much as I can and dive into scrub when I think I hear marching or the beating of leathery wings.

By dusk, I'm dizzy with hunger and my feet are an agony of burst blisters. Even walking up a small hill makes spots dance before my eyes. I drink freezing water from the spring, but there's nothing to eat in this barren, wintry landscape.

At nightfall, I spy some outbuildings set back from a dark little house, and I'm desperate and cold enough to approach them. My stomach aches from hunger and my fingers and toes are stiff and swollen.

Inside one of the outbuildings, I climb a ladder into the hayloft with painfully frozen fingers and bleeding toes. I heap hay over myself and lay there shivering, trying to ignore my twisting, aching belly.

Something moves against my leg, and I nearly scream, thinking it's a rat come to gnaw on my body before I'm even dead. I sit up and see the shape of something small and furry in the dark. Bigger than a rat, and fluffier too.

I breathe a sigh of relief when I realize it's a cat with green eyes, a great deal of tawny fur, and tabby markings. It yawns luxuriously and stretches its forelegs, extending ten sharp claws. Its eyes half close, and it seems about to put its head back down and drift off to sleep again when there's a clattering from downstairs.

While the cat seems unbothered, I freeze.

"Puss-puss!" a woman calls.

I put my eye to a crack in the boards and see that a woman has placed a saucer of milk down by the door. The cat gets to its feet, arches its back, and pads its way through the hay to the ladder.

I listen as the woman's footsteps fade away before

following the cat down the ladder and lifting it away from the saucer before it can start lapping. "Sorry about this."

I'm not that sorry, though. This cat is soft around the belly and feels like it consumes saucers of milk night and day.

The cat watches with an affronted expression as I take a mouthful from its saucer of creamy milk. I don't think I've tasted anything more delicious, but I've barely swallowed it down when there's a screech behind me.

"Who in the bleeding hell are you? A cowardly deserter in my barn? Get gone with you, back to where you came from."

The woman has come back and she has a broom in her hands, raised high.

"I'm not a—"

She swings the broom right at my head. I drop the saucer and it smashes on the ground, sending shards of ceramic and splashes of milk everywhere. The cat streaks away in panic. I duck away and run for the door, narrowly missing a swipe of the broom, and race out into the night.

I keep running until I'm lost among the trees, trip over a root, and go sprawling through the freezing mud.

Whimpering and shaking, I peel myself off the ground and limp over to the base of a large tree. I can't see anything in the dark, so I curl into a ball and try not to cry. The cold night air bites into my ears and fingers, and I start shivering violently.

Maybe I should just give up.

Lie down in the dirt and wait to die. It probably won't be long. Between my hunger and the cold, I'm weak enough that half an inch of snowfall would finish me off. No one cares about me, and not a soul knows where I am. My family will think I died by dragonfire in a monastery, loyal to Maledin to the end. It's probably best they don't know I was nearly sacrificed, or that I ran from the Brethren the first chance I got.

I wish I had been able to say goodbye. A year ago, when I was forced into a Brethren cart, Anise was still in her hiding place in the woods where I warned her to stay no matter what. Waylen was crying, frantic, high-pitched cries. Ma was sobbing and Dad looked like he was torn between ripping his hair out from grief and attacking the Brethren Guard.

I had just enough time to call out a frantic, *I love you*, before the door of the cart slammed closed and the horses set off. I was locked in the shuddering darkness, but it wasn't just me who was taken from their village that day. There were three girls already in the cart, and by the time we reached the monastery that evening, there were nine of us all together. It was a bad harvest that year, and it seemed like everyone was paying the tithe with their daughters.

I wonder what would be happening to me right now if I'd stayed at the invader's camp. Maybe he would have draped a warm fur around my shoulders by now and we'd be sharing a hot meal by candlelight. I almost start to regret my decision, until I remember that I'm just as much the enemy to him as he is to me, and he'd more likely be hitting me or hurting me in some other terrible way than making me cozy and sharing his food. Any man who has power is dangerous with it.

A deep, mocking laugh reaches my ears. The familiar sound of the High Priest laughing at me while I'm being beaten and I'm struggling not to cry out. He would personally supervise many of my punishments, and it always amused him when I finally whimpered in pain.

For a moment, I think I feel him grab hold of me in the dark. I must be hallucinating from hunger because when I open my eyes and raise my head, all is silent apart from the wind. All the same, I can't help the feeling that I'm being stalked in the dark. By a wolf. By a Brethren Guard. By one of those nimble silver blurs. By an invader and his dragon.

As cold and hungry as I am, I don't expect I will fall asleep, but exhaustion overwhelms me, and I fall into a fitful doze, filled with dreams of being hunted and thrown into burning flames. I awake with the heat of a fire about to consume me alive—until I open my eyes and realize it's the golden rays of dawn in a clear sky piercing my vision.

Unwinding my stiff body, I get slowly to my feet and take a look around. The woods are empty and coated in frost, as are my boots and sleeves. For months and months, I've awoken in the dormitories with the other Veiled Virgins. We weren't permitted to talk to one another and would wash and dress in silence, eat in silence, and then don our veils to pray in church, all with our gazes fixed firmly on the ground.

I haven't died in the night. I can raise my chin to the sky and look where I choose. I'm no longer a prisoner of the Brethren, and I'm on my way home, so perhaps all is not yet lost.

I walk as fast as I can all morning, hoping that I'm heading in the right direction. Smoke and clouds have obscured the horizon, but I feel like every now and then I catch sight of a familiar landmark. Mid-morning, I find a small bush of winterberries and cram some into my mouth, filling my pockets with the rest to eat as I walk along.

It's late afternoon when I finally crest a hill and see my village of Amriste spread below. With my heart in my mouth, I scour every cottage, every garden, every frost-laced vegetable patch. Nothing is on fire or a smoking wreckage, and I breathe a sigh of relief.

As I hobble on bleeding feet down the path to the village square, nothing moves except for a handful of ravens that stand out starkly against the frost. One is perched on the well in the middle of the square and eyes me beadily as snowflakes blow across the cobbles. The village is silent the way only an empty village can be silent; a deserted, bleak silence.

I tear the helm from my head and throw it aside, allowing my tangled hair to fall around my shoulders before hurrying up to a cottage door, knocking and calling out.

"It's me, Isavelle Harrow. Is anyone there?"

There's no answer there and no answer at the next cottage either. The next three have their front doors hanging open and leaves have blown inside.

After eight cottages, including my own, I give up hope.

"Is nobody here?" I call out, turning slowly on the spot. "Nobody at all? It's Isavelle Harrow. Are the Cantrells here? The Ackworths? Has anyone seen my family?"

Silence swallows my shouts. I'm too late. The village has been abandoned, and with dragons haunting the skies, I can't imagine when they'll come back. Overcome by despair and exhaustion, I sink down onto the ground, tears welling up and streaming down my face.

A harsh, high voice, as cracked as a dry riverbed, splits the air. "Aye, sit there and cry. Give up before you've even tried. As sorry as a half-drowned kitten, aren't you?"

I scramble to my feet and whirl around to see a hunched old woman dressed in black rags, her gnarled hand grips a walking stick and an unlit pipe dangles from her lips.

"Mistress Hawthorne?" I say, wiping the tears from my cheeks. Biddy Hawthorne lives in a ramshackle cottage in the village, and she's rarely seen in the village square. She always terrified me, but right now, I'm grateful to be looking at her tangled white hair and hooked nose. Someone who knows me. Someone who can tell me where my family has gone.

I hurry over. "Have you seen Mother and Father? Or my brother and sister, Anise and Waylen?"

She squints at me. "Ah, you're the Harrow maid. You were tithed the harvest before last because none could bear to part with their pigs."

"Yes, Isavelle Harrow," I reply, though I don't enjoy being remembered in such a demeaning manner. I was taken by the Brethren because otherwise, the villagers would have starved.

Mistress Hawthorne gives a derisive sniff. "If you're looking for your family, they fled, didn't they? Packed everything onto oxen and donkeys and into carts days ago and took their old and young and carried them off."

I feel a stab of guilt on behalf of my village that no one thought to help Biddy Hawthorne to safety. Everyone always went to see the old woman for medicine or advice when a child or an animal was sick. She was respected, but no one liked her. It's difficult to like an old woman who mutters and cackles to herself in the street. Witchcraft is outlawed and witches are burned, and even though no one said it, everyone knows that Biddy Hawthorne is a witch.

"I'm sorry you were abandoned. It isn't right that you were left behind."

The old woman draws herself up. "Abandoned? I wasn't abandoned. I wasn't going to leave my home to be taken over by those stumble-headed fribbles."

"The invaders?"

Biddy Hawthorne gives me an outraged look. "The *Brethren*, you stupid girl. Now, come with me and we'll see to your feet."

With that, she turns and shuffles up the path in the direction of her cottage. I follow, and even in my wretched state, I have trouble keeping up with a bent-over old woman. If the Brethren or dragons show up now, I won't be able to run.

Biddy's cottage is just how I remember it a year ago, with its peeling front door, ragged thatched roof with weeds growing among the straw, and a garden fence that looks as though it will collapse if a single bird alights on one of the posts. I feel another twinge of remorse that no one in the village offered to replace her thatch, put in another fence, or weed her garden.

Inside the dark, smoky cottage, Biddy pushes me toward a three-legged stool and tells me to sit down and take off my boots. She walks laboriously around the room with her cane in one hand, filling a small cauldron with water, various herbs, and powders, then hanging it on a chain in the fireplace.

I try to help her, only to be pushed out of the way. "I'm not dead yet, girl."

With my fingers knotted together in my lap, "Please, can you tell me where everyone's gone?"

"Where? Oh, away somewhere," Biddy says, in an offhand manner that doesn't suit the situation. There are dragons in the skies and everyone in the village has disappeared. Isn't she paying attention?

"I see more than you know," Biddy snaps, answering the question that I didn't ask out loud.

I know she's just good at reading people and faces.

At least, I think that's all it is. I've seen women burned alive for the crime of being witches, but if they were truly witches, they could have saved themselves from the flames. I just think the Brethren like to tell lies to keep us scared and obedient.

But they also said there were no such things as dragons.

"Is it true that the dragons came out of the northern mountains?"

"You've heard the stories, girl."

"Yes, I've heard *stories.*"

"Well, then," Biddy says as she crumbles a dried herb into the cauldron, as if that explains everything.

There are few things as frustrating as pointing out how bizarre everything suddenly is, only to have someone shrug it off as if today is any other winter's day. I stew in silence along with whatever concoction Biddy is brewing. It doesn't matter where the dragons came from or whether the stories are true. Between the invaders and the Brethren, what remains of this country will descend into fire and ash.

Wherever the refugees have fled, I will follow.

"I can probably catch up with my family if I can find some proper shoes," I say, thinking aloud. There may still be some of my belongings in our cottage. I can crawl in through a window if they haven't all been boarded up.

Biddy Hawthorne stirs the steaming cauldron. "You think they're worth going after when they left you behind?"

"Of course they are! I belong with Ma and Dad." My parents were inconsolable with grief when I was taken away. They offered up everything they had to keep me even if it would mean they would starve, but the Brethren wouldn't listen. Even so, I feel a pang of sadness that they left without trying to discover if I was alive or dead.

Biddy uses a metal hook to take the cauldron off the flames, and she tips the hot water, herbs and all, into a basin. "Put your feet in there."

I unlace my boots and carefully ease them off my blistered and bleeding feet. "Did anyone say where they were all going? A destination, a road they planned to take?"

"No one said anything to me except, *We're leaving, Mistress Hawthorne. You'll have your throat slit or be eaten by dragons if you stay here.*" Biddy puts a clean folded cloth into my hand. "Load of nonsense. Take that, girl."

Biddy sits down and puffs her pipe as she watches me place my feet into the steaming basin and use the cloth to gently draw the water up my bruised calves. I groan in relief as the heat and whatever she's put into the water eases the pain.

"Did you see which way they went at least?"

The old woman blows a cloud of smoke. "I wasn't looking."

I glower at her. It's like she's trying to be unhelpful. Unlike her, I think our chances of being killed or eaten are alarmingly high.

For a few minutes, there's only the crackle of the flames and the hiss of burning tobacco every time Biddy sucks on her pipe.

If only there was some way to see where my family is right now.

A magical way.

A *forbidden* way.

I gaze thoughtfully at the old woman, and years and years

of strange tales about her swirl in my head. I ask carefully, "Is there a way for us to find out where my family is right at this moment?"

"Of course not, girl."

"Are you sure?"

A nasty grin spreads over Biddy's face and she points her pipe at me. "You've been listening to stories in the firelight."

"I've heard all the tales, and they've had an alarming habit of coming true lately. There are a great many told about you, Mistress Hawthorne. Old Mister Groat said you once told him where to find a whole herd of his sheep that were lost in a snow drift."

The old woman nods sharply. "Aye. I fancied some spring lamb, and when he paid me in a leg, I dressed it with mint out of my garden."

"How were you able to do that?"

"I was hungry."

Does she really expect me to believe she was able to save a whole herd merely because she was hungry? "My family is also lost, in a manner of speaking, and I thought that if you could try and look—"

"Why would I see them? They're your family, and it's your heart that's hankering after them."

"But couldn't you ask your heart to—"

"It doesn't work like that."

"But the sheep—"

"We would have all starved without those sheep. I saw what the village needed me to see, what *I* needed me to see, not what one silly girl wants to get herself killed over."

Biddy Hawthorne is watching me as beadily as the raven that sat on the well and watched me enter the village. I have the feeling that she's not saying no. She's waiting for me to figure something out.

"How did you know I was here? This cottage is on the other side of the village from where I walked in."

She points her pipe at me. "Ahh, now you're asking the right questions."

Silence stretches until I blurt out, "Well, are you going to answer me, please?"

Biddy Hawthorne puffs on her pipe, examining me with her cloudy blue eyes. "You were the chit who would walk off whenever your mother's back was turned, and when you were carried home again, you would cry and say you could hear something in the mountains."

The old witch remembers something about me that I don't remember myself, though I was told about it often enough over the years. Apparently I liked the old folktales so much as a child, I thought they were true.

But they are true. What did I know then that I've since forgotten? Could I really hear something in the mountains?

The old woman reaches out and seizes my wrist, her jagged yellow nails digging into my flesh. I gasp and try to wrench myself away, but suddenly I'm not in the smoky little room anymore.

I'm not anywhere.

It's a terrifying feeling, like suddenly I don't exist.

The world has turned black.

Blacker than black.

Is this death?

Several shapes form in the darkness. A soft glow that becomes pinpoints of light from candelabras. Dozens of candelabras. I'm standing in a room, and there's not much to see except for lines and shapes carved into the floor.

Then something moves.

A figure turns toward me, a tall man in long robes. For a sickening moment, I think he's one of the Brethren, but his hoodless robes are tailored and fitted rather than loose and billowy, with decorations around the cuffs and throat.

His blue-gray eyes lock onto mine, and he seems as shocked to see me standing here as I am to see him. He has long brown hair spilling around his broad shoulders, a handsome face with thick brows, a long, regal nose, and a mouth with a full, soft-looking lower lip. I've never seen this man before. I've never even seen anyone like him before, a man with authority in his bearing and intelligence sparkling in his eyes. Right at this moment, his expression is perplexed.

The man reaches out for me, and suddenly there's so much yearning on his face. My own hand lifts to meet his.

Is this real?

Our fingertips almost touch—and then the vision snaps out of existence.

I open my eyes in Biddy Hawthorne's cottage, overbalance on the rickety stool, and fall in a heap on the ground. The basin of water and herbs tips over and floods the floor.

"Did you get your answer?" Biddy asks mildly, watching me struggle on the ground from her seat in the armchair.

Who was that man? *Where* was he? Did he have anything to do with my family? Perhaps they could be near him, but there was no one else close by that I could see. I wish there had at least been a window so I could tell if he was in a forest or a town or up a mountain. His clothing didn't look like anything I'd seen on a villager or a lord or even the Brethren, so perhaps he was in another country.

But more importantly, why did I see him when I was hoping to see my family?

"You could have warned me you were going to do that," I grumble, getting to my feet and watching water drip from my clothes. "Was that your vision? I didn't see anything I wanted to see."

"Mayhap you saw something that you *needed* to see."

What I *need* is to find my family. "Are visions supposed to look back at you?"

Biddy's eyes open wide, and I realize that no, they most definitely are not supposed to do that. She leans closer to me, her eyes narrowing. "Have you been having dreams, girl?"

I suddenly feel hot all over. "No. Well, yes. Everyone has dreams, don't they? Last week I dreamed that I turned into a maypole and everyone in the village decorated me with flowers and danced around me."

I can tell from the old woman's severe expression that those are not the kind of dreams she means. She means strange dreams that feel like being flung violently into darkness with *things* that are hungering and trapped and desperate to escape. I don't like remembering those dreams.

There's raucous cawing overhead, as if ravens are swooping and wheeling over the cottage.

Biddy's gaze is blank and fixed, and she's staring at something outside this room. "He's hunting you."

Trepidation skitters down my spine. "Who?"

"The mountain prisoner."

I glance toward the door, expecting someone to come crashing through it right that second.

The vision I had just now—if it was a vision—was that the mountain prisoner? The floor seemed to be carved from stone, though I could see little but darkness beyond the flickering candlelight.

I thought that dragons were only a story until a few days ago, but now I've taken a ride on one. If the king under the mountain is looking for me, I'd better get moving. I don't need him adding to my problems.

Biddy searches among the clutter on the table at her elbow, grasps something small, and thrusts it into my hand. "Take this and keep it safe. Use it if you ever need to hide from him."

The object she's given me is a bottle made of murky glass and sealed with wax. Inside is a dark green liquid. A shiver passes down my spine. *Use it if you ever need to hide from him.* Hiding seems like my only chance to survive. "How do I—"

Biddy half lifts herself from her seat, her expression frantic. "Put it away, girl. He's coming."

I shove the bottle down the front of my stays. Footsteps grow louder and louder. Terror seizes my throat as I remember the frightening places from my dreams, and I wonder if I'm about to be dragged beneath the mountains and into the darkness.

The door rips open, and my heart plunges through the floor and then rebounds back up and lodges in my throat.

4

Zabriel

My mate. She's here.

Scourge pulls in his wings and plummets toward the ground, landing with a deafening *whomp* and sending clouds of dust up into the sky. As it settles around us, I slide from the saddle and draw my sword, hunting in the shadows between cottages for enemies. The village seems deserted, but after the events of the past week, I trust nothing and walk nowhere in Maledin without a blade in my hand.

Everything is silent apart from the wind gusting through the thatched eaves.

Scourge opens his jaws and bares his teeth. He's not readying to roar or send a plume of fire toward the wooden houses. Rather, he's exposing the sensitive scent receptors in his gums and lining his throat. He turns this way and that, and then rears up and stomps his forelegs on the ground.

The girl's scent is everywhere, but it's fading and he can't find her. With a growl of frustration, I realize this must have been her village. She once lived here and knocked on every door. Drew water from that stone well. Walked over the cobbles. Perhaps she was here recently, but now she's gone.

I close my eyes and inhale deeply, and I breathe her in.

Honeysuckle on a dewy morning. The earth after rain. The color turquoise and a joyous flash of sunshine. Sticky sweet apple fritters and kites dancing in the wind. As I savor the nuance of her scent, I can feel her coming to life around me. Everything to a mature dragonrider has a scent. Sights, sounds, even emotions. This girl's scent is sweet and playful, and it's filled with my favorite things.

I've hoped and yearned all my life for my Omega. I was beginning to believe that I would never find the one true mate that every Alpha craves. The one who he is fated to love and protect. The mate he recognizes as soon as he scents her.

The tension in my body melts into bliss, and even the hand gripping my sword grows loose as I keep breathing her in. Is that a hint of wind-whipped sky? Every inhalation brings new things to enjoy. I could live in her scent forever. I want to drown in it. I've held her in my arms. I pressed my face into her throat and knew a moment of perfection.

I had her, but then she slipped through my fingers.

There's a muffled sound from our left. I open my eyes, and both Scourge and I turn sharply in that direction. There's nothing to see.

But there's something there.

We're not alone after all.

I swing my body in that direction and stride across the square. With every step I take, the girl's scent grows stronger and stronger. She *is* here. Rage mounts in my chest, and I raise my sword. Someone's keeping her hidden from me. I'll drive my blade through their heart for daring to imprison my mate.

The muffled sounds are coming from inside a ramshackle cottage on the edge of the village, up a dark and winding lane. Trees have overgrown the road, creating a tunnel of branches that block out the sun. The fence is rotted and leans drunkenly inward, and the tiny front garden is overgrown with a variety of weeds.

I stride up the path, shove the front door open, and bend nearly double as I burst into the room. The door slams shut behind me.

A voice shrieks angrily in the darkness. "Who dares enter this place with steel drawn? I'll roast your gizzards on my fire if you don't turn around and leave at once."

I blink to adjust my eyesight and try to straighten up, but I knock my head against the ancient, iron-hard oak beams overhead.

"Blast you with dragonfire," I growl through my teeth as I'm showered with soot and rub my scalp. "Who's there?"

A crone dressed in black rags is sitting in an old stuffed chair, the seat of which sags on the ground like the belly of an old tabby cat. One of the woman's gnarled hands is braced before her on an equally knotted and gnarled walking stick. Her other hand cups a putrid and smoking pipe. She sits bolt upright in the low chair, like a queen on her throne, surveying me with a wickedly sharp gaze.

"You're too late. They took her hours ago."

I breathe in deeply and sense that she's telling the truth. The girl's scent is here, but it's fading away. I sheathe my sword with a muttered curse, anguish piercing my heart.

Where has she gone?

Why did she flee from me?

"Did the Brethren take her, Grandmother?"

Grandmother is a term of respect for an old woman, especially one who knows things that others don't. Secret, dangerous things.

The hag cackles, plumes of smoke erupting from her mouth and nose. "Grandmother? You have six times more years than mine, though you look better than me for them, I'll give you that."

"Has it been so long?"

"Aye."

Devastation washes over me. None of the dragonriders or my soldiers have been able to discern how long we slept under that mountain. Maledin looks different, but I had hoped we only slumbered for a decade or two, not hundreds upon hundreds of years.

I fix the old woman with a narrow stare. "You seem to know me."

Her expression grows proud and flinty. "We're not all ignorant around these parts. Some of us pay close attention to the stories, and we know they aren't merely tales to tell around the fire." Her gaze flicks scornfully over my armor. "So he's returned, gods preserve us."

I exhale sharply through my nose, an expression of displeasure I've picked up from Scourge. Apparently she doesn't think much of the man currently filling her tiny room.

The first person in Maledin who knows who I am, and this is the welcome I receive?

"Where did they take the girl?" I growl.

"Your dragons are invading. The whole country is in an uproar of sparks and smoke. Why do you care about one little village girl?"

"Because she's mine," I snarl. I know my eyes must be burning red in the darkness, but if the old woman is afraid, she doesn't show it.

"Have you scented your mate, *Ma'len*? Is she comely?" the hag asks slyly. "Does she have lovely pink cheeks and bright, glittering eyes?"

My teeth clench together. "I don't know. I haven't seen her face."

The woman nods slowly. "So it is like that. A true *Ma'len*, and a true *Ma'len's* mate. Hard found, and carelessly lost."

An Alpha king and an Omega queen. Meant to be together. Meant to rule together. It's the stars telling me I will win this war—if I hadn't lost her.

"I was not careless," I snap. "I left the battleground and flew with her to my camp where she would be safe."

"And then?"

"She ran away," I grind out through clenched teeth.

The hag cackles again. Mocking my frustration. Delighting in my failure.

"I have known the chit all her life, and I can tell you if she is a beauty," the hag offers. "What she's like. Her temperament and her charms."

"It doesn't matter what she looks like. Scourge and I have other methods to find her, and the rest I will discover for myself."

I found her veil in a tent back at camp. She'd pulled it off and cast it aside, ruining my hopes to draw it back from her face and gaze down at her for the first time. I *hungered* for that moment, but the girl crumpled it up and hid it beneath a stinking sleeping pallet, along with her dress. Both garments are still bathed in her scent, but they also reek of sweaty, unwashed soldiers. It's obscene that her garments smell of any man but me.

The hag casts me a coquettish expression, which looks strange on her haggard old face. "But don't you want to know for certain that she's as comely as *Ma'len's* bride should be? What if you waste your time hunting her, only to discover she doesn't please you?"

I hunker down on my heels before the crone and put my face close to hers, grinning nastily. "Not be pleased by my mate? I will look upon her and see the most beautiful woman in the world. Even if she is your twin."

The hag's expression turns sour. "I was a beauty once. You should have seen me before that trickster, Time, stole all my gifts."

I wave a dismissive hand. I wouldn't have been interested in her even if she was the Goddess of Beauty herself. "You still have gifts for me. Your clever mind. Your powers of foresight, of farseeking. Where have the Brethren taken my bride?"

"Me? Have powers? I am an old woman who boils weeds in a cauldron. I have no talents to interest you."

"Lies," I seethe, moving so close that my nose is nearly touching her hooked one. "The stench of witchcraft is upon you."

The hag mutters, sitting back. She regards me for a moment, and then snaps, "I have no strength left for farseeking. With my help, the girl had a vision not two hours hence, and it drained me so much that I could not flee for my life if this cottage caught fire."

My mate had a vision?

"Of what?" I ask calmly, though my heart is suddenly beating wildly. Was it of me? Of us? Did she see us together? As we are meant to be. As we *will* be. If she did, it probably terrified her because she knows nothing of our ways. Apparently, no Maledinni does except for those who escaped the mountain with me and this hag before me.

The woman hesitates, leaning closer with gleaming eyes. My breath catches in my throat as I anticipate what she's about to tell me of my mate's vision.

"I can't say. She didn't tell me what she saw."

I get to my feet, nearly cracking my skull on the ceiling once more. The hag cackles at her own jest, and I dearly want to put my fist through the wall. How much of the gods' favor would I lose for running one of their blessed through with my sword?

I'm barely holding back the Brethren, and I've lost my mate within minutes of finding her. I can't risk it.

And I'm wasting time.

I turn toward the door, but the hag calls to me, "What will you do if you never find your bride again? Or if she is killed by your enemies? For it is into your enemy's hands she has fallen."

I turn and say coldly, "If they kill her, I'll round up every enemy soldier in Maledin and every priest in the Brethren, and they will die slow and painful deaths." And then I'll throw myself on my sword because I will never be a true king without her.

The hag eyes me with interest, smoking that disgusting pipe. "Do you wish to know her name?"

I watch her through narrowed eyes. The witch knows I do not possess it. "What do you want in exchange for my mate's name?"

She puffs her pipe thoughtfully. "Nothing. A trifle."

A gift from a hag always comes with a price, and though I have no doubt that I can repay such a debt, I will not trade for secrets about my *sha'len*. "I will have that gift from her lips, not yours."

I yank open the front door with such force that I almost rip it off its hinges, then let it slam shut behind me.

Scourge is waiting for me back in the main square, his long tail coiled around a squat little house. When he sees me, his red eyes blaze with interest and his nostrils flare—only for him to snort with fury when he realizes I'm alone.

"I know. I thought we had her," I mutter. It was a waste of time coming here, and the hag will no doubt want payment in the future for telling me that the Brethren have stolen my bride away from me, something I could have figured out for myself.

I climb up into the saddle, anger raging so violently in my chest that I feel like I could breathe fire along with my dragon.

I'll find her. Even if I have to raze the whole of Maledin to the ground to get her back.

5

Isavelle

My screams echo around the tiny cell. I writhe in pain, my wrists rubbed red and raw against iron manacles. The High Priest watches on, his hands in his sleeves and his eyes burning with sadistic delight as the Brethren strike my bare back again and again with a birch cane.

"Ungrateful, selfish girl. Our king has passed into the afterlife without a bride because of you." The High Priest's voice is a low hiss, but he can't disguise the delight in his voice that he has yet another reason to punish me. He's never gone this far before. My back feels like a river of pain and blood. Bright red drops spatter on my feet.

"*Harder*. She has not yet learned her lesson."

The Brethren grunts with effort and doubles the speed of his strikes. A guttural scream tears from my throat. There's no point in telling him that I didn't summon the dragons that attacked the funeral. I could beg for my life, but I learned a long time ago that the High Priest takes sadistic pleasure in girls who tearfully beg him for mercy. He never laid a hand on me himself, and I've never seen him touch any of the other girls. Sometimes I've wondered if he's impotent and this is how he finds his pleasure, or if he gets off on wielding one subordinate to punish another.

The cane slices my flesh again and again. The pain in my back reaches a crescendo, and I must pass out because, the next thing I know, I'm being sluiced with freezing water, my cuffs are unlocked, and I slump to the ground in a heap.

With my cheek pressed against the wet, gritty ground, I take painful, panting breaths. My back feels like it's on fire. Hopefully this is when they kill me because I can't take much more.

The door to my cell clangs shut and the lock grates, and I'm left alone, but not in silence.

I'm deep within the cloisters, but even feet upon feet of mud and stone can't mute the furious screams of dragons in the sky. What a dream it would be to be burned to a crisp by a dragon right now. I hope they attack and tear this place apart —and me with it. There's only so much suffering one person can take. Hunger claws at my stomach, and that saucer of fresh milk seems like decades ago. It was a mistake to return to my village. Of course the Brethren sent guards to search for me there. Stupid, Isavelle. Stupid, *stupid.*

I wonder where my family is now and how far they've traveled from Maledin. A chasm of despair opens inside me as I wonder if I'll ever see them again.

I'm so alone.

They left me behind, and now I'm trapped in the dark.

Time passes slowly, and every second is filled with pain and misery. Eventually, there's a tramping sound from above, growing louder and louder, and the door of my cell swings open. Two guards come in and haul me up by my armpits and half drag me, half carry me out and upstairs.

In the main hall, someone is waiting for me, surrounded by Brethren Guard. Torchlight flickers on his gray robes. I can see his cruel mouth, but the hood he wears conceals his eyes. The High Priest. Whenever something horrible happens to me, he's always there. When I was tithed and dragged from my home. When I was punished for not keeping my eyes lowered and for not speaking my prayers. When I was nearly burned alive for the sake of a dead king.

I have no doubt that something horrible is going to happen now. We look at each other without saying anything.

I gather what little moisture there is in my mouth and spit in the High Priest's face.

One of the Brethren Guard raises his hand and delivers a stinging backhand blow to my face. Pain explodes in my mouth and I taste blood.

"That's enough bruises on her face," the High Priest says when the Brethren Guard lifts his hand again, but without much urgency in his voice.

My heart thumps painfully in my chest. Why can't there be too many bruises on my face? Who am I supposed to marry now?

The High Priest catches the gleam of fear in my eyes and gives me a gloating smile. "That's right. The Shadow King can't wait to meet you, girl. When he does, I hope he rips the living flesh from your ungrateful bones."

That story is true as well? The Shadow King is real?

"What has this Shadow King promised you in return for a beaten and half-starved girl? You think you'll be saved from the dragons if you give me to him?" I wrench myself back and forth in the soldier's grip. "Let me go and find my family, you bastards. *Let me go.*"

As usual, my struggling and screaming do nothing but exhaust me, and I'm dragged outside and into the fresh air. It's nighttime, and there are a dozen Brethren Guard on horses holding flaming torches.

My wrists are tied in front of me as I'm put up onto a horse led by one of the guards and told to hold on to the saddle.

In the distance to the north, there's a red glow on the horizon that must be the flames of battle. The dragons and their riders are still fighting for Maledin. For some reason, the sight gladdens my heart.

"The Proxen Road is still passable. We'll take her that way," I hear one Brethren Guard say to another.

Proxen is far to the south, away from the capital, Lenhale, and the worst of the fighting. There's wasteland and mountains to the south, mountains that are said to be more treacherous than the Bodan Mountains to the north. And little else. Few people, fewer settlements. No kings that I've heard of.

The Brethren Guard set off at a trot and then a gallop, and my horse goes with them. I hold on to the saddle for dear life, wondering who or what the Brethren have promised me to.

We ride for hours, alternately galloping and walking. The screams of dragons fade away, and when I glance behind us, I can no longer see the red glow on the horizon, something that makes me ache with desolation. I don't know why. It's not like the dragons are going to take me to my family.

There are fewer and fewer trees and signs of habitation the longer we ride. The flat, dusty road is edged with scrub, and wind cuts across the plains. I shiver on the back of my mount because I'm dressed only in the shirt and breeches that I stole from the invader's camp, and my torn-up feet are bare. I'm so cold and in such pain that I think longingly of those moments I spent in the invader's arms, wrapped in his warm cloak with my cheek pillowed against his furred collar. I felt safe and protected for the first time since I was taken from my village over a year ago.

I close my eyes and shake my head. Don't think about him. Just because he held me close and had a voice like velvet and thunder doesn't mean he isn't dangerous. With that sword and dragon, he's more dangerous than the High Priest and all the Brethren Guard put together.

I try to think on the bright side as I cling to the saddle of the galloping horse with my hands and thighs. If I am to be married, it sounds as if my bridegroom is at least living this time. Only living men care if their brides have bruised faces, and if I'm alive, I can look for a way to escape.

The drumming of the horses' hooves on the road drowns out every sound except for the rushing of wind in my ears, but the nape of my neck begins to prickle. I have the sensation that something is closing in on us. Something big. Enormous in fact, and a moment later I hear a muted beating that I've heard once before. I look up at the sky but all is inky blackness and stars.

Or is it? As I watch, a patch of stars winks out and then reappears as if something has passed in front of them. The soldier on the horse next to mine notices what I'm staring at. Our gazes lock for a moment, and his expression turns fearful.

The beating grows louder. The soldier's fear turns into panic, and he shouts, "Dragons incoming!"

Overhead and just in front of us, a light appears in the sky that resembles a furnace trapped within a scaly membrane, which makes absolutely no sense because why would a furnace be in the sky? Then I realize what I'm looking at.

The underside of a dragon's throat.

A dragon that's preparing to breathe fire.

The red glow rises up the dragon's neck, and suddenly the creature is lit up as liquid fire streams from its open jaws. The night is painted red and gold as the fire hits the ground and erupts into a wall of flames. There are more dragons in the sky. Four, five, six circling over us. The fire-breathing dragon banks and circles around us, blistering rage still spilling from its jaws and setting the ground afire. A very large dragon.

A very large *black* dragon with burning red eyes.

The horses scream and rear. I can't hold on to my mount, and I go tumbling from the saddle and land in a heap on the road. There are hooves stamping all around me, and I roll into a ball and cover my head. I need to get back on one of the horses and take my chances in all the chaos to run.

But when I finally sit up and look around, I find there's no escape. We're enveloped in a ring of fire, and the flames are six feet high and scorching hot. They light up the darkness almost as bright as daylight.

The Brethren Guard and I watch with open mouths as the enormous black dragon finishes its revolution and lands within the circle, its wings beating the flames into a frantic dance. I'm not wearing a veil this time, and I can see every detail of the fearsome creature. It's glistening, supple black body. The burning red eyes. The pointed spines that decorate its sleek head. Once all four of its clawed feet are on the ground, it opens its jaws and roars at the soldiers, a guttural, deafening sound that causes ripples in the air around its sharp teeth.

A man is sitting atop the dragon, perched just in front of its wings. He wears gleaming plate armor, and the wind snatches at his long black hair and red-lined cloak. He swings his leg over the saddle and slides down the dragon's flank to the ground.

As he straightens up, he glares around the circle with burning red eyes. No one moves. No one makes a sound. He's hunting among us for something.

For someone.

I'm hidden among the nervously dancing horses, peering at the soldier through their legs. A guard draws an arrow in his bow and aims it at the man's chest, and I have the strangest urge to shout a warning.

The archer lets loose his shot. The invader draws his sword in a lightning-fast arc and deflects the missile.

I gawp at the huge man. How was that even possible?

He strides toward us, sword drawn, murder glittering in his red eyes. While the archer stares in shock at the invader, something comes swooping out of the sky, talons first. I see a flash of snow-white scales. The white dragon snatches the man up in its claws, banks hard, and flings the archer far away into the darkness on a fading scream.

"Get back," the invader snarls at the Brethren Guard. "Move those horses."

The soldiers scramble to obey him as if he's their commanding officer and not the enemy, snatching at bridles and hurrying to the farthest reaches of the flaming circle.

Revealing me.

Sitting in a heap in the dust with my hands tied in front of me.

The invader stops dead and stares at me, recognition and outrage blooming on his face. His expression is like he's been searching desperately for someone. Someone beloved.

Only to find them hurt and suffering.

I know it's him. I know it even though I've never seen his face. This is the invader who landed his dragon on the dead king's funeral pyre and carried me away on dragonback. It's not only that his dragon seems to be the same dragon or that I can see this man has long, silky hair, or that the inside of his cloak flashes crimson in the wind. I just *feel* it's him. I felt he was near even before I saw the dragons in the sky.

The invader sheathes his sword, walks over to me in three long strides, and goes down on one knee. I lift my chin high to gaze up at him.

He's huge. Bigger than any man I've ever seen before. I already knew that from the way he held me against him, but now that he's looming over me, I feel like a piece of dust before a mountain.

The firelight moves across his face, and I feel a jolt of recognition. I *have* seen his face before, or someone very like him. That jawline. That long, straight nose. His fierce brow. The way his long hair frames his handsome face. He's the stranger from my vision in Biddy Hawthorne's cottage.

Only he's...different. This man's hair is jet black, not

brown, and rather than them being blue gray, the man kneeling before me has burning red eyes.

Demon.

That's what the Brethren called him, and he looks every inch like he just walked out of hell.

He draws a knife and brandishes it in his fist. I shrink away in fear—until he gently takes hold of my wrists in his gauntleted hands and cuts through the ropes.

"I came as fast as I could, *sha'len*," he says in a low, angry voice. "No one shall tie you up ever again."

Behind him, several of the Brethren Guard have noticed that he's sheathed his sword and are drawing their own. A soldier charges toward him, sword raised.

I gasp a warning before I remember that I'm not on the invader's side. I'm not on anyone's side but my own, but the words still break from my lips. "Be care—"

The invader stands up and draws his sword, parrying the guard's weapon with a roar. It's such a violent deflection that the guard is thrown off his feet and skids across the ground on his back. With his teeth bared, the invader takes his sword's hilt in both hands and thrusts the blade through the man's armor and rib cage. I flinch at the sound of crunching bones and metal and the man's last gurgling breath. Bracing the dead soldier's body with his foot, the invader yanks out his sword with a spray of blood.

The black dragon lunges forward, grasps the dead man with his teeth, and flings him out of the flaming circle.

The invader turns slowly on the spot, his sword held at his side with the dripping point directed at the ground, inviting anyone else to attack him if they dare.

No one moves.

Satisfied, the invader sheathes his weapon and turns back to me, kneeling once more.

With the black dragon peering over his shoulder at me with the same burning red eyes, I feel like I'm being looked at by the same demon twice. Their red gazes fasten on my bruised mouth, and they narrow and grow searing hot.

"They hit you? They *hurt* you?" the invader seethes. "Which of these men did this to you?"

"I..." I open my mouth, but I can only shake my head helplessly. I stopped paying attention a long time ago to which of the Brethren and their guards beat me. So many of them hit me and the other Veiled Virgins over the past year that I couldn't point out one man over another. "I don't know."

The invader gets to his feet and shouts, "*Hel mai.*"

Half a dozen invaders wearing armor step through the wall of flames and into the circle, as easily as if they are walking through an open doorway. Most are men, and though none are so tall and broad as the invader in the red-lined cloak, they're far bigger than the Brethren Guard. There are some women as well. I've never seen a woman dressed in armor and carrying weapons, but they look as dangerous and fierce as the men.

"On your knees," he seethes at the Brethren Guard.

When no one moves, the invader soldiers force the guards to the ground until they're kneeling in a row before us.

"Who is leading this unit?" the invader asks them.

The only sound is the crackling of flames.

Tentatively, a man toward the end of the row says in a shaky voice, "I-I am."

The invader strides along the row until he's standing in front of him. "Where were you taking my mate?"

His *what?*

Is he talking about me?

The guard stumbles over his words. He's never faced an enemy soldier before, only bullied young women and threatened unarmed villagers. I relish the fact that he's just about wetting himself. "That's not...I don't... My orders are to..."

The invader grasps the front of the soldier's uniform and drags him up until his feet are dangling off the ground. The soldier wears half his poundage in armor, but the huge invader is holding him aloft with one hand as if he weighs nothing.

"*I said*, where were you taking my mate?"

"To the end of the Proxen Road," the man gasps, twisting back and forth. "We were told that someone would meet us there. That's all I know."

With a snarl of rage, the invader hurls the man away from him, and he lands in the flames. With a scream of pain, the guard rolls back into the circle. One of the dragon's clawed feet descends and pins the man in place. The creature lowers its monstrous head until the tip of its snout nearly touches the guard's nose and snarls.

The invader strides over to him. "Did you hurt my mate? If you lie to me, Scourge will know, and he'll rip your head off."

The guard's eyes are bulging and he struggles to draw breath into his lungs. "Only her face. She spat at the High Priest. The rest wasn't me."

"The *rest*?" The invader's face goes blank, then it suffuses with even more rage than before. With burning eyes, he strides back to me and scours every part of my flesh that he can see. The shirt that I stole from one of his men is slipping from my shoulder, and I can imagine how my skin looks. Fresh red and blue-black bruises over fading yellow and purple ones. Thin, vicious stripes of the cane, some fading, some vivid red.

The invader exhales slowly through his nose as if barely clinging to his temper. "How much of you doesn't hurt right now?" he asks in a low, furious voice.

I moisten my lips and gaze up at him, not wanting to answer.

"I thought so," he growls, turning away.

The invader and the dragon meet each other's eyes, and I have the strangest idea that they're communicating silently. The dragon clenches its claws, driving them through the guard's armor and into his flesh. The soldier screams, but the scream is cut short when the dragon rips his head off with one bite and tosses it through the flames. Blood gouts from his severed neck, a grisly sight that I can't tear my eyes away from.

A moment later, a shriek of panic claims my attention. The invader has drawn a dagger and pulls the nearest guard to his feet. The man is begging for mercy, but the invader slashes his throat with the blade. With a roar of anger, he throws the dying man aside and grabs another, slitting his throat as well. Two men are gurgling and clutching their throats at his feet, but his thirst for blood isn't slaked. A third man tries to run, but the invader is too fast for him. With a savage grab and a wrench of the blade across the guard's throat, another man dies, and the invader tosses him aside.

Breathing hard and with blood gleaming on his chest

plate, the invader says to his soldiers, "Kill them all, and then leave this place."

The soldiers obey without a word, drawing their swords and plunging them down inside the guards' armor at the neck. One by one, the bodies topple forward into the dust.

The invader's soldiers turn away and walk back through the flames, which are finally beginning to die down. One by one, they climb up onto the backs of their waiting dragons—all different shades, all different sizes—and fly away.

The horses have had enough of dragons and screaming and blood, and they bolt into the darkness.

Silence falls, and I'm alone with the invader and the dragon that he called Scourge. The man sheathes his knife and strides over to me, holding out his hand to help me up.

There's blood all over his palm.

I get to my feet by myself, gazing at all the dead bodies. This war is crueler than the life I've always known. "You killed them all. Why did you kill them all?"

I have no love for the Brethren Guard. They chained me to a wall and beat me for the crime of not wishing to be burned alive. They terrorized everyone in Maledin for decades. Centuries. They beat helpless girls and old women. These were not good men.

"Because they hurt you, and no one hurts my mate and lives. And because you wished for it, *sha'len*."

"I never said that."

He gives me a dangerous smile. "Not out loud, but I could smell it on you at the funeral pyre, and I can smell it on you now. You craved their deaths."

Maybe I did. With a gut-knotting sensation, I recall my

last thoughts before I was about to be hurled onto the funeral pyre.

I hope the dragons burn them all.

I'm about to ask him if he can read minds, but I'm distracted as he reaches for my throat. His hand is huge, made even bigger by the jointed armor that covers the backs of his hands and each finger, and I flinch away from him. I'm not fast enough, however, and he gently brushes my hair back. At the same time, he draws me closer to him. "I need to see your neck."

I stiffen, and my hands land on his bloody chest plate. "Why?"

A gentle finger caresses the nape of my neck. Past the invader's arm, his dragon is watching me with intense focus. Whatever he's looking for, he doesn't see it—or perhaps he does—and he heaves a sigh of relief.

"*Previet k'len,*" he groans, closing his eyes and leaning down to rest his forehead against mine.

How strange this man is. It's clear he doesn't want to kill me, but I can't tell what he does want. I study him while he holds my face in both his hands. His nostrils flare slightly as he breathes, and despite the blood spattered on his face, his strong features are entrancing. He's the most striking man I've ever seen, and he's holding me like I'm the most precious thing in the world to him.

The silence is excruciating, and I blurt out the question that's upmost in my mind. "What do you want?"

He opens his eyes and gazes at me with an expression so full of yearning that it makes my heart jolt. "You."

"But I don't know you."

"You will."

That sounds like a threat. Cold wind cuts through my clothes and I shiver.

The invader takes his cloak from his shoulders and wraps the huge garment around me. I'm enveloped in warmth. For a moment my nostrils catch a tantalizing scent, and I'm consumed with the need to smell it again. I breathe in deeply. I even raise my elbow, bury my face in the cloth, and inhale. Smoke from fires. Blood and metal. A musky suggestion of the man standing before me. I thought there was more, but I must have been mistaken.

I lift my gaze to his neck, right where the wind is teasing his long hair. For an insane moment, I feel the urge to beg him to lift me up in his arms so I can bury my face right there.

I want...something.

The invader is watching me closely and seems to be holding his breath.

"What?" I ask.

He hesitates, and then shakes his head.

"Have we met before? Apart from at the funeral pyre."

"We have never met. It's impossible for us to have ever met before." He smiles, and his hard, chiseled features soften into breathtaking good looks. This man is preternaturally handsome.

"Are you a demon?"

His smile widens and then he laughs. The sound delves deep inside me, warming me from the inside out. "Only to my enemies. I'm Maledinni, just like you. My name is Zabriel."

Zabriel. I've never heard that name before, and I doubt he's telling the truth about being from Maledin. He must have invaded from another country, but where did the dragons come from? I would have heard if there were dragons and riders in another land near ours, unless the Brethren kept the truth from us. It seems like something they would do.

"And your name?" Zabriel asks, wrapping his cloak even tighter around me and drawing me into his arms. The fur collar tickles my cheek.

I want to tell him it's none of his business what my name is, but the same warm, liquid feeling as when he held me in his arms on dragonback is stealing over me. The night wind teases strands of his long hair.

He'll save me? Protect me? But men don't save. They punish and gloat and take what they want while inflicting unimaginable pain and torment.

But this man feels...different.

"Isavelle," I whisper, gazing up at him.

Zabriel crooks a finger under my chin and draws my mouth up toward his. Bending down from his great height so that his face is close to mine, his voice is a smoky whisper as he says, "Isavelle."

He draws the *Isa* luxuriously over his tongue, and there's far more bite than usual in the *velle*.

"I've found you at last, Isavelle."

I'm captivated by his touch and the way he says my name. His dark lashes are fluttering closed, and his lips are descending toward mine.

6

Zabriel

Isavelle breathes in sharply, then turns her head to the side, denying me her mouth.

I freeze, my lips a fraction of an inch from her softly curving cheek. "Give me your lips, *sha'len*."

"I won't, Zabriel."

I groan softly. My name sounds so delectable in her mouth. "Please grant me one kiss. I've waited five hundred years to meet you."

"Five hundred?" Her expression transforms in shock. "You will tell such lies just to claim a kiss? Besides, you're covered in blood, and we've only just met."

"But the blood of your enemies is my second favorite scent in the world." I'm playing with a tress of her hair, enjoying the way her scent rises around me. I could stand like this for hours, just breathing her in.

An Omega should instantly melt when she's given an order from her Alpha, uttering a breathy, cock-hardening, *Yes, Alpha,* before her lips part for mine. For that matter, she should never have run from me. I should have found her in my bed, buried beneath my sleeping furs and blankets, drunk on my scent, and whimpering for me to bury my knot inside her.

We've only just met doesn't mean anything when fated mates find each other at last.

I want so much more than her lips. I want to undress her in my bed and squeeze every delicious handful of her. I crave her slick against my fingers and her heavy panting in my mouth. For her to wrap her hand around my knot and *squeeze.* Isavelle must be able to smell her Alpha's desire for her. My hunger for her touch and overwhelming need to protect her.

Can't she?

Suddenly I'm not so sure. My Omega isn't behaving as I've heard all Omegas do when a fated pair finally meet. She should be gazing up at me like I'm her whole world, but maybe she hasn't realized who I am yet.

That must be it. The poor girl has been living through a war. She's barely had a moment to inhale my scent.

I go down on one knee and pat my thigh, my gauntleted hand clanking against my leg armor. "Sit here. I know steel plate isn't the most comfortable place to sit, but you can wrap your arms around my neck and get your face in my gland."

Isavelle takes half a step back, alarm on her features. "Your...what? Why would I want to get my face in anything?"

I blink in surprise. "So you recognize me, of course." Since when were Maledinni so clueless about each other's bodies? Our kind has scent glands in the wrists and the sides and backs of our necks. The gland at the nape of the neck is the most sensitive and fragrant of all.

What the hell has been happening in Maledin while I've been locked up under a mountain?

Isavelle shakes her head. "No, thank you. You've already told me we've never met. I don't know you."

"Not my face. My scent. I'm your mate."

I was prepared for a small frown. A little skepticism. Isavelle glares at me like I've insulted her scent. "You are *not* my mate. I don't even know what that means, but you can't decide whatever you like about me."

I leap to my feet, shock slamming through me. "You dare say I'm not your mate? Why are you tormenting me like this? Have I wronged you somehow?"

Has there been some kind of Omega revolution while I was trapped beneath the mountains? Instead of being good and sweet and loving their Alphas, do all Omegas now thumb their noses at them?

"First of all, you're an enemy invader."

An invader? Maledin is my home and the home of my people, and it always has been. At this moment, I should be reclaiming what's mine, but I've been tearing Maledin apart looking for her. I've *killed* for her. She calls me her enemy?

My mate should recognize me as fast as I recognize her. That's the way this works for our kind and always has.

I take a rough breath, reminding myself of the number of years that have passed. The centuries. Isavelle has never ridden a dragon. Never even seen a dragon until a week ago. Could it be that she doesn't even know what a mate is? What an Alpha or an Omega is? Alphas are leaders. They're physically strong, swift, dangerous, and resilient. They give the orders and everyone else follows. There are many Alphas, but Omegas are very rare. Precious. They're also at the very bottom of the pecking order. They don't naturally take to battle or leadership, and they're physically small. That should make them insignificant, but Omegas are so prized because male Alphas and female Omegas breed the strongest, cleverest, and most beautiful offspring.

And they're totally, completely irresistible to each other.

There's nothing so deep or intense as the love between an Alpha and an Omega. It's an instant, irrevocable bond that only deepens over time. Alphas find their Omegas utterly irresistible, adorable, and sexy, and Omegas crave their Alpha's touch, protection, and voices more than anything in the world.

"What do you smell when you are close to me?" I ask her.

Isavelle wrinkles her nose. "Blood. Dust. Ash and fire like a blacksmith's forge, which I think is from that fire-breathing monster behind you."

Over my shoulder, Scourge snorts in irritation that he's been called a monster.

She's named only mundane things that a human would smell. A Maledinni scenting her mate should be overwhelmed by a wondrous bouquet that leaves her dizzy and hungry for more. I've always wondered what I'd smell like to my Omega when she finally appeared, if she finally appeared, and the fact that Isavelle detects nothing in particular is a crushing disappointment.

"Why, what am I supposed to smell?" she asks.

I lift my hand and let it fall.

Me.

Us.

I know that Isavelle is Maledinni like me because I can smell it on her. I know that she's my mate. There's no question about that. For the past five hundred years, my people have been living like humans. Could it be that the part of her that should recognize me is asleep, as I was beneath the mountain?

I'll just have to wake that part of her up.

I reach for Isavelle, but she backs away with a soft gasp like she thinks I'm going to hurt her. My hand is enormous compared to hers. I'm towering over her, clad in armor and carrying weapons. She's defenseless, wearing the clothes she stole days ago from my camp, her feet bloodied and torn, and her body covered in cuts and bruises.

A pang goes through my heart. Isavelle doesn't care that I've saved her life twice. All she sees when she looks at me is a killer.

Though it causes me physical pain, I take a step back from her. "I'm not your enemy. The ones you call the Brethren are my enemy—my only enemy. You and every other Maledinni between the northern and southern mountains are my people, and I'm here to save you from these zealots."

Isavelle says nothing, but her distrustful expression doesn't change. She wraps her arms around herself and then winces as she squeezes her injured flesh.

I'm a terrible, thoughtless Alpha, seeing my Omega in pain but doing nothing about it. Shame spirals through me. "You're hurt and injured, *sha'len*. I will fly you somewhere that will ease your pain."

She shakes her head. "I don't want to go anywhere with you, especially not on that creature."

"I'm not leaving you here to suffer and die. We are miles from safety and there are many Brethren still abroad."

Isavelle glares around into the darkness. There are no lights that might indicate a nearby village or even a house. We're alone out here with Scourge and a pile of dead bodies, and the horses have long since fled.

Her gaze lingers on my dragon. "All I want is to find my family. Ma and Dad fled our village with my two younger siblings when the fighting broke out, and I don't know where they've gone." Her voice trembles with emotion and her scent is awash with loneliness and despair.

My poor little Omega. How well I know the pain of losing your family, though she has the hope of recovering hers. "I will do everything in my power to help you find your family. I want nothing but for the people of this country to feel safe in their homes once more."

"You say that, but I've watched your dragon eat people. How do I know he won't eat me as well?"

The corner of my mouth tilts up. "Scourge, eat people? Humans have a disgusting taste, and eating Maledinni would be akin to cannibalism. He prefers to hunt deer and sea creatures. I promise that you and everyone in Maledin are safe from Scourge—as long as they don't attack me or you."

I hold out my arm, inviting her to step closer to him. Scourge is our only way out of here to safety. Isavelle takes a tentative step forward, and Scourge swings his enormous head around to look at her. His eyes gleam red and his nostrils flare.

My mate freezes. Then she does a surprising thing. Isavelle turns away from him and squeezes her eyes shut, saying through gritted teeth, "Do it like you did it before. If I have to get on that dragon, then take me up there. I can't make myself do it."

Her arms are wrapped so tightly around herself, and she's shaking in fear. Seen through her eyes, my enormous black dragon is indeed a monster. Fire-breathing. Flesh-rending. A wild creature, but entirely tame for me, and for her, though she hasn't realized it yet.

I draw my mate closer, murmuring softly as I gather her to my chest and lift her up, a warm, soft bundle in my arms. Finally, I get to touch her again. Hold her. "I've got you, *sha'len*. No one is going to hurt you ever again. No one will take you from me."

She fits perfectly against me, a part of me that I've always known I was missing.

A wave of her delicious scent blooms around me, and I carefully press my face to her neck where there aren't any cuts. I feel my own scent glands tingle as they respond to my need to comfort and protect her, just as they did the first time I held her. As my scent wafts around her, she relaxes into me just a little.

"You're doing it again," she whispers drowsily. "That... something. I don't know what it is, but you're doing it."

"I am." How strange that she's not conscious of my scent but her body still responds to it.

I carry her atop Scourge and settle her between my thighs, carefully making sure her shaking body is secure.

"I'm holding you so tightly," I murmur, my lips against the top of her head. "You're safe. You will never fall. Nothing can hurt you when you're with me."

Scourge's body bunches beneath us, and then he launches into the air. My dragon undulates continuously as his wings beat and we gain height. These wavelike motions seem to upset Isavelle the most, and she whimpers and clutches my arm.

"I don't like flying. I'm going to throw up."

I pull her closer and tuck her face against my throat. "Breathe deeply. Close your eyes and take steady breaths."

"You smell good," she mumbles woozily a moment later. "Why do you smell so good? It's like—like—oh, it's gone again."

My heart zooms around inside my chest. Did she catch my scent for a moment? Dragons' teeth, I hope so. "I smell good to you because you're my Omega."

It's thrilling to say it out loud. *My Omega.* I still can't believe I've found her. What if I'd never woken up and she'd lived her whole life and died while I was still trapped beneath the mountain? Pain slices through my chest, and I hold her even tighter. This is the most precious thing that has ever happened to me. Isavelle will understand that I'm her Alpha and she'll learn to trust me completely. I won't waste this stars-sent chance.

"I'm your what?" she murmurs.

I suspected that she might have never heard the word, but her confirmation is no less disappointing. "You don't know what an Omega is?"

"No. Should I?"

I press my face into her hair and take another breath of her. Bliss. Pure bliss. "Isavelle. Why do you think I've been searching for you for days and days in the midst of fighting for my country?"

Her voice is dreamy over the rushing wind. "I have no idea. I'm not important, or beautiful, or noble. I stopped trying to understand why the High Priest was so obsessed with me long ago. I suppose I'm one of those people who powerful people like to hurt."

Fury and revulsion gather in my chest. Wherever this High Priest is hiding, I will find him, and I will shred the flesh from his bones.

"Zabriel? You feel...angry."

I quickly push away the burning hot emotion and focus on soothing my mate. "I'm sorry. I was thinking about that High Priest. We've climbed as high as we're going to, and Scourge is flying fast. It won't be long until we reach our destination."

We skim beneath the occasional cloud. The sky all around us is heavy with stars. I never fought for anything in my life as much as I've battled to reclaim each and every one of them.

But the fight isn't over yet.

I was imprisoned in that mountain as an untested youth, but I've emerged to prove I'm a man. I will be the mate that Isavelle needs, and the ruler the people of Maledin deserve.

I wonder when my father felt like the rightful ruler of Maledin. Was it when they placed a crown on his head, or when he mated Mother? I wonder if he ever truly felt like a king, or if he was only playing a role. It makes my heart ache to think so poorly of my father, but he was a lazy king. A foolish king. He neglected the people and ignored the treachery that was brewing under his nose until we lost everything.

I gaze down at the girl nestled in my arms, her eyes gently

closed and gripping a fistful of my cloak. I won't make the same mistakes my father did. Isavelle needs me, but so do the people of Maledin. I will retake our lands, and they will never know such suffering again.

As Scourge makes his descent, I scour the ground in the hope that this place has remained the same after all these centuries. I visited these hot springs hundreds of times in the past. The only way to reach them, high in a mountain valley, is by dragon.

With a stiff beating of his wings, Scourge lands on a stretch of grass by a steep cliff. Moonlight bathes steaming pools of water with silver light.

Keeping a secure hold on Isavelle, I carry her to the ground and try to set her on her feet, but she has her fingers curled so tightly into my cloak. With a smile, I realize my Omega is clinging to me, just as I was always told she would.

I *found* her.

I can't believe the gods have granted me an Omega, and that I found her so soon after waking beneath the mountain.

Keeping hold of Isavelle, I unbuckle my armor with my other hand while Scourge uses his strong talons to clamber up the mountainside. He settles there to guard us and watch the skies.

I manage to get all my armor and my clothes off while holding Isavelle against me, but I can't manage her clothes while she's huddled into me. They'll get wet, but I'll wrap her naked in my cloak for the flight back to Lenhale.

With my drowsy Omega in my arms, I walk into the steaming hot pool and sink into the water. Isavelle moans in relief as the soothing water envelops her, and some of the hurt in my heart lightens.

From now on, no one is going to be cruel to my woman. She'll know only happiness.

"What happened to your feet, *sha'len*?" I murmur in her ear, gently rubbing her arches beneath the water.

Isavelle's cheek is resting against my chest. "The boots I stole didn't fit, and I walked and walked in them. They gave me blisters. I left them in Mistress Hawthorne's cottage, and I've been barefoot ever since."

Slowly, her red and swollen feet begin to look less swollen and sore. I gently stroke water over her bruised and bloody lip with the pad of my thumb. Then I lean down and lick it. An Alpha's saliva is meant to heal his Omega, and she wouldn't let me kiss her earlier.

When she feels the brush of my tongue, she laughs softly and cuddles even closer against me. My heart swells, and I gather her closer. It's not the only thing that's swelling. I can feel my knot start to grow and ache beneath the water.

My hand skims over her bare skin where the shirt has slipped from her shoulder. "Who is responsible for all these bruises?"

Isavelle winces and buries her face in my chest. "The High Priest. He never hit me himself, but he made the other priests do it."

Anger mounts in my chest, but I make myself remain calm so it doesn't invade my scent and upset my mate. "Have I killed him yet?"

"Maybe you have, but he wasn't there tonight."

"What about at the funeral where you were nearly sacrificed?"

Isavelle nods. "He was there. He tried to grab hold of me

when you all landed on your dragons, but I ran the other way."

I feel my eyes narrow. I think I remember the man she's talking about. He wore a cowl, and I could see little of his face except that he had a dark beard with silver in it.

"You were clever to run. You ran right to me, *sha'len*, because you knew your mate would protect you."

Tears fill her eyes and roll down her cheeks, silvering them in the moonlight. "I've been all alone and so afraid. I didn't know who I could trust."

I cradle her in my arms and press a kiss to her brow. "You're safe now. I won't let anything happen to you."

We lay in the steaming water for some time while stars twinkle overhead and the moon carves a path through the heavens.

"I've never seen this place before," Isavelle says, gazing at the rising steam.

"This is a favorite place of mine. The water is soothing and heals your injuries. Are you feeling better?"

Isavelle whispers, "So much better."

We should leave soon, but before we do, I should get her out of these wet clothes. As I tug at the first button, she blinks and frowns, and raises her head. The effects of my scent seem to be wearing off.

"Are you naked?" She looks down at herself and sees that I'm undoing her shirt. "Wait, what are you doing?"

Isavelle pulls herself out of my grasp and starts to stand up in the thigh-deep water. Well, waist deep on her. Then she realizes her shirt is plastered to her body and turned see-through, and ducks down into the water again.

"How dare you try to undress me? What's going on?" she splutters.

I suppose it's only natural for my starved and injured Omega to become confused and upset by everything that's been happening.

"You can't get out of the water in wet clothes. I'll give you my cloak to wrap yourself in. It's bigger than you are and very warm." I reach for her, but she jerks away from me.

"I'll just wear wet clothes."

"No, you won't. You'll take off your clothes and put my cloak on. You're so weakened that wet clothes will make you ill."

Isavelle glances to the side of the pool where my cloak lays, and she seems to see the sense in that. "I'll take my own clothes off. Turn around, please."

"Why would I turn around?"

Her eyes widen in surprise. "So you don't see me naked."

"Why does it matter if I see you naked when you're mine?"

Isavelle glares at me. "I do not belong to you, and if you really believe that then I'm leaving. I'd rather be lost on this mountain than stay here with you."

Suppressing a snarl, I turn about-face and fold my arms. I'm not allowed to kiss my Omega, and I'm not allowed to look at her either? Every inch of her belongs to me to adore.

My Omega doesn't trust me. Whoever heard of such a thing? An Alpha would never in a thousand eons hurt his Omega or make her feel like she's anything less than precious and adored.

I wonder how humans court each other, and whether Isavelle is expecting something like that from me. I think hard for a moment, but I know so little about human culture that I come up with nothing. I suppose I'll have to show her that her Alpha can be kind and patient.

My lip curls at the thought.

Patient.

Now that I've found my mate, I want to run patience through with a sword, haul my Omega over my shoulder, and carry her to my bed. I stare straight ahead, fuming as I listen to Isavelle's wet clothes hit the edge of the pool.

"Oh, this is wonderful," Isavelle moans.

I turn back to see her chin-deep in the steaming pool. Her eyes drift closed, and she strokes her hands back and forth through the water. "I feel better already."

The relief in her voice soothes my ragged nerves. I've done something that my Omega approves of at last. I'm not the worst Alpha in the world.

I'm keenly aware of the aches and pains of battle in my body and the blood and dust coating my skin. My eyes are on Isavelle, drifting and soaking serenely in the steaming water. I stand up and move toward her, thigh-deep in the water. I need to be close to her, but I won't touch her if that's what she wants. If Isavelle needs me to be patient, then I'll be patient for her. I didn't wait five hundred years only to ruin everything by being hotheaded.

When I'm a few feet away, Isavelle opens her eyes, then opens them wider. She stares right at me, or I should say, a very specific part of me. Shock is writ so large on her face that I glance down at myself, wondering what's wrong. I'm thickened from being close to her, but I'm nowhere near erect and am very far from falling into a rut. My knot is a little swollen, but that's because I've been holding her in my arms. There's nothing about me that should alarm an inexperienced Omega. Even if I were in a rut, I wouldn't jump on her.

She gasps and whirls around, sinking even farther into the water so that it's up to her ears. "Zabriel, what are you doing?"

I frown at her in confusion. "Is there something wrong with me? Do I displease you?"

"You—you—" she stammers. "You're standing up in the water and you haven't got any clothes on."

"Neither have you," I point out, but I submerge myself and lay back against the smooth stones, letting the hot water work its magic on my aching body.

"What is..." She lifts her hand out of the water and steam rises from her fingers.

"What is what?"

Isavelle glances over her shoulder, sees that my body is beneath the water, and turns around. "That thing on your... um, never mind. Maybe we should have taken turns in the water."

"It's normal for people to bathe together," I murmur, catching sight of her dusky nipples beneath the water. Talons and fire, she's so beautiful. Not only her face but her body as well. Her breasts are full and luminous in the soft moonlight, but I make myself look away before she realizes that I'm staring.

"Children, yes. But not adults, and especially not men and women who barely know each other."

"That's not true."

"Yes, it is. Maybe you bathe naked with whomever you please where you come from, but in Maledin we don't do that."

"I'm from Maledin," I tell her, and a pang goes through my heart that I even need to say it. We're the same, her and me, but she looks upon me as if I came from a faraway star instead of trod the same ground as she did all my life.

"No, you're not. I would have noticed if someone like you had been flying around on a dragon."

I move closer to her in the water, and she stiffens. "Please don't flee. I promise I won't hurt you. I'm not armed, and I won't even touch you." I spread my arms beneath the water, inviting her to look at me. My long hair is wet and clinging to my shoulders. The hot springs have washed all the blood and dirt from my skin. Hopefully I don't look so terrifying anymore.

Isavelle lets her gaze travel over my face, my throat, my chest. "I would have noticed someone like you."

Take her in your arms and squeeze that lush body against your hard one. The instinct is almost overwhelming.

"Someone *like* me?" I murmur, moving closer to her. "Or me?"

Isavelle hesitates but stays where she is. She tilts her face up so she can look into my eyes, and she's close enough to place her palms on my chest if she wanted to. "There aren't many men over seven feet tall stomping around Maledin. There aren't any dragons, either."

"I was always here, *sha'len*. I haven't stepped foot out of Maledin in many, many centuries. Neither has Scourge. Neither have any of the other riders or their dragons."

Her brow wrinkles. "But how is that possible?"

"A long time ago, the rulers of Maledin were killed, and their soldiers and dragons were trapped beneath the Bodan Mountains by a powerful spell cast by a devious wizard."

"Are you talking about 'The Mountain Prisoner'? But that's just a story."

Relief pours through me. If she knows the story, then my people and I haven't completely disappeared from the memories of the people of Maledin. "The hag of your village knew me the moment she saw me, but you know how strange hags can be. I wasn't sure if anyone else would know what happened to me and my riders."

"Biddy Hawthorne knew you?"

"Is that her name? Yes, Mistress Hawthorne is a canny old witch." A horrible thought occurs to me. "Wait, do you think that no one else in Maledin knows who I am? I'm just a story to everyone but the witches?"

"I don't know. Who are you?"

I study Isavelle's beautiful face with its sweet little nose, adorably curved cheeks, and lush pink mouth. She truly doesn't know. She's heard the stories, but they're so old and implausible that they couldn't possibly be true.

I'm not real to her.

Hopelessness and exhaustion wash over me. Everything I've ever known and loved has vanished from Maledin. Reclaiming this country is going to be a lot harder than winning the war if my people don't know who I am.

"You only mentioned other dragonriders. Where's your family, Zabriel?"

I watch steam rising from her bare shoulders and say flatly, "They're all dead. They died a long time ago."

I miss my mother terribly, and my sister as well.

The rest? They can rot in hell.

"I'm sorry," she whispers. "I truly am. I just want to find my family. I think they might still be alive, but they won't stay that way if this war continues. You're a commander, so maybe you can do something. Please stop attacking Maledin."

What she's asking for is impossible. We won't stop until we've reclaimed every square inch of Maledin.

"We're here to protect you all. We have no quarrel with the people, human or Maledinni. It's the Brethren and their guards we're fighting. Do you have sympathy for the Brethren? Do you wish for things to carry on as they have been? These people were going to throw you on a funeral pyre and burn you to death."

"But at least before my family was safe in their village," she cries.

I take a deep breath. "Listen. We've taken the capital. In a few days, we will have driven all the Brethren out of Maledin and the people can return to their villages. Your family and everyone else will hear word that it's safe to come home."

The moonlight has turned Isavelle's eyelashes silver and her lips press together. I can feel her wanting to believe me, but she doesn't know if she can.

"Is that true?"

"I swear it. Everything would have been over by now, but I was distracted by looking for someone." I give Isavelle a small smile.

She doesn't return it.

"Life will be better for everyone in Maledin from now on," I promise.

Isavelle doesn't jump for joy and throw herself into my arms, but she doesn't doubt me either. I nearly reach out to her in the water. My mate is naked and right there in front of me, and we should be wrapped around each other, tasting each other with our tongues and stroking each other with our fingers. She should be learning my scent. Feeling her Omega awaken. If the designations have grown dormant in the people of Maledin while they've been separated from the dragons, then everyone is going to need to wake up. I'm impatient for it to happen to my mate. I wonder how long it's going to take. I can smell Isavelle's Omega, and she responds to me soothing her, so it should happen soon.

Maybe I can find a way to help Isavelle's Omega wake up. *Let Alpha lavish your clit with his tongue. Dig your little talons into my muscles. Wrap your fingers in my hair and pull my face into your sex as you climax.*

I swallow a groan and force myself to think about something else. I'm a long way from any of that with her.

"We can all go home? Do you really mean that, Zabriel?"

"The villagers and townspeople of Maledin, yes. I swear it on my sword. On my *life*."

"Can you even promise that? On what authority?"

"I'm the commander of the dragonriders. You saw for yourself tonight how the soldiers follow my orders." A little voice in the back of my mind prevents me from uttering the words, *and I'm their future king*. Isavelle has probably had a gutful of kings for now.

"Your people will honor your oath?"

"*Our* people. Yours and mine."

She shakes her head. "I don't know about that. To me, you're the invaders who have forced us from our homes, and now you give me this strange story about the mountains and an evil wizard."

Not so strange. She's heard that story all her life from the sounds of it. She just didn't realize every word of it was true, and that it was about her mate.

"You will see soon enough how we all fit together. The dragonriders and the people of Maledin. You and me." My hungry gaze slips down her body without me realizing what I'm doing.

Isavelle turns pink—even pinker than the hot water has made her—and spins quickly away from me.

"I'm sorry," I say, and cut my gaze to the left. I can't help my frustration and ask, "You don't like me to look at you? I don't mind if you look at me. I would *love* for you to look at me."

"We're naked," she replies in an uncertain whisper. "It's not right to look upon each other naked."

"Who says?"

"Everyone. The Brethren."

I move around Isavelle until we're face to face again but keep my eyes above the waterline. "The same Brethren who beat you and starved you? You think they told you the truth about anything? You and I share a bond, *sha'len*. Water is a sacred place, and it pleases me to be close to you here. I won't touch you unless you want me to, but there's nothing to be ashamed of in enjoying these springs together."

She gazes at the water droplets gleaming on my chest in the moonlight. "I'm not ashamed. You're—you're just a lot."

I smile at her. "Where am I a lot?"

"All over." Her eyes fly open as she realizes what she's said. "I mean—you're tall."

Oh, my sweet blushing Omega. I saw you staring at my knot.

If Isavelle wasn't so shy, I'd invite her to wrap her fingers around me and feel me swell even bigger by her touch.

"And you're a delicious armful," I murmur, remembering

how she's plump and soft in my arms. I've never felt anything so delectable.

Isavelle swallows, hard. "Thank you for saving me from the Brethren, twice. I really do appreciate it. I don't know why you and your friends came to Maledin, but you're here now, and you seem to be winning, so please try not to be worse than the Brethren and the last king."

My eyes narrow as Isavelle makes her little speech. It sounds like she's working her way up to bidding me goodbye.

"I'm heading toward the southwest because that's the closest border to my village, and I think my family may have fled that way. I know you're probably a busy man, being a commander in the army, but may I please ask you to fly me somewhere that's a little south of my village? I'll ask around to discover if anyone has seen people from my home."

I gaze down my nose and grit my teeth against the torrent of outrage that wants to spill from my lips. Take her toward the south, in the direction that the Brethren have fled?

When Scourge's dragonfire turns to ice, I'll take her south.

"I can't do that."

Her face falls. "Oh. Well, can you please point me in that direction? I'll walk."

"I can't do that either," I growl.

"Can't, or won't?"

"Absolutely, positively won't. You're coming with me to Lenhale."

Isavelle's expression smolders with frustration. The scent of my outraged Omega washes over me, and I harden my heart to the knowledge that I'm making her furious. I don't care that she's furious with me.

Better furious than dead.

7

Isavelle

Zabriel is towering over me with a thunderous expression. Tears sting my eyes, and my voice shakes as I say, "But you said that I could go home."

More tears well up. I hold my breath so I don't sob like a child.

While I was a prisoner of the Brethren, I once asked the High Priest when I would be allowed to go home. Sometimes the Veiled Virgins return to their villages after serving for a year or two. Some ask to stay longer. The High Priest laughed cruelly and rubbed his fingers across his salt-and-pepper jaw, saying, *What makes you think I'm letting you go, Harrow?*

The days and weeks were long and cruel, and they stretched on and on, seemingly forever. I wanted to die. I craved to be turned to ash and blown away on the wind so I'd finally be free.

I never understood why the High Priest hated me so much. Sometimes I caught him staring at me, a furious expression on his face as if he didn't understand it either. I have no doubt that throwing me onto the king's funeral pyre was his idea. He was probably excited to see me burn.

The moonlight paints harsh shadows on Zabriel's face, and his eyes glow red. "I said the people of Maledin could go home."

The words he spoke were not the words I thought I heard. "Am I not a person to you?"

Zabriel clutches my upper arms. "You are *everything* to me. You were always meant to be mine."

"Please, please let me go," I beg him, and I can't hold the tears back any longer. They spill down my cheeks in fat drops. "I won't tell anyone we met. I'm not dangerous to you. I just want my family and then I'll leave Maledin forever. I'll do anything you want, just please let me go."

I can't stop myself from sobbing brokenly.

Zabriel presses his full lips together and shakes his head.

Hopeless tears spill down my cheeks. "Why are you doing this to me? I'm not beautiful and rich, or witty and charming. Is it that I can't fight back? Is that exciting to you? Is there something about me that invites people to hurt me and push me around? Please tell me because I need to understand why this keeps happening."

Zabriel makes a sound like he's in pain. In a harsh whisper he says, "I should have been here to protect you. In a way, you are right. There's a hierarchy in Maledinni society, and you're at the bottom of it. The people around you can sense it, and when you fight back, they want to punish you for not giving them the obedience they crave."

I wipe the tears from my cheeks, hiccupping as I try to catch my breath. Punish me for not giving them the obedience they crave? That's exactly what the High Priest was doing. I kept defying him, and his cruelty worsened. The other Veiled Virgins told me to grovel before him, but I couldn't stop fighting.

"So that's why you want me," I say in a broken whisper. Maybe it will be less painful just to give up.

"No, Isavelle. That's not why I want you. You're my only hope, and I'm yours."

"Hope of what?"

Zabriel's expression is heartfelt. Desperate. "If I don't have you, I may as well turn to ashes and float away on the wind."

That might be the craziest thing he's said so far, and he claims he was trapped under the Bodan Mountains for centuries.

I shake my head. "You're strong and you're clever. You have a dragon and a sword. You'll be fine without me."

Zabriel's jaw is tight, and the muscles on either side of his throat are flexing. I must be insane, making this enormous man furious with me. We're all alone in the middle of the night, and we're naked together. If he wanted to hurt me, there would be nothing I could do to stop him.

He sighs and rakes his fingers through his long hair, water running down his bicep and dripping from his elbow. "It's late. We're both exhausted and hungry, and Scourge needs to rest and feed after so many battles. All I care about right now is keeping the two of you safe."

I wince. Am I his pet? That's as terrible as being his prisoner. I'm something to put in a cage and play with when he's bored, and as soon as he's tired of me, I'll be discarded.

He stands up so fast that I don't have time to look away, and water cascades down his sculpted body. The man is more naked than it should be possible to be naked. With his dark hair spilling down his chest, his lower half stands out in stark relief, and I catch sight of that thing again.

Not his...manhood. Oh, stars, am I really calling it that? His...length? His organ? I hate words. Who decided we should start naming things but make the names absolutely, excruciatingly embarrassing?

It's not *that* part of him that's making me writhe in mortification, though it's long and thick enough to make me wonder how he carries it around all day. What I don't understand is why it's got a swelling right at the base. Men don't have that. At least, I think they don't. I'm not completely sure, though.

That bulge makes me feel strange. I shouldn't be thinking about it, but suddenly it's the only thing on my mind. Something inside me is highly interested in that specific part of him, and I'm not only curious about it, I'm so excited that I want to throw it a parade.

Zabriel reaches out a hand to me and waits for me to take it.

I cover my eyes, blushing red to the tips of my ears. "Please. You don't want me. I promise you don't. I'm damaged goods. I'm weak and injured. It's best that I find my family and leave Maledin with them."

"Why would you leave Maledin? The war is nearly over. The old king is dead and a new one will soon be crowned. There will never be another war in Maledin in your lifetime."

I peep up at him through my fingers, and he's still standing right there, lit up by moonlight. "Can you please cover yourself? I can't think when you're standing there with your whole everything out."

"I am going to have to write myself a list in order to keep up with your demands," he growls, an edge to his voice.

I flinch away from his sharp words. I suppose his soldiers jump to it whenever Commander Zabriel gives them an order. "If I go with you, then I'll have to get down on my knees for your new king. I can't bow to an invader king."

"He never asked you to," Zabriel snaps.

They never ask, but they expect. I turn away and wade toward the edge of the pool, but Zabriel reaches out and gently grasps my fingers.

"Listen to me, Isavelle. Please. Refugees are already passing through Lenhale to collect food and supplies to repair damage to homes and farms. Representatives from every town and village, including yours, are being asked to report to the capital for aid. The best place to find your family, if they plan on returning for you, is there."

If they plan on returning for me. Fear and loneliness tug at my chest. I haven't seen my family in over a year, but they wouldn't just leave me behind. Would they?

I glance at Zabriel's fingers holding mine and try to sound like I believe it when I say, "Of course they plan on returning for me."

"Then Lenhale is where you will find them or hear news of them. I don't say this to persuade you to do what I want. You will see for yourself on this very day that I'm telling the truth. If you're not satisfied, then we'll think of something else. Together."

I nibble on my lower lip. My village is five days' journey on foot from the capital. If Zabriel is lying or tries to keep me prisoner, I can escape and find my way home on my own. "What will you expect from me while I'm in Lenhale? Soldiers expect spoils of war."

"I don't know what *spoils of war* means." He releases me and steps back. "If you're worried that I'll force you or hurt you, I claim nothing that you're not willing to give. I can wait."

I meet his eyes, which is difficult to do when I'm crouched in the water and my head doesn't clear his thighs. "You'll... wait? You presume I'll change my mind?"

A smile spreads over his lips and he laughs darkly. Then he shouts, "*Scourge*," making me jump. To me, he says, "Come on. It's time to go."

"Please turn around so I can get out of the water."

He does as he is asked, and I'm treated to a view of his muscular ass. This man is a work of very touchable art, and I force myself to look away and concentrate on getting out of the water and pulling on my wet, ragged clothes so I don't sneak looks at him.

The dragon clambers down the mountainside, his red eyes fixed on my naked body, and I hurry to finish getting dressed. Scourge's eyes feel suspiciously like Zabriel's eyes.

"I can call Scourge with my mind, but I thought you might get scared if he suddenly landed next to you."

Well, that's certainly true.

I wait with my back turned while Zabriel gets out of the water and pulls his clothes on. I can hear his armor clanking and the sound of leather bag flaps being opened and closed. Maybe he's packing it all away rather than putting it back on.

There's a soft step behind me. Zabriel puts a hand on my waist, and the next thing I know, I'm scooped up with his arm behind my knees. I'm suddenly very high off the ground, and I gasp and wrap my arms around his neck automatically.

This is the first time he's held me when he's not wearing armor, and his muscular body is yielding and inviting. The well-washed fabric of his black shirt feels soft against my fingers, and the nape of his neck is warm and smooth.

"I've been dying to hold you like this, *sha'len*," he whispers against my ear, carrying me over to Scourge. His lips delicately trace my jaw. My throat. "You feel like heaven in my arms and you smell even better." He buries his face in my neck and groans, "Fuck, you make my knot ache."

His knot? What's a knot? But I don't have time to ask before he grabs hold of Scourge's leather harness and carries me up onto the dragon.

As Scourge prepares to take off, I push my face in Zabriel's shoulder and tighten my arms around his neck. "I really don't like this. Doesn't flying make you sick?"

"Our kind were made to ride dragons. You will learn to love it."

I doubt that. It feels like we leave my stomach behind as we lurch into the air, but then it rebounds with a vengeance.

Zabriel wraps his cloak around me. This is absolutely the last time I'm getting on a dragon, and I won't be getting this close to my captor ever again, but for now, I snuggle into him for warmth and that delicious sensation of sinking down, down, down into decadent comfort. I don't know how he does that. It must be some kind of magic.

We've been flying for some time when Zabriel murmurs, "*Sha'len*, look. My home."

I sleepily drag my eyes open, but I can't make myself peel my cheek away from his chest. "Hmm?"

The sun has begun to rise.

I see it. Lenhale.

The dawn has painted the sky in shades of gold and blue and turned the underside of feathery clouds to blush pink. The landscape sweeps upward, and fields and forests turn into farms, which run up against a city wall. Within the walls, there are wide streets and twisting, turning laneways. Manor houses and rows of cottages. Walled gardens and orchards. Nothing seems to have been planned out, and yet everything fits together without a scrap of wasted space.

Crowning the city is a vast palace of creamy stone, lit golden by the sun with crenelated walls and pointed turrets thrusting up into the sky. The sight is breathtaking. Intimidating. I can't imagine not getting lost inside that vast space. This is where the kings and queens of Maledin have dwelled for hundreds of years, yet Zabriel called this place his home.

Beyond the palace, there's a shallow valley and a strip of bare ground before a cliff that rises steeply. It's to this place that Scourge takes us. There are things moving about on the ground and the cliff face as well. Huge, strange things of many colors.

Dragons.

Dozens of the monsters.

My stomach lurches as we come into land, but thankfully I manage not to retch. The dust settles, and every dragon in the field or perched on the cliff is staring at us.

Zabriel follows my gaze. "They won't hurt you. Dragons are as intelligent as you and me, and they understand that you're welcome here."

Zabriel carries me carefully down Scourge's flank and places me on the ground. Half a dozen curious dragons have drawn closer and extended their heads on their long necks toward me. Their nostrils flare, and several have their jaws parted, revealing an alarming number of fine, sharp teeth.

"Are they smelling me?"

"Scent is important to all dragons and Maledinni."

When a midnight blue dragon thrusts its head and shoulders past the others as if it means to eat me, I gasp and shrink back. Scourge roars at the blue dragon until it backs off. The other dragons move away as well. I wonder if Scourge is in charge of the…flock? Herd? He's by far the largest of the dragons that I can see.

Zabriel puts a protective arm around my shoulder. "They won't hurt you, but they can be overly curious. Come on, this way."

He leads me through the field, which is a lot bigger on the ground than it looks from the air. The dragons stay back, but I can feel myself being watched by many pairs of bright, predatory eyes.

We cross a stone bridge over the valley, pass through a gate, and then we're inside the towering castle walls made from pale stone.

"We only took the capital two days ago," Zabriel explains as we pass through a courtyard with broken wooden fortifications in a scorched heap. "King Alaster fled and left it almost defenseless. The castle seems to be secure, but there will be many soldiers on guard while we brace for more attacks. You'll be safe as long as you remain inside the walls."

As we enter the castle, the various men and women on duty stand to attention and then bow as Zabriel goes by. How strange. I suppose he must outrank all these soldiers.

I try to keep track of which way we go, but I lose my way

as fatigue overwhelms me, and we walk down dozens of corridors and up flights of stairs. Zabriel seems to know where we're going, but I don't think I could find my way back. This place is enormous.

"How do you know where we're going?" I ask him with a yawn.

"I've walked these halls a thousand times before."

We pass a flag hanging on a wall that I recognize as belonging to the dead king, the one to whom I was going to be sacrificed. Zabriel yanks it down with an angry snarl and grinds it beneath his boot.

Finally we reach a door, and Zabriel pushes it open. "I asked for this room to be prepared for you. I hope it's to your liking, *sha'len*."

While he was hunting for me, and before he even knew he'd find me? I peek inside and see a huge room with thick, ornate tapestries on the walls, an enormous fireplace, rugs, and a canopied bed heaped with blankets.

I'm not important enough for a room like this. Zabriel is trying to trick and humiliate me. I turn back to him, saying, "Please don't make fun of me. Just take me to my real room so I can get some sleep."

His eyebrows shoot up. "This is your room."

"Do you really expect me to believe that? This room is far too luxurious."

"I'm too tired to jest. This is where you will sleep."

I hunt his expression for even a hint of mockery. "Wait, really? You mean that? If I step inside, you won't laugh at me or beat me for trespassing somewhere I shouldn't?"

"You were beaten for that kind of thing?" he growls, fury flashing over his expression.

I was beaten for the smallest of reasons. For no reason.

I'm so tired and that bed looks inviting. A room of my own instead of a cell or a freezing dormitory is a strange thing indeed. "Thank you. I'll go in and sleep."

"Take care in the palace, Isavelle, and don't wander too far. Never forget that there are enemies beyond these castle walls and people who would do anything to get their hands on you. Now, close the door and lock it behind you. I won't leave until you do."

I take a look at the door and see that the lock is on the inside rather than the outside. That makes a surprising change. "I'm allowed to leave this room if I want to?"

He points down the corridor. "The Great Hall is that way. If you turn right before you reach it, you will find the main courtyard. I will look for you here and in those places. They are all well-guarded, and you will be safe."

What I hear is that there will be soldiers watching my every move.

Zabriel waits as if he's expecting me to thank him, but I regard him in silence. I've been told my eyes are too expressive for my own good, so he can probably tell that I'm not feeling grateful for my captivity.

"I'll bid you farewell, Isavelle. One last thing." He takes my hand and raises it to his lips. For a moment I think he's going to kiss my palm, but then he buries his nose in my wrist, closes his eyes, and breathes in deeply.

Zabriel's countenance softens and this enormous man looks...endearing. He changes so utterly from smelling my wrist?

He lets me go and stands back.

"Why did you do that?" I ask in surprise.

"To get me through until the next time I see you. It will feel like another five hundred years. Now, lock this door. I'll send someone with food in a few minutes."

I close the door. There's a big brass key in the lock, and I twist it until I feel the lock slide into place. A door with the lock on the inside instead of on the outside? This prison cell is nothing like I've ever known before, and it's bigger and more luxurious than any room at the monastery.

I listen to Commander Zabriel's footsteps receding down the corridor. He is without a doubt the strangest man I've ever met.

The room is surprisingly cozy for such a large space. The fire crackles and the candlelight is soft. Someone has left a chest open against one wall, and I see clean clothing inside. I pick out garment after garment. Some of the underclothes seem fine, but the dresses are ridiculous. Or rather, they'd look ridiculous on someone like me. Long, trailing things in rich colors, and so luxurious that I feel like I might drown in them. I drop them back in. I can't wear these.

There's a knock on my door, and I stand before it in an agony of fear and indecision.

"Lady Isavelle?" calls an unfamiliar male voice.

"What is it?" I reply, my voice high and tight with fear.

"Commander Zabriel asked me to bring you food."

My stomach convulses in response. Food. I haven't eaten since that mouthful of milk days ago. With trembling fingers, I unlock the door and open it just a few inches to reveal a soldier in a black and silver uniform holding a wooden platter. My mouth waters at the sight of bread, meat, cheese, and fruit, but I still can't make myself open the door.

"Would you like all your meals brought to you in your

room? Or you may eat in the Great Hall if you prefer," the soldier offers.

Have all my meals brought to me like a fine lady expects? This soldier must think I'm important for some reason. How he'll laugh when he realizes who I really am. Besides, leaving this room for my meals will be a good excuse to hunt for a way to escape. "Thank you, but I will eat in the Great Hall for my future meals. And just Isavelle is fine. Sorry, what was your name?"

The man respectfully bows his head. "Captain Ashton, wingrunner." He has brown, curly hair, tanned olive skin, and a serious face with scars along his jaw. Serious, but kind.

"You ride a dragon?"

"A wyvern, my lady."

I wonder what wyverns are as I carefully open the door a little wider and take the platter from him. The food looks delicious, but I hesitate before I close the door. "Captain, I'm sorry to ask you this, but can you please bring me a dress that a maid would wear?"

The soldier frowns. "Commander Zabriel arranged for there to be dresses in your room. Are they not to your liking?"

"They...aren't the right size. Thank you, I appreciate it," I say before he can argue, and I shut the door.

I set the platter on a table by the fire and immediately stuff three grapes into my mouth. I groan in pleasure as the sweet fruit bursts over my tongue.

A few minutes later, I've gobbled up half the fruit and Captain Ashton is back. He hands me two well-worn and patched dresses with simple bodices and skirts, though he's frowning as he does it.

"Thank you, Captain," I say, closing the door once more.

"You're welcome, Lady Isavelle."

"Just Isavelle, please. I'm not a lady," I call through the wood as I turn the lock.

I lay the dresses on my bed for now and finish eating while standing before the fire. Soon I'm warm and my belly is so full that I'm falling asleep on my feet. I drink some of the wine that came with the food, and a long draft of cold water from a nearby ewer, before stumbling over to the bed.

I take off the ragged soldier's clothes, get between the sheets, and pull the blankets up over my head. My bruised body sinks into the soft mattress, and I groan in pleasure. The hot springs dulled a lot of the pain, and food and a warm bed are finishing me off.

With my eyes closed, I think about where I am and wonder what's going to happen tomorrow. The moment I was tithed, the Brethren began to beat me. Break me. Lock me up. Zabriel has given me the key to this room, but I didn't want to come here, and I still feel like a prisoner. I will feel like a prisoner until I find my family and go home.

~

Flames.

Licking up my legs. Scorching my feet. Consuming my charred flesh and turning me to ash. No matter how much I struggle, I can't move, can't run, can't *escape*—

I sit up with a frantic gasp, clawing at my hair until I realize that I'm not being suffocated by smoke, but by a blanket that was covering my face. I push my hair out of my face and take a few calming breaths, willing the nightmare to recede. Where am I?

The fire in the grate has died down, but there's golden light edging a tapestry. I get out of bed and pull it back. There are still a few more hours of daylight. I haven't slept the whole day away.

I look out, taking a moment to get my bearings. I'm in a room high in the keep from the looks of things, and I can see soldiers and other people below, and beyond the castle walls, the city. On the distant horizon, a dragon beats its majestic wings.

So, this is the capital.

I never imagined I'd be here or even see it. Who could ever have predicted that there would be dragons in the skies over Maledin?

I pour water from the ewer into the basin, give myself a wash with a handcloth, and pull on some underclothes and then one of the maid's dresses. Captain Ashton chose a good size, but the dress still trails on the ground a little. I pull some soft shoes onto my feet and wrap a cloak around my shoulders.

Leaving my room, I head in the direction of the Great Hall. There are a number of people around, but in my homespun dress, no one pays me a lick of attention, and that's exactly how I like it. I dodge around tall people in armor who look like they might be dragonriders, and others in black and silver uniforms, who could be wingrunners like Captain Ashton.

Then there are people who seem to find the dragonriders and wingrunners as strange as I do, but they are getting on with their work. I wonder if these people have always worked in the castle. It seems strange that whoever is in charge here trusts them to move around freely.

I take an apple and a slice of pie from a platter that has been set out, find a seat on a bench in a corner, and devour the food. All the while I watch people coming and going, tensing up every time someone armed goes near one of the servants. It was normal to see the Brethren strike their novices or the Veiled Virgins several times a day. Their robes weren't neat enough. They raised their eyes. They were walking too fast. Too slow. Any excuse would do. If you cried out when someone else was beaten or tried to protect them, your beating was even worse.

I sit by the wall for some time, but nothing whatsoever happens except for people eating, fetching, carrying, talking. Even laughing.

At the far end of the hall, one of the huge double doors is ajar, and a thin shaft of weak winter sunlight is streaming inside. I wonder what will happen if I go that way. Zabriel warned me not to wander too far, but I should test how far is far.

I follow a man hauling a basket of pears as he heads out the main doors and into a huge, dusty courtyard.

And I stop dead.

There are dozens and dozens of people gathered there. No, not just people.

Villagers.

Tears fill my eyes as I recognize the simple clothes and hairstyles that belong to the people of Maledin, and among them, there's not a single robed Brethren or an armored soldier. It's been so long since I've seen so many of my people gathered in one place. There are children, too. Girls in smocks and boys in breeches and shirts. Everyone looks ragged and tired, their faces pinched with sleeplessness and worry, but they're uninjured. They're alive. Most of them are resting or eating, and some of the children are even playing games.

A little boy of about two runs across the courtyard away from his mother, who has a baby in her arms and another child clinging to her skirt. The toddler is oblivious to a donkey and cart being led across the flagstones.

"Poul, no—!" the mother calls.

I scoop the little boy up in my arms and stand back to allow the donkey and cart to pass, and then take him over to his mother. The little boy, frustrated in his ambitions to reach the other side of the courtyard, starts to scream.

The woman seems close to bursting into tears as the baby starts to cry in her arms. "Thank you for your kindness. I'm about at my wit's end with these three. Their father has gone to see about a cart for us, but I don't have much hope."

I sit down beside her on a log with the boy in my arms and fashion a straw dolly with some wisps of hay that are on the ground. Poul's cries quieten as he watches me work, and he grabs at bits of hay. "He's a beautiful little boy. I'm Isavelle, by the way. Isavelle Harrow of Amriste. Over by Gunster, in the west," I add when the woman gives me a blank look. No one's ever heard of Amriste.

"Ah, the west. Never been there myself. Aster Yackley of Nobble. I thought we had a long walk home, but if you're past Gunster, then I hope you have a pair of sturdy shoes."

We both look at my bare and blistered feet. "I won't be setting off yet. I'm looking for people from over my way who might be able to tell me about my family. I haven't seen them in over a year, and I've just discovered my village was abandoned."

"Like every village near and far. Curse those dragons," she mutters and glares at a nearby soldier.

"Did the invaders kill people in your village?" I ask.

She shakes her head. "No one was hurt, but they set fire to the church, and we weren't waiting around to see what would be next. We thought we'd be safe in Lenhale, but then all the Brethren Guard deserted the place and the invaders came here as well." She glances nervously around and then whispers, "What strange people they are. Some of them have purple eyes. Golden eyes, even. They've said we can return to our village tomorrow. Do you think we can believe them?"

I bounce Poul on my knee and waggle the dolly before his eyes so he takes it from me. "I don't know, but if that's what they've promised you, we'll find out in the morning if the invaders will honor their word."

The woman nods and swallows, placing the baby in a wicker bassinet. "That we will. I'll be praying that it will be so."

I wince as I hear the word *pray*. No one was very fond of the Brethren, but people still take their praying seriously. I gave up that anyone was listening long ago. If someone was listening to me, then they weren't on my side.

My neck prickles, and I see something out of the corner of my eye. Someone is making their way toward me across the courtyard.

Someone large and dressed in black and crimson.

Aster sucks in a breath. "It's that invader who told us we could leave tomorrow. He's absolutely terrif— Oh, God's balls, he's coming this way."

My arms tighten reflexively around Poul as Zabriel marches over and stops right in front of me. My eyes travel slowly up his muddy leather boots, black breeches and doublet, and that long cloak lined with crimson.

Zabriel watches me intently, looking from my face to the toddler in my arms and back again, a smile turning up the corner of his lips. "How wonderful to see you up and about so soon. Did you sleep well, *sha'len*?"

Aster's mouth falls open, and I feel my face burn. The two of us were having a conversation, villager to villager, and now I look like some kind of traitor. A traitor who's been sleeping in an invader's bed.

I swallow hard and pass the boy back to his mother. "This soldier saved my life the other day, and I haven't been able to shake him off since. Good luck with your journey tomorrow. I hope you make it safely home." I want to add, *I didn't sleep in his bed*, but I don't know how without sounding like I'm protesting too much.

Aster gives me a doubtful look. There's chilliness in her expression, and she doesn't say goodbye as I stand up. I should have been honest with her instead of pretending I was another refugee just like her. I'm not like her. I slept the day away in a soft, warm bed, and a soldier personally brought me food and clothes.

I move past Zabriel and hurry away, but he follows me and catches my hand, pulling me around to face him. "Something's wrong. What has upset you?"

Dozens of pairs of eyes have fastened on this huge invader soldier holding on to my hand.

"Nothing. Don't." I try to pull my hand back from his but he won't let go.

"Tell me," he growls.

"I feel like a traitor because you're giving me special treatment. Please, can you just leave me be while I wait for news of my family? No one here will trust me if they think I'm on your side and not theirs."

Both his eyebrows rise. "We're all on the same side. I explained that to you last night."

"These people don't believe that. You invaded on *dragons*."

Slowly, Zabriel lets go of my hand. I brace for him to order me back to my room. To tell me I should be on his side, not theirs, and spout that nonsense about us being mates and destined for each other. He gazes around the courtyard at the broken-down, desperate, and hungry people who were driven from their homes by him and the other dragonriders.

"Have you found anyone from your village? Seen anyone you know?"

I shake my head.

"I'm sorry to hear that," he murmurs, and I'm surprised to hear genuine remorse in his voice.

"Why did you and the other dragonriders burn all the villages?"

Zabriel folds his arms and frowns down his long, regal nose at me. "We didn't. We burned the churches. The monasteries. The barracks that belonged to the Brethren Guard. We destroyed the interlopers' buildings, but we have no quarrel with the people of Maledin. Your village had no Brethren buildings. Was it touched? You walked for days to reach your home. Was every town and village burned to the ground, or was it only the Brethren buildings that were destroyed? Were crops razed? Animals slaughtered? Women and children dead in the streets?"

I think about this carefully. It was difficult to tell which buildings were destroyed, but I don't remember seeing burning fields or dead villagers. "No, but… Everyone is terrified. Why did you even invade Maledin in the first place?"

"Because it's ours," he snarls, and his dull red eyes glow ferociously hot.

I flinch back. There's the dragon in him. The part that hungers and consumes.

Zabriel takes a deep breath and the flames ebb from his eyes. "I promise we're not here to destroy and kill. We wish to reclaim and liberate."

"You terrified a whole country. It's going to take a long time for anyone to trust you."

Zabriel nods, his expression serious. "I know. That's why we've already started." He glances around at the refugees. "What do they need to be more comfortable through the night?"

I look around the courtyard. "More hay and blankets so that they are warm. Carts for traveling home. Shelters so that they have some privacy and a sense of safety. Some people who are not carrying weapons or dressed in armor to help with the children."

"I shall see that this all happens immediately." His expression softens as he gazes at me, and he says in a low voice, "Thank you, *sha'len*. I am more grateful to you than you can know."

Sha'len. That's what he called me when I was tied up and veiled, and he's said it several times since. "Why don't you call me by my name instead of whatever that word is? What does it mean?"

A smile tugs the corner of his beautiful lips. "*Sha'len*? It means little dragon."

"I'm not a dragon."

Zabriel's eyes dance with amusement, and he steps closer to me. "Anyone can call you Isavelle, but this is a special name. It means that you're just for me."

Though he's not touching me, his possessiveness wraps around me like a physical embrace. I throw it off with a flippant question. "What do you want me to call you? Big dragon?"

He tips back his head and roars with laughter. When his shoulders stop shaking, the gaze he pins me with is smoldering. Bending close, he whispers, "I have a few ideas for what you can call me, but that's for another time."

My face flames red, and I don't even know why.

Taking advantage of the fact that I'm already close to him, he dips his head and his nose skims my cheek by my ear as he breathes, "Please stay within these courtyards, and don't overwork yourself. One more hour, and then go and rest." He touches my face and then cups my chin, drawing my face up to his. "I worry about you, *sha'len*. You are still recovering from what those monsters did to you."

I gasp softly at his touch and the heat suddenly rippling through my body.

He stares at my mouth and his own lips part. For a wild second, I think he's going to kiss me. I'm frozen to the spot by those red eyes, and if he does kiss me, there'll be nothing I can do to stop him.

Zabriel strokes his thumb over my chin, and then says in a murmur, "You are full of surprises. I love the sight of you with a baby in your arms, *sha'len*."

He steps back and strides away.

Finally, I can breathe again. A baby in my arms? What's that supposed to mean?

As I glance around, everyone in the courtyard quickly looks away and acts busy.

On the other side of the courtyard, Zabriel approaches a row of guards and talks to them for a moment before turning and looking in my direction and giving me a small smile. The guards all nod and keep their eyes on me as Zabriel leaves the courtyard.

Soon after that, hay, blankets, and tents are brought to the courtyard, and I help to distribute them, but as I work, I can feel the guards following my every move. It seems I'm being watched at all times. As kind as he wants me to believe he is, Zabriel doesn't seem to trust me.

Night falls, and I don't want to go back to my room. I belong here with my people, and so I find a place beneath a shelter, drag a blanket over my body, and settle down on the hay. I'm so tired that I'm out like a candle being snuffed.

Sometime later, I awaken when someone shakes my shoulder and whispers, "*Sha'len*? You can't sleep here."

"Mmph." I'm too exhausted to even open my eyes. The man sighs, I hear the hay scrunch beside me, then a massive warm body wraps around my own.

There's a heavy breath in my ear as he settles down to sleep, and he huffs, "Someone should have warned me that Omegas could be so stubborn."

I AWAKEN in the thin gray light of dawn and feel the empty straw around me. I thought that Zabriel was here, sleeping against me. Or did I merely dream it? My hand lands on a warm spot on the straw as if someone lay there not long ago, and there's a strange feeling low in my belly as I picture him curled around me all night.

A soft whisper caresses the back of my mind. *Zabriel craves to protect me*, and an answering flush of heat courses through my body.

I shove the blanket off and get up, angrily shaking the hay from my skirts. I won't simper over that man. He's the enemy, and he's dangerous.

The refugees are all awake and packing away their possessions in carts and onto donkeys. I help where I can, then stand to one side as they line up by the locked gates, anxious to leave this place. There are a great deal of whispers about whether they'll be able to leave at all, and people spare fearful glances at the guards.

The mood in the courtyard and in my belly is anxious, and I find myself gripping my thumbs in my fists and begging silently, *Please, please, please don't be a liar on top of everything else, Zabriel. Let these people go. Prove that you and your people will keep your word.*

The soldiers walk up and down the line, checking that cartwheels are sound, saddles are cinched, and handing out fresh loaves wrapped in clean cloths. My heart is in my throat as the refugees grow more and more restless.

Just let them go, I think, my nails digging into my arms now. *They can worry about their own donkeys' saddles.*

Finally, one of the soldiers waves to the men on top of the gatehouse, and the portcullis is raised. I breathe a sigh of relief as the refugees begin to walk out the gates.

I spot Aster and her family among the crowd. She avoided me last night and seemed close to tears at times, no doubt worried about her children's fate. There's an expression of relief on her face now as she walks toward the gates.

I wave to her, hoping that her journey will be a swift one. Aster looks confused for a moment, then looks quickly away.

There's a lump in my throat as I watch them descending the road into the city. Some families are going home, but I'm still stuck here waiting for news of mine.

8

Zabriel

"That is the last load, *Ma'len*."

The wingrunner bows to me, and then leads the horse and cart back across the stone bridge to the castle. Before me is a massive mound of colored fabric. All the human kings' foul decorations have been stripped from my home. Their gaudy flags. Their false banners. The tapestries depicting them slaying our dragons.

My lip curls in disgust. They didn't slay any dragons. These humans can't even fight their own wars.

Scourge comes walking across the field, head extended forward, huge limbs thudding against the earth.

Burn it.

I rarely speak aloud to my dragon as there's a connection between us deep within our minds. This is just one of the many things that the people of Maledin have forgotten. Their own history and culture were stripped away, buried, and replaced. I'll bring it back, piece by piece, until the people of Maledin finally know who they are once more.

It begins by destroying what never should have been.

Scourge's head rears back on his long neck, he opens his jaws, and a steady stream of dragonfire ignites the pile. It burns fiercely, turning the bright colors black and then to crumbling ash.

Soon there will be dragon banners flying from every turret and the Great Hall will be festooned with true Maledinni decorations.

As I walk back across the dragongrounds toward the castle, dragons take off and land. I raise my hand in greeting to the riders. There are wyverns in the skies too, dragon-like creatures, only smaller and silver and with two legs instead of four. Their riders are called wingrunners and they are the swiftest and most nimble of my army.

The sight of wings in the skies restores my strength and reinforces my resolve. Maledin will be strong once more, and we will rid the land of anyone who's ever hurt my people.

My right-hand man, Godric, meets me at the gate, and after, he greets me with a brief bow. Godric has sandy hair, a hooked nose, and a sturdy, dependable expression. He commands the foot soldiers and has been my friend since we were in swaddling clothes.

"*Ma'len*. Brethren have been spotted fleeing toward the southern mountains." He presses his lips together in a grim line and adds, "The dragonriders have reported the stench of dark sorcery."

A growl rises up the back of my throat. After all these years, the southern mountains still shelter wizards who practice the foulest arts. Whoever is protecting the Brethren, I will personally rip his heart out, turn it into a hot coal, and shove it down his worthless throat.

"And the Brethren that fled the Fliesch Monastery?" The monastery where Isavelle was held captive and beaten after she was recaptured. Two days ago, I led several dragons and a unit of wingrunners in an attack on the place. The Brethren ferociously defended it, and the battle lasted many hours. We rescued dozens of young women who were dressed the same as Isavelle when I first saw her.

I had hoped to find the High Priest cowering within and to watch as Scourge tore him to pieces. Instead, I discovered Isavelle's scent in one of the underground cells, laced with misery and pain. Her tears and blood were all over a set of manacles. The wall where her cheek was pressed against the stone. The ground where she lay and wept in the dark.

I had that place razed to the ground in a fiery inferno.

"We think they have headed south, including the High Priest."

I thank Godric and head over the stone bridge toward the castle. Isavelle's vile torturer is still breathing.

I detect a sweet and luscious scent in the air and move to a nearby low wall and look down into a courtyard below. My mate is moving among a group of forty or so young women in scuffed white dresses. The Veiled Virgins we rescued. They've all discarded their veils and sit huddled together. Like Isavelle, they'll have no idea where their families are, but I hope they're able to discover other refugees from their villages in the coming days.

Godric has moved to my side and is looking down into the courtyard. As I watch, Isavelle puts her hand to her mouth and smothers a yawn, then scrubs a hand over her face.

"Is this your future queen, *Ma'len*?"

A smile spreads over my face. My queen. "She works too hard and sleeps too little." Every night she sleeps on the hay with the refugees, and I have to hunt her down in the dark before lying with her. Most nights her sleep is broken by nightmares, and I have to hold her tight to my chest to soothe her.

"She devotes herself to the people instead of to the king," Godric mutters.

I glance sideways at my friend. "Must you be so gloomy while I'm admiring my bride? She hasn't accepted me as her mate, and she doesn't even know I'm the future king. Leave the girl be."

Godric makes a noncommittal noise and continues to cast his eyes over the scene below. While we watch, a dragon swoops low overhead, and every girl in the courtyard flinches, and some of them scream.

I detect another whiff of hostility from Godric as he says, "Those Veiled Virgins your bride fusses over are mostly human. Probably even all human, without a drop of Maledinni blood in them."

I have no quarrel with humans. My kind has always interbred with them, and I imagine that after five hundred years there are tens of thousands of them living among the Maledinni. Now is not the time to tear families apart because the mother is human and the father is Maledinni, nor will it ever be the time.

"I have no doubt, and no concern about it either," I tell

him, moving away and calling over my shoulder, "Tell me about the preparations for the coronation."

After a moment, Godric looks away from the women and follows me.

While we discuss the day when I'll be crowned King of Maledin, we survey the damage that the castle and city suffered during our attack and the repairs that are being made. The day is a long one, and everywhere we go in the city, we encounter more and more refugees pouring into the capital.

Every now and then I stop and talk to some of them, ask where they have come from and the condition of their villages. I never fail to inquire whether they've heard of anyone from Amriste or any place to the west, but no one has.

"Why do you ask after Amriste, *Ma'len*? I thought your mother was from Gunster," Godric says as we begin the long climb back up the hill to the castle.

"Lady Isavelle's family is from Amriste. She hasn't seen them in over a year, and she's worried about them."

Godric's expression grows a shade more serious. "Should you wish for your bride to hear news of her family? What is to prevent her from leaving Lenhale as soon as she finds them?"

I stop in the road and turn to Godric. "What will prevent her? Me, of course, and I won't stop her from leaving. I'll ask her."

"Will she heed your request?"

"I'm her Alpha," I growl. I've had enough of his negativity for today. Isavelle isn't going anywhere. She sleeps in my arms night after night, surrounded by my scent. No Omega can resist that.

Godric seems to realize he's been testing my patience. "Of course, *Ma'len*. I only wish to consider things from all sides." Godric is a Beta, and he oversees all the soldiers in the castle. Me included.

I give him a wry smile. "As you always have, and I'm grateful for it."

A wingrunner is hurrying down the street toward me. I recognize Captain Ashton, and the moment he reaches me, he gasps, "*Ma'len*, Lady Isavelle has collapsed."

I stare at the captain in shock, then break into a run.

"She's in the—"

"I know where she is." I can smell her from here, and her scent spikes with a sickly overtone.

In a moment I'm through the castle gates and racing across the grounds until I reach the courtyard where the Veiled Virgins are sheltering.

Isavelle collapsed in their midst, sprawled on the ground with her long hair scattered on the flagstones.

"Isavelle!" I pull her into my lap and cradle her in my arms. "*Sha'len*, can you hear me?"

My mate's eyes are closed, but she's breathing. A dragon swoops overhead on the way to the dragongrounds. Some of the girls are crying as they watch Isavelle, and then they shriek and sob even harder as the dragon's shadow passes over us.

The refugees really don't like our dragons.

I give Isavelle a gentle shake, and finally, she rouses, her eyelashes fluttering. "Isavelle. Can you hear me?"

"Zabriel?" She looks around, seeming surprised to find herself on the ground gazing up at me. "What am I… Oh. I'm fine. I just didn't eat breakfast yet."

"Breakfast was two meals ago. You're supposed to be taking care of yourself," I growl and pick her up in my arms. I don't want an Omega who will always quietly and obediently do exactly what she's told, but it would be nice if she did *something* I asked of her. "I told you that you could help the refugees as long as you didn't exhaust yourself. If you won't follow your Alpha's orders, I'll have to make you."

I carry her into the keep and up to her room. She needs a proper rest, and I need to make more time to ensure that she eats well. I thought she looked too gaunt when she arrived at the castle, but now her cheeks are thinner and her complexion is a ghastly gray.

I tuck her beneath the blankets of her bed and press a kiss to her forehead. "Sleep, *sha'len*. You must stay here for now."

She grasps my sleeve as I turn to go. "Please don't lock me up. I can't bear it. I've been in the dark for so long."

I sit on the edge of the bed and take her face between my hands. "Isavelle. No one is locking you up. You're not a prisoner here."

"I feel like a prisoner."

"Has anyone in the castle prevented you from going anywhere you wish?"

Isavelle gazes up at me with clear green eyes. "I think that's only because I haven't tried to go beyond the walls yet."

Go beyond the walls? Absolutely not. I'm not going to keep Isavelle from her family, but the truth is, it's too dangerous for her outside the castle. I can't risk losing my mate when I've only just found her.

"Everything I'm doing is to keep you safe. Things will make sense to you soon." By the gods, I hope so anyway. How long will it take to wake up a dormant Omega?

"You won't explain why you're keeping me here against my will?"

Because she's not human, she's a rare and precious Omega, and she and I are destined to rule this country together. She's my ultimate weakness, and my enemies will prey on her if they find out who she is, and she has enough enemies of her own. Words aren't enough to make her believe me. When her body starts changing, when she feels what she is for herself, when she catches her Alpha's scent, everything will become clear.

"You're more precious than you can know. Not just to me, but to everyone in Maledin."

She frowns. "I don't understand."

I tuck the blankets in around her. "I know, and I'm sorry. We can talk more about it later. For now, you have to stay here."

"Because you say so?"

I lean closer and glower at her, hoping my red eyes will convince her how serious I am. "Yes. Your Alpha says so. Now get some sleep."

Isavelle's lips part in surprise, but I can't tell if she's reacting to the word *Alpha* or the flare in my eyes.

Outside her room, Godric is waiting for me.

"She's all right. She just needs to rest and eat something," I tell him.

He glances at her closed door. "I'm not sure that it's safe for you to be alone with her."

I growl and pass my hand over my brow. Godric is getting on my last nerve today. "I'll pretend you didn't just imply I'm an Alpha who can't control himself."

"That's not what I mean, *Ma'len*. Maledin is crawling with

enemy Brethren. This girl was their prisoner a long time. As the dead king's bride, she—"

My temper flares hearing my bride attached to another man. "She's not the dead king's bride. She's my bride, her name is Lady Isavelle, and you will address her as such."

"Of course, *Ma'len*. I meant no disrespect to you or the lady." He waits, and it's clear that he has more to say.

"Speak your mind, quickly. I have things to do."

"Lady Isavelle believes she's human, and she was in deep with the Brethren. She could be a spy. She may attempt to assassinate you."

"She didn't know I existed before she was about to be thrown on the king's funeral pyre."

"But there were days and days she was separated from you and held captive in the monastery. The High Priest is your most dangerous enemy right now, and she was with him. Now the lady is working among the refugees, and any one of them could secretly be Brethren and pass instructions to her. I only ask you to consider your safety. The guards you have around her are an excellent idea, but perhaps there should be more of them."

"There are guards around Isavelle to protect her, not to protect me, and I will be alone with my mate as often as she and I both wish it. She is of the people. She's a true queen in that respect, just like my mother was."

"Your mother knew her place was by her husband's side, and she understood what it meant to be Maledinni."

I narrow my eyes at the other man. "It sounds as if you are suggesting I cast my Omega aside."

"You don't need to give her up, but you don't have to make her your queen."

I advance on Godric with a snarl, "Lady Isavelle is my mate, my future wife, and she will be your queen. You and I have been friends since the cradle, but don't suppose for a moment I won't demand you draw your sword and fight me if you insult my mate one more time."

Godric drops his head into a solemn bow. "Forgive me, *Ma'len*. I will speak no more on the matter."

I study the top of his head. He's my oldest friend in the world, and I've never once ordered him to be quiet on any matter. Hundreds, perhaps thousands of times I witnessed my father demand people hold their tongues about important matters. I told myself that when the time came, I wouldn't rule in the same tyrannical way.

I've been the ruler of this castle for less than a week, and already I'm breaking promises to myself.

But Isavelle is my mate. She's going to be my queen. It goes against every instinct beating in my chest to hear one word spoken against her.

Gripping the hilt of my sword, I turn on my heel and stride away. Damn Godric to hell for making me feel like my father before there is even a crown on my head.

~

Isavelle stays in bed for a few hours, but that night she sleeps outside with the refugees again. As I lay awake beside her on the hay, watching her sleep, I console myself with the thought that at least I get to hold her during these dark hours. Isavelle isn't used to the kind of affection I wish to lavish on her, and I doubt she'd permit me to sleep in her bed.

While the stars twinkle beyond the tent flap, I press a kiss to the nape of her neck. Isavelle stretches sleepily and wriggles back into my warmth.

"Zabriel," she whispers, and my lips curve into a smile against her skin.

So she does know I'm here.

I'm always gone before the sun begins to edge over the horizon, but my scent remains on her all day, whether she knows it or not.

The refugees are just one of my concerns, but I find that my attention lingers on them because Isavelle spends all her time tending to their needs. The dragons flying over the castle seem to upset them, but I remind myself that they will get used to them in time. In Old Maledin, ordinary villagers would rarely see a dragon and would often be in awe of them.

Several days later, a dozen dragons and their riders are returning from a skirmish with Brethren Guard, and the battle must have been a successful one as several of them take victory laps of the sky over the castle, swooping close to the battlements and unleashing bursts of dragonfire.

I'm on the balcony in my room, holding a scroll but smiling up at the sky, watching the riders celebrating their triumph. They make Maledin feel like home again.

I hear a scream, shrill and panicked.

My mate's.

I drop the scroll and run.

There are three corridors and four staircases between my chambers and the courtyard where Isavelle is working, and I don't think my feet touch the ground as I fly along them. When I burst into the courtyard, Isavelle has her arms spread protectively while dozens of refugees cower behind her against the gates. My mate's eye sparkle with angry tears as she stares up at the skies, but I see nothing more alarming than several dragons flying over on their way to the bluff.

"You have to let them out. They don't want to stay here. Can't you see they're scared?" she calls to the soldiers, and I realize she wants them to open the gates. It seems unwise to allow terrified people to run through the streets where they may get hurt or panic others.

Isavelle sees me hurrying toward her, and the scent of her terror and fury hits me like a wave. "Whoever is in charge here has gone out of their way to frighten the refugees. Why are the soldiers doing nothing instead of opening these gates?"

The guards glance nervously at me, the person who is in charge here, though Isavelle doesn't know it. I'd rather she has a little more time to get used to me and this place before she finds that out.

"I assure you that we're doing everything we can to aid the refugees. I will open the gates if that's what you desire, but I worry that people will get hurt if they run in a blind panic. What's making them so afraid?"

Isavelle gazes distractedly at the weeping women and girls. "The dragons, of course. Dragons attacked the monastery, and now they're flying over us, roaring and spewing flames as if they mean to attack again."

I glance up at the skies, feeling stupid for not realizing why they're so afraid. There is just one dragon left in the sky now, gray with a violet iridescent sheen. Damla, with her rider Tish on her back. She flies upward, then tumbles into a dive before spreading her wings and heading for the bluff. To me and my fellow Maledinni, it's a sight that stirs our hearts and gives us hope.

Behind Isavelle, the Veiled Virgins whimper and cry.

"They're not attacking. The dragons are returning home from battle to the dragongrounds."

"Must they fly around and around the castle, diving and swooping and terrifying everyone? Is it necessary to breathe fire until everyone is screaming and crying?"

I hesitate. It's not necessary, but it is their custom. As the Flame King, anything that curtails a dragon and rider exercising their freedom feels like an outrage but looking at Isavelle and the women cowering behind her, it's clear that harm is being caused.

"I know the dragonmaster," I tell her. "I'll speak to him about the dragons approaching from the northeast instead of over the castle and ask them not to display their victory when they're returning from battle. For a time. Just until everyone becomes used to their presence."

The anguish fades from Isavelle's face, as she says in a quieter tone, "You can just order that?"

Of course I can. I'm the Flame King, but I say vaguely, "I will suggest it to him."

"Will he listen to you, this dragonmaster?"

My mouth twitches at the idea of any of my soldiers disobeying a direct order from me. Even Stesha. "I have earned enough goodwill to be granted this request. Besides, the dragonmaster is an old friend of mine."

I doubt Stesha would call me a friend, but I've known him all my life and he understands duty and respects the royal line.

Isavelle's expression softens from anger into relief. "Thank you, Zabriel. These poor women are terrified, and I worry that some villagers won't approach the capital if they see dragons flying overhead. There's been no one arriving from the southwest. No one at all."

I step closer to her and murmur, "You will find your family, Isavelle. All the people of Maledin will soon return to their homes and life will be peaceful once more."

Isavelle brushes stray hairs out of her eyes, pretending she's not swiping away tears that have gathered on her lashes. "I hope so."

"Is there anything else?"

She looks up at me in surprise. "Pardon?"

"What else can be done to reassure the refugees that they're safe while they remain here?" It's important that the refugees take good memories of Lenhale and their new king home to their villages.

Isavelle glances around. "I don't know. I've mainly been seeing to it that there are enough blankets and food. Maybe there's someone who can report to you or one of the other Maledinni about the refugees' needs."

"Why don't you do it?" I suggest. Who better than Isavelle, who will one day rule Maledin alongside me? She understands the villagers, and it's clear that my people don't.

Isavelle gapes up at me. "Me? I can't do that."

I smile at her. "Why not? You're already doing it, and you're good at it."

Isavelle's scent is filled with doubt. She hasn't realized how important she's been for the refugees these past few days. I've seen how people are less lost and afraid after she's talked to them. She moves among them with ease, dispensing hope as well as blankets and food. Even now, the women behind Isavelle are calming down as they see how Isavelle isn't afraid anymore.

"Can I think about it?" she asks.

"Of course, *sha'len*. In the meantime, I will speak with the dragonmaster." I want to kiss a tress of her hair, but instead, I kiss my fingers in farewell while gazing into her eyes. Isavelle watches me do it, staring at my mouth, her gaze a little out of focus.

I could swear she just felt that on her lips.

I walk up the cobbled road and head around the castle, taking the opportunity to look down into the walled city below. Parts look deserted, and no smoke rises from the chimneys. Here and there in squares, I see that some people are gathered, but they huddle close to the walls and look fearfully up at the skies. An utterly wretched sight to behold for the future King of Maledin.

I sigh. All I can do is keep working and hope that life returns to the capital, and everywhere else in Maledin.

I find the dragonmaster at the dragongrounds, a white-haired Alpha in his prime. Stesha is a man of thirty years who has held his high position since before he was my age. All Alphas are proud and stubborn, but Stesha is also hypercritical, cantankerous, and has an evil temper. He has little patience for people, especially other Alphas, but he's fiercely protective of the dragons, or as he likes to call them, his dragons.

As I approach, I see that he's wrapping soaked marseng leaves around a young Beta dragon's injured foreleg. She's a vivid raspberry-pink color with a creamy underbelly and metallic rosy gold eyes and talons.

"Hold still a little longer. Good girl," Stesha murmurs soothingly, tucking in the edge of the bandage and checking it's secure.

The Beta dragon makes a sad little noise in the back of her throat and then nuzzles Stesha's shoulder with the top of her head, expressing her gratitude to him.

"There's no need for that. I wasn't going to let it fester." He gets to his feet and smooths a hand along the dragon's neck.

A dozen or so feet away, Stesha's crystalline white Alpha dragon watches over them with her serene, pale blue eyes half closed. Nilak is the most elegant dragon in the flare, which shouldn't be possible considering her prodigious size, but she carries her muscle and wingspan with ease. She's also one of the fiercest dragons and has a quick, snarling temper. Just like her rider.

Nilak draws closer to the Beta dragon and nibbles delicately on her wing bones and around the pink dragon's crest, while Stesha continues to stroke her neck. It's a great privilege for a Beta to be fussed over by two Alphas at once, and the pink dragon seems to forget about her injury amid this flattering attention. She closes her eyes and trills happily.

"How are the dragons?" I call as I approach.

Stesha turns, and I see how the gentle look in his eyes hardens as he realizes someone's intruding on his work. Worse, it's another Alpha. Stesha has the same coloring as his dragon, his long hair ice-white, and his eyes a frosty blue.

He assumes a relaxed pose, the heel of his hand resting on the pommel of his sword, but his eyes narrow. "Omaira was injured in the attack on the Fliesch Monastery, but she's doing fine, Zabriel. May I help you with something?"

He's being scrupulously polite, but since we took the capital, everyone has been calling me *Ma'len*, though I have yet to be crowned. Everyone except Stesha. I wonder if this is forgetfulness on his part or if he's resisting addressing an Alpha who is younger than him with an honorific. For all Stesha's life, my father was *Ma'len*.

I'll let it go for now and trust that the coronation reminds him who outranks who even though he's older and just as large and violent as I am.

I open my mouth to tell him why I'm here, but I'm interrupted by a high, thin shriek. Together, we watch as a dragon soars over the city, its rider flying a full revolution and a half around the castle before bringing their mount into land on the far end of the field.

"A wonderful sight," Stesha says with a thin smile of satisfaction. "After all these years, I never thought I'd see it again."

"You remember time passing beneath the mountain?"

A line appears between the Alpha's brows and his gaze turns inward. "I don't know. So many hundreds of years went by, and it was as if I was lost in a long, disjointed dream."

"I feel the same way. Asleep, yet conscious that I was trapped."

Stesha nods. "But we're free now, and we'll find out who was responsible and make them suffer. No one will dare thwart the dragonriders of Maledin again."

I rub my hand over my jaw. "Speaking of the dragons, I need the dragonriders to approach the castle from the northeast instead of over the city, and land right away."

Stesha frowns. "I don't understand."

"No flying displays over the city. No laps of the skies or bursts of fire. It's upsetting the refugees."

Stesha's pale eyes flash with anger, and he grips the hilt of his broadsword. "What are you talking about, Zabriel? For the first time in hundreds of years there are dragons flying over your castle, and you want to put a stop to that? We wouldn't be standing right here if not for our dragons."

The dragonriders are all proud and enjoy the spectacle they create. We've just fought a war, and we want to prove how fierce we are, and even under normal circumstances, there are plenty of reasons to show off. If a dragonrider is courting someone, their displays are especially noisy and flashy. I'd love to be up there on Scourge showing off to Isavelle, but his roars and plumes of fire would have the opposite effect on my mate right now. Maybe one day she'll hunt the skies for the sight of Scourge and smile when she realizes we're coming home to her. Fuck, I hope so.

"I know. But the refugees don't like seeing the dragons in the skies. It feels like the invasion all over again."

Stesha stares around the field as if he's searching for the person who put me up to this terrible joke. "We liberated the refugees from a death cult and gave them back their country. They are Maledinni just like us, and dragons are in their blood. If they're human, we're protecting them as well. Dozens, hundreds, thousands of designations will be emerging in the coming months, and the people will finally understand what being Maledinni means. Some will be privileged enough to become dragonriders and wingrunners, and when we fly overhead, they don't *like it*?"

I grit my teeth as Stesha goes on his rant, reminding myself not to interrupt him and his concerns are valid. Countless times I saw my father speak over one of his subjects and dismiss their concerns, and situations he could have easily fixed only grew worse. I didn't learn a lot about how to rule from my father, but I did learn how not to do it.

"I know it's frustrating, Stesha, but all these people know right now is that dragons attacked out of nowhere and killed their king. It will take time for them to accept who they really are, but right now, we must take care not to terrify them unnecessarily."

"I don't believe they're scared. Who has been telling you such dragonshit?" Stesha growls.

"I saw their terror for myself, and I spoke to someone who is working with me to help the refugees. We discussed how the dragons can modify their route to the dragongrounds for a little while."

"Who the hell do they think they are?" he demands.

Stesha has been ferociously busy leading battles and caring for the dragons, and he hasn't had time to glimpse Isavelle or even hear of her.

"My Omega."

A myriad of emotions flicker over Stesha's face. Shock. Yearning. Resentment.

Jealousy.

"An Omega? *You* have an Omega?" Stesha's fists tighten as he bites out, "A forthcoming coronation and an Omega. You must be a busy man, Zabriel." He turns on his heel and strides away, leaving only his scent in his wake.

A wave of it hits me, blown by a gust of wind. I recognize Stesha's familiar scent of sulfur and fine ash. White winter crocuses. The crispness of the wind at the highest breathable reaches of the skies. His pride in our dragons is a strong fragrance, as is his outrage at the idea that their liberty must be curtailed in any way, but one emotion in particular dominates his scent.

Despair.

My former riding master reeks of it.

9

Isavelle

Red dragon silhouettes on white backgrounds, all fluttering in the breeze.

Half a dozen seamstresses are sitting in a patch of winter sunshine with banners spread over their laps, needles moving in and out of the fabric. I just finished my breakfast of split pea porridge with blackberries when I emerged into one of the inner courtyards to find a group of women I've never seen before, working and chattering away.

"Are these for the coronation?" I ask, and all the women stop sewing and look up in surprise. I give them a smile. "Sorry, I didn't mean to interrupt."

A red-headed woman squints at me through the sunshine. "These banners are to be hung in the Great Hall. Are you a castle maid? I've not seen your face before."

I glance down at myself and realize I'm wearing the same dress as they are.

"Oh, no I'm not. One of the soldiers found this for me to wear. I was a Veiled Virgin at the Fliesch Monastery, and I'm from Amriste, near Gunster. Have any of you talked to anyone from over that way lately?"

The seamstresses all glance at each other and shake their heads. It was worth a try. I won't stop trying, though my hopes are becoming more desperate day by day.

An old woman with a mole on her chin tuts sadly, shaking her head. "Those poor girls, and you as well, dearie. Taken from your homes and locked up in the cloisters. You only have to look at those whimpering little things huddled over in that courtyard to know they were put through something terrible." She nods toward where the Veiled Virgins have been sheltering these past few days. Everyone looks at me expectantly.

There are plenty of gruesome things I could tell these curious women, but instead I ask them, "Did you all work here under the last king?"

"Stumble-headed Alaster?" asks the redhead. "We did. I heard he was burned to a crisp by a dragon. I wouldn't be surprised if he walked right into his mouth."

The others all laugh.

"He was stomped into the dust by a dragon," I tell them. "Well, his funeral pyre was. I don't know how he died."

The old woman sniffs. "It was probably his own fault, for he was a coward as well as a fool. The next one can't be worse."

Maybe. Maybe not. I wonder who he'll be.

"We don't know what we're getting with this new king," I point out. "He could be much worse."

"Worse," a raven-haired woman mutters with scorn. "You're not from these parts, so let me tell you that we knew tyrants here. My husband was imprisoned in the dungeons going on two years for the crime of missing church to care for his sick mother. I don't care for dragons, but this new lot let him come home to me, so I'll sew their banners and drink to the new king's health."

"So far they haven't beaten anyone," adds the redhead, and she asks me, "Have you seen anyone being beaten?"

I shake my head. The bruises on my body are fading for the first time in over a year. Not being beaten makes a wonderful change, though I won't be drinking to this new king's health just yet. He could have worse torments in store for us.

The youngest of the seamstresses gives the others a mischievous smile. "These new soldiers are striking men and women. So big and handsome in their armor."

I recall the sight of Zabriel dressed in his plate armor, standing amid flames. Then without his armor in the moonlight. The tips of my ears grow hot.

Well, so what? No beatings—yet—and some of them are good-looking. Is that all it takes to win people's loyalty?

The woman who has her husband back hasn't stopped smiling the whole time she's been sewing. If one of these dragonriders brought me my family, I might find my heart softening toward them as well.

"Who is the new king? I haven't had time to find that out," I ask, glancing around as if he might appear that very moment.

"A big soldier who rides a dragon, that's what I've heard," says one of the women.

"They seem to worship their dragons," adds another.

One of the women shakes out a finished banner and examines it. "That they do, but as long as they don't feed me to one of them, I'll be happy with a new king, and them flying beasts and all."

All the seamstresses nod in agreement and laugh, and I wish them farewell.

I have a lot to think about as I continue through the courtyards and over to the main gates. Another group of refugees is leaving, heading for their homes, and the group of Veiled Virgins watch on sadly as they head out the gates.

They should be on their way back to their own villages by now, but many of them are orphans. Orphans are always the first ones in a village to be tithed.

A thin girl called Posette with her hair in a messy plait is chewing mournfully on a piece of bread and honey, watching the departing refugees. "I wish I was going home, but I was told never to return to my village after the Brethren took me." She glances around at the battlements. "Maybe I could stay here if there are jobs within the castle."

Another called Santha nods in agreement. "I'd like to stay. It's not so bad here now the dragons have stopped flying overhead."

I glance up at the skies to find them free of wings, and a smile spreads over my face. So they have. Zabriel really did that for us?

"If only we knew how to go about getting a job here," Posette grumbles.

A little thread of excitement shoots through me. Maybe

there is someone who can help them get jobs in the castle. The seamstresses seemed content, and I wonder if I could talk to the kitchen maids and chamber maids and find out if they're similarly well-treated.

"I think I might know a way," I tell Posette and Santha. "Let me ask around for you, and I'll see what I can come up with. It will be hard work, though."

"I'll scrub floors and boil linens if it means I don't have to go back to the cloisters or my old village," Posette says, and Santha nods in agreement.

As I head back into the Great Hall, I remember what Zabriel suggested. Me, be a spokesperson for the refugees. I wonder if this is his crafty way of tying me to this castle, and by extension, him.

I remember how things were in my village and that when there was someone who needed help, people would stand around and say, "Someone should do something," but nothing would ever get done. With a spike of guilt, I remember the sorry state of Biddy Hawthorne's home. Someone should have done something for her. I can't help her now, but I can speak up here, and if I stir up trouble and it gets me thrown out? So be it.

The only person I know in this place with even a smattering of authority is Zabriel, and I wonder if he'll tell me to stop wasting his time if I ask him about castle jobs for the former Veiled Virgins.

I spot a tired-looking boy carrying platters back to the kitchen and ask him, "Excuse me, have you seen Zabriel?"

The boy gives me a baffled look. "Who?"

Someone clears their throat behind me, and I turn and see Captain Ashton of the wingrunners. "Commander

Zabriel is in the cellars. Through that door, turn left, and down the stairs."

I offer him a smile as I hurry away. "Thank you."

The cellars turn out to be a cavernous underground space that smells of oak, hops, and pickled vegetables. There seems to be enough food down here to outlast a year-long siege, which I suppose is a good idea in a castle.

There's a light flickering up ahead, and I follow it and turn a corner. Zabriel is lit by lamplight, hauling barrels over to a wooden platform where they're hauled up through a trap door. Barrels of salted fish, from the smell of them.

My soft shoes aren't making any noise, but as I approach, Zabriel freezes and turns around. He's stripped down to his shirt, which is sticking to his sweaty body in a way that makes him look almost as naked as when I saw him in the water. His long, dark hair tumbles around his shoulders, and golden light dances over his sculpted features.

For a split second, my gaze drops to his tight breeches, and I remember in lurid detail what other parts of him looked like at the hot pools. I guiltily cut my eyes away.

"You came looking for me?" Zabriel asks, leaning on a barrel with a smile and a spark in those red eyes. "How can I help the lovely Isavelle?"

An indistinct voice calls from above, and Zabriel shouts back without taking his eyes off me, "Just one moment, Ulf. I'm talking to Lady Isavelle."

Lady Isavelle.

What a charmer Zabriel thinks he is with his smiles and flattery. I may not have been around many men in my life, especially not men like him, but there's no sincere reason for him to be acting this way. I would bet a week of hot dinners that the moment I gave in to his charms and let him kiss me, he'd lose all interest. Well, he probably wouldn't stop at kissing. He hasn't said it out loud, but he'd find a way to get me into his bed.

The mental image of being in bed with Zabriel, surrounded by heaping piles of soft blankets and no one in the world to interrupt us, is shockingly vivid. His mouth on mine. His large hand cradling the back of my head while his other deftly undresses me. I know the basic mechanics of what happens between men and women, but few of the details. I imagine Zabriel gets creative with the details.

Zabriel smiles wider. "Your scent is very interesting all of a sudden, *sha'len.* Care to tell me what you're thinking about?"

I give myself a little shake, and quickly divert the conversation elsewhere. "It's about work for the Veiled Virgins. Maybe you can help, or I could meet with some kind of overseer. The castle steward if there is one."

Zabriel steps toward me as if drawn closer by an invisible force, his eyes hungry and his nostrils flaring. I have a feeling he hasn't heard a word I've said. A man so dusty and sweaty should probably smell offensive, but the fresh saltiness of his sweat is making me breathe deeper and deeper, trying to drag every hint of him from the air and into my lungs.

"You can ask me for whatever you want," he murmurs, and then adds as he reaches for my hand, "Have you noticed how we never seem to be alone?"

As he grasps my fingers, there are zero thoughts in my mind all of a sudden. Thanks to our height differences, I have a close-up view of his muscled chest where his shirt parts and the silky ends of his hair, as black as a raven's wing. "That's because there is so much to do and many things the people need."

"Yes, isn't there," Zabriel murmurs, though I suspect he didn't hear that either. "I love that you came to find me. What else is on your mind?"

He traces his fingers down the side of my face, over my jaw, and they linger on my throat.

I swallow hard as I gaze up at him. "I'm wondering if we have to do everything ourselves. Where is this king that I've heard about?"

Zabriel is staring at my neck. If it was my breasts, I could tell him he's a vulgar leech, but staring at my neck is baffling.

"The king? Oh, don't worry about the king," Zabriel murmurs. "I can help you with whatever you need."

He cups my cheek and lowers his face to mine. My mouth is tingling. His red eyes are hypnotic. Suddenly, I need a lot of things, and they all involve putting my arms around Zabriel's neck and opening my lips to receive his.

What am I supposed to be doing again? I was here about...jobs. Talking to the steward. Or something.

"I suppose the king is organizing his coronation," I murmur vaguely. "Thinking about feasts and showing off to all the important people of Maledin."

"Is that so," Zabriel whispers, and his lips are so close to mine that I feel him speak the words.

"I hear lords and ladies are traveling here from all over the country when they should be at home looking after their people. This new king will probably be worse than the last."

Zabriel's eyes widen in surprise, and then he smiles. "I bet you wouldn't say that to his face."

"I would." I doubt I'd do anything of the sort.

Zabriel's red eyes burn with wicked delight. As he smiles, I get a close-up view of his strong white teeth and see how his canines are longer and pointier than they should be. It doesn't seem right. It doesn't seem *human*.

"Are you a vampire?" I blurt out.

"Am I a what?"

"A cursed corpse that drinks human blood. They're supposed to only exist in stories, but you're only supposed to exist in stories, so I don't know what to believe anymore. Your red eyes. That hungry expression. Your pointed teeth. If you bite me, I'll scream."

His pupils dilate, and he mutters something under his breath that sounds like, *Fuck, I hope so.*

"What?"

He smiles again and touches the tip of his tongue to a pointed tooth. "What, my dragines? Made for biting necks and sucking blood? Good guess. Very good guess, *sha'len*."

The sight of his tongue and his open mouth makes heat ripple down my spine. I wait for him to tell me why he has pointed teeth, but he doesn't elaborate.

"I can take this shirt off if you like. You can even take it with you if it's what you came for."

"What?" I realize I've got both fists clenched on his shirt and let go. "Oh! No, I came for..."

A group of soldiers enter the cellar, stop smartly in front of Zabriel, and bow their heads with their fists over their hearts. "*Ma'len*."

I've seen the way the dragonriders and other soldiers greet each other during my days spent at the castle. Subordinates greet their superiors with their hands on the hilts of their swords and a brief bow. I've never heard anyone say *Ma'len*, whatever that means.

Silence fills the cellar, and I feel the irresistible urge to fill it. "Why are they all bowing to you like that?"

Zabriel takes one of my hands in his. "What is it, Godric?"

"*Ma'len*," Godric says again in tones of deep respect, then glances at me.

"You may speak freely in front of Lady Isavelle."

In my homespun dress, I'm not fooling anyone into believing I'm a lady, and yet Godric gives me a courteous nod before turning back to the man he came to see.

"We have finished our search of the areas surrounding the five largest monasteries. Several enemy priests were captured, but there was no sign of the High Priest. It appears our suspicions were correct and he's fled south."

My stomach swoops at the mention of the High Priest, and the realization that he's still out there somewhere.

Zabriel mutters under his breath in a language I don't understand. "Thank you. You may go."

After Godric and the other soldiers have left the cellar, Zabriel turns to me with an expression of regret.

"I'm sorry. I hoped to present you with his corpse by now."

That is disappointing, but I'm thinking about something else. "Why are they calling you *Ma'len*? What does it mean?"

"It means Flame Dragon. We don't speak the ancient tongue anymore except for honorifics. And curses. It's pleasing to swear in the old language."

Flame Dragon. What a strange thing to call a soldier, even if he is a commander. "And why do they call you that? Is it because you have that big black dragon?"

Zabriel hesitates, and then says, “It also means Flame King. It’s how my people address their ruler.”

A faint buzzing begins in the base of my skull. “Their...what?”

For once, there’s not a trace of teasing on his face. “I’m sorry. I didn’t know how to tell you. I didn’t *want* to tell you because I knew you’d look at me like I’ve sprouted two heads.”

Zabriel is the new ruler.

Zabriel invaded my country, and he’s responsible for the misery and distress of every single person in Maledin.

Zabriel won the war and now he’s my king. He let me go on and on about what a terrible job the king is doing and all the while he listened to my ranting without warning me I was crossing so many lines.

“I have been in this castle for many days,” I whisper. “I talked to people about a soldier called Zabriel. I asked people if they had seen Zabriel as if I had the right to demand your whereabouts. I cursed Commander Zabriel to hell and back when the dragons flew overhead, and no one told me to stop talking myself into my own execution.” I look up at him. “Are you going to cut my head off now?”

Zabriel sighs. “Can we go back a few minutes to when you thought I was a vampire? That was much more fun.”

“Why didn’t anyone tell me that you’re the king?” I cry.

A voice calls down through the trap door, “Do you need assistance, *Ma’len*?”

“I’m all right. I wouldn’t be the Flame King if I couldn’t handle a few sparks,” Zabriel calls back. Addressing me, he says, “I told my people to give you whatever you asked for but not to tell you who I am. Everyone else will learn who I am the day of my coronation."

"Why are you keeping it a secret?"

"It's not a secret." He stares at our joined fingers with his dark brows drawn together. "I had my reasons for keeping it quiet. Please forgive me for keeping it from you."

"You should have told me yourself."

He lifts his red eyes to mine. "But then you wouldn't have come to see me, *sha'len*. You wouldn't have wanted to talk to me or even look at me. The last time you were wedded to a king, you were nearly thrown onto a burning pyre. Marrying me will be a lot more pleasurable, I promise you."

Marry him?

He winds his fingers even tighter around mine. His fingers are far longer and thicker than any of mine, and he wears a heavy gold signet ring in the shape of a dragon on his pinkie. Like a king would wear.

I'm such a fool.

He commands the army. He rides the biggest dragon. He carries himself with the arrogance of a man who knows he is the most important person in the castle. Why didn't I realize who he was?

"*Ma'len*. Is that what I should call you?"

Zabriel gives me a smoldering look. "Absolutely not. There are better things for you to call me. Would you like to hear them?"

"No, thank you. *Ma'len* is just fine."

"Zabriel," he insists. "Just call me Zabriel, please. And yes, I can see to it that the Veiled Virgins find work in the castle. I'm pleased they want to stay."

I stare at him in surprise. Whoever heard of a king

helping a group of refugees? Whoever heard of a king hauling barrels around in a cellar? "Really?"

Zabriel smiles. "Of course. There are as many jobs as there are people who want them. I'll send someone to talk to the women, and please spread the word among the other refugees that they're welcome to stay."

I step back from him and draw my fingers out of his, not knowing what to say.

"One more thing," Zabriel says, and he sounds so serious that I turn toward him. "Kiss me before you go."

"You stink of fish." He doesn't.

"If I smell of anything, it's not fish."

There's a bitter taste on my tongue and anger blooms in my heart. "If you're hoping for a mistress, you can look elsewhere. I'm not interested." I turn and walk out of the cellar.

"I don't want a mistress. I want a queen," he calls after me as I hurry up the stairs.

I feel sick as I walk along the corridor. Posette and Santha will be pleased, and I'll be happy knowing there are a few familiar faces within the castle, but I don't know what to do with this new information about Zabriel. Commander Zabriel was formidable enough with his armor and his sword and his dragon. The soldiers he led and the enemies he killed. I thought that Commander Zabriel had taken a liking to me. I would have refused his advances, but did I walk around this castle with a mite more confidence because I'd caught the attention of a man whom I thought was just a little bit important here?

Now I know for sure that he's been playing with me because there's no way that a king can marry a commoner, or even want to.

There are too many people in the Great Hall. I turn the other way down the corridor and keep walking down twists and turns until I come to a window in an alcove covered by a tapestry. I duck beneath the tapestry and huddle against small, thick panes of glass. My throat feels tight. My eyes sting. In the distance, I can make out a dragon that's little more than a smudge flying on the horizon.

Why does my chest ache like it does? I will not cry because a man I don't even want is so far out of my reach that he may as well live on the moon.

I dash tears from my cheeks, take a deep breath, and I pull myself together.

Posette and Santha are where I left them, and I force a smile onto my lips as I tell them, "I have good news for you both."

OVER THE FOLLOWING DAYS, every time I catch sight of Zabriel, I flee.

I'm not proud of my behavior. I know he knows I'm running from him. I'm a hare fleeing a fox, whisking myself away down corridors and up narrow lanes in this warren of a castle. Suddenly it seems like he's everywhere, and if it's not him who's tormenting me, it's dragon banners, dragon flags, dragon shields, cakes baked into the shape of dragons, pastry dragons, flower bouquet dragons, and children running around with dragon kites. The coronation is just days away, and the whole castle has gone Flame King crazy.

The secret of who the new king is has spread. People point Zabriel out in excited whispers whenever he walks by.

Everyone has a story to tell about Zabriel from during the invasion or seeing him around the castle. Everyone is keen to say that they know the Flame King.

Posette, Santha, and several more former Veiled Virgins have joined the kitchen staff and thrown themselves into preparations for the big day. Dozens more refugees have embraced life at the castle and are now working in the kitchens, the armory, and the gardens. Meanwhile, I still have no news about my family and find myself standing forlornly amid coronation excitement, gazing at a boy who reminds me of my brother, or watching a woman teaching her daughter who looks like Anise how to darn a stocking.

The day of the coronation dawns bright and clear. Even the dragons seem to be excited, and I can hear roars and the beating of wings from the dragongrounds. The castle gates are open, and a long train of horse-drawn carriages enter one by one. I recognize the crests of many important cities of Maledin. The people who emerge are dressed in fine clothes. They once paid homage to King Alaster, and now they've come to witness the crowning of the Flame King, a man who rides a dragon and took the country from the former king by force.

At midday, every dragon at the bluff launches into the air and flies in a wide arc around the capital. They're careful not to draw too close as they spit flames into the sky, but as the people rush to the walls to get a better view of the spectacle, I see that no one's frightened of the creatures anymore. Their faces are filled with wonder, not terror.

From within the Great Hall, horns blare. It seems to be the signal that the coronation is about to begin, and everyone hurries through the enormous open doors.

I stay where I am, watching the skies as the dragons fly and swoop. I don't know if I want to see Zabriel today. I remember our first meeting, how he froze mid-battle to call me *sha'len* and pull me atop his dragon. At our second meeting, he killed every Brethren Guard who tried to take me from him. He was an impulsive soldier when he did those things, but he's not a soldier anymore. As much as I secretly and very deep down wish he would remain a soldier, I have to accept he's not, and so I join the line and file inside with everyone else.

Even if I wanted to get close to the front of the hall, I couldn't. The important families have taken all the best spots. The Great Hall is filled to bursting with spectators. It seems like everyone else at the castle and in Lenhale has flooded inside.

The wingrunners and soldiers stand to attention around the edges of the room. A few minutes later, the dragonriders file into the hall and line up in front of the huge, empty golden throne on the dais.

Only then does Zabriel arrive at the double doors to the Great Hall, gleaming brighter than the sun in golden armor. Everyone turns around to look, and I suck in a breath at the sight of him. His face is proud and determined as he strides forward, the crowd parting for him. He's the biggest man in the room, and in that gleaming armor, he's pure flame and power.

He walks the length of the hall to the dais, turns, and surveys us all. He seems to look at every single person as his red gaze roves around the room.

After a moment, he goes down on one knee and braces his forearm against his thigh. An older woman in red flowing robes steps forward with a gleaming golden crown in her hands, and she places it atop Zabriel's flowing black locks.

Everyone is staring at him with rapt attention, and I notice how the young women from the important families are gazing up at Zabriel with more than interest. An unmarried king requires a queen, and they're the most likely candidates to catch his eye. The ache gnaws at my chest.

The moment Zabriel takes his seat on his throne, all the dragonriders go down on one knee and say, "*Ma'len.*"

They're echoed a moment later by the wingrunners and soldiers doing the same thing. Everyone else, the people who never knew dragons and Flame Kings existed until a few weeks ago, sink to the floor and say in hallowed tones, "*Ma'len.*"

I recall the conversation we had at the hot pools. *Enjoy bending the knee to your new king, but an invader will never see me bow to him.*

He never asked you to.

Zabriel doesn't need to ask. He merely presents himself to us and everyone is inspired to kneel. I sink down with the rest of the crowd, the memory of all the stupid, haughty things I said to him burning in my veins. The High Priest tried to beat my pride out of me, and now I wish he had. Zabriel's up there, and I'm down here on my knees where I'm supposed to be.

I never saw the old king until he was lying on a funeral pyre, but the stories were that he was lazy, decadent, and could barely hold his crown up, let alone a sword. I've felt Zabriel's palms, and they're callused from fighting. His arms around me were strong, and he wields that weapon at his hip as fiercely as if it were his own arm, though it must weigh almost as much as I do. Zabriel looks like a real king.

There's a tightness in my chest and throat, and I have to look away from him. I don't want to remember him this way. I want to remember Zabriel, a dragonrider, a commander in the army with blood and mud spattering his jaw. Someone important to the people of Maledin, but not everyone in Maledin.

As much as it hurts, I make myself raise my chin and fix my eyes on the Flame King.

Take a good, long look at that man. Do you see him up there in his gilded armor with that crown upon his head? Do see how everyone in this Great Hall is marveling at him? Bowing to him? Falling in love with him? Get this through your thick skull, Isavelle. You may as well be an ant to someone like him. You are *an ant.*

And what's wrong with being an ant? You never minded being an ant before. A little nobody person from a little nobody village in an insignificant part of Maledin. Remember how peaceful your life was before anyone knew you existed? As soon as you find your parents, or someone who has seen your parents, or just anyone from your village, you're going back there. People who sit on thrones in golden armor won't even notice you're gone.

And that's the way it should be.

I take a final look at Zabriel, and then I turn and leave the Great Hall, pushing through the crowd as they strain for every glimpse they can of their new king.

10

Zabriel

I step out onto the balcony from my rooms, and a deafening cheer goes up. I thought the Great Hall was filled to bursting, but it feels like everyone in Maledin has crowded into the courtyard below and onto the streets of the capital. The festive atmosphere of the day has disposed everyone to jubilance, but I don't fool myself that it will be easy from now on. The hard work is only just beginning.

The hardest part is that I have no idea what I'm doing.

I want to be a good and just king, and that ambition is all I have to guide me. That, and the determination not to make the same mistakes my father did. I feel the weight of these responsibilities resting on my shoulders, heavier than my golden armor.

There's one person in particular I wanted to share this moment with, but she's been running from me for days. I scan the crowd below, hunting for a head of dark gold hair and a beautiful, heart-shaped face. I couldn't see her in the Great Hall, and I can't see her in the crowd.

Godric is standing to attention behind me, and I call over the cheers of the crowd, "Where is Lady Isavelle? Have you seen her?"

He shakes his head. "The last I saw, she was out by the stables seeing to the villagers' mounts, but that was this morning."

I stand on the balcony for several more minutes, trying to appear regal and focused, but my thoughts are consumed by my mate. After another ten minutes, I wave to the crowd, head back inside, and stride down the corridors to the rear of the castle.

Out by the stables, Isavelle is bent double, examining a donkey's fetlock.

"One more. Come on, don't be stubborn," she coaxes. The donkey flicks its ears in irritation and stamps its foot, but finally allows her to haul it up and examine it.

At the sound of my approach, she glances up, and her eyes widen in surprise. Then she stares at my crown, and her face falls.

She hates that I'm king, I can feel it. If I was intimidating before, I'm completely unapproachable now.

Slowly, she straightens up and brushes the dirt from her fingers, but she says nothing. Her eyes fall to the ground and they stay there.

"Did you watch the coronation?"

She nibbles briefly on her lower lip, not lifting her gaze. "I was out here working, *Ma'len*. As is my place."

I don't like the way she says any of that, but I particularly hate the sound of that formal address on her lips. "Don't call me that."

Isavelle picks a piece of hay from the donkey's gray coat and shrugs. "Then what should I call you?"

Alpha. Call me Alpha when we're alone. But Isavelle's a long way from wanting to call me that. Whole deserts of time. "Zabriel. Just Zabriel, like you always have."

"I can't. You're the king and everyone must address you as such."

"Not you," I say firmly.

She finally lifts her eyes, and they're confused. "Why?"

"You know why." I take a step forward, aching to touch her but keeping my hands to myself. How sweet she looks in her simple dress, and the apron tied tightly to emphasize the lush curves of her body. Strands of dark gold hair are falling out of her braid. She gazes up at me, those beautiful lips parting as everything fades into the background.

Then Isavelle's eyes fall to my golden armor, and she looks away quickly and studies the stable wall. "There were ever so many young ladies dressed in finery arriving at the castle earlier. I had no idea we had so many lords' daughters in Maledin, but of course, I'm coming to realize that there's a lot I don't know about Maledin." Her tone is bitter.

"Other young ladies? I didn't notice any."

Isavelle sniffs and leans down to haul the donkey's fetlock up again. "I doubt that."

I go over and crouch down next to my mate beside the donkey's legs and peer into her face. So that's what upset her. She believes that I will lavish attention on someone who's not my Omega.

"I was aware of the people in their finery," I tell her, and she tries not to, but she flinches and then attacks a rock in the donkey's foot with a hoof knife. "But I didn't notice them in any detail. I saw all my people. Old and young. Men and women. But I was only looking for you. You needn't be jealous."

Isavelle dislodges the rock and glares at the underside of the donkey's hoof. "Who's jealous? I was just making an observation."

"There is a feast in the Great Hall to celebrate my coronation. I want you beside me, *sha'len.*"

She raises her eyes to mine. "How come you can call me *sha'len,* but I'm not allowed to call you *Ma'len*?"

"*Sha'len* is an affectionate name. *Ma'len* is a title. And don't change the subject."

Isavelle shakes her head and picks at mud in the donkey's hoof. "I had better not come. It will make all the young ladies angry to see drab little me sitting beside their new king."

"What do I care for the tempers of young ladies who aren't my mate? And you couldn't be drab if you tried."

Isavelle's expression softens, and she risks a glance up at me. She doesn't understand what *my mate* means, but she doesn't dislike it. Maybe she's even starting to respond to it.

She shakes her head again. "It will displease your lords if you ignore their daughters. There's already been enough strife in Maledin."

"That's not how Maledin works."

"Oh? How does it work then?"

I cover her hand with mine and draw her to her feet. "Come to the feast, and I will tell you."

"I'm not hungry," she protests, but without much conviction.

I take the hoof knife from her and set it atop a wall. "You can slake your curiosity at least. Come see what the Great Hall looks like on a feast day."

My mate is reluctant, but she allows me to draw her inside and walks with me. The murmuring of voices gets louder and louder as we approach the Great Hall.

At the doorway, she digs her heels in and shakes her head. "I can't go in there with you looking like that. You have a crown on your head. Your armor is gold. I have hay sticking to my old, darned dress, and there's mud on my apron. Just leave me here."

I take the golden cloak from my shoulders and wrap it around her. "There. Now we match, and no one can say you didn't dress for the occasion."

She touches the silken fabric, hesitating. "I look silly in this cloak over my old clothes."

On the contrary, it's perfect. Every single one of my soldiers will see the king's Omega wearing his cloak and assume that Isavelle begged for something soft and scented of mine to comfort her on an important occasion. That, or they'll think she's approaching a heat and needs comfort and my scent for that reason.

Her heat. How I long for the day when she will cling to me, hot, slicked, restless, and needy, and I feel a growl rise in my throat at the thought.

Swallowing it down, I tell her, "It's perfect for a Maledinni woman, I promise."

As I enter the hall, still holding tight to Isavelle's hand, the talking stops and everyone stands up and sinks into bows and curtseys. Long trestle tables run the length of the room and have been placed on the dais as well.

As I walk the length of the hall with Isavelle at my side, the sense of something being missing all day dissipates. With Isavelle's hand in mine, I finally feel like a king.

A king is nothing without his queen.

We take our seats at the top table, and there's a rustling of fabric and scraping of chairs as everyone resumes their seats. I pour my mate some wine into her gleaming goblet and notice she's twisting her dress in her lap, her gaze darting around the room.

"Is something the matter, *sha'len*?"

"Everyone is staring at me," she whispers.

I glance around and notice that the dragonriders, wingrunners, and soldiers have expressions of mild interest on their faces as they look at Isavelle. The members of the important families of Maledin, people who had no idea that dragons existed until recently, are staring at Isavelle in shock. I glare at several of them until they drop their gazes and turn to reassure my mate. "Everyone is curious. New people are always of interest, but they will get used to you in a few moments."

"Kings of Maledin don't sit at the high table with village nobodies," Isavelle hisses under her breath.

"They did in my time, and now they are again. The people of this country have a whole set of customs to remember. Are you hungry?"

There are dozens of dishes placed on the table within arm's reach, and I serve my mate and then myself. Half the dishes I don't recognize, and I suppose they must be human. I examine something circular with a hard crust. "What on earth..."

"That's a pie," Isavelle explains. "Cut it open and you'll find out what's inside."

It turns out to be pheasant and winterberry, and it tastes pleasing. "I wonder why humans hide something delicious inside something secretive and unassuming."

"It's cooked that way so the meat is tender and juicy, and it keeps better in the larder. Do your people like to show off when you do everything, even ordinary things like cooking and eating?"

I glance at her in surprise and smile. "And why wouldn't we? What's life without a little showing off?"

"The Brethren told us that too much enjoyment and pride are sinful."

The people eating below at the trestle tables are speaking politely to one another. Plates are being passed around with somber nods. No one is singing or cheering or dancing, and couples aren't sneaking away to steal kisses and other sweet moments in the corridors.

I barely recognize the place. How quiet Maledin is, but I have no doubt it will liven up as soon as designations start to emerge. Alphas love a celebration, but Betas love them even more as it gives them a chance to demonstrate how their numbers far exceed the Alphas and Omegas put together, and all parties are actually about them. That's how they see it, at least. Alphas let them have their way as long as things don't get too out of hand. As for Omegas, they're so rare that they never lack any attention.

Isavelle has no idea how precious she is. My people and hers still haven't stopped staring at her, and she still hasn't taken a bite of her food.

I push Isavelle's plate toward her. "You must eat. I know

the Brethren starved you, and you haven't been eating properly since you came to the castle. You were plumper not long ago."

"How do you know that?" she asks in astonishment.

I take a morsel of cheese from my plate, lean closer, and hold it to her lips. Our eyes lock, her mouth parts, and she nibbles the cheese from my fingers. Fuck, that was cute. A hot, restless feeling stirs in my lower belly. "I don't know how I know. I've never had one of you before."

Isavelle swallows and arches an eyebrow at me. "A prisoner?"

"A mate." I know she was once rounder. Softer. Happier. It hurts my heart to see how the Brethren have bruised her, inside and out.

"If I'm not a prisoner that means I can leave."

I reach out for her hand, curl my fingers around hers, and tighten them. "No, you can't. This is where you belong."

"The lords and ladies are all staring at me, a commoner, sitting with the king. Your people are probably finding me lacking as well, for a whole host of reasons I have no idea about. I don't know where you get the idea that this is where I belong, but you're the only one who thinks so."

I lean closer to her, my eyes narrowing. "Either eat, or I'll haul you into my lap and feed you myself."

"In front of everyone?" she squeaks.

"In front of everyone."

Isavelle seems to realize I'm serious and hastily picks up her spoon. When she takes a mouthful of a grain dish, I sit back and start to eat as well.

As the minutes pass and everyone finds something else to

look at, Isavelle slowly relaxes. She sneaks looks at me as she eats.

"How long ago did you and your people rule Maledin?" she asks.

"Five hundred years, I'm told." I asked the scholars to look into it after we reclaimed the capital, and my blood boiled when they showed me the proof that we'd been imprisoned for that long.

"Such a long time. How old were you when you were imprisoned?"

I rub my hand over my smooth jaw and smile at her. "How old do I look?"

She examines me with her head on one side. "It's hard to tell when you seem inhuman with those red eyes and such dark hair. If I had to guess, I'd say you were around twenty-five."

I don't look human because I'm not human, and neither is she. "I was twenty-three when I was imprisoned. I still feel twenty-three because I was more asleep than awake for those five hundred years."

Being trapped beneath the mountain was like being in an endless, despairing dream. I sensed Maledin's empty skies and the people's true nature draining away as the Brethren told them lies and made them believe they were human. My people became nothing but stories to them. Stories they didn't believe in.

"It's strange being the king of a people who don't know they're my people," I murmur, studying her beautiful face. "At least, they don't know it *yet*. There will be many like you in the weeks, months, and years to come. Now that the dragons are back, the people in Maledin will rediscover their designations."

The *Hratha'len* Crone, the keeper of all our knowledge and dragon magic, has explained it to me. Our designations are linked to the presence of dragons in Maledin. Dragons are our culture and history, and dragons also influence our bodies so that we can bond with them and each other. Without the dragons, life is colorless, scentless, and pointless.

Keeping my gold cloak wrapped tightly around her, Isavelle eats her dinner. Our first meal together, and I'm flooded with gratitude at the sight. I do my best to keep my pleasure to myself so I don't overwhelm her, but this moment feels even more significant than the coronation.

"There's something I was hoping you'd help me with," I say when she's nearly finished with her plate. I have my hand around my wine goblet, and I'm making quarter turns with it on the tablecloth.

"Oh? What's that?"

"I was raised to be my father's successor. I know my duties as king, but I don't know Maledin anymore. The people and what you've suffered for the past five hundred years. How things have changed. What remains the same. What you all need." I glance at her. "That's where I was hoping you'd help me."

"Me? I don't know anything. I was raised in a tiny village in an out-of-the-way place."

"Yes, Amriste. I recognized the place when Scourge and I landed in the village square. The happiest May Day celebrations in all of Maledin are held at Amriste, and after the maypole dancing, everyone eats—"

"Apple fritters," Isavelle finishes, staring at me in astonishment. "You knew Amriste? No one knows Amriste."

"My mother was from Gunster," I tell her with a smile, naming a market town a few miles to the south. "She took us—me—there several times for the spring celebrations when I was a boy." The warm glow from that happy memory fades as I remember Mother dead with a gaping wound in her throat. She is dust now. She is nowhere.

Isavelle looks up at me with liquid green eyes and asks softly, "Was it recently that you lost your parents? For you, I mean."

"For me, it was just a few weeks ago. I saw my parents lying dead from their wounds just before we were all locked beneath the mountain. I don't know what happened to their bodies." They wouldn't have been given a respectful funeral. No doubt their bodies lay in the open air for the vultures to pick down to the bones.

"I'm sorry," Isavelle whispers, slipping her fingers into mine and squeezing. This is the first time she's touched me of her own free will. I'm flooded with her scent, and as welcome as it always is, there's no love for me in her perfume, only sympathy and pity. I draw my hand away from hers. An Omega pitying her Alpha is all wrong. Wrong and shameful.

Isavelle stares straight ahead, her expression confused.

I shouldn't be so proud. That was one reason for my father's downfall. It's often an Alpha's downfall, not listening to others and thinking they know best.

I reach out and grasp her hand once more. "Thank you. That means a lot to me. Will you tell me when I'm being too stubborn or hotheaded? You seem to like doing that."

Isavelle's lips twitch. "I don't dislike it, but I'm afraid you might cut my head off if I keep doing it."

"Alphas can be touchy about their Omegas talking back to them, but I was never comfortable with the way Omegas are sometimes treated." I keep a pleasant smile on my face, though I'm remembering the dozens of times that I saw my mother with a bleeding lip or a black eye.

"How are they treated?"

Like they're the bottom of the heap because, technically, they are. Omegas might be their Alpha's whole world, but to everyone else, they're someone's fancy little plaything. "It depends on how important their Alphas are, but unfortunately, they don't get much of a say about many things."

Isavelle shrugs this off. "Sounds horrible, but I'm not one of those, so that's not my problem."

I choke on my wine and wipe my mouth with the back of my hand. We'll have to have this talk again when her designation starts to emerge. Omegas are supposed to enjoy the total protection and adoration that comes from belonging to an Alpha.

"How did you come to be with the Brethren?" I ask to change the subject. I know so little about Isavelle, and I'm hungry for more details.

Isavelle's expression darkens. "When a village cannot meet their tithe obligations, the Brethren take a girl child instead."

I'm familiar with the idea of a tithe. There was a similar system under my father's rule, though it was levied in the market towns on goods sold and traded, not on the food that villagers needed to survive.

"So, you were handed over like a bag of wheat or a side of bacon?" I growl, and she nods.

"They wanted my sister or one of the other young girls, but I hid them, so they had to take me."

Pain pierces my heart. My mate would have been spared all this pain if they'd taken her sister instead. I don't want to wish Isavelle's suffering on anyone, but she's mine, and she's the one who matters to me. "You hid them and presented yourself?"

"No, I hid as well. I didn't want them taking me, but they still found me."

"But why did you help the other girls when they were the ones the Brethren wanted?"

She presses her lips together and shakes her head. "They were so little and so scared. It hurt so much to see them crying."

I touch my thumb to her cheek, wiping away a tear that isn't there. "Didn't you cry, too?"

Isavelle doesn't say anything.

She did cry, but not where anyone could have seen her.

"And then what happened?" I ask, an edge to my voice.

Isavelle glances at me and shakes her head. "You don't want to hear about this. Today's your coronation and this is a celebration."

"I want all of you. The good and the painful. I'm hungry to know everything that happened to you before we met."

Isavelle takes a deep breath. "You remember the man who was at the pyre? The biggest man who was yelling commands. He was the High Priest, and he's in charge of all the Brethren. The moment I met him, everything became so much worse. He seemed to single me out as a bad apple for some reason. I had to be corrected and punished because there was something wrong with me, but he never said what. The other priests loved to please him and so they were delighted to drag me before him whenever I did something wrong. My parents were never strict about the church's teachings in our home, so I did a lot of things wrong accidentally. When I finally learned the rules and tried to stick to them so they wouldn't beat me, they started making up transgressions. Several of the priests would take turns spying on me, even when I was asleep, or washing, or dressing."

Isavelle shudders at the memory, and pain slices my heart as I remember how upset she was at the idea of bathing in front of me. No wonder it was painful for her. I didn't know, *sha'len*. I'm sorry.

"One day I was washing myself…" Her face flames and she says in a rush, "Between my legs. I know some people touch themselves between their legs for gratification and that's wrong, but all I was doing was washing myself."

My eyes widen in shock. Since when was making yourself come a crime? I nearly tell her that's not what the Maledinni believe, but she's finally confiding in me, and I shouldn't interrupt.

"The High Priest made me stand on a chair in the middle of the dining room where all the other girls could see me while he gave a lecture on how disgusting and degrading it was to your soul to touch yourself, and only degenerates did that because they were listening to the demons. It was awful," she trails off in a whisper, rubbing her upper arms as if she's cold.

The Brethren shouted *demon* at me during battle, presumably because of my red eyes. I bring myself off often, so I suppose that makes me a degenerate and a demon. I'd laugh if my poor Omega wasn't so utterly miserable right now.

"And then of course, I was beaten again. That was one of the worst times because the High Priest was obsessed with stamping out anything dirty. I couldn't walk for days after."

I put both my hands on her waist and pull her into my lap until she's sitting astride my thighs.

"Zabriel! What are you doing?"

"If you're going to tell me such a sad fucking story and break my heart, you're going to be dragged into my arms so I can comfort you." She's a warm bundle of soft flesh and gold cloak in my arms, and I press my face into her throat and breathe in.

She's here. She survived. I'll make everyone who hurt her pay in blood.

There's wry amusement in Isavelle's voice as she says, "It sounds more like you're the one who needs comforting."

I pull back and look at her. "Me? I'm the Flame King. The supreme Alpha in all Maledin." My lips twitch. Maybe I do need a little comfort from my Omega, just to assure myself that she's all right. "Will you help me be the best king I can be?"

Isavelle hesitates. "As an adviser?"

"As my wife. My queen."

"But I'm a commoner," she says desperately.

"Like I said, my mother was a commoner. The king caught her scent one day, and that was that. An Alpha found his Omega, and he mated her."

"Your people don't know me. My people don't want a commoner as their queen. I'm going to cause trouble for you, and it's not going to be much fun for me either, being singled out like this."

She's very strange for an Omega. In my time, her designation would have started to emerge around thirteen years of age, and she would have grown into a woman knowing it was her place to do as she was told. She should hear my voice and melt when I command her to do something.

"I have the answer to that."

"What is it?"

"*I* want you, and people will do what I say."

Isavelle puts her little nose in the air and turns away from me, but with my arms around her, she's not going anywhere.

"I have enjoyed helping the refugees. I might like being your adviser for a little while, but I don't know you, and I'm not going to be your wife just because my smell turns you into a lunatic."

"You're not allowed to say no. You're only allowed to say *I'll think about it.* I told you, I'm a patient man. I can wait however long it takes for you to beat down my bedroom door and beg me to make you mine."

Isavelle splutters in outrage. "You're an *arrogant* man. Fine, I'll think about it, but I'll be thinking about it for the rest of my life, so there."

I laugh softly. "She didn't say no. *Previet k'len,*" I murmur, stroking my finger up the underside of her jaw. Isavelle looks up at me, her mouth just inches from mine.

Kiss her. Kiss her. Kiss her.

My Alpha is practically roaring at me to claim her lips, but I grit my teeth and make myself wait. I want her breathless from my kisses. I want her beautiful cheeks to overheat and her slick to coat my thighs. If I can't have that, I don't want anything.

Isavelle frowns. "I've heard you say that before. What does it mean?"

"*Previet k'len*? It means thank the gods."

"But *len* means dragon, doesn't it? And flame and king. *Ma'len* is *my king*."

"That's right, but the word for *dragon*, *flame*, *king*, and *god* are all the same in Maledinni."

"So, when people address you as *my king,* they're calling you their god? No wonder your ego is bigger than the Bodan Mountains."

I laugh and rub a hand over my jaw. "Well, it depends on the context." I give her a smoldering look. "I hear some women cry *ma'len* to their mates in the throes of passion. Apparently it comes easily to the tongue."

Isavelle's face turns red.

I rub the blade of my nose up her warm cheek and murmur, "I'm looking forward to finding out what comes easily to your tongue, *sha'len*."

"Stop it. Everyone's looking."

"Good," I bite out. "I want everyone to know you're mine and what my intentions are for you."

Isavelle squirms in my lap. The platters are cleared and replaced with tarts, sugar animals, and fruit. The centerpiece is a dragon made of marzipan. I break off a wing and share it with her, and she eats some grapes and nectar plums as well.

While she's distracted licking plum nectar from her fingers, I plant a kiss on her throat. "Mm. Good girl for eating your dinner."

Isavelle freezes and her eyes widen, but a moment later

she pretends she didn't hear me and goes back to licking her fingers.

After that, my mate starts to yawn.

"Are you sleepy? I'll take you to your room."

"I know the way, thank you."

She does, but she hasn't been sleeping there. I'll make sure she does tonight because she needs a good rest. I stand up with her in my arms and head for the stairs up to the keep. There's a hasty scraping of chairs as everyone gets up to bow and curtsy us out of the room.

Isavelle's scent is thick with embarrassment, and mine turns soothing in response. Her face is buried in my neck and she becomes drenched with it, and she slowly relaxes by the time we reach her room.

We're alone in the corridor. I loosen my grip, and Isavelle slides down my body until she's standing on her feet. I wish I could feel her against my clothes, or better yet my naked body, but since I'm wearing armor, I'll just have to appreciate as much of her as I can.

Isavelle doesn't immediately move away. Her fingertips trail over my gauntlets as she gazes up at me. "I didn't expect a man to ever carry me around. Some of the girls in my village would tease me that I'd squash my husband on our wedding night."

My eyes open wide in astonishment. "What? You're tiny."

"No, I'm not. You're just enormous."

"I have to bend double to kiss you. Not that you've let me kiss you," I add darkly. I take her waist in my hands and marvel at her, wondering how she or anybody could not think she's perfect. "When I squeeze you, your lovely body is soft and yielding and you swell between my fingers," I murmur, and start peeling the cloak from her shoulders, my gaze fixed on her beautiful skin. "I lie awake at night imagining both my hands cupping your ass while I suck one of your br—"

She slaps her hands over my mouth. "Stop that. It's your coronation day. You're supposed to be kingly."

"Mrp mm brmm mmlee."

She moves her hand from my lips. "What?"

"I am being kingly. What's kinglier than wanting to bed your queen?"

"I'm not your queen. There will be no squeezing and no bedding. I'm going to find my family and then I'm going home."

She turns away, but I put my hand against the wall, barring her way, and lean down to speak directly into her ear.

"You are the most disobedient of your kind I've ever met. Always talking back. Always arguing with me. You're my bride and my mate, but you don't have to believe me just because I say so. I don't need to persuade you to melt for me because it's going to happen anyway, and it's going to be fucking delicious." I lower the pitch of my voice to a velvety purr. "Soon I'll be all you can think about, and you'll beg me to make you mine."

11

Isavelle

I stare up at Zabriel in shock. He's leaning over me with a smirk on his lips, his body massive in golden armor and that crown sitting atop his head, looking for all the world like a man who can have anything he wants.

I duck inside my room, my cheeks blazing with heat. Who *talks* like that? Isn't Zabriel ashamed to talk so openly about squeezing and bedding and craving to touch me? The Brethren taught us that it's sinful to say such things out loud or want them, even if you're married. Because...because...I don't know why, but I suppose people wouldn't be working hard, praying, and obeying if they were thinking lustful thoughts. Like what that giant of a man looks like in the moonlight with water droplets on his broad, muscular chest.

I moan softly at the memory and heat ripples up my body. What on earth is wrong with me? I've never had lustful thoughts about anyone, and I shouldn't be having them about the King of Maledin. I wish...

I shouldn't wish because it's dangerous to wish. A childhood spent dreaming of dragons and fairytale kings has taught me that. I can't help but remember Zabriel as he held me close just now. Not the way he looked or his aura of power, but the way our bodies seem to hum together.

I wish he were a soldier with dust on his cheek, hauling barrels of salted fish. Maybe I would have let that man kiss me, even squeeze me a little, as sinful as it is, but the King of Maledin?

I'm still wrapped in Zabriel's golden cloak. My fingers stroke the soft, sleek fabric, remembering the sight of him atop the throne. Whenever he's close to me, he takes the opportunity to sniff my hair or bury his face in my neck and breathe in. I don't understand why, but I drag his cloak from my shoulders and lift it to my face.

I smell...nothing. It's just a cloak, and I throw it aside and go to bed.

THAT NIGHT I dream that Scourge is hunting me.

I'm in the middle of the dragongrounds, and there's nowhere to hide. I'm running and running toward the stone bridge, but it never gets any closer. I feel rather than see the dark shape above me, and then the dragon opens his jaws and unleashes a stream of dragonfire, burning me to a crisp.

I wake up with doom flooding my body. I lay there sweating for some time, wishing that it were morning already, and then fall back into the same terrifying dream.

As the first shades of dawn light my room, I sit up and rub the nape of my neck. It's aching like I've been bitten, and I'm covered in sweat. My lower belly and back hurt like I've been throwing bags of wheat onto carts for market. I didn't even do that much yesterday, just worked with the refugees' mounts, watched the coronation, and then ate with Zabriel at the high table before he carried me back to this room.

I get out of bed, dip a washcloth in cool water, and press it over my suddenly burning cheeks. Zabriel. What a spectacle we must have looked to everyone at the feast, the seven-foot-tall newly crowned king with red eyes and a dragon, pulling a short, fat little nobody into his lap so he can feed her and squeeze her and whisper things into her ear.

I don't need to persuade you to melt for me because it's going to happen anyway. Soon I'll be all you can think about.

I seem to be all he can think about, but stars know why. I'm perfectly content with the way I look, and I'm grateful for two strong legs and a pair of hands that allow me to work hard, but I have no illusions about the kind of beauty that inspires a king to declare again and again that he must marry you. That kind of beauty I just don't have. Not one girl in ten thousand has that kind of beauty, tall or short, fat or skinny. Not one girl in a million.

Maybe being buried alive beneath the Bodan Mountains for five hundred years has addled Zabriel's brain.

My gaze falls upon his gold cloak on the floor, and I have the strangest urge to snatch it up and bury my face in it. I even take half a step toward it, my hand reaching for the soft satin.

Absolutely not.

I'm not here to melt for the new king.

Today, I'm going to go everywhere, speak to everyone, look in every place within the castle walls. Someone must know something about the fate of the people to the west. I'm redoubling my efforts.

I start in the Great Hall as I have a few bites of breakfast, asking the wingrunners and the soldiers if they've heard any news, and then talk to Posette and Santha as they lay out loaves on the tables. Both of them look relaxed, rosy-cheeked, and happier than I've ever seen them before, but they haven't got any news for me.

For the rest of the morning and into the afternoon, I walk from courtyard to courtyard, hunting down every last refugee and emissary from the villages. There are fewer refugees now, and I'm pleased about that for their sake. They're all from the north of the country, or the east or the south. None from the west. It's the same for the emissaries, though they're the most difficult to engage in conversation when they're more interested in being heard than listening to anyone else.

Who's going to pay for my burned-down barn, that's what I want to know.

There's the spring planting to think of, I can't be wasting time in the capital.

My lambs are going to be lost in the snow if I don't get back home right away.

Who knows what tithes and taxes this new king shall levy. We could all starve in the streets next winter. Or be eaten by dragons.

I can understand their anxieties because I have plenty of my own, and they grow and grow as the sun continues its journey through the sky. I'm deep in conversation with a woman from an eastern town, and I walk with her and her fellow villagers as she tells me in detail about the injured wyvern that crash-landed through her runner bean frames.

"Broke the whole lot of them," she snaps, filled with righteous indignation. "I've been compensated, but it's not as if I don't have a hundred other things to do before the spring."

I commiserate with her, then find a way to steer the conversation toward Amriste. She's never heard of the place or crossed paths with my family. I swallow my sigh. It was worth a try.

A moment later, I notice we're about to pass through a huge stone archway with a raised portcullis. I realize with a jolt that I've been so absorbed by our conversation that I've walked a considerable distance with the woman and stop dead.

"Wait, what are these gates? Are we leaving the castle?"

The woman shakes her head. "These are the city gates, girl. I told you I'm going home."

I watch with an open mouth as she and the rest of the refugees pour out the city gates and head down the road into the open fields beyond, before wheeling around and staring in shock at the castle all the way back up the hill. I've escaped by accident.

My captor isn't going to believe that.

I dither on the cobbles, wondering whether I feel elated or terrified. Does a songbird feel relieved when her cage door is left open, or does she huddle in a corner hoping someone will slam it closed again?

Beyond the city walls are fields with cottages dotted here and there. It's a long walk to my village, and with no money or food, I probably won't make it. I have no desire to relive those freezing, hungry days on the run.

Turning around, I take in the city.

The *city*.

Now, this place could actually be useful to me. It's teeming with people, many of them from all around Maledin. In my homespun dress and with my unremarkable appearance, I blend in so well that no one is going to notice me. I'll explore for a little while, and then I'll head back to the castle before Zabriel even notices I'm gone.

For an hour or more, my hopes are high. Lenhale is filled with people from all over Maledin, and they're happy to talk to me. Many have never been farther than a few miles from home. I'm starting to understand that while it was usual for the Brethren to travel between the five monasteries in Maledin, dragging the Veiled Virgins along with them to wash their clothes and cook their meals, common folk rarely went farther than their closest market town. Very few people know of Gunster, and almost no one's heard of Amriste. I start to feel like I'm going mad and wonder if I've imagined a whole region of Maledin and the hundreds, even thousands, of people who lived there.

I've been sweaty and uncomfortable since I got out of bed, and my empty stomach feels queasy. The roads of the capital are twisty and unpredictable, crowded with people, and are overlooked by tall, haphazard buildings. I glimpse an open square and hurry toward it, hoping I'll get my bearings, when I trip on a cobble and go flying.

I land on my hands and knees, scraping them against stone and gravel. My pride takes a bruising as well, which isn't helped by the fact that a dozen people walk past me like I'm not even there.

"You poor thing. Are you very hurt? Come and sit here."

Someone puts her hands on my elbows and helps me to my feet. There's a water pump over a stone basin nearby, and the woman encourages me to sit on the edge while she dips the corner of her apron in the cool water and washes the dirt and gravel from my palms.

I take a breath to calm my racing heart, and I see that the person who has come to my aid is a young woman, my age or a year or two older. She has a kind, pretty face, and dark brown hair, and she's currently soiling her dress and apron with dirt and my blood.

"You didn't need to do that. Thank you. I'm Isavelle, by the way."

"Odanna. I'm a stable hand at that travelers' inn over yonder, and I saw you go flying," replies the young woman. She's crouching before me and looks up at me with a smile. Then she hesitates and peers more closely at me. "Did I see you sitting in the Flame King's lap at his coronation feast yesterday?"

My face turns scarlet.

No one inside the castle mentioned it to me this morning, though I was aware of a few curious looks, but since then I've forgotten all about the spectacle that Zabriel and I must have made.

Odanna smiles and shakes her head. "Don't be embarrassed, I thought it was romantic. I crept up to the door in the middle of the feast so I could peep inside. A lot of us did. We were all saying to each other that maybe the Flame King won't be a tyrant if he can so sweetly feed an ordinary Maledinni woman with his fingers." She hesitates, and I can see the question in her eyes that she's dying to ask.

A lump of frustration rises in my throat. "I should be on my way. Thank you for stopping to help me up."

Odanna puts her hand on my arm, and in a tone of remorse says, "I'm so sorry. Listen to me gossip. Let me make up for my nosiness by helping you if I can. Come with me, and I'll buy you a cup of silkmallow tea."

The young woman has such a sweet, gentle way about her, and I'm too tired and overwrought to resist as she leads me over to a tea stall. We sit on low wooden stools and Odanna places a wooden cup of pale pink tea into my hands, and its warmth soothes my injured hands. It feels strange to have someone looking after me instead of me trying to comfort everyone else.

I take a shaky breath. "Thank you. This is very kind of you. As you can see, I'm not having a good day."

"Are you new to the capital?" Odanna asks, interest lighting her eyes. Her dark hair is in a loose bun at the nape of her neck and loose tendrils frame her face.

It's a simple question that doesn't require more than a yes or no, but suddenly my despair fills right to the brim and spills down my cheeks. "I've been in the castle for over a week, but this is my first time in the city. I'm looking for my family, or even news of anyone from their region of Maledin. Anyone at all. I feel so wretched about them that I don't know what I'm going to do."

Odanna presses my sleeve, her light brown eyes filling with sympathy. "Oh, you poor thing. I've never been outside Lenhale, but I might know someone who has been there. Where are they from?"

Without much hope, I describe Amriste and Gunster to

Odanna, and I'm not surprised when she gives a sad shake of her head.

"I haven't heard of anyone from that region. I'm truly sorry. We have a lot of travelers passing through the inn. I will listen for news and will let you know if I hear anything that might help you." Odanna has a pleasant, throaty voice, and I hear the sincerity in her words.

"That's very kind of you to help a stranger like this."

"We're all in need of a little help right now. There's been so much upheaval since the invasion. Perhaps some roads or bridges have been destroyed that prevent news or people from reaching the capital from that region."

I nod and make myself smile a little. It's a thin hope, but it's still a hope. What I fear is that something terrible has happened around Amriste, or that everyone in that region has fled across the western border and they don't know it's safe to return. That's assuming it is safe to return and the fighting isn't going to start again.

"Is your family safe?" I ask Odanna, taking a sip of my drink. Silkmallow tea has a delicate, sweet taste, and though these dried blooms must have been in storage for nearly a year, they have enough flavor to remind me that spring is just around the corner.

She hesitates. "My mother passed away several years ago. My father was a Brethren priest."

I gaze at her in shock. Brethren take vows of celibacy, and they can't have wives or lovers, though I've heard rumors of them forcing themselves on vulnerable women who haven't got anyone to protect them.

Odanna must realize where my mind went and she

hurries to correct me. "It wasn't like that. They were in love, but of course they weren't allowed to be together."

"That must have been hard for both of them." I hesitate, and then add, "I was one of the Veiled Virgins until not long ago, and it's difficult for me to imagine any of those men acting out of so tender a feeling as love. Did you know him well?"

The dark-haired girl shakes her head. "I never met him, but Mother always spoke so highly of him as a man, even if he wasn't a good priest. I have to believe he had a good heart."

Odanna looks so wistful that even though it turns my stomach to do it, I force myself to say, "I'm sure he did."

We finish our tea, and then Odanna suggests that we talk to the innkeepers about my family as they overhear gossip from all corners of Maledin. It's a good idea, one I should have thought of, and we give our empty cups back to the stall-holder and walk across the square.

It's starting to snow, with a few flakes drifting down. My attention is on those rather than the people around us when I hear an exclamation of shock from Odanna. She's been pulled roughly aside by two men.

At first, I think they're trying to steal the satchel she has hanging from her shoulder, but then they turn to me. Their faces are in shadow beneath caps and their clothes are as ordinary as any traveler that I've seen in the city, until I see that they both have leather ties around their necks. The ties disappear inside their shirts, but I can guess that there's a shiny triple chevron hanging from the leather.

The symbol of the Brethren.

One of them pulls a length of rope from his pocket. The other is gripping a piece of cloth and has a shapeless robe over his arm. Together they close in on me, throw the robes over my head, and one tries to gag me with the cloth while the other snatches at my wrists.

Memories of the day I was bound and gagged and nearly thrown onto a funeral pyre overwhelm me, and I scream and thrash around in their grip. I yank my wrist from the bruising hold of one strong hand, only for it to be snatched and wrenched behind my back by another. The robe slips from my head and I can see again. For a moment I think I'm going to fight my way free, and then one of the Brethren punches me in the stomach so hard that I can no longer drag breath into my lungs. Black spots dance before my eyes.

Odanna is standing a few feet away. The young woman's face is totally blank as she stares at me. It's not even blank with shock. Her expression has been wiped clean.

"Run, Odanna," I manage to wheeze.

There's an angry roar from the skies, and as cries go up from people around the square, my fear escalates to panic.

A dragon.

A moment later, there's the thunder of wings and a deafening *whomp* as an enormous black beast lands in the square. Scourge fills the space—overfills it, as one of his back legs braces atop a stone dwelling and his tail disappears over a house and down an alley.

He rears his head up and looms over me and my two assailants, and then opens his jaws and roars his fury. We all flinch as we're struck by a wall of noise and the stench of sulfur. The Brethren attempt to drag me away from the dragon but, lightning fast, Scourge snaps at one of them with his teeth, catches his clothing, and flings him against the wall on the other side of the square. He falls to the ground in a heap and lies still.

The other assailant cries out in horror and runs to help him up, and I hear an ominous rumbling. Scourge has his jaws closed, but his red eyes are glowing brighter and brighter. Heat radiates from him and smoke curls from his nostrils.

The dragon opens his mouth and dragonfire streams out, hitting the men and enveloping them in blistering flames. I fling myself backward and cover my head with my arms, anticipating that the fire will burst all over the square and burn everyone and everything in its wake.

Scourge closes his jaws and the two men burn to death on the cobbles. Dragonfire doesn't behave like normal fire. It seems to possess destructive properties because, in a few moments, the two men aren't even recognizable as humans anymore, and their bones begin to crumble away.

The black dragon turns in my direction and parts his jaws. His nostrils flare as he stalks closer. The heat coming off him is incredible, and his red eyes fill with rage.

This is the dream I've been having.

My *nightmare.*

I scramble backward, but I'm not fast enough, and then the dragon is on top of me. He stands over me, great taloned forelegs on either side of my body. This is the same stance he used when he landed on top the dead king's funeral pyre while I was sprawled beneath him, and I realize he's not here to eat me or burn me alive.

He's protecting me.

I slowly lower the arm I've raised. Scourge's black scales

are roasting hot. I can hear a rumbling, as if more liquid fire is churning within him and he'll unleash it if necessary.

Scourge angles his head down at me and pins me with his red eyes. Every time I've been this close to the black dragon, Zabriel has been with me. Strangely, I feel like he's with me now.

Half a dozen soldiers wearing castle uniforms burst into the square, and Scourge whips his head around and roars at them, warning them to stay away. These are men and women who are used to dragons, but even they stumble backward at the sight of so many pointed teeth.

"Scourge, those are Zabriel's soldiers. They're not going to hurt me."

The dragon keeps his fierce gaze on the soldiers and doesn't back off.

One of the soldiers calls to me, "We'll stay back and wait, Lady Isavelle. Scourge won't let you move or let anyone else approach."

Wait for what? Am I stuck here beneath a furious black dragon until he calms down and realizes the threat has passed?

A crowd has gathered, awestruck by the enormous beast, and every time someone gets too close, Scourge snaps his jaws at them. This can't be doing much to help improve people's opinions of dragons.

Scourge slowly raises his head and peers in the direction of the castle. It seems he can hear something or sense something that no one else can. Or someone.

A moment later that someone strides into the square, a thunderous expression on his face as his cloak and long hair billow behind him. Zabriel is dressed in his usual black attire of a close-fitting long jacket, breeches, and boots, and he has a death grip on the sword at his hip, ready to draw it in a heartbeat if necessary. He takes in the crowd of people around the edges of the square, the unit of soldiers keeping them back, his enormous black dragon taking up just about every inch of space, and finally me, sitting on the cobblestones between Scourge's front legs.

Above my head, Scourge gives a short, sharp huff of satisfaction, and only then does he raise himself out of his protective crouch and move back a little.

Zabriel spies the pile of ash and blackened bone that reeks of burnt flesh, and his hand tightens on the hilt of his sword as if wishing he had someone to use it on.

He hunkers down on his heels before me, a tendril of black hair falling over his forehead into his ferociously burning eyes as he studies me. Reaching out, he takes my hands and turns them palms up.

His expression grows more thunderous as he sees my scrapes, and he seethes, "They hurt you."

I shake my head. "I did this by accident. I was thinking about my family, and I fell down. Those men, the Brethren—"

Zabriel yanks me suddenly into his arms and holds me tight, burying my face in his shoulder with his cheek against my temple while he shudders with rage. "They could have taken you away from me. They could have *killed* you."

I swallow hard, his anguish feeling like my anguish. "I fought so hard," I whisper to him. "I wouldn't have let them take me back to that place." That place is filled with darkness and misery. A hopeless place of pain and punishment. I'd rather die than go back there.

"I know, *sha'len*. You fought with everything you had. I can smell it on you," Zabriel says in a roughened voice. He draws back and takes my face between my hands. "But it wasn't enough."

Panic leaps into my throat. I want to convince him that I was fine, and not even so he won't be angry with me. I want to erase the despair in his face. "Scourge protected me. I didn't understand why he came, but he burned those men and then he wouldn't let anyone else come near me."

"Of course Scourge protected you. You belong to both of us from the moment we both saw you. From the moment we awoke beneath the mountain."

He braces a fist against the ground and glares at the cobbles, fury radiating from him in waves. Suddenly, he looks up, his eyes burning red.

"I didn't wait five hundred years for my queen to be killed by insane cultists who are too foolish to realize they've already lost the war," he bites out. "What are you doing outside the castle walls, Isavelle? Did you not realize how dangerous this would be?"

12

Zabriel

Liquid, seething rage boils through me at the sight of my mate lying injured with dead Brethren around her yet again. How can I call myself the King of Maledin when I can't even keep my future queen safe?

Isavelle swallows hard and fear bleeds into her expression. "Are you going to beat me as well?"

I rear back in shock. "What?"

"I left the castle grounds by accident. I didn't return as soon as I realized my mistake, so I suppose you want to punish me for that." She turns around and stands up, pulling her hair aside so I can see her upper back and a glimpse of the nape of her neck. "Most of my bruises have faded and cuts have healed, so your fresh ones will show if that's what you want."

Isavelle thinks I'm going to beat her like the Brethren did.

I stand up and put my hands on her shoulders and draw her around to face me. "I'm angry with myself, not with you."

What I *want* is for Isavelle to hurry up and become my mate. If she were my mate, I'd fly with her to some private place and fuck her until she could barely walk and was promising never to put herself in danger ever again. Even by accident. I want to hear her beg her Alpha for forgiveness. Reassure me that she's still alive and safe in my arms by climaxing hard and taking my knot.

Isavelle blinks in surprise. "Why are you angry with yourself?"

I lean down and press my forehead against hers. "Because it's my fault you're in danger. My enemies will kill you because you're my mate and the future Queen of Maledin. I will only ever have one mate. If you die, it will rip my heart out, and I will never have children. There will be no one to inherit the throne, and Maledin will be plunged into yet another war upon my death."

Isavelle's face goes blank with shock. I shouldn't have laid it all out in such dire terms for her when there's enough I'm already heaping on her shoulders. "Everything's planned out so far ahead? Your fate and mine?"

Her designation is supposed to take care of that for us. Isavelle should be begging me to knot her and make her pregnant. If not now, then soon.

A pang of longing and desire shoots through me. Please, make it soon.

Isavelle shakes her head. "You're thinking years ahead, but I can't see past the end of this week. Now that I've seen how many travelers are passing through this city, I believe that someone here will be able to help me. I'm not your mate or your queen. I don't think someone smelling nice is the basis for a sane relationship."

I glare down my nose at my defiant Omega, hungering to slant my mouth over hers and part her lips with my tongue. There's nothing sane about the way I feel about Isavelle.

"You want to wander around this city? Alone? I gave you the limit of the castle walls where there are plenty of refugees for you to talk to. That's all I'm offering. Help the people as you want, ask around for your family, but stay within the castle grounds and return to your room to sleep."

Over our heads, Scourge snarls, telling my mate to do as she's told and obey me. Any Omega that receives snarls from her Alpha's dragon should be whimpering and promising to do whatever he asks. Isavelle merely glowers at Scourge in annoyance and turns back to me with folded arms, inadvertently pushing her breasts up. Her green eyes are sparking with defiance.

"Then you'll have to lock me up in chains because I'm not going to agree to that."

She's so lovely.

Lovely and *infuriating*.

I grind my teeth together. How long is this going to take? Where's my good little Omega who will always do what her Alpha asks of her? Who *loves* doing what her Alpha asks of her? It's supposed to make her a panting little mess to do what pleases me.

I scrub my hand over my face, smothering a growl. The gods have proclaimed that she's the mate that I need, and I'm the mate she needs. If this is hard now, it must be for a reason.

I want her to find her family. My mate deserves every

happiness, and I'm not afraid that she'll abandon me when she finds them. Once her designation emerges, she won't want to leave my side.

I take a tress of her hair and draw it up to my nose, inhaling deeply. I smell frustration. I smell fear. I smell those fucking Brethren who put their hands on her. Last night she seemed to react more when I told her *good girl*, and today her scent is richer than usual. Could it be that something is beginning to stir in her at last? Or am I just being hopeful?

"A compromise," I tell her, keeping her silky hair close to my face and stroking it with my thumb. "You may go out into the city while the sun is up."

"Thank you," she says pertly, pulls her hair out of my fingers, and turns to go, her cute little nose in the air.

I catch her gently by the arm and pull her back toward me, my mouth twitching as I try not to smile. Tiny as she is, she has so much spirit. "I haven't finished yet. You may go out, but you're taking bodyguards with you. And I'm choosing your bodyguards."

"People who can spy on me for you?"

I shake my head. "They're to protect you. Not tell tales to me about you. Think of them as your new heavily armored friends. I'll choose two soldiers who were under the mountain with me, so you can ask them everything you wish to know about Maledin as it was before."

Isavelle considers this. "I can still talk to whomever I want and go wherever I want?"

Yes, Alpha, thank you, Alpha. A man can dream. "Within the city, yes. I'm trying to keep you safe, not lock you up. Is that agreeable to you?"

Isavelle nods, but her eyes fill with sadness. "You say I'm

not a prisoner, but you don't seem to be giving me much choice, Zabriel."

She pulls out of my grip, and I reluctantly let her go. There's an ache in my chest that she still thinks of herself as my prisoner, and a horrible thought occurs to me. What if she never stops feeling that way? What if she hates being an Omega?

Her designation means she'll be looked down on by everyone, even as the Flame King's mate. People will assume that she's a pretty ornament at the best of times and a scared waif at the worst, and Isavelle has proved to me a thousand times since we met that she's not either and she would never want to be. Will she feel disgusted with herself that she suddenly craves my touch? Will she hate the breathless, wet, messy Omega instinct to cling to her Alpha and beg for his affection and attention? I want that from her so fucking much, to bond with her and feel how much she trusts me to protect her and care for her. To lavish her with kisses, make her come, protect her from the world, and make her mine, mine, *mine.*

The ache in my chest grows even fiercer. I don't know what I'll do if Isavelle rejects me. I may as well not be the Flame King, and instead step aside for another Alpha who has won the trust of their mate.

I put my hand on Scourge's flank, sending him my gratitude that he protected her. Scourge makes a low sound in response and takes off in a gust of wind.

I follow Isavelle back up the road to the castle, aware that everyone is staring at Isavelle, the petite girl in the maid's dress, walking fast, and me, the Flame King, striding after her. We don't make quite the pretty picture today as we did yesterday when she was in my lap.

At the castle gates, Isavelle hurries through a doorway and disappears inside. With a gusty sigh, I head to the wingrunners barracks, intending to sort out the matter of Isavelle's bodyguards immediately.

At the sparring grounds, I see two Betas dressed in the black and silver uniforms of the wingrunners. Wyverns are remarkably versatile creatures that are ridden like horses but can also take to the skies and attack from the air. They're ferocious in battle, and though they're not as powerful and destructive as dragons, they're nimbler and more versatile.

This pair, a man and a woman, are sparring with halberds, a pole weapon topped with an axe blade and spike that can be used from wyvernback.

They're both lightning fast as they train, and they're laughing and chatting between bouts. It must be nice being a Beta. Someone else will shoulder the worries and responsibilities.

I lift my chin and call out to them, "You two. Come here."

"Yes, *Ma'len*," they say, straightening up and hurrying over to me, and stand to attention with their halberds gripped in their right hands.

"What are your names?"

"Fiala," the woman says.

"Dusan," replies the man.

"Fiala and Dusan, my mate needs bodyguards at all times when I'm not with her. I want her guards to be able to carry her swiftly to safety if the need arises. I have the utmost respect for wingrunners. The two of you were at the Battle of Fliesch Monastery, weren't you?"

They seem astonished that I know this, but I saw these two wingrunners take out a detachment of Brethren archers, alternating dive attacks from the air with ground attacks.

"Yes, we were, *Ma'len*."

"I'm asking if you would like to volunteer to guard my mate." I fold my arms and regard them solemnly. "Think carefully before accepting. She's a handful for an Omega, and I value her life more highly than I value my own."

The two wingrunners glance at each other, have a short but silent conversation that consists of raised eyebrows and small nods, and then turn back to me.

"We would be honored, *Ma'len*."

"Are you certain?" I ask, a grim note entering my voice. "If anything happens to my Omega while I'm not with her, if she so much as stubs her toe, I'll take you up into the skies and hurl you from Scourge."

"Yes, *Ma'len*," they say smartly in unison.

I think I can trust them to protect her. The wingrunners are some of my most tenacious, committed soldiers, and they go above and beyond in battle. These two seem as energetic as any of them. It's not just their prowess that I'm thinking about. They will spend a great deal of time with Isavelle, talking to her about Maledin and probably about me as well, and hopefully they will become her friends. She's bound to ask them questions that she should be asking me.

"My mate has been raised as a human, and as her Alpha, it's my duty to teach her what our designations mean. My duty. Not yours. Is that clear?"

I watch the pair of them through narrowed eyes, hunting for the tiniest flicker of derision or amusement. Secretly,

Betas think of Alphas as snorting, shouting pains in the neck who overreact to every provocation.

They're correct.

We are exactly like that.

But if an Alpha is losing their shit, it's usually for a good reason. I don't want a couple of Betas to fill her head with a load of nonsense about what goes on between Alphas and their Omegas, or to teach Isavelle to ignore or make fun of my very real concerns for her safety. I'm her mate, and it's my duty to see that she's protected and happy, even if sometimes they're watching over her in my stead.

"Yes, *Ma'len*," they say again, without a flicker of impertinence in their eyes. No doubt it's there, Betas are just *like* that, but hopefully the threat of my wrath is enough for them to hold their damn tongues.

I relax a little and say, "Good. Thank you. Please go and introduce yourselves to Isavelle. Knowing my mate, she'll tell you she doesn't want bodyguards, so you'll have to convince her that she wants you around."

"How do we do that, *Ma'len*?"

I rest my wrist on the hilt of my sword and give them a bored look. "I don't know. You Betas are always bragging that you're so relaxing to be around. Why don't you show my mate an average good time at some of your neither excellent nor terrible Beta haunts? She could probably use some downtime after being dazzled by me for days on end." I allow the corner of my mouth to turn up so they know I'm not being totally serious.

I am dazzling, though.

Both the wingrunners' mouths twitch. "As you wish, *Ma'len*," they say, before bowing their heads.

I turn away and head back into the castle. Hopefully they'll help Isavelle relax into life in the capital as well as keep her safe. She's been miserable, afraid, and in pain for more than a year, and the constant intensity when we're close to each other isn't making her happy. Isavelle's happiness means more to me than she can possibly know.

13

Isavelle

I pass a terrible night in my bed, tossing and turning while my stomach churns. The brief moments when I am asleep, I'm plagued by nightmares of being burned alive. When I awaken with a gasp, I see over and over in my mind's eye the moment that Scourge incinerated those two Brethren.

Zabriel. Where is Zabriel? He's here in the castle and must be sleeping somewhere nearby. I could go to him and slip into his strong embrace. I think I'd feel safe in his arms, but then what? Mate this. Queen that. The man is impossible.

Instead, I lay miserably in my bed and long for him, and then I feel disgusted with myself for it.

At breakfast, the doors to the Great Hall are open and the clouds are heavy and oppressive as I nibble unhappily at a pear. Yesterday I was filled with energy and determination, but now I feel like I've been trampled into the dirt by a herd of stampeding dragons. I rub the nape of my neck, wincing. Why does it *ache* so?

I get to my feet and head outside for something to do when a voice drifts over from another table.

"...back to Joryan tomorrow."

I whirl around and grab hold of the speaker's shoulder. "I'm sorry, did you just say you're from Joryan?" Joryan is a town at least twenty miles from Amriste, but if this person is from there, that's closer than anyone else I've talked to.

It's a young man, and he looks startled that I've suddenly intruded on his conversation and grabbed him. I'm distantly aware that six people at the table are staring at me.

I make myself let go of him and force myself to smile. "I'm anxious for news from anyone in that part of Maledin. My family is from Amriste. It's small. You might not know it."

The young man relaxes a little. "I know it. Your apples are sometimes in our marketplace. Ma and Dad might have heard something. They're down in the tanner's district selling their wares, and then they'll be..."

I don't wait to hear what his mother and father will be doing next. If they're down in the tanner's district right now, then that's where I'm going.

As I exit the doors to the Great Hall, two soldiers holding long poles topped with spiked axes step in front of me. One is a sandy-haired man with a big smile, and the other is a smaller, stocky dark-haired woman.

The man greets me cheerfully. "It's your lucky day, Lady Isavelle. Fiala and I are your new bodyguards. My name's Dusan, and you don't know how fortunate you are to have the two of us protecting you."

They're wearing uniforms that are similar to what Captain Ashton wears, so they must be wingrunners.

"Sorry, I haven't got time to say hello. I might have news about where my family is," I tell them breathlessly.

They hurry after me, the man wearing an apologetic look. "Ah, well, you see, that's a bit sticky for us. We need to be your bodyguards, otherwise, King Zabriel will feed us to his dragon."

"No, he won't. Dragons don't like the taste of people."

"I told you she wouldn't buy that," Fiala snaps, and Dusan looks crestfallen. "Let me do the talking, you great big oaf. Lady Isavelle, you seem like you are on your way outside the castle grounds. Let us accompany you, and I promise you won't even know we're there. Unless something like yesterday's unfortunate event occurs, and then we'll gut the Brethren bastards like fish." Fiala brandishes her weapon, an expression in her eyes like she's hoping she gets the chance.

There's a familiar beating sound in the distance, and I see three dots on the horizon, growing larger and larger as they approach the castle. Dragons. They no longer fly in circles over the city and castle, but they pass close to where we're standing as they head for the dragongrounds and disappear. A moment later we hear the thud of them coming into land.

"Do you think they made it through the barrier?" Dusan asks his friend.

Fiala sighs dismally. "I doubt it. If I'm locked under the mountain for another five hundred years, I will lose my blasted mind."

I turn to them. "What barrier?"

Dusan opens his mouth to answer, but Fiala's gray eyes

flare and she cuts him off. "Lady Isavelle, we will happily tell you all you wish to know."

She remains silent, and I glance between the two of them. "Please go on."

"We will tell you all wish to know…once you accept us as your bodyguards. Do you accept us?"

"What does it mean if I accept you?"

"We are your protectors in *Ma'len's* stead. We will accompany you whenever you wish to leave the castle. Our wyverns will fly with your dragon. We will lay down our lives for you if necessary."

That startling sentiment has me shaking my head. "Please don't. I'm not important enough for you to lay down your lives for, and I don't have a dragon."

Fiala and Dusan go down on one knee before me with bowed heads, and Fiala says, "We pledge to protect you, Lady Isavelle, up to and including with our lives. Do you accept us?"

I don't want to go down into the city alone where I can get lost or be attacked, and if I'm attacked by more Brethren, they'll help me fight them off. I'm just not used to people wanting to do things for me and make my life better. I don't feel like I deserve it. "Um, that's very kind of you. Thank you."

"Then we are your blade and shield." They get to their feet, Fiala's expression somber and Dusan with a grin on his face.

"I need to go outside the castle walls. Will you come with me?" I ask them.

"Certainly. Anywhere you want to go, we'll follow," Dusan replies cheerfully, and I find myself smiling at them.

"Then let's go now. I just overhead there are people from a

town near mine down in the city, and I need to talk to them. They're in the tanner's district, but I don't know where that is."

"We'll show you, my lady," Fiala replies. "When was the last time you saw your family?"

I explain briefly everything that's happened, from being taken by the Brethren to nearly being killed by them, and then being saved twice and brought here by Zabriel.

Dusan rubs his jaw thoughtfully. "I wish I could give you some news, but the wingrunners haven't had much cause to fly over that part of Maledin."

"We can put the word out and discover if anyone will be heading that way," Fiala offers. "Meantime, Lady Isavelle should question this person from Joryan. It sounds as if it's a promising lead."

My chest feels tight, and I try to smile at them, but I think I must look like I'm in pain.

"Lady Isavelle?" Dusan asks with a frown.

"You're both on my side? Just like that?"

"Whose side would we be on?" Fiala asks, a baffled expression on her face.

Dusan slings a friendly arm around my shoulders. "Good news, Lady Isavelle. We're on your side. In fact, every Maledinni is on your side. But especially the two of us."

"*Ma'len* doesn't want your stink all over his mate," Fiala scolds, knocking his arm away again.

I find myself laughing as we head through the gates and into the city. With the sun shining and two companions walking by my side, there's hope in my heart. I ask my bodyguards where the tanner's district is, and we head for the western part of Lenhale.

"Tell me about this barrier you mentioned," I ask as we walk.

Fiala's serious expression grows even more serious. "It's a magical barrier that has appeared near the southern border, and nothing from our side can pass through it. All the enemy soldiers have fled that way, and we fear they are regrouping for a fresh attack on Maledin."

"We don't even know who their leader is. I don't know if you heard, Lady Isavelle, but their former king is dead."

"Oh, I heard," I say, and tell them about my up-close experience with the dead king.

Dusan brandishes his weapon in both hands as if he's prepared to fight the memory of my brush with death. "How dare they attempt to sacrifice a Maledinni to their god. It's obscene, and they all deserve to die for such an offense."

"Zabriel and the other dragonriders killed most of them," I tell him, and he and Fiala both nod in approval.

"They must be serving someone," Fiala muses. "A powerful wizard, if that magical barrier is anything to go by."

"The Brethren call him the Shadow King," I tell them.

They both stare at me in surprise. "The who?"

"While you were all asleep beneath the mountain, I was forced to be in service to the Brethren. I heard rumors that the true ruler of Maledin wasn't our king, but someone powerful who lived in the southern mountains. I think he's called the Shadow King because he pulled on King Alaster's strings like a puppet master. The High Priest said he was taking me to him."

"Well, whatever he's called, he's a pain in our asses," Dusan grumbles. "We'll know more when we've breached the barrier and discovered what's on the other side."

He holds out his arm and directs me around a wagon that's stopped in the street, and he and Fiala chat about how the city has changed in five hundred years. Apparently, it's a lot muddier and dirtier, and many of the houses are in shambles compared to their time. It's pleasant to listen to them talk.

"You both seem quite normal for Maledinni. I've mostly been around my people, and you both feel like you're my people."

Dusan brightens. "Thank you for saying so, Lady Isavelle. It's because we're Betas. Most of the Maledinni you will meet are Betas."

"What's a Beta?"

"We're the sane ones," Dusan says, and from his grin, I know he's not being totally serious. "We're the Maledinni who get things done and don't create a fuss over nothing."

Fiala clears her throat meaningfully, and Dusan stops talking.

"Most people? Even Captain Ashton and Sir Godric? They seem more like Zabriel to me," I say.

Dusan nods. "They're Betas, though pretty high up on the chain, as close as a Beta can get to being an Alpha."

"Are there more Alphas around here? Have I met any?" I glance around, wondering if I can spot one right this moment.

"You'll know an Alpha when you meet them," Fiala says with a sour twist to her mouth, which tells me all I need to know about what she thinks of Alphas.

As we cross a square, a figure comes hurrying toward us. She's holding on to her skirts and her eyes are fixed on me, and my heart lightens when I realize it's Odanna.

Dusan immediately steps in front of me and brandishes his halberd. I put my hand on his arm. "It's all right. She's a friend."

I step around my guards and feel them follow me as Odanna reaches my side. She asks in her throaty voice, "Isavelle, are you all right? I've been so worried about you."

I assure her that I'm fine and introduce her to my bodyguards. "Fiala and Dusan of the wingrunners. Wingrunners ride the wyverns, which are the smaller flying creatures that we've seen in the sky."

Odanna flinches at the sight of their weapons, but a moment later she forces a smile and greets the guards. Fiala watches Odanna with a frown, but that could just be her usual expression.

She turns to me, her expression wretched. "I'm so sorry, Isavelle. I froze when you were attacked, and then I ran away and left you when I heard the dragon coming. I'm so sorry I abandoned you."

"I promise you don't have to feel bad about that," I assure her. "There's nothing you could have done about the Brethren, and Scourge terrifies me as well. I wouldn't blame you if you never got used to dragons being around. Scourge killed two people right in front of us."

The memory of the man being eaten away by dragonfire makes me shudder. What a horrible way to go.

Odanna rubs her hands against her arms as if she's cold, and hesitates before she adds, "It's terrifying seeing the dragons up close." For a moment, she searches the skies for wings, and I wonder if that wasn't the first time she's come close to a furious dragon.

"What happened here during the invasion?" I ask.

Odanna describes a sky that seemed to be filled with dragons. People screaming and panicking in the streets. Children crying. Men brandishing axes and pitchforks as if they would do them any good against dragons.

"I hid in the stables, holding a hammer, wondering if I would be burned to death, trying to gather the courage to fight. Thankfully, no one needed to because when the Maledinni soldiers entered the city, they made it clear they had no interest in hurting us."

As Odanna evokes the smoky, terror-filled day, I can't help but picture my own village and wonder what happened there. If dragons flew overhead making Waylen sob in terror. If Anise grabbed a gardening implement, bravely resolving to fight the dragons herself if she had to. Wherever they are now, I know that Anise will be protecting our little brother. A lump rises in my throat as I remember her huge, scared eyes when the Brethren came for a village girl. The way she gripped my wrist and refused to let go at first, insisting I hide with her. Maybe she knew something that I wouldn't admit even to myself, that I was going to hide poorly so I would be the one taken. Maybe she knew because it's something she would have done herself to protect Waylen.

Odanna must realize that I'm thinking about my family as she says, "I've been asking around in a few taverns about your family and hometown. I wish I had some news for you, but all anyone wanted to talk about was you and the Flame King."

I smile at her, my heart lightening. "Thank you for trying. I appreciate it more than you can know."

"Speaking of you and the Flame King..." The young

woman trails off and bites her lip. I think she's trying to be a good friend and stifle her curiosity.

"Go on. Ask me what's on your mind."

"The word around the city is that you don't want to marry him, but why not? He's so handsome, and he's the king. If he wants to marry you, you'll be Queen of Maledin and live in luxury for the rest of your life."

"All the Flame King wants is for me to fall at his feet, but I'm not in a falling mood." I picture going down on my knees before him and kissing his fingertips while gazing up at him with a flirtatious expression. Soon my mind is wandering down heated little pathways where I feel him cup my face with his large hand. He gazes at me adoringly. Lets me suck his fingers while he tells me how beautiful I am.

Zabriel would love all that.

I don't want that, though. Absolutely not.

Odanna nods sadly. "I can imagine that wouldn't be possible for you, and that's all right. What I wouldn't give to..." She trails off and sighs. "I was in love once."

"Oh? What happened?"

"He didn't love me back." Odanna puts her arm through mine and walks with me down the street. We arrive at some stables, and I guess that this is where Odanna works because she starts introducing me to the horses. A brown and white mare snuffles affectionately at my hand. Fiala and Dusan are standing quietly a few feet away.

"I'm sorry to hear that you had your heart broken," I say.

"He tried. He really did, but I think that just made it worse in the end. I knew what his kisses felt like. What his protection meant to me. But never his love." Her face scrunches at the memory like she's about to cry. "Sometimes I can't breathe when I remember just how long ago it was. Isn't that funny?"

Odanna forces a smile and a husky laugh, but there's nothing funny about it.

She strokes the black horse's nose, a faraway expression in her eyes. "If the Flame King loves you, really loves you, then you're blessed to have the love of a man like him."

I gaze at the young, dark-haired woman before me and sense so much sadness radiating from her. I don't think she's had an easy life.

I hug Odanna and promise to come back and see her as soon as I can. "It means more to me than I can say that you were asking after my family. I'm getting closer, I can feel it."

"Good luck, and I'll keep trying." She gives me a hopeful smile and a wave as we head off.

In the tanner's district, I ask around about a couple from Joryan until a blacksmith's apprentice points me toward a man and woman who are selling what looks like the last of their tanned leathers to a shoemaker.

I wait until they've concluded their business, then approach and explain that I met their son at the castle and that I'm looking for my family from Amriste.

The woman peers closely at me, then at my bodyguards, and then grabs her husband's sleeve in horror. "My-my lady. I apologize, for we didn't recognize you." In a loud whisper, she tells the man standing next to her, "This is the king's betrothed. The one that the dragon protected so fiercely yesterday."

They both sink into curtseys, the flustered husband copying his wife until he realizes his mistake and changes it to a wobbly bow.

A dozen pairs of eyes are drawn in this direction, and I feel myself flush. "Please don't. Before the invasion, I was a Veiled Virgin, and before that, I lived in Amriste. I'm not anyone special."

The woman looks uncertain, but as she straightens up, she says, "I know of Amriste, but I'm sorry, my lady, we fled this way and never went through those parts. I will keep my ears open for news on our journey home, if it pleases you?"

I try to conceal my disappointment that I've turned down yet another dead end. "Thank you. I appreciate it. Have a good journey home."

"I daresay the king's dragon could fly you to Amriste in a mere moment," the husband calls after me as we turn and head for the castle.

Yes, Scourge could, couldn't he? And a wyvern is supposed to be even faster than a dragon.

I turn to my bodyguards as we walk. "Can your wyverns carry a second passenger?"

Fiala straightens up proudly. "Of course. Wyverns are strong fliers, my lady. They can carry two people and a generous load of supplies."

"Can you fly me to my village?"

Dusan laughs. "Take the Flame King's mate hundreds of miles from the castle without his permission? I don't fancy being ripped to pieces by Scourge, my lady."

Fiala gives me an apologetic look. "We will accompany you wherever you wish to go, but for a journey like that, we will need the Flame King's permission."

I expected that's what they would say. "Then you had better take me to wherever the Flame King is right now, please. I have a question for him."

Fiala and Dusan exchange haunted looks as we head for the castle, and I wonder if they're afraid Zabriel is going to think they put the idea to fly to Amriste in my head. "Don't worry. Zabriel knows I'm capable of having crazy ideas all on my own."

This makes Dusan laugh, but it sounds hollow.

We find Zabriel in a large room a short distance from the Great Hall, brooding over an enormous map of Maledin that's covering a table. From where he sits, he has an expansive view of the dragongrounds and the northern mountain from a large terrace with a balcony.

He's so sunk in thought that he doesn't seem to hear me approach. His nostrils flare, then he looks up from the map in surprise to see me standing at his elbow.

I give him my sweetest smile. "It's your lucky day, Zabriel. I have a favor to ask you, and when you grant it, I'm going to be eternally grateful to you."

14

Zabriel

Isavelle is smiling at me. I'm instantly suspicious. My suspicions grow when I notice how Fiala and Dusan are staring at their feet.

I fold my arms, gazing down at my mate severely. "You'll bestow your eternal gratitude on me? And how may I accomplish this miracle?"

"By allowing me to fly to Amriste with Fiala and Dusan on their wyverns."

The world cracks at the edges and turns red. Isavelle leaving the safety of the city, which is dangerous enough to be getting on with. Isavelle returning to her village and wandering around in the open where she could be attacked by a hundred Brethren. Isavelle making herself vulnerable to being snatched away by the High Priest, thrown onto another funeral pyre, or presented to another king.

Absolutely fucking not.

I glance behind her at her two guards who appear to be trying to sink through solid stone, and growl, "I suppose she got this idea from the two of you."

Isavelle moves until she's blocking my sight of them. "It was my idea. I have hunted all over this castle and the city for news of anyone from my region and have come up with nothing. This isn't just about my family anymore. This is about all your people in western Maledin. Aren't you worried about them?"

The people of western Maledin? I turn around to the map and study it.

Isavelle moves to my side and points out a western town closest to the capital. "That's Joryan. This morning I met a family from there, but the rest of the region?" She draws her finger in a circle, encompassing an area that makes up at least a fifth of Maledin's landmass. A humble region of dotted villages and a few low-ranked lords, which is doubtless why no one but Isavelle has been beating down my door about it. "I have encountered no one from these towns and villages. Don't you find that alarming?"

That does seem strange. The people may have fled to the far west, into the vast and empty Silk Reed Plains that belong to neighboring Grendu, or it could be something more sinister could have happened. Killed. Captured. Something else.

"All right," I say, nodding slowly. "You've convinced me that the area should be investigated."

Her eyes widen in delight. "Really? I can fly to Amriste with my bodyguards?"

"No. You're flying with me on Scourge. Fiala and Dusan may accompany us to give you additional protection."

Isavelle's face falls as I mention my dragon. "On Scourge? Surely you're too busy."

I glance out the window at the sky and see that the sun is just tipping past noon. A little over an hour to fly there and the same to come back. The magical barrier is occupying most of my mind, but the people of the west are important too, and if seeing her village for herself is what Isavelle needs to assure herself that she's doing everything she can to find her family, then I can spare the time.

Besides, if I say no, she'll go and do it anyway, and at least she's safe with me.

"I'm never too busy for you, *sha'len*. But we'll eat first." I signal to one of the attendants to bring us food.

Dusan and Fiala both bow and murmur, "*Ma'len*. Lady Isavelle."

"Meet us at the dragongrounds and ask Captain Ashton for two more wingrunners to protect Lady Isavelle."

"Yes, *Ma'len*," Fiala says, and she and Dusan leave the room.

There are comfortable chairs by the fire, and I draw my mate that way and invite her to sit down. A few minutes later, the attendant brings platters of bread, fruit, cheese, and sweets, as well as a carafe of watered wine sweetened with winterberry juice. I make up a plate for Isavelle and pass it to her, only to find that her expression is pained and she's fidgeting. I think I know what's preoccupying her.

"Scourge will never hurt you, on purpose or by accident," I assure my mate. "He's big, but he's aware of you at all times."

I'm starting to believe that he purposefully landed with

Isavelle safely between his front legs at the funeral pyre because he understood immediately that she must be protected. He sensed her before I did. He scented her before me. My dragon found my mate for me, and if I wasn't already eternally devoted to Scourge, I would be just for that.

Isavelle twists a grape in her fingers. "I believe you, but it makes me feel so ill to ride on a dragon. I don't think I'll ever get used to it."

"I'll help you so you don't feel sick, and you don't need to keep your eyes open." How sad if Isavelle never discovers for herself the joy of flying. There are Maledinni who never ride, but I always expected that my mate would be a dragonrider.

Isavelle is watching me closely. "You're disappointed, aren't you? You want me to love flying, not merely endure it."

I give her a quick smile. "I don't care at all. There are a thousand other things we can share. Now, eat."

As we eat our meal, Isavelle tells me about the people she has encountered and their fears and challenges. "Are you sure you want to hear about villagers and crop planting? These aren't the kind of people that interest a king."

They probably didn't interest King Alaster, and they absolutely didn't interest my father, but as both those kings met a bloody end, I don't much care for their preferences. "All my people are important, and I don't have much time to get to know them at present. You're helping me immensely. I'm understanding them through you."

Isavelle considers this, and then continues to tell me about the former Veiled Virgins who are now working in my kitchens, and some refugee men who have shown interest in the wingrunners.

I glance over and see with pleasure that her empty plate is

dotted with crumbs. She's eating well. Her body has healed from all her injuries. She smells *divine*.

Before I can stop myself, I put my arms around Isavelle and scoop her into my lap. She feels softer than she did the first time I held her in my arms, and a golden feeling of happiness spreads through me. "Good girl for eating so well. I just want to squeeze you. I just want to *eat* you."

I imagine the delicious bounce of her breasts as I thrust into her and moan, pressing my face into her neck to inhale even more of her delicious scent.

"Eat me?" she squeaks, her eyes going wide in alarm.

"Yes, the big, bad dragon eating up the princess because he's *ravenous* for her. You're so plump and juicy."

"Actually, I'm usually bigger than this, and I'll get that way again if you keep feeding me."

"Good," I purr, sliding my hand possessively around her thigh, pulling her closer, and licking slowly up her neck, right over her sensitive gland. I don't know how sensitive it is yet, but Isavelle gasps softly, and I feel her melt a little in my arms.

There's a plate of sweets that we haven't touched yet, so I pick up a creamy tart and hold it for her, watching as she bites into it. "*Vru'mai*, your mouth is sexy."

Isavelle licks the corner of her lips and swallows. "What does *vru'mai* mean?"

I smile and stroke the blade of my nose up her cheek. "Say it again and I'll tell you."

Isavelle hesitates, but curiosity wins out. "*Vru'mai*."

She's not got the hang of rolling her *r*'s, but that was pretty good. "Mmm, wonderful. It means *fuck me*. You can use it as a curse or as a request. If you say it before *desh* it means, *fuck me please. Vru'mai desh.* Go on, repeat after me or you'll never learn."

Isavelle hesitates. "I don't think it's appropriate to teach me about your ancient tongue starting with the obscenities."

"*Our* ancient language, and of course it is. The first thing you should learn in a foreign language is how to swear."

"How do you say *fuck you*?"

"*Vru'je.*" I grin wolfishly at her. "But I will never say that to you unless it's proceeded by, *I'm going to.*"

Her cheeks grow red, and I watch her playing with the fastenings on my jacket and then hesitantly drawing her fingers through my black hair.

"It's so silky," she whispers, then rubs a tress of my hair against her cheek. Her fingers go on exploring me, touching my jaw, and then behind my ear. Her fingers brush the sensitive gland on the side of my neck.

"Touch me there. Please," I say in a roughened voice, my eyes closing.

To my delight, she does as I ask, her slender fingers trailing delicately over my flesh. I can feel her eyes on me as she strokes me, fascinated by my enjoyment.

"Is this a special place?" she asks. "Where I'm from, people enjoy being touched here, but they don't enjoy it as much as you seem to."

Pleasure flashes through my knot, and I can feel myself growing rock hard. My mate is curious about what gives me pleasure. "It's a very special place, *sha'len.* The way you're touching me feels wonderful. You're giving me so much pleasure."

I open my eyes and see the way her cheeks are flushed red again from my praise. Another little hint of her designation.

I glance out the window and notice how far the sun has continued its passage through the sky.

"I would love to sit here and teach you all the ways I want you to touch me, but if you have finished eating, there's somewhere we have to be."

Isavelle draws her fingers away from my neck. She tries to get off my lap, but I stand up with her in my arms and carry her out of the room.

"I can walk to the dragongrounds," she protests.

"It's faster if I carry you," I say, lengthening my strides and walking at a pace that would have her running to keep up with me. "And I'm not ready to let go of you. Put your arms around my neck."

She hesitates and then does, and my eyelashes flutter as her fingers touch my nape. The gland there isn't as sensitive or important as hers, but fuck, it still feels amazing when she touches me there.

At the dragongrounds, Fiala and Dusan are standing near Scourge with their wyverns, along with Captain Ashton himself and another wingrunner called Leibel. Half a dozen dragons of the flare have gathered around, interested in what's happening in their midst.

Isavelle clutches my shoulder as we approach. "You should put me down now."

I keep walking with her in my arms with no intention of letting her go. "You'll have to get used to the king giving orders while holding you in his arms because I'm not going to stop."

An exasperated expression crosses her beautiful face. She needn't feel shy. My people are used to Alphas being ultra-protective of their Omegas. In fact, they expect it. No one would bat an eyelash if I sat on my throne issuing decrees with my sleepy Omega napping in my lap.

What a beautiful thought. I hope I can make that happen one day.

I address Captain Ashton. "You're joining us? Thank you for coming personally. Have Fiala and Dusan informed you and Leibel about where we're going and why?"

The captain nods, and so does Leibel, a stoic and battle-scarred wingrunner who wears that Beta air of indifference to everything that goes on between Alphas and Omegas. He doesn't even look twice at Isavelle.

"This could be dangerous. Here's how this is going to work, and why I wanted more wingrunners to join us." As I explain the plan, Isavelle gives a cry of dismay and struggles in my arms, but I won't put her down or change my mind. Either we do this my way, or we don't do this at all.

A few minutes later, I'm carrying my worried mate atop Scourge and settling her into my arms. All around us, the wingrunners are mounting their wyverns and the svelte silver creatures are spreading their wings.

"You haven't seen wingrunners in action, have you?" Dusan calls, beaming at my mate as his mount shoots into the air. "Prepare to be amazed, Lady Isavelle."

~

I WATCH from among the trees as Isavelle hurries through the deserted village square, her cloak pulled up over her head. The day turned overcast as we flew, and flurries of snow are skittering across the cobbles.

As she reaches her cottage, she calls out for her mother and father and raises her hand to knock on the front door.

There's the sound of running feet and half a dozen cloaked figures emerge from the laneways and behind walls and doors. Isavelle screams and runs back toward the square, but she finds no shelter or protection. With her cloak pulled tightly around herself, she peers this way and that, rooted to the spot from fear.

The Brethren are closing in on her, hands reaching to grab her.

A large creature whirrs out of the sky and shoots across the square lightning fast. So fast that the other Brethren don't understand why one of their own is crumpling to the ground, blood cascading down his robes.

Isavelle pulls a short sword out from beneath her cloak and straightens up, her cloak falling back to reveal that it's actually Fiala. The wingrunner wears an expression of bloodthirsty delight as she thrusts the blade up beneath a Brethren's ribs and into his heart.

Wyvern after wyvern dives at the Brethren, either ripping the men with their talons or allowing their riders to sever heads and limbs with their halberds.

Beside me, the real Isavelle huddles into my side, wincing at the carnage but unable to drag her eyes away.

A few moments later, all six of the Brethren lie bleeding on the cobbles, thick rivulets streaming across the gently sloping square. Three wyverns land by the bodies, their talons gleaming red.

Captain Ashton and Leibel dismount and bow as we emerge from the trees and into the square. Dusan slides from his wyvern and grins at my mate.

"Did you see that, Lady Isavelle? That's what wingrunners are all about. Speed, agility, and precise attacks. No roaring, trampling, or fire needed. Impressive, right?"

"You were an amazing sight." Isavelle gazes at the bodies and body parts with a bleak expression. "I don't understand why the High Priest is still trying to take me prisoner."

I presume that the Brethren have discovered that she's important to me, and so she either has to be captured or die.

It's plain to see that the village is still deserted, and we saw no trace of anyone between here and where I landed with Scourge just over a mile away. "Does it seem to you as if anyone has been here since we were last in Amriste?"

Isavelle turns on the spot, examining every cottage, every laneway. Her expression is so downcast as she shakes her head that it makes my chest ache. "It doesn't seem to me like anyone's been here. Could my family and the other villagers have been taken behind the barrier to the south?"

I study her closely, thinking hard. "That is something to consider. They could also have fled into Grendu." By all the gods, please let them be in Grendu and not captured by the Brethren.

Captain Ashton addresses me. "Leibel and I can explore the Silk Reed Plains for signs of the western townsfolk."

Maledin and Grendu always had a strained relationship in my time. They didn't trust our dragons, and we were less than comfortable with their necromancy and animal magic. The one thing we could agree on was trade, and that kept the peace, though I imagine that any incursion onto their lands from my wyverns would anger them.

"Fly along the border but don't pass into Grendu territory," I tell Ashton. "I will arrange for letters to be sent to nearby Grendu towns and their capital to ask the lords and the king whether refugees from Maledin have been sighted."

Isavelle splays her hand against my chest and whispers, "Thank you."

I cover her hand with my own as we watch Captain Ashton and Leibel take to the skies and fly west. We'll know in a few hours if they spot anything, and in a few days if the people of Grendu have anything to tell us.

After they've disappeared over the houses, Isavelle turns to me and opens her mouth to speak, but she hesitates. A raven is perched on the edge of the well, gazing at her. "Mistress Hawthorne, I know that's you."

The raven flaps its wings and flies away, cawing.

As if she was there all along—and perhaps she was—Biddy Hawthorne shuffles out of the shadows between the cottages. The old woman looks from Isavelle to me, then to my hand clasped over my mate's on my chest, and leers at us.

"Has the happy occasion taken place already, *Ma'len*? Surely it's too soon for her first heat. You've only just met."

"My first what?" Isavelle's cheeks turn pink and she draws away from me.

"Don't be shy around your Flame King just because an old woman is watching you, girl."

"Grandmother," I growl in warning. I don't like the witch tormenting my mate, and I don't like her calling Isavelle *girl* either.

"Mistress Hawthorne, have you seen anyone since we last spoke? Or your ravens? Anyone at all?" Isavelle asks without much hope.

The old woman sniffs and plants her walking stick before her in both hands. "Only Brethren. They're watching this place night and day. Go back to the capital with your mate where you belong."

"I belong here. I was born in this village, just like you," Isavelle replies.

"But did you ever want to stay here? No, you were trying to leave the moment you could crawl," the old witch snaps back. "From the moment you heard there was a king under the mountain, you were trying to reach him. Your mother nearly had to tie you to her apron strings to keep you at home."

I eye my mate with interest. Is that so?

The flush in Isavelle's cheeks deepens. "That's not true."

"Aye, it is. I remember, and I knew what was hidden beneath that mountain. Witches know. Witches always know. Why do you think they wanted us all dead? Because we delivered babes and boiled up fever drafts? I knew you never belonged in Amriste, not then and not now, so get gone."

Isavelle is taken aback by the old woman's sharp words, and she stares with a hurt expression at the witch.

I put a hand on Isavelle's shoulder and stroke the nape of her neck with my thumb. "Mistress Hawthorne. That's enough."

Biddy Hawthorne is amused by the way I move closer to my mate. "You can't help yourself, can you, *Ma'len*?"

Protecting and soothing my mate when someone flings sharp words at her? Of course I won't stand idly by and let it happen. "Isavelle will accept how things are in her own time."

My mate shrugs me off and glares at both of us. "If my family has fled to Grendu or been taken behind the barrier to the south, then I'm not going to hide in Lenhale and forget about them."

"We will find everyone who is missing, *sha'len*. In Grendu or the south." I reach for Isavelle's hand, but before I can take it, the old woman speaks up again.

"Whoever has placed that barrier is a powerful wizard. The same wizard that defeated your father, Flame King?"

Black fury erupts in my chest at the memory of that vile entity who murdered my father and mother and sealed every dragon, wyvern, and so many Maledinni beneath the Bodan Mountains. "Five hundred years later? It seems unlikely."

"You're among us five hundred years later," she observes.

My breathing comes faster as my fury mounts. "That wizard from my time has long since come and gone. It can't possibly be the same one."

"Can't we travel beyond the barrier and see who it is for ourselves?" Isavelle asks.

Fiala clears her throat. "Lady Isavelle. Two wingrunners accidentally flew through the barrier when it first appeared. They and their wyverns were killed instantly."

Isavelle's face falls.

I touch Isavelle's chin and draw her gaze up to mine. "My people are working night and day to find a way to bring down that barrier. I won't lose Maledin again, or anyone who belongs here. I swear that I will do everything in my power to bring them home. Do you believe me?"

Slowly, Isavelle nods.

I relax and draw her into my arms, tucking her cheek against my chest. Isavelle's long, honey-gold hair dances against her back in the cold wind, and tiny white ice crystals shine among the strands.

Slowly she pulls away from me and turns to the witch.

"What about you, Mistress Hawthorne? Will you stay here in this village?"

"Of course I shall. This is my home."

I hear her emphasis, and Isavelle must as well. This is *my* home.

Not yours.

~

It's late afternoon when Scourge's talons hit dirt at the dragongrounds. Isavelle has been pressed tightly against me with her eyes closed the entire flight, and I detect no scent of nausea from her as I carry her to the ground. I'm the one who feels sick to my stomach.

Rather than allay her fears or give her hope, the empty village, the carnage, and the doom-laden description of the magical barrier has only made her wretched. "I'm so sorry, *sha'len*. That was a terrible few hours for you, and it has accomplished nothing."

"Not nothing, Zabriel. I know where my family isn't."

She touches my cheek with a small smile on her lips and turns toward the stone bridge. I follow at her side, a clawing sensation in my guts. I have a terrible feeling that Captain Ashton will return with no news from the Grendu border, and the letter that I will write tonight and send to Grendu lands will turn up nothing either.

On the far side of the stone bridge, Godric greets me with a scroll in his hands. "A wingrunner unit was approached by a lone member of the Brethren by the barrier. He was unarmed, and he gave this to me, saying it was for the Flame King."

I turn the scroll over in my hands and see that there's an imprint in the wax seal. A triple chevron.

"That's the High Priest's seal," Isavelle says. "I recognize the markings from his signet ring."

I dart a look at her. The High fucking Priest has written me a letter? I want to hurl it away from me and have Scourge set it aflame. I open it, though it makes my lip curl in disgust to see letters written by his hand.

"Greetings to the usurper king…" I mutter as I start to read. He's off to a great start. As my eyes follow the flourishing, arrogant script, I grow angrier and angrier. "It's a proposal to cease hostilities between us, and a list of demands. If I surrender the capital and all the monasteries, I will be permitted to claim the southern mountain region of Maledin for my people and we will live undisturbed. An emissary will arrive in Lenhale shortly to accept my surrender. If I refuse, they will…" My jaw tightens angrily, and I have to force the words out. "…have no choice but to cleanse our parasitic presence from their homelands, beginning with our dragons."

I ball up the missive angrily in my fists, imagining it's the High Priest's throat I'm twisting, and the crackling of the paper is the bones in his neck. This is the piece of wyvern shit who had my woman beaten and starved. She suffered at his hands, and he dares contemplate for a moment that I will surrender to him?

That man will *burn*.

Scourge has come to the other side of the stone bridge. I throw the balled-up paper into the air and he incinerates it with a blast of his dragonfire that lights us up as bright as a summer's day and heats our faces.

There's a short silence, and then Godric clears his throat. "One of the wingrunners is ready to return to the barrier with your reply."

"I have fucking replied. He can go to hell."

"And their emissary?"

I grasp Isavelle's hand and stalk into the castle. "If that arrogant smear of shit wishes to send someone to bleat at my gates, he can waste his time."

TWO DAYS LATER, I receive letters from unsettlingly intelligent silver falcons. The birds find me wherever I am and flutter to the nearest perch, offering their legs. I know before I read the tiny scrolls that the messages are from Grendu and these birds are influenced by magic.

The falcons bring me no good news from Grendu. Maledinni people haven't been sighted across the border in Grendu. The king's greeting to me is polite and flattering, but reading between the lines he implies that any Maledinni found on his side of the border will be immediately ejected.

"Your people haven't changed in five hundred years," I mutter to the falcon messenger, who pins me with fierce black eyes, ruffles her feathers, and whirrs away.

I've talked with Stesha about the threat to our dragons, and he's stationed guards around the dragons' food and water supplies, and he's cautioned every dragonrider to be mindful of poisons, traps, and spells. The man's temper is never good, but it's been incendiary ever since and he barked at me that it would be wise for me to hurry up and pull down that magical barrier. Thank you, Stesha. I hadn't thought of that.

It's evening, and the sun has already set when Godric comes to me with the news that the emissary from the Brethren is at the capital's gates, asking for admittance.

"What about it?" I snarl, not looking up from the map of Maledin I'm studying.

"Do you wish for him to be sent away?"

I wish for him to die by my hand, but I don't slaughter messengers. "Let him wait at the gates until he grows tired and leaves of his own accord."

"He's asking after Lady Isavelle."

I round on Godric. "He's *what*?"

"The emissary claims that Lady Isavelle is the King of Maledin's bride. Her marriage to King Alaster was thwarted, so she belongs to the next King of Maledin. The Brethren demand that the lady is released from your captivity."

"I'm the King of Maledin, and Lady Isavelle is not a captive," I roar. "How dare they try to take my bride from me."

"The emissary seems to be aware that Lady Isavelle is not..." He winces. "...wedded and bedded, as he put it, and therefore the Brethren want her back."

Wedded and bedded. I suppose that's the human term for mated and married. Of course they would put them in the wrong order, expecting marriage before a couple has pledged themselves to one another, the barbarians. Isavelle and I have not married because her designation hasn't emerged, and I'm not a fucking monster to force my knot on her before she's ready or even wants me.

There's no point explaining the complexities of Maledin wedding traditions to these ignoramuses, and I don't care if they understand or not, but the wedding takes place *after* mating, not before.

I stare at the moonlight spilling over the windowsill. I wonder if the fact that the Brethren are completely ignorant of our ways might come in useful here.

I turn to Godric, my finger tapping thoughtfully on the table. "Admit the emissary to the castle. Once I'm present, bring him to the Great Hall."

"*Ma'len*? Of course, but..."

I'm already striding out of the room. "Keep him waiting in one of the outer rooms and light the candles in the Great Hall. I'm going to fetch my bride."

First, I'll need to change my clothes. As I head for my rooms, a smirk is playing around my lips. What I have planned will protect Isavelle and thwart the Brethren, but I think I'm going to enjoy this.

I change into a silken robe, knot it carelessly around my hips, and drag the tie from my hair that's holding half of it back.

With bare feet and my hair hanging around my shoulders, I make my way to Isavelle's door. I rap softly on the wood and listen for movement from within.

A moment later her voice calls back, "Who is it?"

"It's me. Can I talk to you?"

There's a slight hesitation, and then the door opens. Isavelle hasn't changed into her nightgown yet, and she's still wearing the homespun maid's uniform that I've seen her in ever since she arrived at the castle. I would rather see my bride in silk and velvet, but I don't wish to battle with her about every little thing she does. I'll choose my battles for the important moments, like this one.

I frown at her. "Why wasn't this door locked? Your bodyguards aren't with you and anyone could walk in."

Isavelle takes in my appearance, from my loose hair to my bare chest and the silk robe. A blush coats her cheeks. "Zabriel, you're—you're *naked*."

I glance down at myself and back up at her. "I'm not naked. I'm wearing a robe."

Her eyes dart away only to cut back to me again like she can't help herself, and she whispers, "It's practically falling off you."

I lean against her doorframe and smile. "There's a reason for that."

"Oh, yes?"

"Diplomacy."

Isavelle's brow wrinkles in confusion. "I don't understand."

"I'll explain on the way. Quickly, make yourself look like I've been ravishing you for hours, and we've dragged ourselves from the sheets without bothering to get dressed."

15

Isavelle

"I'm sorry, what? Why would I do that?"

"Diplomacy," Zabriel repeats. His thin, silky red and white robe is crossed loosely over his chest and tied carelessly around his hips. So carelessly that the robe is open to his waist and falling off one muscular shoulder. The sight of so much of his bare flesh is doing things to me. Hot, unsettling things.

"I need to look like you've just bedded me for...diplomacy?"

"For the people of Maledin. A Brethren emissary is here, and I need to send him a clear message." His expression softens. "It's for your sake. I need to make sure they don't try and take you again."

Despite the flirtatious expression in his eyes, this is serious.

If he's found a way to stop Brethren from grabbing me in the street then I'm interested in trying it. "Um, all right. But how do I make myself look like we've been…what you said." Ravishing me for hours. What a dangerously interesting thought.

Zabriel gazes at me with smoldering, hooded eyes. "We've got enough time to muss you up for real if you're willing. Has your slick started yet?"

I have no idea what he's talking about. "Pretense will do."

Zabriel gives a disappointed sigh and examines me critically. First, he reaches out and drags several pins from my hair and loosens my braid. "Your hair is so soft, *sha'len*. I love your braids, but like this you're beautiful. If you take off your dress and come with me in your underclothes, that will be perfect."

While he's been touching my hair, I've been drinking in the sight of his muscles moving across his chest. "I need to be dressed in my underclothes?"

Zabriel's expression grows grim. "The High Priest is demanding that you're handed over to the Brethren. They claim that you're to marry the King of Maledin."

Marry the King of Maledin. Be thrown onto another fire. The High Priest is here and he wants to drag me into some dark, lonely cell and have me beaten senseless, starved, and then burned to death.

Before I know it, I'm breathing faster and faster, and everything feels like it's spiraling out of control.

Zabriel clutches my shoulders and says urgently, "Isavelle, look at me. The High Priest is not here. I would have slaughtered him the moment he stepped beyond the barrier into my territory. He'll never hurt you again. I swear it."

I breathe a little easier hearing this.

Zabriel draws my face gently up to his with his fingers beneath my chin. "The first chance I have, I will kill him, and he will suffer a death that is a thousandfold more painful than what you suffered because of him."

I feel the same strange sensation as when Fiala and Dusan swore to lay down their lives for me. Me? Why me? I'm not special. I'm nobody, and soon Zabriel is going to realize that he's made a mistake, and then all this adoration and comfort will be taken away from me. I shouldn't want the suffering of another person, and I definitely shouldn't get used to anyone treating me with so much kindness, but as I gaze into Zabriel's red eyes, all I can feel is gratitude. I whisper, "Thank you."

"Meanwhile, I have a plan to make that piece of wyvern shit forget about you forever."

That at least I can get behind wholeheartedly. "What's the plan?"

"Show the emissary that we are lovers. If I've claimed you, the High Priest will no longer wish to give you to whatever pretender the Brethren wish to place on the throne."

Lovers. Claimed. Intimidating words, but Zabriel did say that we were going to pretend. "How are we going to convince him of that?"

"It will be innocent, though it won't look innocent. Quickly, get dressed—or rather, undressed. Show off that beautiful body of yours. I'll wait out here." Then he adds with a mutter as he closes the door, "And I'll try not to tear the head off any man who looks at you."

It all sounds very flimsy, but Zabriel was raised to be a king, so I suppose he knows about things like diplomacy and strategy. Inside my room, I go to the trunk of clothes and sort through the garments. One of the chemises is low cut and gauzy. I haven't tried it on yet because it's impractical to wear in this cold weather, but it reminds me of what Zabriel is wearing, so I take off everything and put it on. The thin fabric skates my figure. I'm showing about a mile of cleavage, and I think my nipples might be visible. Oh, stars. Well, if it convinces the High Priest to forget about me forever, then it's worth the embarrassment.

I open the door and stand nervously on the threshold, waiting for Zabriel's approval. When Zabriel looks up, his red eyes widen and his lips part.

"*Sha'len*," Zabriel breathes. "You look..."

He comes toward me slowly, reaching out a forefinger and brushing a lock of hair back from my shoulder.

I can't tear my eyes away from the expression of wonder and desire on Zabriel's face. A man has never looked at me like this before, and it's making my heart beat faster. Does he truly think I'm desirable? He's not making fun of me?

There's not a trace of mocking in his red eyes. They flare with hunger as he draws closer. "You're so—"

Footsteps sound along a corridor at the bottom of the stairs, and Zabriel whips his head around, his dark brows drawing together. Whoever it is, they're not coming this way, but it's enough to remind Zabriel that there are other people around. His face transforms with infuriated jealousy, and he snaps, "Get back in there and put some clothes on."

I jump and nearly run and do as he says, but then I stand my ground. "Wait. Me looking like this was your idea. Are we going to meet the emissary or not?"

Zabriel's body is taut with fury, and he shakes his head,

staring at my breasts. "You're too... I won't share... I've changed my mind. I'll just kill the emissary and every other Brethren that bastard sends my way. No one gets to look at you like this except me."

Zabriel is wound up enough to do something he might regret later. It won't do the people of Maledin any good if the king murders a messenger and escalates tensions with the Brethren. I catch his arm. "One moment. Please stay here."

I go back into my room. When I return, I have Zabriel's gold cloak wrapped around my shoulders, the one he wore for his coronation.

"Did the Flame King have time to wrap me in his cloak before he dragged me from our bed?"

Zabriel's flinty expression relaxes into a smile. "*Sha'len*, you kept it. Has my scent been comforting you every night?"

I shrug. "I left it in a heap on the floor. It smells like cloth to me."

"But you kept it, and it's a perfect idea. You look beautiful." Zabriel takes my hand and leads me down the corridor. I try not to peek at his body in that silky robe, but it flows across the muscles of his back and upper arms like water. The craving to touch this stunning man nearly overwhelms me.

The Great Hall is lit by soft yellow candlelight, giving an intimate feel to the cavernous space. When we reach his throne, Zabriel sits down, still holding on to my fingers.

I hesitate. "Where am I supposed to sit?"

Zabriel pats his thigh.

Oh, blood and stars. Of course I have to sit in his lap. Well, we are pretending to be lovers.

"I'm doing this for the people of Maledin," I tell him warningly.

"Mm-hmm," he murmurs, but I don't think he heard a word I said, because he's focused on the sight of me moving between his thighs, putting my hands on his shoulders, and perching on his leg.

Zabriel's smile is amused. "You look like a bird preparing to take flight, not a woman who has been rutted for hours on end."

"What does rut—" I start to say, but I break off as he hauls my legs across his lap and settles me against his chest. It's intoxicating to be held so close to him like this, and how wonderful he feels with just this thin silky fabric over his muscles. One of my hands is pressed to his chest, and I can feel the strong, heavy beating of his heart.

"That's better," he murmurs, arranging the cloak around me so it shows that I'm in a state of undress but without revealing too much of my body. "Just one more thing." Zabriel cups my cheek with his huge hand and his mouth descends toward mine.

"What are you doing?" I gasp.

His lips part. His red eyes are sharp and intent. "I'm not going to kiss you. I'm only going to bite you."

"You're going to—?"

Before I can finish what I'm saying, he lowers his head and sinks his teeth into my lower lip. I've never been kissed, so I have nothing to compare it to, but his bite is chain lightning erupting through my body. His teeth feel like they were made for my lower lip, and I arch into him with a gasp. He curves his hands around my ass and pulls me tighter against him with a deep groan. The rumble in his chest travels through my fingers and down my body, making fire burst in my belly.

Finally, Zabriel releases me and sits back with a pant.

I ask breathlessly, "Why did you do that?"

"So our guest will believe I've been kissing you hard, and when dragons kiss, they bite." He sharply annunciates the *bite* with a snap of his white teeth.

Zabriel relaxes back, knees spread, with one arm around me and the other along the armrest, a smoldering expression in his red eyes as he gazes at me, looking every inch a king who has exactly what he wants.

A moment later he glances down the Great Hall, and his eyes narrow in anger. A man in Brethren robes coming this way, escorted by two castle soldiers. The soldiers deposit the Brethren priest about twenty feet from us and leave the room.

"Zabriel of the Maledinni," the man calls in greeting, though he doesn't use Zabriel's honorifics or bow to him.

With a stab of fear, I realize I know this priest. He once caught my attention wandering during a service and dragged me outside into the mud, tore off my veil, and beat me with a stick. There's no answering flash of recognition in his eyes as he glances at me cuddled against Zabriel's chest. I'm just another Veiled Virgin whom he punished.

Zabriel feels me tense and puts his lips against my ear. "Who is he? If he ever hurt you, I will kill him."

Just those words are enough to soothe me. I'm not the prisoner of the Brethren, and I slowly relax. "I...just don't want to look at him."

Zabriel cups my cheek and presses a kiss to my brow. "Look at me, *sha'len*. I'm the only one who matters here."

I nestle closer to his broad chest, telling myself it's for the pretense that we're lovers.

While making minor adjustments to the robe that's

around me and stroking his fingers down my bare arm, Zabriel says, "You dragged me from my bed, priest. I understand that you're clueless about such matters, but you should know that your presence here is denying my mate her satisfaction. Speak, and then get out."

Out of the corner of my eye, I see the priest draw himself primly up, but I focus on the hard line of Zabriel's jaw and his full lips in profile. My fingers are playing with the edge of his open robe and my body slowly relaxes into his. I might even melt a little; he's just that warm and comfortable.

"The High Priest of Maledin sends his respects, and he asks that the King of Maledin's bride is returned to us."

Zabriel presses kisses to my cheeks, my eyelids, and my temple. "I'm the King of Maledin, and Isavelle is already mated to me."

"If by mated you mean married in your tradition, then will you be able to produce documents to that effect?"

"I don't mean married. I mean bedded. I took Lady Isavelle to bed the moment I snatched her back from your men. When I want something, I take it immediately. Don't I, *sha'len*?"

I was nestling into Zabriel's warm embrace, but I freeze when I realize I've been asked a question. I don't even know what's being said.

Zabriel puts his lips against my ear and breathes, "Touch me. He won't believe that I've had you already if you don't show him how much you adore me."

I reach up and stroke his throat and trace my fingers down his bare chest. His flesh is warm and smooth beneath my fingers. Zabriel's eyelids flutter and the muscle in his jaw clenches. Seeing him enjoying my touch so much has me melting even further into his lap. Is this what couples do, relish giving each other pleasure? I wonder just how much pleasure we could have, sitting on his throne, our fingers meandering all over our bodies. A ripple of heat goes through me.

"Fuck, your scent," Zabriel murmurs. There are still a few twists in my braid, but he drags his fingers through my hair, loosening it completely.

I stare up at him, transfixed by the sight of him. My braids are undone.

I'm becoming undone.

As he draws his fingers slowly through my hair, Zabriel says, "You're looking at my bride and the future Queen of Maledin. The true Queen of Maledin, who will soon be wedded to the true King of Maledin." His tone sharpens. "I don't like the fact that you're looking at her. I've killed men for less."

"The High Priest..."

Zabriel snarls, "I said, lower your fucking eyes."

A swift pang of pleasure darts through me.

The priest must do as he's ordered. As Zabriel's red eyes dim, he turns back to me and drags the pad of his thumb over my lips. My mouth is tingling and sensitized from his bite, and my lips part for him with a soft pant.

Zabriel smiles down at me. "You may take this message back to the High Priest. Lady Isavelle is likely already expecting my child. I will slaughter any Brethren who dares come to my gates and speaks the name of the mother of my children." To me, Zabriel whispers, "Do you want me?"

I feel knotted up inside from tension and pleasure. The question feels seductively dangerous.

Zabriel tries a different question. "Do you think I'm handsome?"

"Yes," I whisper. I thought he was magnificent from the first moment I laid eyes on him. Even through the veil, feeling his presence and listening to the heavy baritone of his voice, I felt entranced by him.

"Yes, *Alpha*," he corrects with a soft snarl. His eyes are burning red again.

I don't know what *Alpha* means, but inside me, something or someone sits up and takes notice. *Alpha*, she breathes, and I have a sudden urge to shove the gold cloak from my body and pull the straps of my chemise down so he can see all of me.

Zabriel studies me closely. "Say, *Yes, Alpha*. I know you can hear me."

"Who are you talking to?" I ask.

"You, *sha'len*. Only you. Always you. Say, *Yes, Alpha*. Let me hear you, and I'll give you a kiss."

A kiss, moans the voice in my head. *Alpha wants to kiss me. Fall at his feet. Beg for his lips.* I get a sudden mental image of doing just that, my arms wrapped around his knees and whimpering for a scrap of his attention.

"Don't be so pathetic," I whisper, and Zabriel's eyebrows shoot up in surprise.

I clamp both my hands over my mouth. I didn't mean to say that out loud.

There's a strained silence, and then Zabriel bursts out laughing. "You're hearing your designation, aren't you? The things I heard in my head as mine were emerging were sometimes bizarre." He relaxes back on his throne and smiles at me. "Once I nearly fought a tree because my Alpha told me it insulted me by whipping leaves against my face on a windy day. What did you just have the urge to do?"

If I told him I'm craving to kneel at his feet and suck on one of his fingers he'd probably think it was the hottest thing he'd ever heard. "Nothing…specific."

Zabriel pushes ever so slowly up with his hips and smiles wolfishly. "Too shy to tell me? That's all right. I'll tell you something instead. You feel fucking amazing sitting on my lap, *sha'len*."

He catches the edge of the golden cloak and draws it slowly down, uncovering my shoulders. I can't make myself begin to think about stopping him. *Let Alpha see what belongs to him.*

"You shouldn't do that while the priest is watching," I breathe.

"Hm? Oh, he left."

I look around in surprise to see that the Great Hall is empty of everything but golden candlelight. "Oh! Do you think it worked? Will the High Priest leave me alone now?"

"If he doesn't get the message the easy way, I'll start spilling blood."

There are so many emotions and sensations swirling through my body as Zabriel holds me in his arms, and one of them is gratitude. I glance at him shyly from beneath my lashes. "Thank you for protecting me from him."

"I don't need to be thanked for protecting what's mine." His gaze wanders down my throat and to my breasts. He drinks in the sight of me. My nipples tighten and stand out even further against the thin fabric. He adds huskily, "But I love hearing it from you, Omega."

I gaze into the face of the handsome man before me. He

clearly wants to rip this chemise from my body, but he goes on holding me against him, his large hands hot against my flesh. "Why haven't you just barged into my bedroom?"

A line forms between his brows. "Why would I do that?"

I shrug one shoulder slowly. "You have a sword and a dragon. You have a whole army. You're bigger than me. People who are more powerful can just take what they want."

Sadness flashes through his eyes. "It hurts my heart to hear you say that. I know it's because you were treated cruelly in the past. You're my mate, and I want only to cherish and protect you."

I wind my arms around his neck and lean closer to him, my lips parting. Cherished and protected, two things I'm so hungry to feel.

Zabriel lifts a tress of my hair to his nose and inhales deeply. Then he closes his eyes and makes a satisfied noise. "It's getting stronger."

"What is?"

"Your scent. It's going to be all over me tonight in my bed. Sweet torture."

I'm happy just sitting here gazing dreamily at him, but I should probably say something. "Is it really that important, the way I smell?"

Zabriel twines the lock of my hair around his finger, murmuring, "Scent is very important to our kind. It bonds us. For lovers, the more delicious and intense the scent, the stronger the children. The deeper the bond between them. Our scent tells us that we're meant to be together."

But I can't smell anything special about Zabriel. Maybe he's made a mistake and we're not really meant for each other. If he realizes he's mistaken, he'll turn his back on me so fast I won't have time to say goodbye, and then I'll be all alone again. My heart aches at the thought.

He seems to sense my distress and strokes my cheek with his thumb. "Don't fret, *sha'len*. You will smell my scent one day soon. Your designation is still waking up."

"Are you sure you haven't made a mistake? Maybe I'm just an ordinary human."

He shakes his head. "I haven't. Just be patient, and all will be clear in time."

I'm not very good at being patient. I want answers now.

"What was that thing on your..." I bite my lip and trail off. The question is flagrantly intimate.

Both his eyebrows lift. "What was what?"

I squirm on his lap out of sheer embarrassment. Then I feel it. The very thing I'm asking about. I'm not so naïve that I don't know what it means that he's hot and thick beneath my thighs. I've been around livestock all my life, and their organs get bigger and stiffer when they're ready to mate.

"That," I whisper, pointing to his lap while looking past his shoulder, my cheeks flaming with heat.

The corner of his mouth hooks up, and there are suddenly red sparkles in his eyes. "Are you asking about my cock?"

Oh, stars. It would be easier to talk about this if his cock weren't rubbing against my inner thighs right this second. My curiosity will be the death of me. "Um, well, I mean the part of it that..."

"Oh, I see. You're asking about my knot." A sleek smile spreads over his face and his expression says, *Please ask me about my knot. I would love to talk about my knot.*

"Human men don't have those. As far as I'm aware. I mean, I would have heard if they did."

Zabriel's smile grows wider.

I lightly punch his shoulder. "Stop enjoying this so much. What is it for? I mean, I presume it has a function."

"What is what for?"

"You know what."

"I know. But say it."

"Your...knot."

He hums appreciatively and pushes up with his hips. "Fuck, it's hot just hearing you say knot. As curious as a fledgling, aren't you? Shall I carry you to my bed and teach you all about it?"

"No, thank you," I whisper quickly, while that other part of me breathlessly chants, *Yes, yes, yes*.

"Then would you like to touch it? You're already sitting on it."

"We're sitting on your throne," I say, scandalized. There must be rules about this kind of thing.

"It's my throne. If the future Queen of Maledin wants to touch her mate's knot here then she shall."

The cloak has slipped even farther from my shoulders and his eyes on my body feel intense. "Can you tell me what it's for? What it does?"

He muses upon me for a moment. "Give me...a kiss, and I'll tell you whatever you want to know."

I gaze at Zabriel shyly. A kiss? I suppose I can give him a kiss. I might even want to give him a kiss.

I put my palms on his chest, lean in close, and press my lips to his cheekbone. His eyelashes flutter in pleasure.

"A real kiss. On my mouth." He smiles again. "If you think it won't debauch my throne."

Alpha wants a kiss. Alpha wants to make me feel so, so good. Kissing Alpha will feel better than anything I've ever felt before.

That other me is hypnotically convincing, and so are Zabriel's red eyes. He dips his head, his lips closer to mine and slightly parted. His chest lifting and falling against me, and he waits.

My eyes drift closed, and I raise my chin and press my open mouth to his. A true kiss. A lover's kiss. Pleasure swan dives through my body and pools low in my belly. My hand slides up the nape of his neck, and I surrender completely.

Zabriel groans and seals his mouth firmly over mine, crushing me to him with one arm around my waist and his other hand cradling the back of my head. His tongue brushes against my lips, and I open wider for him as he thrusts it into my mouth. I moan at the swift intrusion, my nipples tingling as they brush against his chest. Zabriel growls, deeper and more animalistic than I've ever heard him before. His fingers drag across the nape of my neck, and the sensation floods my body to every extremity. Without thinking, I shift so that I'm straddling him with both knees hugging his hips. This is better. Now we can truly kiss.

He pulses up with his hips again and again, rubbing against a part of me in a way that feels fantastic. All the while he's kissing me hungrily. I can't think; I can only tangle my fingers in his hair and open my mouth to his demanding tongue. Every upward thrust of his hips sends pleasure shooting through me that's growing in intensity. There's something hard and swollen shifting against me.

"Do you feel that?" he asks in a deep, roughened voice. "That's my knot, and its purpose is to give you pleasure."

Zabriel claims my lips again. I do feel it, thicker than the rest of him, bulging against my sex through his robe and my chemise. I moan into his mouth, my knees clenching his hips tighter and tighter. Just a bit more… I want more… Something good is hovering so close.

A warm, wet sensation gushes between my thighs. My eyes pop open.

I shift on his lap and feel wetness. A lot of wetness.

What the hell is that?

Did that come from me?

I glance down at myself and realize I'm straddling Zabriel's lap with my chemise rucked up past my knees. How on earth did I get here?

Whatever is happening right now, this is your fault, I think furiously at that other voice in my head. *He growled at you and you lost your silly head.*

Let Alpha see, she moans. *He'll be so happy and he'll touch my slick.*

My *what*?

Zabriel thrusts upward again, rolling his knot against me.

"Wait, stop!" I cry.

Zabriel stops moving right away and pulls back, opening his eyes. "*Sha'len*?"

"This is so humiliating," I mutter, clenching both my hands on his bare shoulders. Sometime in the last few minutes, his robe has slipped completely off him. Slick. That's what Zabriel asked earlier. *Has your slick started yet?*

I don't need to persuade you to melt for me because it's going to happen anyway.

Is this what he meant, that I would get drenched between my thighs because of him?

Zabriel stares down between us, a worried frown on his brow. "I hope I didn't hurt you. Was that too much?"

"I'm not hurt," I say. He looks so beautiful with his robe pooling around his waist, and I feel utterly humiliated as I stare at his perfection. "I'm—I'm sorry."

"I doubt that you have anything to be sorry about right now, but tell me what's wrong."

"I..."

But I don't have time to reply because there's a trickling, dripping sensation, and Zabriel feels for himself what's happened. His face transforms in shock and his fingers curl between my thighs, seeking what I'm trying to hide from him. "Oh, fuck. Your slick. It's all over me."

Mortified, I clench my legs together. *All over me.* Could this be any more excruciating?

"*Sha'len,*" he breathes, gazing at me with adoration. "Precious little dragon. This is wonderful."

Occasionally some of the women in my village would make roguish remarks about *gushing like a stream down there* for their husbands, and others would giggle in a way that told me they were talking about what goes on in a marriage bed. I've noticed that after spending time with Zabriel on a handful of occasions, I've been a little too liquid between my thighs, but I brushed that aside as nothing important. Now I've gushed right through my chemise and all over his thighs.

This isn't a stream. It's a waterfall.

"I have to go," I moan. "I need to hurl myself off the stone bridge and into the valley beside the dragongrounds."

He grasps my waist and begs, "Please don't go, *sha'len*. And definitely don't hurl yourself off anything."

But even a man as strong and determined as Zabriel can't keep me in his lap, and I scramble to my feet. There's a shiny wet patch on his robes the size of his hand.

I moan in horror at the sight. "I can never show my face again. I wish Scourge were here so he could incinerate me with one blast of dragonfire. I'm so sorry."

He touches the wet spot on his robes and then clenches it tight in his fist, and when he gazes up at me, his expression is feral. "Sorry? You're sorry? Fuck sorry. This is the most wonderful thing I've ever seen. Ever felt. My Omega's first slick. Come. Here."

I shake my head, backing away, and Zabriel gets to his feet, his robe falling off his top half completely and only held up by the tie around his hips. As he advances on me, the thin fabric flows around his thighs, and something large and thick protrudes there. His cock. His *knot*.

Even filled with burning hot embarrassment, I crave to touch him. I want to grab his hand and drag his fingers against my aching sex while he whispers sweet, filthy words of praise in my ear. I want to wrap my hand around his knot and hold on tight.

Everything is happening too fast. How did I go from thinking he was handsome to making a mess all over him in twenty minutes? I should be beaten. I should be crying and begging for mercy as I bleed. I deserve it.

"Please don't," I beg him, backing down the steps.

"You won't let me feel you? You won't let me soothe some of that aching that I know you must be feeling?"

I shake my head desperately. "I want to go back to my room." Tears well in my eyes and drip down my cheeks.

Zabriel's predatory advance suddenly halts, and he seems to shake himself. "You can go. Of course I will let you go, but I'll escort you."

"You don't—"

He suddenly growls, "If you think I'm letting my mate walk around alone with her slick coating her thighs, her *first* slick, you have a lot to learn about Alphas. Walk. I'll follow."

He picks up his gold cloak and drops it around my shoulders. As I head back to my room, Zabriel's footsteps sound behind me. The urge to turn and fling myself into his arms is strong, but that urge seems to belong to that strange, panting voice I heard, while my shame and embarrassment are all mine, and it's stronger.

The moment I reach my room, I close the door without looking at Zabriel and remember to lock it this time.

Zabriel speaks through the wood. "This is your designation emerging. This is who you are, Isavelle. You're beautiful, every part of you. I crave you so much. You didn't do anything wrong."

I take off my soaked chemise and wash myself with a cloth and cold water from the basin. My designation. I don't know what that means. Why doesn't my body feel like my own anymore?

Once I'm dressed in a clean, dry nightgown, I glance at the door and realize I never heard his footsteps receding. I go over and touch the wood. "Are you still out there?"

His reply is immediate. "Of course I am. There is no other place for me to be than by your side."

My fingers curl against the door. He sounds disappointed.

He sounds upset. I'm flooded with the awful realization that I'm disappointing him. Zabriel's always wanted a mate to love and cherish, but he's stuck with me, and I'm not giving him anything he wants. This *first slick* must be something special he was looking forward to.

"Choose another mate," I beg him through the wood. "I don't know how to give you want you need. I'm broken. I'm ruined."

There's a beat of outraged silence, and I picture Zabriel with his forehead and both fists pressed against the door while he utters strings of silent expletives. "That's not how this works. I am yours and you are mine. Only mine. Forever." He takes a deep breath and continues in a softer tone, "There's nothing broken about you. You're perfect, Isavelle. I'm too intense for you, I know. I will give you the space and time you need. Just don't shut me out for good, *sha'len*. Please."

A bleak note rings in the air between us. I squeeze my eyes shut, wondering how I'll ever feel differently about this than I do right now. My skin is crawling with shame, and I'm appalled at how much I crave to be punished and beaten. I am broken. The High Priest made me hate myself.

"Go to bed and sleep. I'll be out here if you need me," Zabriel says softly.

Does he really mean to stay out there all night in the cold? I hesitate, and then pick up his gold cloak and open the door. "Here. I don't like the thought of you in the cold all alone."

Zabriel stares at me, sadness and longing filling his eyes. His hands curl into fists, and I wonder if he's resisting reaching out and grabbing me.

He shakes his head. "It's yours, and I'm not alone or cold while I have your scent with me."

Taking the door from me, he firmly pushes me back inside and closes it. I stare at the cloak in my hands, then lay it over the end of my bed.

Not knowing what else to do, I blow the candle out and go to bed.

Shame and confusion swirl through me, keeping me awake. If Zabriel thinks my slick is something beautiful, could he be right? Did I panic and ruin a beautiful moment? The thought makes me feel even more anguished. I can't get anything right.

Just as I'm falling asleep, the most delicious smell fills my nose. I jolt awake, my eyes going wide in the dark. My flesh floods with heat, but as I inhale deeply, there's nothing there. I can't smell anything.

It happens again. And then again. The third time I'm jolted awake. I'm hot and sweating, and my thighs are wetter than when I was sitting in Zabriel's lap. Why must my body give me no peace tonight?

Eventually, I drift into restless slumber and awaken in the morning feeling groggy to a knocking on my door. Wrapping a blanket around myself, I go over and unlock it.

Fiala and Dusan are standing on the threshold. The two wingrunners come into the room, their expressions sympathetic. There's no sign of Zabriel outside.

I turn back and go sit on the edge of my bed, rubbing my eyes.

"The Flame King mentioned you might be feeling out of sorts this morning," Dusan tells me, pouring me a cup of water and handing it to me.

"He says your designation is emerging," Fiala says with a concerned wrinkle of her brow. "It's a rough time."

I sip the water, remembering that Zabriel said the same word. Designation.

"Betas don't have a tumultuous time with their designations like Alphas and Omegas do, but it's strange for us as well," Fiala says, sounding gentler than she did the other day.

"Sometimes it can feel like we're being pulled in two different directions," Dusan says. "Lead or obey. Stand out from the crowd or blend in. Keep your head down or talk back."

Fiala nods. "There are a dozen ways to be a Beta, the same as it is with an Omega, and we each have to find our own niche within our designation."

Dusan muses on this. "Well. Not so many ways to be an Omega. I hear it's pretty much following your Alpha's rules and slicking yourself stupid when you're told you're a good little—"

Fiala slams her elbow into Dusan's stomach. He puffs his cheeks out and doubles over with a groan.

"Shut your mouth. Lady Isavelle isn't stupid, and who says she has to be that kind of Omega? Who says any of them do? Maybe it's time we left that nonsense in the past."

"All right, all right. Don't blow your wings off," Dusan grumbles, straightening up.

I shudder inwardly. Slicking myself stupid. That sounds familiar. "What's a designation?"

"It's your place in the Maledinni hierarchy," Fiala explains.

"Fiala and I are Betas, but we're pretty much at the top tier of Betas, as wingrunners," Dusan says, waggling his thumb back and forth between him and Fiala. "There are a lot of smart-talking, competitive Betas in our crew. Like me. But it's fun to play the more submissive type sometimes."

"Lady Isavelle doesn't need to hear about your bedroom escapades," his friend hisses.

"Where else is she going to learn how to have some fun? This is how I learned. By talking to people."

Fiala opens her mouth again, but I shake my head. "Let him speak. I want to hear."

I should have clarified that I wanted to hear about designations, not Dusan's sexual exploits, but it's too late and he launches into them.

"Good choice, now listen up. I had sex with an Alpha once, and it was exhausting. He wanted me in the Omega heat position, and he wouldn't stop *biting* me. The back of my neck was raw for a week."

I frown. "Omega heat position?"

He rolls his eyes. "It's an Omega position where they want you face down with your knees spread and your ass up and they mount you like a—"

"*Dusan*," Fiala hisses. "Cut it out."

"What? Lady Isavelle asked me."

"Remember what we were ordered," Fiala growls through her teeth.

The color drains slowly from his face. "Oh, wyvern piss. I forgot."

I wait for him to go on, but they both stand there in silence. "I still don't understand what a designation is, and I want to know what an Omega heat position is."

Both bodyguards keep their lips firmly closed.

I put down my cup on the bedside table and get to my

feet. "Fine. If you won't tell me, I'll ask Zabriel. Please leave while I get dressed."

The dark-haired wingrunner drags a hand down her face and mutters to Dusan as they leave the room, "Now look what you've done, idiot."

As I get dressed, I can't help thinking, they mount you like a *what?* A strange feeling is revolving in my belly, and I can't tell if it's curiosity or horror.

When I open my door, Fiala steps forward immediately. "Lady Isavelle, please forget we said anything. We're Betas, and we don't know what we're talking about."

"You seem to know more than I do. Look, what is an Omega anyway? Everyone keeps talking about Alphas and Omegas like they're important, but I don't understand why. Zabriel is an Alpha, but what does that really mean?"

I didn't think it was possible for a couple of battle-hardened soldiers to look fearful from merely being asked a question.

"He...he didn't explain it to you?" Dusan stammers. "Nothing at all?"

"Dusan," Fiala growls in warning.

"Zabriel doesn't tell me anything. He says wait and see, and I'll understand later."

Dusan rubs the back of his head and puffs out his cheeks. "Well, yeah, you probably will. Omegas get cravings for all kinds of crazy—"

Fiala punches his shoulder. "*Dusan*. Shut. Up."

I look from Fiala to Dusan, at a complete loss to understand why my normally friendly and relaxed bodyguards are acting so strangely all of a sudden.

"If you have questions about your designation or King

Zabriel's, you need to ask your mate," Fiala says, an apologetic note to her voice. "We can't help you, I'm sorry."

I've had enough of weird things happening to my body and strange conversations I don't understand. "Fine. I will ask him. Slicks. Omegas. Heat positions. Everything."

As I turn and head down the corridor, Dusan mutters under his breath, "Oh, no. What have we done?"

"We? *We?* You're unbelievable, Dusan. Scourge is going to rip both our heads off for this."

16

Zabriel

The hallowed space of the Flame Temple is hushed, and the fire crackling in the Font of First Flames melds with the gentle murmuring of the Temple Mothers going about their work. Occasional flakes of snow drift down from the open vaulted ceiling and settle in my lap and on my hair.

I'm sitting cross-legged on the ground, attempting to meditate and quiet my mind.

My mind won't be quiet.

All I can think about is my mate.

She lost herself in my arms. I grew drunk on her scent as she kissed me and rubbed herself against my knot. I have never been as blissfully happy as I was then, and then I discovered that her first slick had come, and I was drenched in her.

A soft moan escapes me at the memory. I'm getting hard in the temple and my knot is throbbing, which is inappropriate but not too transgressive seeing as this place is devoted to everything that makes Alphas, Betas, and Omegas what they are. I probably shouldn't stand up for a few minutes, though.

Behind me, I sense *Hratha'len* moving around. Polishing the black volcanic stone from which this temple is hewn. Replenishing oil in sconces. Copying out manuscripts. Crafting medicines and drafts for the dragons and their riders in the workrooms in the back of the temple. There is always background bustle here.

I would like to think that Isavelle would enjoy it here, but I fear that it could remind her too much of the Brethren monasteries.

My hands curl into fists and grip my breeches. Those *fucking* Brethren.

I wonder what would have happened to her if her designation had emerged in a Brethren monastery. No doubt she would have been punished until she bled and screamed. If it weren't for them, Isavelle wouldn't have torn herself from my lap last night. They've made her ashamed of who she is. If I didn't already hate them, I would hunt every single one down and kill them just for that.

I slowly get to my feet and gaze into the First Flames, wondering how I'm going to help my terrified Omega. If there was another like her among the dragonriders, I could entrust Isavelle to them to explain some of the changes she's going through, but there isn't another in all of Maledin. I wish my mother were still here. My sister...

One thing is clear. I should have asked the Omegas in my

life a thousand questions when I had the chance. I never imagined a world in which my Omega was the only one.

I turn to leave and see that the Temple Crone, the woman who placed my crown on my head the day of the coronation, is watching me from an upper level. We nod to one another in greeting. She and the Temple Mothers and Temple Maidens have done a wonderful job restoring this place from the ruin of dust and neglect that it suffered during Brethren times. Here, I almost feel like no time has passed at all.

I make my way back through the castle, and a few minutes later, I'm standing at the war table once more, gazing at the map of Maledin. It swims before my eyes, and I blink to clear them. Sitting in the corridor outside Isavelle's room all night has left me feeling wrung out, though I can only imagine how she's feeling this morning. She probably didn't get much sleep either.

As if I've summoned my mate merely by thinking about her, in Isavelle walks. Her complexion is wan and there are dark smudges beneath her eyes, but she walks purposefully toward me and stops a few feet away.

I turn and gaze at her with longing, imagining sweeping her into my arms and pressing a kiss to her lips.

"Do you want to bite me?" she suddenly blurts out.

I open my mouth and close it again. My gaze fastens on her throat. Sinking my aching dragines into her warm flesh and holding on tight would be a delicious pleasure. "Are you offering?"

She draws back in surprise. "Offering? I'm speaking hypothetically."

"Right. Yes. Of course." For fuck's sake, of course she's not interested in me biting her. Wanting her so much is making me stupid.

I scrub a hand over my face. "Sorry, why are you asking me this?"

"I'm curious. Do you want to bite me? I don't know if I want you to bite me. That sounds painful."

"Okay," I say slowly, hoping my brain is going to catch up with what's going on sooner rather than later. "Right this second, I promise not to bite you."

"And what's an..." Isavelle hesitates, and her cheeks turn pink. "...Omega heat position?"

Her blush is nothing compared to the outrage that swells inside me. My mate barely knows what an Omega is yet. How has she heard about things like that? "Where did you hear the phrase *Omega heat position*?"

"Um. I don't remember."

My mate is a terrible liar.

"Godric," I shout. When my second-in-command pokes his head into the room, I growl, "Bring me Lady Isavelle's bodyguards. Now."

Before Godric has a chance to reply, Fiala and Dusan shuffle into the room. Fiala wears an expression of resignation. Dusan is staring at the floor, the apple at his throat bobbing.

"Where did my mate hear the phrase *Omega heat position*?" I growl.

Godric swiftly exits, closing the door behind him. Fiala is staring at a spot over my head with a resigned expression.

Dusan begins to mutter, "Uh, *Ma'len*, well, you see..."

Fury burns through me. I lunge forward, grasp a fistful of his uniform, and drag him toward me. The wingrunner's eyes open wide with terror, and his toes nearly leave the ground as I seethe into his face, "You said these things to my mate? You disobeyed orders from your king?"

Isavelle rushes forward and grabs my elbow, trying to tug it down but not succeeding. "Wait, please. Dusan was talking about something that's common knowledge to him. Common knowledge to Fiala. Common knowledge to *you*. But do I know what you're all talking about? No, and yet apparently, it's about me."

I keep my attention fixed on the man in my grip. "Did you disobey a direct order from your king?"

"Y-yes, *Ma'len*."

I wait to see if he's going to gabble some excuse or another, but at least he has the sense not to try my temper even further.

"Report to Captain Ashton and await my punishment. You are not to leave the castle grounds." I put Dusan down, and snarl at Fiala, "You either. Both of you get out of my sight."

The wingrunners hurry out of the room, and I whirl away toward the terrace, breathing hard with my fists clenched at my sides. I was very fucking specific about what Isavelle's bodyguards were to discuss with her. They were meant to make her feel at home and safe, not fill her head with things she's not ready for. My poor girl is having difficulties confronting simple things like her slick, and they went and told her about the most intimate part of mating. Betas have no right to even gossip about it because it has nothing to do with them. My dragines ache in frustration, and my knot throbs just thinking about it. Inside my mouth, my tongue brushes across a pointed tooth, trying to ease the pain.

Isavelle has come to my side and asks softly, "Zabriel? Why are you so angry about this?"

"Because it's my duty to teach you about this, not them," I roar, and Isavelle flinches.

I pass a hand across my brow. Fuck it all to hell. I'm making things worse. "I'm sorry. Not for what I said to your bodyguards, but for shouting just now and not explaining things to you." I turn and put my hands on her shoulders. "I want to tell you about these things. They're for us. Only for us."

I've been trying so hard to tamp down that primal instinct to haul Isavelle over my shoulder, pin her to my bed, and snarl in her face to obey her Alpha without question. It's always there, hungry and pacing and *wanting* her, naked and obedient and wet. The unreasonable part of me is always pointing out that she should be falling at my feet with gratitude that her Alpha is the Flame King, and if I had an Omega from my own time, then she probably would be doing that. I dream about the moment Isavelle will wrap her arms around my neck and whisper, *Show me what it means for you to be my Alpha.*

"All right," she says slowly. "Your, um, teeth. They're very pointy. Why?"

I put my hand to her neck and stroke my thumb down her throat. My knot throbs in response as I think of the moment I'll sink my teeth into her mating gland and mark her as mine forever. "It's so, um..."

To my astonishment, I feel my face burn. I imagine these things so often but putting them into words for my mate is daunting, and I suddenly realize why I haven't talked about these things with Isavelle. The Temple Crone would laugh if she could see the Flame King now, tongue-tied before his sweet and innocent mate.

Isavelle reaches up and touches my cheek. "You're shy about this too," she whispers.

I nod and cover her hand with my own. "This is important to me. To us. I don't want to get anything wrong and make things worse between us."

Anguish flashes through Isavelle's eyes. "I wish you didn't feel like—"

I press a finger to her lips. "Hush. Don't apologize for something that's not your fault. I've been wishing there were another Omega you could talk to, but I've just remembered someone else who might be useful to us."

"Oh? Who?"

I turn around and beckon Isavelle to follow me. "Come with me. I'll show you."

I rely on Isavelle's natural curiosity, and a moment later, I hear her following me. I lead her through the castle until we reach a massive open doorway made from carved black stone.

"This is the Flame Temple. The *Hratha'len* run the temple and they're the closest thing the Maledinni have to a religious order, but I promise that they're nothing like the Brethren. I was reluctant to introduce you to them given your hardships, but they're the best people I can think of for you to speak openly with. I would have wished my mother or someone like her to help you, but you're the only Omega in Maledin."

Isavelle glances into the Flame Temple. The burning flame. The open sky. The women in bright red dresses who are working in little alcoves or meditating. "It doesn't look anything like the gloomy monasteries I'm used to," she says slowly.

"It's not. You will be welcomed here, not beaten. You can leave whenever you like, and no one is going to force you to pray. Besides, we don't pray. We meditate."

Isavelle's expression lightens even more.

As if she's realized why I've brought my mate here, the Temple Crone has moved to the middle of the temple and is standing with her hands folded before her.

"The Temple Crone is waiting for you," I tell Isavelle softly.

My mate takes a hesitant step across the threshold.

I grasp her shoulders and draw her back. "One thing. One very important thing. A lot of people will tell you what an Omega is and how they act and think and feel, including the *Hratha'len*. Especially the *Hratha'len*. The only right way for you to act and think and feel is how you act, you think, and you feel."

Isavelle moistens her lips and gazes up at me. "Do you really mean that? I...I don't think I'm what you were hoping for."

"I mean every word. The only Omega I've ever wanted was a happy one."

"If I truly am your mate, and you mean that, it's sweet of you to say," Isavelle replies, but I can see she's not convinced about any of this.

"In my time, Alphas, Betas, and Omegas were raised knowing what was expected from them. I thought those expectations were set in stone, but now there's a whole country full of people who have to figure things out as they go along. You and I can do that together."

There are a thousand things I'd like to be doing with Isavelle right now instead of sending her off to speak with the

Temple Crone. I want to crush her to my body, douse her with my scent, and taste her slick, but right now I need to let her go.

I allow myself to cup her chin, but no more than that. "Our instincts drive us, but they don't control us. Make yourself into the Omega you want to be, and I'll love her."

17

Isavelle

I stare up into Zabriel's beautiful face. Strong emotions are warring in his red eyes, and his body is so taut as if he's holding back an avalanche of desire and emotion. "You'll...love me?"

With his fingers beneath my chin, he leans down and presses his forehead against mine and closes his eyes, breathing, "Of course, *sha'len*. You are everything to me. Your happiness is all I desire."

Love was rarely spoken about in our village, and never at the monasteries. The only time I thought about love was when I dreamed of fairy tales that we weren't allowed to tell. The man before me is straight out of one of those fairy tales.

Zabriel draws away from me, and suddenly I don't want him to go.

He nods at an old woman walking sedately toward us.

"This is the Temple Crone. She will answer all of your questions."

I think I recognize her lined face. "Is she the woman who crowned you on your coronation day?"

Zabriel glances at me in surprise. "So you were there."

I bite my lip and feel my cheeks burn. Zabriel has been so honest with me that I want to be honest with him. "I was too proud to admit it at the time, and you were so intimidating in that golden armor. A man like you couldn't possibly be for me."

His beautiful mouth lifts in a smile. "Not for you, *sha'len*? I'm all for you."

Suddenly, he goes down on one knee before me and clasps my hands. Our eyes are on the same level, and I gaze at him in surprise.

"Being worthy of you means I'm worthy of leading the people of Maledin. The golden armor, the crown, my title as king, they mean nothing if I don't have you."

Touch him.

Touch your Alpha.

Hesitantly, I lift my hand and brush a lock of dark hair back from his face. My fingers skim his cheek and hard jaw, and I say, "You are so gentle right now."

He closes his eyes and leans his cheek into my touch. "Do you feel the urge to run from me?"

"No," I whisper.

His smile widens. "That makes me happy, *sha'len*."

Zabriel opens his eyes, gets to his feet, and plants a slow kiss on the inside of my wrist. "Remember this moment when the time comes and I am not so gentle." He turns and walks back the way we came.

What's *that* supposed to mean?

I have no idea, but my inner Omega is quivering in delight.

The Temple Crone has reached my side, and she's gazing down her long, sharp nose at me with pale amethyst eyes.

I don't understand what an Omega is, but I have been told I'm at the bottom of the pecking order, and I sink into a curtsey. I wince as I remember all the times I was forced to my knees before the loathsome High Priest.

Zabriel wouldn't leave me here if he thought anyone was going to hurt me.

The crone's face relaxes into a thin smile. "Welcome to the Flame Temple, *Ma'len's* mate. We are honored by your presence among us."

She turns and drifts inside, and I follow her into the cavernous space. Everywhere is gleaming black stone, except for the vaulted open ceiling.

The Temple Crone wafts a wrinkled hand toward the massive fire that's burning in the middle of the vast space. "This fire was lit by the First Dragon, and it is refreshed every week by the flare's Alpha. It must never be allowed to go out."

A dragon the size of a small dog is sleeping by the flaming font. As I watch, it stretches its forelegs out and yawns, revealing dozens of sharp white teeth, then it loops its tail around itself again and goes back to sleep.

"Did the fire go out when the dragonriders were sealed beneath the mountain five hundred years ago?" I ask.

She nods sadly. "It did. Those were dark times. Scourge relit the fire on *Ma'len's* coronation day, and the *Hratha'len* have been proud to tend it again ever since."

"Is that what you do here? You tend the fire?"

The crone gives me a look that reminds me of Biddy Hawthorne at her shrewdest. I can tell that without her needing to say anything that this woman does a great deal more than tend a fire.

She walks, and I follow along at her side. "We are the guardians of dragon magic. The keepers of history. We guide Alphas, Betas, and Omegas to understand their true nature. At present, we are also meditating on the barrier that is currently separating Maledin from the southern mountains."

Interest blazes through me. "You are? What have you discovered? Have people from Maledin been taken behind that barrier?"

The Temple Crone arrives at an alcove carved into rock, which forms a natural kind of sheltered seat. "*Ma'len* brought you to us to help you understand your Omega nature. The barrier is his concern, not yours. Please be seated."

I want to tell her that I can do both at once, but a lifetime trying to drag secrets out of Biddy Hawthorne has taught me that shrewd old women have to do things in their time and no one else's.

I sit down and fold my hands in my lap with an expectant expression on my face. The crone regally takes her own seat, spreading her red robes around her. She's silent for a moment, letting her gaze travel around the impressive and shiny black temple.

I follow her lead and glance around the enormous black temple with its huge flame. "The Maledinni certainly have a sense of scale and drama."

The crone's smile is tinged with pride. "Our people—yours and mine, *Ma'len's* mate—are an impressive people. Our majestic dragons. Our unique nature. Our careful attention to the role that every Alpha, Beta, and Omega assumes within our society. Everyone has a purpose, including you. Especially you, *Ma'len's* mate."

"So I've heard," I mutter. "Right at the bottom."

The crone inclines her head. "That is so."

I thought she would evade the question or come up with some waffle about how I'm not really at the bottom.

"Are you ashamed of your place, *Ma'len's* mate? You may not have heard how rare you are or realized how much your Alpha craves to protect you and keep you safe. He will love you and cherish you above all others and shower you with praise and affection. You are not lesser to him."

Put that way, it doesn't sound terrible, but I do worry how everyone else will treat me while Zabriel's not looking. "Please call me Isavelle. Zabriel told me that I should find my own way of being an Omega, and this Omega doesn't want to be addressed like she only exists because the king does."

The woman inclines her head. "As you wish, Lady Isavelle. How are you coping with your emerging designation?"

I slump back against hard, cold stone. "Obviously not very well seeing as Zabriel has brought me to see you."

The crone gives me a thin smile. "I used to speak with most emerging Alphas and Omegas in Maledin. I hope to again in this new Maledin, and I promise you that we all struggle with our designations at some time or another."

"That's some comfort I suppose," I mutter.

"Do you believe you are an Omega?"

"Well, Zabriel says I am one."

The Temple Crone gives me another one of her enigmatic

smiles. "*Ma'len* has smelled your scent and he knows you are his mate, but have you ever caught your own scent?"

"I can do that?" I ask in surprise, lifting my wrist to my nose to give it a sniff. I smell nothing.

She lifts her hand and beckons over an attendant dressed in sleeveless red robes that fall to the ground. The young woman has a small bowl of oil on a tray, and she bows to me and smiles before anointing each of my wrists and the sides of my throat.

As the attendant steps back, the crone says, "Before you can understand your mate, first you should understand yourself. These oils enhance your natural Omega scent. Try your wrist again."

I lift my hand to my face and breathe in, not expecting much.

A wave of scent washes over me, and I cry out. The sweetness of honeysuckle. The forest after it rains. Fresh, clean, sweet scents fill my lungs and warm me to the tips of my fingers. "This oil smells amazing."

"It is not the oil, Lady Isavelle. It's you." The crone waves the attendant forward again, who holds the bowl under my nose so I can compare it to the scent coming from my arm. The oil in the bowl has no scent at all.

"That's incredible," I murmur with my wrist to my nose as I study the ground. This is what Zabriel can smell when he breathes in my scent? I wonder if he likes it.

Does Alpha love my scent? Run to him and beg for his praise, whimpers that needy voice, and I hush her.

Does he, though?

I shift in my seat, suddenly eager to know as much as she does.

The crone answers the question I haven't asked. "*Ma'len* loves your scent, and it causes a strong reaction in him and no one else. It speaks to him, just as his scent speaks to you."

My bubble of excitement is suddenly squashed. "But I can't... Do you have anything..." I trail off, afraid of this woman's wrath if I say something that insults her king or reveals I'm a broken Omega.

"You may ask me anything, Lady Isavelle. Permit me to be your guide in all things."

"I can't smell Zabriel. Not in the way he wishes that I could." Saying those words out loud makes a fierce ache open up in my chest and my heart beat sickeningly fast. I hunt the crone's expression for any flicker of disgust or outrage.

At the monasteries, any flaw that was discovered meant punishment. Starvation. Sleep deprivation. Beatings.

The crone nods to the attendant, who disappears. While we wait for her to return, I see another small dragon wander sleepily across the temple to where a woman in red is copying out manuscripts at a table. The dragon flops down with its head on her foot. The woman's quill doesn't stop moving, but she smiles when she feels the sleepy creature using her as a pillow.

The attendant returns and places a small glass bottle into my hands, filled with oil and sealed with a cork and red wax.

"A little of this will help, but only a little. Rub this oil on his neck or his wrists." The Temple Crone's bright amethyst eyes run over me. "I do not think you will need the oil for long. If you have not had your first slick, it will be soon. If you have not endured your first false heat, that will be soon also."

"What's a false heat?"

"My apologies. A heat is when an Omega is fertile and

craves her mate most, and it lasts for several days. A false heat is a prelude to the real thing. They are unpredictable and much shorter."

My eyes drop to my lap and my face flames hearing her speak these things so matter-of-factly. Craves her mate. A woman of a religious order is speaking about me having sex with Zabriel, a man I'm not married to and the king, no less, like it's nothing to be ashamed of. "Endured? Is it some kind of trial?"

She shakes her head and smiles. "Not at all, Lady Isavelle. It is a time for intimacy between you and your mate. A sacred time when you will begin to understand what the two of you mean to one another."

"But what do we mean to one another?" I plead with her. I wish someone would give me a straight answer about what all this is about.

"He is for you and you are for him. The power he has over you is as strong as the power you have over him."

I don't know about that. Given Zabriel's size, position, and dominant nature, I doubt I'll ever have any power over him. I barely have any grasp of my own will right now. I hold the little bottle of oil between my hands in my lap, feeling it grow warm from my touch. It's peaceful in the temple with the flicker and crackle of the flames and the soft snoring of the young dragon sleeping in the fire's warmth.

Do I want to use this oil on Zabriel? If I catch his scent, will I make a fool of myself like I did last night? I want to be sure what I'm getting into before I take such a drastic step.

I stand up and slip the bottle of oil into my pocket. "Thank you for your time, um, Grandmother?" I guess the honorific, remembering how Zabriel addressed Biddy Hawthorne.

The Temple Crone smiles and bows her head, and then draws a scroll out of her robes. "You may return here at any time, as often as you wish. You may meditate here, and it will calm you and bring you peace. Meanwhile, may I ask you for a small favor? Will you please take this message to the dragonmaster? It is important information we have uncovered about dragons and the barrier. You will likely find him at the dragongrounds."

"You're trusting me with such an important message?" I ask in surprise, taking the scroll from her and turning it over, wishing I knew what was written inside.

"*Ma'len's* mate is trusted as *Ma'len* himself is trusted. He is you and you are him."

With that, she gets to her feet and drifts away.

I leave the temple feeling a little more at ease than I did when I awoke this morning. It's comforting having some answers and knowing that I've got somewhere to go to sit and think if things become too confusing. Perhaps I'll even ask one of those women in red to teach me to meditate.

I make my way through the corridors until I reach the stone bridge and cross over it to the dragongrounds. I've never seen anyone else here apart from dozens of enormous dragons, but today a tall man with long white hair and white and tan dragonriding clothes is standing not far from the bridge. As I approach, I see that he's as tall and muscular as Zabriel, and he carries himself with the same air of authority.

I think I'm about to meet my first Alpha since Zabriel.

Before him is a small dragon. Smaller than Scourge, anyway. It stands as high as a Shire horse, with a long, tapering body of pale gold and shimmering turquoise. It has a scroll between its teeth and the dragonmaster is holding on to the other end.

He commands sharply, "Esmeral, stop that. I said *no*."

The dragon snarls and hisses, yanking harder and harder, but the white-haired Alpha holds on to the scroll.

I move around to where he can see me and hold up the scroll from the Temple Crone. "Sorry to interrupt you. I was asked to give this to the dragonmaster."

"I'm the dragonmaster." The man keeps his grip on the letter in Esmeral's teeth, holds out his other hand without looking at me, and snaps his fingers.

Oh? Snapping your fingers at me?

Playing with the scroll in my hands, I say, "It's nice to meet you. My name's Isavelle."

"Dragonmaster Stesha," he says, still glaring at the gold and turquoise dragon.

"Is the dragonmaster the one who looks after all these dragons?"

His nostrils suddenly flare and he glances at me with narrowed, icy blue eyes. "Obviously."

Well, isn't he *charming*.

The turquoise dragon suddenly releases the scroll, making Stesha stumble backward, and she paces over to me. Surprisingly, the dragon sniffs delicately at my ankles, my wrists, and then my neck. She makes cute, sniffly noises against my ear, which tickle so much that I laugh and step away, rubbing my ear with my shoulder.

"Why does everything around here want to smell me?"

Stesha is watching me with that same narrowed, critical

gaze. "You're our first new Omega, and Omegas are very rare. You're interesting to her."

I glance warily at the Alpha, realizing that I have his full attention now. Is he going to sniff me as well? "I'm not interesting to you, am I? I mean, you kind of look like, um, you seem like you're—well, you're very tall," I finish lamely. He's obviously an Alpha. He reminds me of Zabriel, not in looks necessarily, but he's got the same muscular strength, height, and authoritative attitude, though Zabriel is a lot friendlier than this imperious man.

Stars help me if another Alpha gets it in his head that I belong to him.

Stesha gives me a long, unreadable look. "You're only interesting to me because King Zabriel will mate you and make you his queen. Give me that."

He holds out his hand for the scroll. I look the other way. I don't know why, but getting on this man's nerves is suddenly the only thing I want to do.

"Maybe I'm interesting in my own right. I can be very good at making sparkling conversation."

Stesha's glower deepens.

"Why are you and Esmeral having a disagreement?" I ask him.

The dragonmaster grinds his teeth together. "Because Esmeral wants to carry messages to the wingrunners at the barrier, and I said she can't. She won't listen because she's young and she's also extremely stubborn." He says the last part louder while looking pointedly at the dragon.

Esmeral was nosing at my skirts, but she suddenly gives a short, angry snort as if to say, *I'm not stubborn*.

"Why can't she carry messages?"

"Because she's young, inexperienced, riderless, and she's too precious to be in so much danger for no good reason."

Esmeral lunges for the scroll in his hands with her jaws, but it doesn't do her any good as Stesha holds it up out of her reach.

"You are getting on my last nerve today," he growls at her.

I can't help but laugh at Esmeral's antics and delight in the fact that she's annoying this Alpha. "Good work, Esmeral. Keep it up."

Without thinking, I reach out to pat Esmeral's head. It's only as I'm doing it that I realize I'm reaching for something with dozens of dozens of razor-sharp teeth as if it were a house cat. When Esmeral's turquoise and golden eyes flash, panic slams through me, and I'm certain she's about to tear my arm off.

Esmeral knocks her head into my hand so hard that it hurts, and she trills happily. With both eyes closed, she goes on rubbing and butting her head against my palm while Stesha and I gaze on in shock.

"Is this normal?" I ask the dragonmaster.

"Not really," he mutters, frowning at the dragon.

Whatever that means.

"Well. Someone likes praise," I mutter, drawing my sore hand away from Esmeral and shaking it.

"It seems that way."

"Why don't you just let her take the letter? We should all be allowed to do our part for Maledin if we wish."

Esmeral seems to realize I'm on her side and whips around to look at Stesha hopefully. *Please? Please, please, please?*

Stesha narrows his eyes at me. "I'm the dragonmaster, not

you. Watch your rank, your tongue, and your tone, Lady Isavelle."

My mouth falls open. Watch my tongue? I'm only making a suggestion.

Esmeral hisses at Stesha. I wish I could do the same.

"Aren't you fun," I mutter, suppressing the urge to snap, *I'm the king's mate, so* you *should watch your tongue with* me.

Stesha holds out his hand for the Temple Crone's scroll, but I pretend not to notice yet again, and he growls in frustration.

"You were raised human all your life, weren't you?" he asks.

"Of course I was. Like everyone in Maledin."

"I see," he seethes, in a way that tells me he'd like to say a lot more.

I lift my chin and gaze at him. "Speak your mind, please."

He watches me for a long time, his pale blue eyes flickering critically. "You were spoiled and indulged all your life. Always given the finest things and told you were special."

I burst out laughing. "Spoiled and indulged? By the Brethren?"

My amusement only makes his anger deepen. "You talk to me like a hatchling who has never met an Alpha before. If you were my Omega, I'd do something about you being such a brat." He bites off the word *brat* as if he's snapping it with his teeth. "Someone should teach you how the lower designations are meant to address Alphas."

The lower designations. The Temple Crone made being an Omega sound special, but Stesha the dragonmaster clearly wants to walk all over me. "Oh, please tell me."

"Please tell me *dragonmaster*," he snarls, completely

missing my sarcasm. "First of all, proper terms of address. The king is *Ma'len*, not Zabriel. Secondly, stand demurely, not slouching like a tavern wench. Finally, you should be thrown into freezing water and scrubbed red raw to punish you for going before another Alpha reeking of *Hratha'len* Omega oils." Stesha's eyes blaze. "But you have your own Alpha, so that's none of my business. Now give me that scroll and get out of my sight."

Cheeks flooding with furious heat, I slap the scroll into his hand. He turns around and strides away with a scroll in each hand, and a moment later he disappears among the large, scaly bodies of the flare.

"Throw me into freezing water?" I splutter, heading back across the stone bridge. "And I do *not* slouch like a tavern wench. If I call Zabriel by his name then that's my business, not the dragonmaster's."

I'm still muttering to myself as I stalk through the castle in search of Zabriel. I find him in the War Room speaking with Godric and several other soldiers, who fall silent when I march in.

Zabriel looks around in surprise. "Isavelle? Is something wrong?"

My chest is heaving. I must look flushed, and there's flyaway hair all around my face. "I met another Alpha just now."

Jealousy flashes across his handsome face and he takes a step toward me. "Another Alpha?"

"Yes. He's *vile*."

18

Zabriel

The hairs at the nape of my neck are bristling the moment the words *another Alpha* are out of my Omega's mouth. Another Alpha? Another Alpha what? Looked at you? Smelled you?

Touched you?

A vein is throbbing in my temple. I tug Isavelle closer to me, sweep the hair from the nape of her neck, and check for teeth marks. Her flesh is as pristine and unmarked as always, but I still growl at the thought of another Alpha being anywhere close to my unmated woman. Another Alpha what? Where? Who?

"Zabriel, what are you doing?"

I grasp Isavelle's upper arms and peer into her face. "Why were they vile? What did this Alpha do to you? Who was it?"

Isavelle scowls up at me. "Dragonmaster Stesha. The Temple Crone sent me to give him a scroll."

Oh. Him.

Some of my anger abates, and I straighten up. Stesha's got a bad temper, but he wouldn't touch what's mine.

A wave of Isavelle's scent breaks over me, so powerful that for a moment I think she's perfuming and going into heat. Then I remember she just came from the Flame Temple, and the Temple Crone must have anointed her with oils.

"Blood and fire, you smell..." I trail my fingers along her throat.

I can't control myself any longer. I scoop Isavelle against my body and hold her so tight her feet leave the ground. With my nose buried in her neck, I take deep lungfuls of her.

"What are you—oh, the oils. Do I smell more potent to you? I caught my scent for the first time, as you smell it, but it's fading now."

A perfect thing for the Temple Crone to do for my Omega who isn't sure she's an Omega. I wish I'd been there. "Mmm. Sweet little dragon. *Fuck*."

Isavelle laughs. "You sound a little drunk."

I feel a little drunk. What was the Temple Crone thinking by sending Isavelle to Stesha covered in these oils? He smelled her like this before I could. Anger and possessiveness rush through me, but I force myself to focus on my upset mate.

When I straighten up and set Isavelle on her feet, I notice that Godric and the other soldiers have left the room.

I smooth my mate's hair down. "*Sha'len*, what happened with Stesha?"

Isavelle describes her brief conversation with the dragonmaster. "I wasn't the most respectful I could have been, and I didn't hand over the scroll when I knew he wanted it, but he called me a brat and he was so *rude*." She stares up at me, her green eyes sparking with indignation. "Are you furious with him for insulting me like that? Or are you on his side?"

"If I was on his side, would that make you upset?"

Isavelle hesitates. "He was just so awful to me. The Temple Crone said you would always protect me, and that's what this Alpha and Omega relationship was all about."

A hopeful note enters her voice. She's trying to understand what we are to each other. She cares what I think, and she's craving my protection. I could jump for joy.

I fold my arms and gaze down at her sternly. "Isavelle. Did you talk back to an Alpha and defy him?"

Isavelle's eyes fill with resentment and hurt. "I did. And I'd do it again. He was horrible to me."

"He shouldn't have called you a brat and been rude to you, and I'm going to talk to him about that, but there's something I want to say to you first."

Isavelle's chin juts forward and her fists ball at her sides as she anticipates the telling-off I'm about to give her.

I smile and reach out, stroking a forefinger down her cheek. "I'm so proud of you."

Isavelle blinks, her anger melting into surprise. "You are? What for?"

"For standing up to him. I know you're not a brat. Just because you're an Omega doesn't mean you shouldn't expect courtesy from the people in this castle. You were courteous to him, I'm sure."

Isavelle's lips twitch and she gazes up at me from beneath her lashes. "Well, I teased him a little, but only after I tried being friendly and he was just so rude. One of the young dragons was giving him a hard time, and I found that amusing."

I find myself smiling. "I would have found that amusing as well."

Suddenly my Omega has a soft, needy expression in her green eyes. "Do you really mean that? About being proud of me?"

My smile widens. I gaze down at her and feel a thud of heat. Omegas love praise from their Alphas and will do just about anything to get it, but so far, Isavelle hasn't seemed to care about what I think about her and what I say to her. How wonderful that seems to be changing.

Suddenly I want to give her all my praise.

With my tongue.

On her sex.

Whose Alpha's a good fucking girl.

She's standing by a pillar, and I brace my hand against it and lean over her, purring, "My Omega is the most beautiful woman I've ever seen, utterly perfect and delicious in every way. How could I not be proud of her?"

Isavelle gazes up at me and swallows hard. Her eyes are suddenly dark and very liquid, and she whispers breathily, "Oh. Um. Thank you."

My lips ghost over her cheek and then her neck. Fuck, those Omega oils on her body are making me dizzy. "No. Thank you for running to me for comfort and praise. You can do that as much as you want, *sha'len*."

Her small hands press against my stomach and then slide up to my chest, where she plays with a button on my shirt. A little of her pride comes back. "I didn't run to you. I walked quickly."

I grin down at her. "Of course, *sha'len*."

"I feel…all funny," she confesses in a whisper. "I've felt strange since being anointed with oils in the temple. Do you think maybe I am an Omega after all?"

Isavelle already knows what I think. I could kiss the Temple Crone. I could even kiss that surly bastard Stesha. He's done his king a favor without meaning to.

I must be smirking because Isavelle suddenly says, "I know what you're thinking. You're congratulating yourself for being such a reasonable Alpha compared to that man."

"Who, me?" I ask, my smile widening.

I don't seem so overbearing and controlling now, do I, my darling Omega?

If she were Stesha's Omega, he wouldn't have assigned her bodyguards shit-shoveling duty for disobeying his orders. He would have sliced their heads off with his sword. Not once have I ordered Isavelle to watch how she speaks to me or called her names like brat. I am a thoroughly reasonable and loveable Alpha.

I twist my fingers through her locks and let her dark gold hair run through my hand. "When I was learning to ride Scourge, Stesha was my teacher, and I could do nothing right. I was too heavy-handed. I was too laid-back. My dragon wouldn't respect me. I couldn't take instructions without losing my temper. On and on it went until I wanted to toss Stesha off a cliff."

Isavelle bursts out laughing, and a golden feeling rushes through me. I made my mate laugh. "I would have liked to see you do that."

I remember how after a ride on Scourge that felt different, one where I'd felt the connection to my dragon that other riders talked about as feeling like one being rather than two, Stesha gazed at me thoughtfully and then said one word.

Better.

It wasn't much, but that single word lit my whole insides up like fire in the sky, and I felt like a dragonrider at last.

"Don't take Stesha's nasty temper to heart. He's like that with everyone, and the dragons as well. He has to be to keep all those monstrous creatures safe and cared for, and he's suffered a great deal of loss unfortunately. That man will always be stingy with courtesy and patience."

Instantly, Isavelle looks saddened. "Who did he lose?"

I sigh, thinking of all the misery that has clouded Stesha's life. "His family when he was a boy, and then his best friend several years ago. Sorry, hundreds of years ago. Then there's the fact that he's always wanted an Omega but..." I make a helpless gesture and shrug. Every Alpha wants an Omega to call their own, but the fact is that there are never enough Omegas, and it seems to be completely random which Alphas are blessed with one and which are passed over. Stesha was the most powerful Alpha under the former king, the son of an Alpha and Omega pair, but he's watched over the decades as others have found their mates and he's remained mateless.

Most Alphas and Omegas find each other around their seventeenth summer and reach full maturity in their eighteenth or nineteenth years. Stesha is thirty years old. I'm considered unusual for finding my Omega at the late age of twenty-three, so there's no hope for him.

Isavelle seems surprised. "He wants an Omega? It seemed to me like he hates Omegas."

"Alphas want *their* Omega, and you remind him of what he doesn't have." I stroke the pad of my thumb over her lips and murmur, "Now do you understand why I'm so crazy about you? It's a miracle I have you, *sha'len*."

There are a hundred curious questions burning behind her eyes. "How…" she begins.

I rest my palm against the pillar by her head, lean closer, and smile at her. *How does my scent smell to you? How do our kind have sex? How can I possibly take your knot, Alpha?*

All delicious questions that I would love to answer for her.

"How, um…" Isavelle stares at my mouth, her tongue playing over her lip. "What can I…"

I cup her jaw and lower my mouth toward hers. She hesitates, then raises her lips so I can kiss her.

I groan and slant my mouth over hers. My mate tastes as good as she smells, and I hungrily devour her with my tongue until she's panting.

Isavelle moans against my lips and her hands fist my shirt, dragging me closer until her lush body is pressed against mine.

"Anything you want, *sha'len*," I murmur huskily as I press kiss after kiss to her mouth.

"Hmm?" She looks as drunk as I feel. Her expression clears a moment later. "Oh, my question. I was thinking that there must be so many people all over this country whose designations will soon be emerging. What's going to happen to them? I worry that they might be frightened if the things that happen to me start happening to them and they don't know why."

My mate is worried about other Omegas? She truly is a future Queen of Maledin. "That's a very important question, and it's something we should talk about with the *Hratha'len*. I would enjoy having your help with this."

She thinks about this for a moment and nods. "What will happen to the humans? Will they be told to leave Maledin?"

"Of course not. Maledin is for everyone who calls this place home. Humans will be allowed to live in peace and mate with whomever they choose, human or Maledinni. There were humans living here in my time, though not as many as there are now."

"That's a relief. I hope there won't be any trouble between us all."

"So do I. But we were talking about you and me. Thank you for coming to talk to me about all this. You made me very happy, my beautiful little dragon."

Isavelle smiles and pushes lightly on my stomach. "I don't need to be flattered all the time." Then she peeps up at me as if she's hoping I'll say it again.

My smile is smoldering. Sure, you don't, *sha'len*.

"Maybe. But your Alpha is going to say it anyway."

AT DUSK, I fill a pouch with chicken necks, one of Scourge's favorite treats, tie it to my belt, and walk over to the dragongrounds.

The dragonmaster is in the middle of the flare with his dragon, Nilak, polishing her gleaming white neck with a soft cloth. He takes his time with the preening female, lavishing her with attention and care. Between strokes of the cloth, Stesha murmurs to her, and she stretches her neck out to its fullest extent for him and closes her eyes.

I imagine what Scourge would do if I stood for hours polishing his scales. Probably roar in disgust and belt me across the dragongrounds with his spiny head.

The female Beta dragons of the flare are all clustered around Stesha and Nilak, nibbling at each other's wing folds or dozing in the last of the sun's rays.

How strange that Stesha lost his temper at Isavelle. Usually he ignores Omegas, going so far as to walk straight past them and pretending not to hear when they speak. I wonder if he disapproves of Isavelle and believes that the Flame King's mate is too young, weak, and naïve to stand by my side. Perhaps he's heard how she hasn't bonded with a dragon, and doesn't even like to ride a dragon. Or it could be that he's bitter that an Omega is blossoming under his nose and it's not his Omega.

Tough.

He can keep his bitterness and disapproval to himself. I won't have him upsetting my mate again.

I glimpse Scourge up on the bluff, pretending he hasn't scented the raw chicken necks I'm carrying. He uses the pointy part of one of his wing bones to idly scratch his side, but his red gaze is fixed on the pouch at my hip.

I stop a dozen yards from the dragonmaster and fold my arms. "My Omega is a brat, I hear."

Stesha glances over his shoulder and greets me with the tiniest dip of his head possible before turning back to his gleaming white dragon, who's watching me with haughty, icy blue eyes. No apology from Stesha. No explanation.

Stesha and I wondered at one time whether our dragons would mate, but while Scourge and Nilak are courteous and respectful, they've shown no further interest in each other. Personally, I think Scourge finds Nilak stuck-up and boring. Whenever Scourge is roughhousing with another dragon or roars a greeting to me, Nilak makes a show of hunching her wings and clicking her teeth before turning around and sashaying away, as if to say, *Oh, these noisy boys. How tiresome they are. How vulgar.* The only Alpha Nilak has any regard for is her own rider, and he treats her like a queen.

On the other side of the field, Scourge begins battling with one of the other male Alphas. It's not a true fight, and they're not trying to shred scales and flesh from the other, but Scourge deals a blow to the underside of the other dragon's jaw with the bony top of his head, and his sparring mate pulls back, lowering his crest and conceding the fight.

I feel a spurt of pride.

Nilak turns her regal head away and closes her eyes.

I turn my attention back to Stesha. I will have an explanation from him. "Lady Isavelle is adjusting and learning, and I'd appreciate it if you kept your criticisms of her to yourself. She's emerging with no knowledge of what she is and no other Omegas to give her any support."

"She's the king's Omega. She'll be fine," he says dismissively.

"Of course she will, but in the meantime, I expect you to be as courteous to my mate as you were to my mother."

Stesha lowers his grooming cloth and studies it in his hands. "I miss the last queen."

So that's it. He's not ready for a new one. I swallow hard, because I miss the last queen as well.

Stesha turns toward me, and there's true feeling in his voice when he says, "Your mother was a natural queen. I'm sorry that we lost her so soon."

I glance around the dragongrounds. "So am I."

What Isavelle could use right now is a friend. A young woman who she can spend time with. Someone like Stesha's ward. Zenevieve is a beautifully mannered Beta whom Stesha adores, so hopefully he won't object if my "bratty" mate befriends her.

"I know she's a Beta rather than an Omega, but Zenevieve would make an excellent friend for Isavelle. Where is Zenevieve, anyway? I haven't seen..."

The expression on Stesha's face becomes stricken before I even finish what I'm saying.

Zenevieve is dead? She wasn't among us beneath the mountain? No one told me.

"Fuck. Stesha. I'm so sorry."

He grips the polishing cloth in his fist and stares at the ground. His voice is forced and unemotional as he says, "It happened a long time ago."

For her, maybe. For him and me, the grief of our losses is still fresh. Zenevieve is—was—everything to him, his only family after he lost his. Zenevieve's parents died when she was sixteen and Stesha took care of his best friend's daughter until she came of age a few years ago. A few hundred years ago. Stesha never had much time for other people, but he doted on the pretty, raven-haired, green-eyed young Beta.

"There's no sign of Minta, either?" Minta is Zenevieve's beautiful dark green and black dragon, a Beta like her rider and one of the sweetest in the flare. She has excellent speed and agility for a dragon, and she could give the wingrunners an aeronautical challenge.

Stesha shakes his head. "Nilak didn't sense her under the mountain, and she hasn't scented her either. They're both just...gone."

"Do you think—"

"That's enough, Zabriel," Stesha snaps.

I close my mouth. I guess we're not talking about it. For a few minutes, there's silence while I try to think of a way to draw the conversation back to Isavelle.

"Do you think Isavelle will bond with a dragon? I want my Omega to become a dragonrider more than anything so I can share the skies with her." With her aversion to flight and the sickness it causes her sometimes, I worry she'll be dragonless.

"Why, were you hoping to give Minta to your mate?"

"For fuck's sake, Stesha. Of course not."

But Stesha's grief has tipped over into fury, and he unleashes a short, sharp tirade. "Your Omega is a brat, and so is her dragon. Good luck to you and Scourge. You're both going to need it."

My folded arms loosen in shock. Her dragon? Isavelle has a dragon? "Wait, what?"

The dragonmaster turns back to Nilak and sweeps the cloth down her flank.

"Stesha—" But I'm distracted by a tugging at my hip. I look around and see that a turquoise and gold dragon has clamped her teeth around the pouch of chicken necks and is trying to yank it from my belt. She's small, her haunches are the same height as my head, but she's strong. As she tugs, I'm jerked toward her, and she begins to snarl as she doesn't get what she wants.

"Hey! Stop that. Those aren't for you." I grasp hold of the pouch and pull back. The dragon's back legs slip and slide as they try to gain traction. A moment later, the ties snap, and the dragon straightens up, her prize held proudly in her teeth. Her eyes blaze with triumph and her wings unfurl.

"Drop that right now," I shout. "Don't you dare take off."

But the turquoise dragon ignores me, launches into the sky, and flies away toward the bluff. Nilak screams in outrage and lunges for the little thief, but the turquoise dragon is too fast, and Nilak's teeth click on empty air.

Stesha glares at the turquoise dragon as she reaches the cliff and settles on a ledge, but does absolutely nothing to call her back.

"Oh, no you don't." I set off after the dragon at a run. Those are Scourge's chicken necks, not hers. When I finally catch up and heave myself onto the ledge, she's ripped open the pouch and has already devoured the chicken necks.

I snatch the torn pouch up and shake it at her. "You little thief. Those were for Scourge, your Alpha and the leader of this flare. How dare you steal from him."

The dragon ducks her head sheepishly and gazes up at me with beautiful turquoise eyes, rimmed with gold. Shuffling closer with her belly low to the ground, she pushes her head into my hand and nuzzles it, making pleading little noises.

I feel my temper draining away and automatically caress her scales. Well, she's young, and maybe she didn't know she was misbehaving or she couldn't help herself when she smelled chicken. Really excellent battle dragons are spirited in their youth, and this one is beautiful as well. From the looks of her, she hasn't yet presented her designation, but she reminds me of Isavelle when she has her rare moments of sweetness.

I stop scratching the dragon's jaw and stare at her, remembering what Stesha just said.

Your Omega is a brat, and so is her dragon.

Dragonfire and piss.

I study the turquoise dragon. Small size. Hungry for treats because she's at the bottom of the flare. Coaxing an Alpha to make a fuss of her and forgive her when she's misbehaved. Beautiful coloring and a surprisingly adorable appearance for a creature with sharp teeth and talons.

I scrub a hand down my face and mutter a curse. Two Omegas. Two Omegas who are rapidly realizing they're irresistible and know how to wrap me around their little claws. Two Omegas to worry about, keep happy, and protect.

The dragon thumps her rear leg on the ground, shrieks to get my attention, and then nuzzles against my hand. When I don't immediately stroke her scales, she nips at my fingers.

Make a fuss of me or I will EAT you, her furious gold-rimmed eyes say.

If this dragon decides Isavelle is her rider and Scourge is her mate, I'm going to have my hands full.

19

Isavelle

As the days pass, my heart aches for any whisper about the people of western Maledin. If they're not in Grendu, then the only other place they can be is to the south, behind that barrier.

The mysterious barrier consumes my thoughts.

From what I've heard, the barrier is a colorless, shimmering veil that's impassable to all who've tried to cross it. The dragonriders and wingrunners mutter darkly about the two wyverns who accidentally flew through it with their riders. All four bodies were found on our side of the barrier, dead and mutilated in ghastly ways. No one's sure if it's the barrier that ripped them apart or whatever lives beyond it.

Posette and Santha do their best to keep my spirits up and are always happy to accept my help when I go looking for them. Losing myself in work with them helps me control my worries.

One crisp, gray morning, the three of us are churning butter in a freezing outbuilding in the kitchen courtyard. We all have pink cheeks and are slightly out of breath, and my arms are aching as I work the wooden churn over and over again. The contraption is almost as tall as I am, and the plunger grows heavy as the curds thicken.

"We heard that you and the Flame King received an emissary from the Brethren in the Great Hall a few days ago," Santha says, pausing to drag the back of her hand across her sweaty upper lip.

I keep my head ducked as I feel my cheeks burn even harder. I expect Posette to giggle and waggle her eyebrows at me, but neither girl seems to know anything that went on between Zabriel and me that night, thank the stars.

"Um. Yes. The High Priest asked for my return, and Zabriel refused."

If my family is behind the barrier, I wonder if they're all right. The Brethren have always left my family alone, and I hope that it stays that way.

"That's because he's in love with you and he's going to make you his queen," Posette says with a dreamy smile on her face. "I wonder what a Flame King's wedding is like. I imagine it will be spectacular."

"Zabriel and I barely know each other. You're getting ahead of yourself."

"If you're going to be the high and mighty queen of this castle, you'll need ladies' maids. That could be us," Santha says, waggling her thumb between herself and Posette.

"Me, have maids? What does a lady's maid even do?"

Santha thinks carefully about this. "We can brush your hair. Lay out your dresses."

"I can brush my own hair and put on my own dresses."

Posette's eyes gleam with excitement. "There's supposed to be all sorts of intrigue at a royal court. We can relay secret messages to handsome knights."

"There aren't any knights here."

"Handsome dragonriders, then," Santha says.

I laugh and go back to churning the butter. "If you want to send messages to dragonriders, go right ahead."

"Maybe I will," Santha says with a smile. "Have you seen that tall, white-haired dragonrider? He's gorgeous and so fierce."

I scowl at the memory of Stesha calling me a brat. "Don't bother writing letters to him. He's mean, and he's not even handsome."

Posette stares at me in astonishment. "Are you crazy? Every time he walks past, I feel like I'm about to have a nosebleed he's so sexy."

I sniff in derision. Stesha wishes he were a tenth as good-looking as Zabriel.

When I'm not working, I find myself drawn to the Flame Temple. The carved obsidian walls seem to absorb the heat of the ceremonial flame, and the hushed space is always warm, even though it is open to the sky. One of the Temple Mothers teaches me to meditate, and I sit cross-legged on a mat with my eyes closed, my mind drifting as I'm dimly aware of the sinuous pattern of the flames behind my eyelids.

Sometimes I'll open my eyes to find three or four baby dragons fast asleep around me. Hatchlings, they're called. They can't yet fly and their mothers drop them through the open ceiling on their way to patrol the skies or hunt. They flutter clumsily to the ground, wings frantically flapping. When they land, they shake themselves off from snout to tail and then find somewhere comfortable to snooze. I suppose they find their own way back to the dragongrounds eventually.

As I'm sitting and meditating one day, I hear a beating of strong wings and guess that one of the dragon mothers is passing overhead with her young. The flapping grows louder and louder, and I open my eyes to see a turquoise and gold dragon descending into the temple. She flies in tight circles until she lands on the temple floor with a click of talons and a gust of wind that sends the flame dancing around in the font.

There's an outraged cry from the other side of the temple, and the Temple Crone marches forward, her red robes billowing behind her. "Esmeral! What do you think you are doing?"

The turquoise dragon scuttles behind me and cowers as if she's hiding, which makes my mouth twitch considering that she's as long as a corridor.

"Are fledgling dragons not meant to come into the Flame Temple?" I ask, pleased that I've remembered what young dragons who can fly are called.

"Esmeral is not a fledgling. She may be small, but she's almost fully mature, and her designation is emerging. Her place is with the flare, not in the temple." The Temple Crone points to the open sky and glowers at the dragon. "Out of here at once, or I'll speak with the dragonmaster about you."

Esmeral lowers her head, hunches her shoulders, and smoke pours from her nostrils. She looks like she's sulking. The dragon and the Temple Mother stare at each other for a moment, and then Esmeral huffs and takes off. If a dragon can be said to flounce into the air, then Esmeral does. I watch her circle upward, then disappear into the sky.

"What a strange dragon she is," I say, watching her.

"Esmeral is unusually strong-minded for what she is," says the Temple Crone as she begins to turn away. "She will be very like her rider, I believe."

I scramble to my feet, unwilling to waste this opportunity to talk to the crone. "Could I please ask you something, Grandmother?"

When she pauses, I hurry to her side.

"I'm aware that you and the Temple Mothers are meditating on the barrier to the south. I wonder if I can offer you any assistance in that matter."

Maybe I should have stopped at *Could I please ask you something, Grandmother?* The Temple Crone's amethyst eyes bore into mine, and the sharp silence goes on and on. I seem to have gravely offended her.

Finally, she says, "Yes, your help would be appreciated, Lady Isavelle."

"It would?" I ask in amazement.

She smiles a little. "Not with the barrier, but there are some duties that we would be grateful for you to fulfill so that we may have more time to focus on the barrier. You grew up in western Maledin, I believe. Are you familiar with the tsetsor plant?"

"I think so. It has small, orange flowers and narrow leaves, and it blooms after a winter melt?"

"That is correct. The winds have been warmer these past two days, so the tsetsors should be blooming in the fields below the city walls. If you could collect me a basketful of tsetsor tubers I would be grateful. We use these to enhance our meditations."

A task that will take me beyond the city walls. I will need to take Dusan and Fiala with me, and they will want Zabriel's permission before taking me outside.

I find Zabriel in a corridor off the Great Hall, dressed in plate armor and pulling on his dragonriding gauntlets. The sight of him sets off sparks in my belly, and I realize how eager I was to go and find him. He gives me a smoldering look, and his gaze locks on my lips, which tingle in response.

I meant to inform him where I was going, with whom, and why, but at the sight of him looking so handsome and impressive, my stomach flutters, and I twist my fingers together, suddenly desperate for his touch, his kisses, his smiles.

"The Temple Crone has requested I dig up some roots for her, but I'll have to go outside the city walls."

An indulgent smile spreads over Zabriel's face. He steps closer and wraps his gauntleted hand around the nape of my neck. "Did you come to ask permission from your Alpha to do something dangerous?"

My lips twitch. He's just loving this. "My bodyguards need your permission. They're terrified of you."

He grins at me, showing his pointed dragines. "As they should be."

His smile dims, and a moment later he slams his mouth over mine in a hungry kiss. I go up on my toes and wrap my arms around his neck. This man's kisses are dangerously addictive. When his teeth sink into my lower lip, I moan.

When dragons kiss, they bite.

Zabriel releases me slowly, planting half a dozen more

kisses on my lips for good measure. "Enjoy the fresh air, *sha'len*. I'll be back soon if you need anything. I'm taking Scourge on patrol."

He kisses the top of my head, and a dozen fluffy ducklings dance in my chest.

Then he growls, "Tell your bodyguards that my mate comes back before sunset or I'll hang them by their ankles from the castle walls."

I promise to pass on his message.

I find my bodyguards in the Great Hall, and they are delighted to have an excuse not to return to their punishment. Shoveling wyvern shit is apparently an appalling job.

"I'm sorry I got you both into so much trouble," I tell them as we head through the castle together.

Fiala glowers at Dusan. "Don't worry about it, Lady Isavelle. He got us into trouble all on his own."

"Did you manage to discover the answers to your questions, Lady Isavelle?" Dusan asks me.

I hesitate and my cheeks turn red. If I asked one of the Temple Mothers or even Zabriel what goes on between an Alpha and Omega when she's in her heat, they would probably tell me, but I'm too shy to ask the question just yet.

Kisses from Zabriel? Heavenly. Delicious.

More than that from Zabriel? I feel locked up with panic, shame, and desire.

I think he knows that, and he's being patient with me, which I can't help but feel grateful about.

Ten minutes later, the three of us walk outside the city gates and into fields and farmland. The air is slightly warmer than it was a few days ago, but spring is still a long way off, and I have no doubt that winter will shroud us in ice crystals again soon.

Fiala points down a cart track toward a stretch of woods. "The open ground by the trees would be an ideal place to start looking for tsetsor flowers, Lady Isavelle."

"Then we'll start there," I tell her with a smile.

While they stand guard a few feet away, gripping their halberds, I kneel on the exposed ground and take a trowel out of my basket. There's a patch of tsetsor flowers, and I get to work digging each of them up.

A few minutes later, there's a rapid beating sound overhead, and I look up to see something bright flashing in the sunlight. A turquoise and golden dragon flutters down beside me.

I sit back on my heels and gaze at her in surprise. "What are you doing here?"

Esmeral trots over and snuffles around in the dirt and then at my skirts. She butts her head against my hand, begging for me to stroke her scales.

I do, and she trills happily.

There's a sound high in the sky, and Esmeral and I both look up to see Scourge flying overhead, presumably with Zabriel on his back. The black dragon shoots a plume of fire into the sky, banks hard, his black scales flash red in the firelight, and then he carries on his way.

"Show off," I murmur with a smile, referring to Zabriel, not Scourge, but continuing to admire them. Esmeral is craning her neck after Scourge and doesn't return her attention to me until the dragon and his rider have disappeared over the horizon.

I get back to my digging, but I've only managed to extricate three tsetsor tubers from the ground when we're interrupted by yet another dragon.

A huge, majestic white creature flutters gracefully to the ground and gleams a more radiant white than the snow. Its rider, dressed in white and tan leathers, swings his leg over the saddle and slides to the ground. I immediately recognize his haughty expression and long white hair.

Stesha.

He pretends to ignore me, turning around to check his dragon's harness, so I ignore him.

Esmeral is gazing in awe at the beautiful white dragon, which is nosing around in the snow. Stesha pulls his riding gloves off one finger at a time as he watches her chewing on something crunchy. The dragon comes closer and closer to the patch of ground where I'm working.

I call out to him, "Is your dragon eating tsetsor tubers?"

Stesha doesn't look at me. "Dandelion roots. She likes them in the winter."

And he brought her here? That dragon has the whole world in which to dig for dandelion roots. "Did Zabriel tell you to keep an eye on me? He needn't be so overprotective when I have my bodyguards."

Stesha snorts in disgust. Even the white dragon pauses in her digging to glare disapprovingly at me. "I don't babysit for other Alphas."

But as he says it, he glances at Esmeral.

Maybe he's here for her, not me. That would make more sense.

As I continue to work, Stesha keeps his eye on the turquoise dragon. She's figured out what I'm digging for and scrabbles in the dirt with her talons. She uncovers a tuber, grasps it with her teeth, and pulls.

"Esmeral, please don't—" The tuber snaps in two, one half in the ground and one half in the dragon's mouth. I sit back on my heels and sigh. "This dragon does whatever she wants."

"Annoying, isn't it?" Stesha mutters.

Irritation prickles down my spine. He's finding new ways to tell me I'm a brat.

Realizing I don't want it anymore, Esmeral chews the broken tuber and swallows it down. While I'm glaring at the dragonmaster, she sidles up beside me and sticks her head in my basket, which I quickly hold out of her reach. "Don't eat those. They're for the Temple Crone, and I don't know if they're good for dragons."

Esmeral gives an apologetic trill and steps back.

I watch her for a moment, wondering if she understands what I'm saying to her. She really is a pretty dragon. Hesitantly, I reach out and stroke my fingers along her smooth neck. Her scales are nothing like I've ever touched before. Supple and smooth, with a slight ridge where each scale meets. The scales are thicker and tougher along her spine and legs, but the underside of her neck is soft. Esmeral closes her eyes as I stroke her, delighting in the attention.

While I stroke her, my attention strays to the white dragon. It seems vaguely familiar somehow, and I realize why. I've seen it before in the skies during the invasion and along the Proxen Road when Zabriel stole me back from the Brethren.

"Is this your dragon?" I ask Stesha.

"She is. This is Nilak," he says, and a proud look comes

into his eyes.

I watch as the man who called me a brat reaches out to touch his dragon, his expression softens as he caresses the enormous white beast. He loves his dragon. Totally adores her. I wonder if he's ever felt the same way about a person. Somehow I doubt it.

While he's in a relatively good mood, I risk continuing the conversation. "I think I saw you during the invasion. Well, I saw Nilak. After I was nearly sacrificed and ran away, I saw her in the skies."

"Yes, I was searching for the runaway instead of doing the thousand other things I should have been doing to reclaim my country," he says, with an edge to his voice.

Stesha's good moods have shorter lifespans than hot cups of tea.

"I saw you again on the Proxen Road. An archer shot at Zabriel and Nilak grabbed him and threw him out of the circle of fire."

"Yes, I know. I was there. I killed for you that night." He flicks me a glare. "You're welcome."

Irritation spikes in my chest. I was going to compliment Nilak for being such a formidable and talented dragon, but now I'm not going to. "You killed the Brethren Guard because Zabriel ordered it. You didn't do it for me."

"Yet here you are, alive and safe at the capital, thanks in part to Nilak and me."

I roll my eyes and go back to digging, vowing that the words *Thank you, dragonmaster* will never pass my lips. I dig up four more tubers, resenting Stesha's presence more and more. "I wish you'd take Nilak to look for dandelion roots somewhere else."

"I will return to the dragongrounds when Esmeral does."

I use my forearm to brush hair out of my eyes and glance up at him. "Why? Isn't she allowed to leave the flare alone?"

Stesha is watching the small dragon with a line between his brows. "She hasn't got a rider or a mate to watch over her, and I think she'll go into heat soon. I don't know how many wild dragons there are in Maledin anymore, but I don't want the newest Omega in the flare to be torn to pieces when she starts to perfume."

Attacked? Poor Esmeral. She's only small and looks entirely defenseless. "That's thoughtful of you."

"It's not thoughtful. It's my duty. I'm the dragonmaster, and Esmeral is in my flare. I don't need to be told I'm doing a good job by a clueless Omega."

I grip the trowel tighter, wishing I could shove it up Stesha's ass. Every time I try to hold out an olive branch to this man, he beats me over the head with it.

Esmeral has wandered over to Nilak and is nosing in the dirt around where the white dragon is digging. Nilak seems to resent the smaller dragon's presence, and she lashes out with a snarl. Esmeral cringes away from her.

Poor little Esmeral. I feel so sorry for her that I can't stop myself from saying, "Nilak, she's only small. Leave her alone."

"Nilak is teaching a lower-ranked dragon her place," Stesha tells me. "Why do you care if Esmeral is being corrected by a bigger and older dragon?"

"I don't." But I do think Nilak is being a bitch and Esmeral can't help being curious.

"I don't *dragonmaster*," Stesha prompts, but I ignore him. He's not my dragonmaster. He's a pompous jerk.

When I don't respond, he says, "It's only natural that you

care. Haven't you figured it out yet?"

"Figured what out?"

"Figured what out *dragonmaster*," he growls. "Esmeral is trying to bond with you. She wants you to be her rider, and if you would do your duty, it would make my life easier. Her rider is meant to be the one to take care of her at times like this."

Esmeral perks up at the word *rider*. Excitedly, she comes around behind me and rests her snout on my shoulder. It's something I've seen some of the other dragons doing with their riders. It seems like a sign of affection or comradeship. Me, be her rider? Something else to tie me to this place when all I want to do is find my family and go home?

I duck out from under Esmeral and back away, shaking my head. "Oh, no. No, no, no. No, thank you. I don't want a dragon."

"But you're Maledinni," Stesha points out, advancing on me. "Riding dragons is your birthright, and it's an honor to be chosen by a dragon. Why would you refuse?"

I don't feel Maledinni, and I definitely don't feel like a dragonrider. I'm nothing like Zabriel and Stesha with their flashing eyes, proud features, and boundless confidence. I feel much more at home among the palace servants or the refugees. I feel sick when I ride a dragon, and besides, they're terrifying. Even if I wanted to become a dragonrider, it would mean spending days on end with Stesha, who clearly hates me, while he berates me over what a terrible rider I am. I can't think of anything worse.

"There's no point in me learning how to ride a dragon because I'm not staying in the capital. I'm waiting to find out where my family is and then I'm going home."

Stesha's eyes widen in astonishment and then narrow with outrage. Over his shoulder, Nilak is giving me the same ferocious glare. "You are unbelievable, child. The King of Maledin has declared you're his mate, and he's working night and day to keep you safe. Now a dragon of the king's flare wants to bond with you, giving you the chance to repay his hard work by becoming a dragonrider who can defend her country, and you refuse?"

Stesha could just accept my refusal, but he can't, can he? He's an Alpha, and Alphas are always right. "Zabriel *demanded* I be his mate. I don't want to bond with a dragon or ride into battle—and don't call me child."

Stesha doesn't move, but Nilak draws her snout back from her teeth and snarls at me.

She can snarl all she likes. I don't care what the dragonmaster and his haughty dragon expect of me. I decide what happens in my life, not them.

Without saying goodbye, I pick up my basket and head for the castle with Fiala and Dusan following behind me. Esmeral utters a soft, sad trill as she watches me go, which sends a pang through my heart.

She's lonely.

I don't know how I know that, but I do. She's small, strong-willed, and picked on. She doesn't feel she belongs here, or anywhere for that matter, and the future is a frightening and uncertain place. I nearly run back to her and wrap my arms around her neck because I know exactly how she feels. It would be cruel to bond with her only to leave her behind. It's impossible that I could ever have a dragon at Amriste. She belongs with her flare, and I belong in my village.

When we're safe inside the castle walls once more, Dusan sighs. "Back to shit-shoveling duty."

Fiala studies me for a moment. "You could give riding a try, Lady Isavelle. I've never met a Maledinni who doesn't love flying."

"Things are different these days," I tell them. "It's impossible for me."

I wave goodbye to them and head for the Flame Temple to deliver the tsetsor tubers, and even though I don't have as many as I would have liked, the Temple Crone thanks me for my work.

Later at sunset, I'm standing on the castle walls, gazing out across the dragongrounds. Esmeral is easy to spot among the bigger bodies.

She moves among them, and the bigger dragons snap at her as she passes. The turquoise dragon huddles at the edges of the flare, and the others ignore her. No one grooms her wings.

I wonder if this is my fault. I've rejected her, and that's made her an outcast within the flare. As I watch, a muscular red dragon with a golden sheen strides into Esmeral, knocking her aside. I can't help but feel he's done it deliberately, and yet he rounds on her, opens his jaws, and snarls. Esmeral cringes back and slinks away, keeping close to the ground. Making herself small. Apologizing for her existence.

Finally, she takes shelter beneath a low overhang where the bigger dragons can't get to her. For a long time, I stand by the wall and watch her, but she doesn't come out.

When I open my eyes in the morning, I'm struck with a wave of loneliness. I lay on my back for a long time in the bed, filled with a wretched, helpless feeling like I haven't known since I was imprisoned at the monasteries. It's strange because I haven't felt lonely since I arrived at the castle. If it weren't for my missing family, I think I'd be happy here with Dusan and Fiala, Posette and Santha, and Odanna down in the city. I've never had so many friends before. Then there's Zabriel, and while my feelings for him are complicated, I certainly don't feel lonely around him.

This feeling of loneliness doesn't seem to belong to me. I think it must belong to Esmeral.

I roll over and press my face into the pillow with a groan. It's already happening. I'm bonding with Esmeral after a few brief encounters. I tried to resist it, but it's happening anyway. Being Maledinni is nothing like being human, something that keeps catching me unawares. Feelings are so much stronger. Connections are more intense. I wanted to go home to my village still feeling human, but maybe that's impossible now. Maybe it always has been, and I was fooling myself trying to be something I'm not.

After I eat in the Great Hall, I still can't get my mind off Esmeral, and I decide to go check on her. Just from a distance. I don't know if dragons can hope, but I don't want to get her hopes up, and I don't want to run into Stesha either.

It doesn't take me long to make my way through the castle and to approach the dragongrounds, but I haven't even crossed the stone bridge when I stop dead.

The sight before me makes my blood boil.

How *dare* he?

20

Zabriel

I'm in the middle of a meeting with Godric and Ashton when Isavelle hurries in out of breath with her hair flying around her face.

I step toward her quickly, searching for signs of injury on her body. "Are you all right? What's happened?"

She points toward the terrace that overlooks the dragongrounds, and pants, "Your dragon."

Alarm races through me. "Something's happened to Scourge?"

Isavelle draws herself up in outrage and exclaims, "He's bullying Esmeral."

I frown at her. The little Omega dragon? That makes no sense. He mostly ignores the smaller dragons unless they need his protection. "Scourge is the flare's Alpha. He's not a bully."

"Come and see for yourself." Isavelle catches my hand and tugs me toward the terrace overlooking the dragongrounds. "Look! Just look at what he's doing."

Below us and beyond the bridge, Scourge is standing in the middle of the dragongrounds, looming over something turquoise and golden at his feet.

My concern melts into realization. I see what's happening. In fact, I should have expected this.

"Let's go down there. Come with me." I hold tighter to Isavelle's hand and steer her out of the room, calling to my men that I'll return soon.

Isavelle and I cross the stone bridge together, but I draw her to a halt before we step onto the dragongrounds. Scourge is in pride of place in the middle of the flare, scales gleaming darkly in the wintry sunlight, wings partly unfurled. Crouching at his enormous taloned feet is Esmeral, less than a third of his size. She's somehow crept or flown past a dozen higher-ranked dragons to reach him and looks tiny against his huge, black bulk.

The little dragon is quite literally playing with fire as she arches the back of her neck, baring the vulnerable flesh beneath her crest. Scourge darts at her with his massive jaws open, and his teeth snap together just inches from her scales.

A smirk spreads over my face as the turquoise dragon cringes even closer to the ground, but she doesn't try to flee.

"This isn't funny," Isavelle exclaims. "He's going to hurt her. You need to call him off."

I fold my arms and fix Isavelle with a severe look. "I heard you don't care what happens to Esmeral. She's not your dragon, and you don't want to be her rider."

Stesha wasted no time seeking me out to tell me that

Isavelle was refusing the dragon who wanted to bond with her and had talked back to him yet again. He has enough to do without chasing an unmated and riderless Omega dragon all over the capital, and so on and so on.

When I informed Stesha that an Alpha shouldn't lose his temper so easily over two little Omegas, he ground his teeth together so hard that I thought they were going to shatter in his mouth.

"That doesn't mean I'll stand idly by while your beast of a dragon is cruel to her. I know what that feels like."

"Of course you wouldn't," I say softly and stoke Isavelle's cheek. Then a wicked smile curves my lips. "But what if Esmeral doesn't need saving from Scourge? What if she's playing a game with him, one they both like?"

Isavelle gazes in surprise at me, and then at the dragons. "Don't be silly. The whole flare has been snapping at Esmeral for days and now even Scourge is joining in."

There's so much she doesn't understand about my kind. *Our* kind. Doesn't she sense it yet? Doesn't she feel what's happening?

I put both my hands on my mate's shoulders and turn her to face Scourge and Esmeral. Isavelle gasps slightly at the sensation of my hands touching her bare flesh.

"Esmeral isn't afraid of Scourge. Esmeral went to Scourge," I murmur in her ear.

She still seems confused. "For protection?"

"That's part of what he'll give her, but it's not what she craves the most. She wants his attention. She's hoping he'll show signs that he's interested in her."

"So why is he being so threatening?"

"He's showing her he's an Alpha," I say softly, stroking a

finger down her neck. "He's testing her daring. Her courage. It's fascinating to him how such a tiny little thing like her is baring her neck to his teeth."

Isavelle relaxes against me as I speak in a deep, slow voice, and her words are a little breathy as she asks, "Shouldn't he test one of the bigger, more experienced females?"

"Why would he, when she's the one he wants?"

My mate is gazing at the dragons, but she flexes her neck to one side, unconsciously inviting the stroke of my fingers. Her eyelashes flutter a little as I run my fingers over her scent gland. I can feel that it's a little swollen. It will probably start to ache soon and a false heat will begin. Desire and longing shoot through me at the thought, and I feel my knot thicken. Finally, I'll be able to make Isavelle mine.

"Are you sure he's not bullying her?" Isavelle whispers.

"It's bonding behavior. They're flirting." I lean down and press my nose to the side of her throat. Her scent is growing richer, and my knot pulses in response. I'm going to be hard nonstop while Isavelle's in a false heat. I move my hands from her shoulders, wrap them around her waist, and pull her against me. Isavelle's eyelashes flutter in response to my touch and she covers my hands with her own. Watching our dragons engage in a mating ritual is making us both want each other even more.

"I didn't know dragons flirted with each other. Are you sure they're a good match? Esmeral looks so tiny compared to him."

I glance down at my mate, who barely comes up to my chest. Omegas are always small compared to their Alphas. Alphas worry the same thing, that they'll bite or scratch or fuck too hard, but Omegas are tougher than they look. When she's in her true heat, I hope Isavelle will beg me to be rough with her.

"Esmeral may be small, but she's determined to get what she wants, and it seems she wants Scourge." The sweet, chirrupy little dragon is destined for my mate, and she's destined for my dragon as well. It doesn't always happen this way between mates who are Alpha and Omega, but it's a wonderful sign that our union will be stronger if our dragons are mated too.

Scourge opens his jaws and clamps them around the back of Esmeral's neck, and Isavelle inhales sharply as if she can feel his teeth. My dragines ache in my mouth. Isavelle's tender flesh is so fragrant, and I crave to get my teeth in her. I want it so badly I can barely see straight.

But not yet. I don't want to push Isavelle too fast, and I don't have to. Soon she'll be begging me for everything. I can smell it on her.

Despite how fearsome Scourge is, the little turquoise dragon isn't afraid of the monster looming over her. She risked being torn to pieces by the larger females for daring to approach the king at the center of the flare, but that wasn't going to stop her.

She wants him.

She *needs* him.

Scourge runs his snout up Esmeral's neck. I do the same to Isavelle, and she moans in response. What Alpha can resist his Omega? Isavelle's eyes have grown heavy lidded. I wonder if slick is pooling between her thighs. If she's aching between her thighs. She's so relaxed in my arms that if I let her go, I think she'd fall down.

Nilak reaches out her long neck and snaps at the smaller dragon, probably irritated that a low-ranked dragon has moved past her and approached the center of the flare.

Scourge spreads his wings, opens his jaw, and roars at the Alpha female. Nilak screws her eyes up, and a moment later turns away and starts aggressively grooming one of the Betas. She seems to be covering up her embarrassment at not being allowed to push an Omega back into line.

When I glance down at Isavelle, there's a satisfied smile on her lips.

I stroke my fingers through her hair and even more of her heavenly scent is released, and for a moment, I close my eyes and savor her. Scourge keeps his wings unfurled to shelter his mate, settles on the ground, and half closes his eyes. Esmeral stretches her elongated body against his and rests her snout on his foreleg. A moment later she closes her eyes and falls into a doze.

Scourge's mate trusts him already to let down her guard with him. Envy stabs me through my chest as I gaze at the dragons. If Isavelle had been born in my time, to Maledinni parents and surrounded by Alphas and Betas, would she feel safe enough to embrace her Omega nature?

When I glance down at Isavelle, I'm surprised to find her gazing as longingly at them as I feel. Maybe it won't be much time until she does.

"Do you think they look good together?" I murmur.

"They're beautiful," she whispers. "Are they going to mate soon?"

I shake my head. "She hasn't begun her heat cycles yet, just as you haven't. But he'll wait for her. He'll wait as long as it takes because she's worth it."

Isavelle turns her head and gazes up at me. Not to ask me a question. Not to puzzle out what I'm thinking. She's simply waiting, and with a jolt, I realize what she's waiting for.

A kiss.

My hand slides up her throat to capture her chin, and I lower my mouth toward hers, stroking her jaw with my thumb. Reveling in the sensation of my mate relaxed in my arms, her soft body nestled against mine, a dreamy look in her eyes, and her lips parted.

I draw out the moment for a few seconds longer, breathing in her scent and her surrender, and then I press my lips to hers. Isavelle's mouth is so sweet and yielding against mine, and I sink into her. With an intake of breath, she parts her lips and I sweep my tongue into her mouth. I draw back a few inches and caress her face.

Isavelle slowly licks her lips as if savoring my taste. "Do Maledinni kiss out in the open?"

"The King of Maledin kisses his mate wherever he chooses," I tell her, kissing her again. This time her mouth opens immediately for my tongue, and I slide it deeper into her mouth. Her body yielding to mine makes me groan. Good Omega. Very good Omega, letting your Alpha take charge of this kiss and giving you the adoration and pleasure you deserve.

"I love the way you kiss, Alpha," Isavelle whispers, a needy little upward tilt to her inner brows.

A spasm goes through my balls. *Alpha*.

"I love it when you call me Alpha," I groan, and kiss her again, messily this time, softly sucking her lips and the tip of her tongue, both our mouths wet. I hope she looks and sounds just like this when she's begging for me to knot her.

Isavelle reaches up and cups my neck, stroking me softly and gazing at me with dilated pupils. "Alpha, do you..." She stops stroking me and her eyes grow vacant.

"Isavelle?"

No response.

I touch her cheek, but she doesn't seem to hear me. "*Isavelle.*"

A moment later she breathes in sharply and refocuses on my face. Then she lowers her chin and looks toward the flare. Esmeral is sleeping peacefully and Scourge is sheltering her with his wings.

"I thought I saw..." Isavelle pulls herself from my arms and takes a few steps forward, searching the dragongrounds. "Is there a coral-colored dragon in the flare? Does her rider have silver hair?"

"Damla and Tish? Yes, they're here somewhere, and if not, they will be back soon. I saw them leave on patrol a few hours ago."

"Oh, no," Isavelle moans, hurrying to the left and then to the right, peering among the dragons. "Damla is the coral dragon? I can't see Damla anywhere."

Isavelle is so frantic that there are tears in her eyes. As far as I know, my mate has never encountered Damla or her rider, Tish.

My mate whirls around and hurries back to me, and when I catch her scent, it's laced with panic. "Something's happened. Damla and Tish have been attacked, somewhere along the Proxen Road. I think I saw the barrier."

"You *saw* it?"

Isavelle nibbles on her lip, shaking her head. "Don't ask

me how I know. I don't know how. But Damla and Tish are hurt. I think they're dying."

I gaze at my mate, several thoughts at once crowding into my mind. Biddy Hawthorne claimed that my mate saw a vision in her cottage. As a small child, she sensed there was something trapped within the Bodan Mountains and it was calling to her. Scourge found her before she was thrown onto the funeral pyre, and again when she was being taken south on the Proxen Road, and in the city when she was attacked by Brethren. He shouldn't have been able to do that. Dragons don't share a connection with anyone except their rider. Dragons can't call out in their minds to anyone but their rider.

But witches can.

I grasp Isavelle's shoulders and ask her urgently, "Do you know where Damla and her rider were attacked? Do you think you could find them if I took you there?"

Isavelle glances toward the southwest. "I think I could but..." Her eyes fill with tears again. She turns back to me and she grasps my forearms, her beautiful face filled with despair. "Zabriel, I think they might already be dead."

21

Isavelle

The sun is dipping low on the horizon as Scourge skims as close to the ground as he can. Zabriel has an arm wrapped around my waist while I grip the saddle with one hand and lean out as far as I dare, scouring the ground. Hunting for any sign of the downed dragon and rider. Up ahead, the southern mountains shimmer strangely, as if veiled by heat or water.

The barrier.

I can feel it like a malevolent, living thing, hungry for blood and death. Whoever made it is like no one I've ever encountered before. Even in his worst moments, the High Priest didn't feel this evil.

The shadows are lengthening on the ground. Soon there won't be any light by which to search for Tish and Damla. Before we took off on Scourge, Zabriel shouted an order to a soldier from a wingrunner unit that at least three dragonriders were to follow us immediately and search the Proxen Road close to the barrier for a downed rider, but there's no sign yet of anyone else joining the search.

I'm so focused on what I'm doing that I almost don't feel sick. Almost.

The vision. I need to remember the vision. What did I see while I was in Zabriel's arms? I close my eyes and attempt to recall it in my mind. The coral-colored dragon screaming and tumbling out of the sky. Her rider desperately clinging on. Both of them crashing into the unyielding, rocky ground. There was something dark beyond them. A crease of darkness in the ground, and beyond that, a pale line winding through the landscape...

I open my eyes and turn toward Zabriel. "Is there a blind canyon nearby? East of the road?"

Zabriel's dark brows draw together. He nods, and a moment later, Scourge swerves in that direction. He banks so hard that my stomach lurches, and I clap a hand over my mouth.

"*Sha'len*, you're feeling sick, aren't you?"

I swallow hard and gasp, "I'm fine. Don't worry about me."

Zabriel can't seem to help worrying about me, and he pulls his cloak around us and holds me securely against his chest. I can see him searching the ground in my peripheral vision as I hunt every shape in the landscape for a hint of coral or the shape of a wing.

A moment later, I spot the blind canyon, deep in shadow by now and not far from it, the outstretched neck of a supine dragon.

"There," I exclaim, pointing to the spot. Excitement

sweeps over me as Scourge arrows toward the spot, but it's rapidly replaced by foreboding. There's an ominous red-black stain in the dust around the dragon.

Scourge circles to land. The ground rushes up to meet us, and for a moment his beating wings conceal the sight of the downed dragon and rider from us. Zabriel holds me tight as he swings his leg over the saddle and slides heels first toward the ground, faster than usual when he has me in his arms but still setting me gently on my feet.

"Stay here. Don't look, *sha'len*," he urges in a low voice, moving me closer to Scourge. The enormous black dragon twists his head around, shielding my gaze from the sight of Damla and Tish.

But I have to look. I'm the one who saw them in a vision, and I feel like I owe it to the rider and her dragon to see for myself what's become of them. I place my hand against Scourge's side and move along his body until I see Zabriel crouched by the coral dragon's forelegs. There's an enormous gash in the dragon's breastbone that's several feet long. A woman is lying beneath Damla, her lower body crushed beneath the dragon's forelegs. Blood has trickled from her nose and staring eyes.

A sickly, metallic scent washes over me in a wave. They're dead. They're both dead.

My stomach churns. Spots rush upward over my vision, and a cold sweat breaks over my body. I stagger to Scourge's other side, just making it around his forelegs before I lose the contents of my stomach all over the ground. I heave again and again, holding on to Scourge's harness as my body feels like it's trying to turn itself inside out. Tears swim in my eyes and trickle over my cheeks.

There's a beating of wings, and a moment later, I hear the muted thump of something heavy hitting the ground. I scrub my sleeve over my mouth and eyes. When I look up, I expect to see Captain Ashton or one of my bodyguards, but instead, I gaze into a pair of beautiful turquoise eyes, flecked with gold.

"Esmeral," I say, my voice husky with tears and coughing. "What are you doing here?"

The dragon trills, sounding concerned, and patters across the dust toward me. Gently, she pushes her head into my hand. A strange feeling passes from her into me, but I'm too overwhelmed to focus on it.

I feel hands on my back, and Zabriel draws me into his arms and reaches for my mouth. I realize he means to wipe my lips. "No, don't—"

But I'm too late, and his thumb smooths over my lips. There's a pained, sympathetic expression on his handsome features. "Not take care of my mate? Don't be foolish, *sha'len*. Hold still and let me dry your eyes."

With a corner of his cloak, Zabriel gently wipes the tears from my cheeks. He should be focusing on the dead dragon and rider, but instead, he has to waste his time with a woman who throws up because she can't ride a dragon or stand the smell of blood.

"I'm sorry I'm so weak."

"You're not. Never think that." Zabriel dabs my cheeks with his cloak. "Can I make you feel better with my scent? I can't bear that you're so unwell."

I swallow, and my stomach feels like it might revolt again, but I don't trust how loopy I become when he does that for me. "You don't need to do that. I'm not sure how I feel about it."

"All right. I won't, but let me hold you until you feel better." He scoops me up in his arms and cradles my face to his neck, holding me easily against his chest. His strength and body are soothing, but I can't smell anything. I wonder what my Alpha's scent is like.

Zabriel is already so alluring. If I start to smell his scent the way he can smell mine, I'm in danger of becoming addicted to this man. I wrap my arms around him and burrow my face into his throat, trying to focus on taking slow and steady breaths.

A few minutes later, Zabriel places me gently on my feet and straightens up, cupping my face with his large hands. "Are you feeling better?"

I reach up and touch his wrists. "I am, thank you. Can you tell me what happened to Damla and Tish?"

His lips press into a grim line. "Something made Damla fall out of the sky, but I can't tell what. Just as concerning is the fact that her *riesta* is missing."

"What a *riesta*?"

"A soul core. Every dragon has one deep within their chests. It's where a dragon makes its fire, but it's also what gives a dragon their scent, designation, and the ability to bond with Maledinni. Everything that makes a dragon strong, powerful, and unique is contained in that core. If a soul had physical form, it would be a *riesta*."

Someone went to the trouble of cutting a dragon open and stealing a powerful organ? That seems ominous. I move back around Scourge, but Zabriel squeezes my hand.

"You can stay here with Esmeral. Let her comfort you. You don't have to look."

Esmeral moves close to my other side, flanking me. His offer is tempting, but I've never closed my eyes to life's horrors, and I'm not going to start now. "I'm fine now. I'd like to see."

When we move around Scourge, I see that Captain Ashton and my bodyguards have arrived on their wyverns and are gazing solemnly at the downed dragon and rider. Nilak is a little way off, as still as stone with her head bowed, and a silvery dragon stands beside her. Stesha is crouched down by the gaping wound in Damla's chest. A female dragonrider has Tish's head in her lap and she's weeping. A lump rises in my throat at the sight of her despair. I wish this war would be over already.

"Will we take them back to Lenhale for a funeral?" I ask Zabriel.

He shakes his head. "Riders who go down with their dragons prefer different last rites. Together, as they always were, and will always want to be."

Stesha gets to his feet and moves back, and his eyes are bleak and hollow when they meet Zabriel's.

Crying softly, the female rider kisses Tish's brow and arranges the woman's arms so that she holds her sword in her hands, and then she draws back to stand with the wingrunners.

After a few moments of stillness and silence, the deep rose of dusk begins to fade into night, and one by one, stars appear in the empty sky.

The dragons move to surround Damla and Tish. Scourge on one side. Nilak and the silver dragon on the other. There's a flash of turquoise and gold, and I realize that Esmeral has moved up beside Scourge.

Zabriel reaches out to hold my hand. His expression is bleak as he gazes at the rider and dragon who died for Maledin. Who died for him. What a heavy weight the crown must be in moments like this.

There's a muted rumbling sound, and I feel heat coming off the dragons. They open their jaws, and fire bursts forth, bathing Tish and Damla. Scourge's stream of fire is the thickest, and Esmeral's is tiny in comparison, but the four of them work together until dragon and rider are fiercely ablaze. The dragonfire eats through flesh at a rapid pace and burns white-hot.

"Forever flying," Zabriel murmurs, and I hear the words echoed by Stesha, Ashton, and the female dragonrider.

I must be squeezing Zabriel's hand as he leans down and murmurs, "Does the fire make you afraid, *sha'len*?"

I shake my head. I'm a little nervous, but I don't feel panicked as I know no one here wishes to toss me into the flames.

A short time later, the two figures are no longer recognizable as what they once were. A little while after that, all that remains of Tish and Damla is a heap of glowing embers. All the dragons line up on one side and begin to beat their wings, sending the embers and ash high where they're snatched on the wind and fill the sky with golden points of light. It's a simple ceremony, and I'm touched by the beauty of these final rites. Damla and Tish are now ash on the wind, forever flying.

Zabriel squeezes my hand. "We should go back. It's not safe out here in the open."

I follow him to Scourge's side, and he crouches down so I can wrap my arms around his neck. I do, and he pulls me against his body and straightens up until my feet leave the ground.

Our eyes lock. Zabriel doesn't move. Our faces are very close.

"This is the first time you and I have worked together for Maledin, and though the deed is bittersweet, I hope it won't be the last. I'm fiercely grateful that you're by my side. And I'm proud of you, *sha'len*."

I shake my head, feeling a lump in my throat. "I didn't do anything." Anything except throw up and cry.

"I don't think Damla and Tish would agree with you. We were able to give Tish and Damla the farewell that they would have wanted."

"But we were too late to save them. If only—"

Zabriel presses a swift but gentle kiss to my lips. "No *if onlys*, *sha'len*. You did everything that you could with love and courage in your heart, and that's all anyone can expect from a future Queen of Maledin."

A future Queen of Maledin. Terrifying words. Beautiful words. Intimidating words. I don't feel like I'm anywhere near living up to them.

Zabriel climbs up onto Scourge, taking me with him and settling us both into the saddle.

"What do you think it means that her *riesta* was taken?" I ask him.

Scourge spreads his wings and leaps into the air. Esmeral follows a moment later, flying by his side.

Zabriel casts a final dark look at the crumbling, glowing

ashes spiraling away beneath us and shakes his head. "Nothing good."

A FEW DAYS later I'm returning from the city to the castle with Fiala and Dusan when something large and turquoise zooms out of the sky and lands before me on the cobbles. Esmeral's wings brush the houses on either side of the street before she furls them and turns toward me.

I fold my arms and raise an eyebrow. "Well, hello. You've come to see me, have you? Finally torn yourself away from your handsome dragon lover?"

I ran to Zabriel in a panic to defend this dragon from her "bully" and she was doing perfectly fine, thank you very much. In fact, she was snagging the Alpha of the flare for her mate. I'd say she was living her best dragon life.

Esmeral trills and buffets her head against my body, almost knocking me off my feet.

"Yes, I know. You're in dragon love. I'm thrilled for you."

I keep moving through the streets, trying to act like I don't see the huge turquoise and gold creature keeping pace with me. All the while, I'm thinking about the kiss.

That kiss.

The one Zabriel and I shared on the stone bridge to the dragongrounds. He's given me several toe-curling kisses, but that one was the best. We watched the tiny Omega dragon allow the flare's Alpha to bite and dominate her, which made heat and desire coil through my belly. The small, sweet Omega that no one likes or wants is protected and possessed by the fiercest Alpha in the flare. Esmeral has embraced her instincts like I've never dared.

Until that moment, when I raised my lips to Zabriel and silently begged for a kiss. His kisses are as hungry as fire consuming dry tinder, and my body went up in flames.

Alpha knew what I wanted.

Alpha gave me what I was craving.

It's a little alarming that "the voice" I've been hearing which says the silliest, most embarrassing things is starting to sound more and more like my own voice.

There's a tug on my dress, and I look down and see that Esmeral has her teeth clamped on my skirts and she's pulling me toward a side street. "Esmeral, what are you doing? I'm not going that way."

"She wants you to go to the dragongrounds with her," Fiala tells me. "That's the quickest way to walk there."

"Why?"

"Probably so the two of you can go flying." Dusan reaches out and touches Esmeral's scales, but the dragon rounds on him with a snarl and snaps her teeth at him. He leaps back, his nearly bitten fingers clutched to his chest.

Fiala tuts and shakes her head. "You know better than to go touching someone else's dragon."

"I forgot. Lady Isavelle's dragon is so cute," Dusan grumbles, shaking his fingers.

"She's not my dragon," I say, turning to walk along the street in the direction I want to go. "I'm sorry, Esmeral, I can't come."

Esmeral follows hopefully along beside me, but a few minutes later, she slows down until finally, I don't hear her behind us anymore. I turn and glance behind me and see her gazing after me with a bereft, confused expression in those gold and turquoise eyes.

All the strings of my heart are plucked, and every note sounds sad. I turn away and keep walking, but I feel like I've kicked a hatchling.

As we pass along a laneway, I ask my bodyguards, "What's it like to fly on your own dragon or wyvern?"

Dusan smiles mysteriously. "I can't tell you that. You'll have to find out for yourself."

"It's the only thing worth doing if you ask me," Fiala says, and then points to the right. "The western gate is up this way. It's the quickest way back."

I haven't come this way before. The gate opens to a different part of the castle grounds. We pass by the barracks and the training grounds, a large, open space where dozens of soldiers are watching a sparring match.

Two large men are fighting, their swords flashing. My belly squirms with pleasure when I realize the bigger of the two men is Zabriel, and he's training with a man who I suspect is another Alpha I don't recognize. My feet slow to a stop as I watch the king deftly parry a blow that was about to split his head open.

The sunlight glints on his proud cheekbones, and the blade he carries is as sharp as his jawline. Even the way he moves is beautiful. A show of strength, precision, and deadly elegance. Is it just my imagination, or is Zabriel getting even better-looking? I absentmindedly rub the back of my neck, which is suddenly aching.

Alpha is the most talented swordsman in Maledin. Such a big, thick sword.

My cheeks burn red. Oh, shut up. Stupid voice. The breathy, needy voice that sounds exactly like my own.

The sparring grows more intense. Zabriel's partner swings his blade in a vicious arc and slices open his shirt. I breathe in sharply in panic, but the sword hasn't cut into Zabriel's flesh. While his partner is overbalanced, Zabriel brings his sword down and stops just short of the other man's wrist.

"Disarmed," he announces.

They both relax and step back. With one hand, Zabriel rips his torn shirt off and casts it aside. Sunlight glints on his sweaty muscles, and his chest rises and falls with his heavy breathing. Silky black hair adorns his broad shoulders. Thick, hard lines on either side of his hips arrow down into his pants, and my eyes swan dive with them. Tight pants. I think I see the outline of something swollen inside them. Unwittingly, my teeth sink into my lower lip.

Zabriel looks up and sees me.

And smirks.

He twirls the practice sword with a flourish and sinks into a bow. "Lady Isavelle. What a pleasure it is to have you observe me today." His smirk tells me he caught me staring at his knot.

Stars above, he's so smug.

Every soldier on the training grounds follows his lead and bows. Flustered, I glance this way and that, wondering if I'm supposed to curtsey to all these men in return.

Fiala whispers behind me, "Do nothing, my lady. Chin up and look proud."

I straighten up a little and try to look like I know what I'm doing. After they've bowed to me, the soldiers go back to whatever they were doing, and Zabriel places his sword on a rack and saunters toward me.

"What brings you this way, *sha'len*? Were you looking for me?" Zabriel asks when he's standing in front of me. I barely notice that he's half naked.

I want to lick Alpha's chest.

I can think whole thoughts in my head about many complex things.

Does Alpha think I look pretty today?

"There's such a lovely color in your cheeks, *sha'len*," Zabriel murmurs. "Did you eat well today? I hope you've been drinking enough silkmallow tea and winterberry juice."

I feel rather than see Fiala and Dusan draw back to give Zabriel and me some privacy.

"I'm fine, thank you. Why are you asking about tea?"

Zabriel often shows concern that I'm eating enough, but he's never asked if I'm drinking enough before.

He smiles wolfishly at me. "Omegas sometimes get thirsty."

I realize what he's implying. That I slicked myself while watching him win a sparring match. I rub the back of my neck and squint at the sky. "Is it hot today? Everything feels itchy. Even my clothes are annoying me." I tug at my neckline and flex my neck to one side.

Zabriel toys with one of his sharp teeth with his tongue, his red gaze fixed on my throat. It's the look he gets when he's thinking about kissing me.

"Don't look at me like that when I'm feeling so wretched."

"I'm sorry, *sha'len*. Your mate can't help but hunger for you when your scent is so fragrant. Is your neck aching?"

"Yes. Everything aches, actually."

He smiles at me. "My little Omega's first false heat is nearly here. How wonderful."

I stare at him in shock. Panic makes my stomach spasm. "Are you sure? Maybe I'm just getting sick."

Zabriel touches my cheeks, his eyes softened with sympathy. "It's nothing to be afraid of. There will be discomfort and strange feelings. Your body will feel a little out of your control for a while, but I'll protect you throughout."

"Out of control? You mean there's more to this than the silly thoughts I've been having about you?"

He laughs darkly. "What silly thoughts have you had about me?"

"Um. Nothing."

He raises a skeptical brow.

I roll my eyes, a smile tugging at my lips. "What a big sword he's got. He seems to know how to use it."

A devilish smile spreads over his face. "Are you curious about my sword? You only have to ask if you want to find out."

"You can keep your sword to yourself, thank you."

Zabriel growls softly, his eyes lighting up. Men can't do that. It must be a Maledinni thing, or an Alpha thing. I have the urge to bite one of his fingers so he bites me back harder.

I gasp in shock. "Oh, stars, we're doing what Scourge and Esmeral were doing. Fighting and flirting."

Zabriel slips a finger into my neckline, dragging me closer to him. Lowering his head to mine, he whispers, "If my sweet little Omega wants to provoke her Alpha into pushing her to the ground and getting his teeth into her neck, that's more than fine with me. I'll show you I'm your Alpha any time you need it."

Heat erupts through my body. There's a surge of wetness between my thighs, and I have to swallow a whimper. Is that what I'm doing, provoking Zabriel into dominating me?

Zabriel's eyelids grow heavy as he inhales. "Fuck, your scent. Your false heat is going to happen any day now. Any hour. As soon as it happens, send Fiala or Dusan to come find me, all right?"

His eyes are on my lips, but he glances around us and seems to remember that this courtyard is full of his men. "I want to kiss you, but there are Alphas here, and they don't get to see what my Omega looks like with my teeth in her bottom lip. Let me help you with your aching neck."

Zabriel pulls me into his arms and presses my face into the crook of his arm. He slides his hand into my hair at the nape of my neck and grips it in his fist. The slow, strong pull on my hair feels so intense and delicious that I moan. The aching subsides. The relief is intense.

"Shh..." Zabriel murmurs softly, his lips against my temple. "Not so loud that anyone but me can hear you. Good girl."

My arms clench his muscular waist. I nearly moan louder at the *good girl.*

Slowly, Zabriel lets me go and steps back, smoothing my hair from my face and kissing my brow. "Anything you need, come find me. No matter how crazy it seems to you." To Fiala and Dusan, he calls, "Take my mate to her room to rest, or to the Flame Temple and ask one of the mothers to tend to her and keep a closer eye than usual on her."

"Yes, *Ma'len.*"

"Of course, *Ma'len.*"

Zabriel gives me a last, lingering look, and then turns and goes back to his men.

I miss him like a physical ache.

I'm barely aware of my surroundings as Fiala and Dusan lead me through the castle, but I realize where I am when we pass the corridor leading to my room. "Leave me here. I'll be fine, thank you."

Fiala and Dusan insist on seeing me to my door, and I enter and close it behind me. Is my designation truly emerging now, and so soon? I certainly feel different today. I'm snappier, hungrier, my breasts are more tender than usual, and there's an ache between my legs. An ache that begs, touch me, don't touch me, hold me, leave me alone. I feel like I'm being pulled in so many different directions. This feels like the dragon version of getting your moon cycle. The cramps are probably going to be vicious when they arrive. Everything to do with dragons has teeth.

I go to the trunk to find something more comfortable to wear, and I hear a soft clinking at the bottom. Drawing out the object, I see the bottle of oil that the Temple Crone gave me that will enhance Zabriel's scent, and the one from Biddy Hawthorne that will conceal my own.

Use this if you ever wish to hide from him.

That gives me an idea. I think I will go to the Flame Temple after all.

The warmth and peace of the Flame Temple soothe me as I stand before the ceremonial fire. I notice something new today, a table spread with long strands of dried plant material.

One of the Temple Maidens sees me looking at it and explains, "This is fire grass. People come and knot the grass into shapes to be burned slowly in the Temple Flame in remembrance of someone they've lost."

When I glance into the crucible, I see that there are hundreds of knots inside, all different, and all enduring in the flames far longer than grass should.

"Are these for Tish and Damla?" I ask, and she nods. "May I make one?"

The Temple Maidens smiles and shows me how to twist, loop, and fold the strands into a simple shape. I make the next one by myself. Holding the offerings in my hands, I gaze into the flames for a while. I've never had strong ideas about gods and the afterlife. Sometimes I envied the other Veiled Virgins who were able to take the Brethren's teachings to heart and were so certain that there was only one God and one correct way to live.

I open my hands and gaze at the fire grass knots. I don't know what I'm doing, and I'm not certain about anything, but I hope that Tish and Damla didn't suffer at the end of their lives. I hope my family isn't suffering wherever they are, and they somehow know that I'm thinking about them. Wishing for them. Needing them to come home.

It's with these small but very dear hopes I cast the fire grass into the flames and watch them burst into fiery knots of light.

When I turn away from the fire, I see the Temple Crone standing behind me at a polite distance. Her eyes are on the flames, but I have the impression that she's been waiting for me.

I approach her and bow my head. "Grandmother."

The old woman regards me with shrewd eyes and then speaks without preamble. "*Ma'len* told me you are having visions. We've never had a dragonrider who is also a witch. I checked the records."

I've seen enough charred corpses tied to the stake in Gunster on market day that the word *witch* feels like an accusation. "Am I going to be jailed and executed for knowing that Tish and Damla were attacked?"

"Witches were outlawed by the Brethren, but they are welcome and protected under a Maledinni king and always have been. They were rare in Old Maledin because, in those times, humans living among us were rare. Witches are born from one Maledinni parent and one human parent. There are many more humans in Maledin now, so I suspect we will see a great deal more witches in the years to come."

The Temple Crone glances at the Temple Flame where I stood just moments ago.

"You feel regret." It's a statement, not a question.

"My vision came too late to help Tish and Damla. I can't help but wish I never saw it instead of seeing it and being unable to prevent their deaths."

"Perhaps you saw for a reason other than to save."

I pick at my sleeve but say nothing. If I'm a witch then I'm far less useful than Biddy Hawthorne, who can find lost sheep and heal the sick. I'd rather not be a witch at all than be tortured with terrible things I can do nothing to prevent.

"Maybe I'm just not strong enough yet. Can you teach me how to use my visions so they're actually useful?"

The Temple Crone shakes her head. "The *Hratha'len* practice dragon magic, which is nothing like witchcraft. You will need a witch to train you, though that may be difficult considering how many killed by the Brethren."

"I know a witch and where to find her. She gave me this,

actually." I fish the small glass vial from my skirts and hold it out to the Temple Crone. "I was on the run and she told me it's useful for hiding, but now I wonder if it might have other purposes."

The old woman holds the bottle up to the light, and then uncorks it and takes a sniff. "She is a canny witch to know about such things. This will conceal one mate's scent from the other. It is sometimes used if a couple wishes to delay a heat or a rut."

"So it is scent that causes these things? I can't even smell Zabriel's scent, yet my body is changing."

"That's correct. Your mate's scent is bringing on your first false heat, even though you're not aware that you're smelling him."

I gaze at the bottle in my hand. "If I put this on Zabriel, will that prevent my designation from emerging?"

The Temple Crone gives me a long, searching look, and I have the sense that she's disappointed by my question. "May I answer a question that you didn't ask?" I nod, and she says, "It is him you fear, or yourself?"

I think about that. "I haven't had much say in my own life in some time, and it has been powerful men who've made me suffer the most. I suppose it's both. If I could just have a little more time," I ask desperately. "Once this happens, I'm afraid there will be no going back."

The crone's expression fills with sympathy. "My dear Lady Isavelle. Once the dragons woke beneath the mountains, there was no going back, not for you or any other Maledinni in the country. An oil will not change who you are or your bond with your mate, a bond that is a privilege that so many of our kind hope for."

I think about Stesha, so cold and cantankerous because he's been denied a mate he feels he deserves, but I can't be thankful for what I have merely because others want it.

Temple Crone's expression softens and suddenly she doesn't look as imperious as the High Priest, or as severe as Biddy Hawthorne. In her eyes, I see a flash of my own mother, and I miss her so much that it makes my heart ache.

"I know you are brave, Lady Isavelle. The moment you knew Tish and Damla were in trouble, you wished to fly and save them with no concern for your own safety. It's natural to feel afraid of change, especially when it is out of our hands. Your mate will support you in the coming weeks and months. The temple will welcome you day and night. You are not alone in this, Lady Isavelle. No one in Maledin is, and when the other Omegas emerge in the days and weeks to come, they will look to you to inspire their own bravery."

The old woman places the bottle back into my hands and closes my fingers around them. "Use this as you see fit. These oils are tools, and they can help you in the short term, but they will not change who or what you are. The dragons have returned to Maledin, and all with Maledinni blood are connected with them, and our blood sings with theirs."

I slip the glass bottles back into my pocket and thank the Temple Crone for her time.

I had hoped to put these changes off, maybe forever, but apparently, there's nothing I can do about what's happening to me without sealing every dragon beneath the Bodan Mountains once more, and this time forever.

TWO DAYS LATER, I'm out by the stables when a shivery feeling comes over me. I rub my arms and gaze at the sky, wondering if the wind has suddenly turned colder or if I'm coming down with something. I really hope I'm not getting sick when there's so much work to do. The Temple Mothers ride out of the city to meditate at the convergence of ley lines and other sacred, secret places, and study the barrier. Afterward, their horses need tending to, and that's what I do. It's not much, but it's something to help their important work.

I've tried meditating and tapping into my own magic, but the problem is, I'm not sure what it is or how to access it. I don't understand what a witch is and what she does. All I know is my mind showed me Tish and Damla's death and that inexplicable vision or visitation with Zabriel. Only he wasn't the Zabriel that I know.

It's all so confusing and frustrating. I gaze at the sky, wondering if it's about to start snowing. The clouds gathering are dark and ominous, and the back of my neck prickles and aches. If I were a mouse, I'd assume that a bird of prey was hovering overhead, ready to snatch me up and rip me to pieces for its dinner.

Get inside.

I frown at the sound of my own voice commanding me. Fiala and Dusan are in the stables, and if I go anywhere else, they'll worry. Besides, why should I go inside when a little rain won't—

Inside, inside, inside.

I glance through the open door into the darkened outbuilding, and nothing has ever looked so inviting or important. I dash inside, and inside feels better. Inside feels *safe*, though I'm still racked with cold and start to shiver. I climb the ladder into the loft and dive into the loose hay, desperate to warm up.

My shivers slowly subside, and I grow warmer. I wish there were more weight on me. I fantasize about someone dumping a whole cartful of hay on top me so that my whole world is safe, cozy, and dark.

"Isavelle?" A soft, deep voice.

"Mm?" I reply without opening my eyes. Unless this person is going to drop a load of hay on top of me, I don't want to be disturbed.

I hear the soft crunch of footsteps approaching, and then a large pair of hands feel around for me, uncovering me as he goes.

"No," I moan, trying to scoop the hay back on top of me. "Cover me up. I don't like it."

"I know, *sha'len*. I know. But it's too cold for you here. Put your arms around my neck, and I'll cover you with my cloak. I'm going to carry you down the ladder."

Zabriel lifts me up and holds me securely against him with one arm, wrapping his cloak carefully around me. It's like he understands that the light of day is horrible, and I need to be held very, very tightly.

He carries me out of the hay loft, and as we emerge into the courtyard, the daylight hurts my eyes, even with my head covered.

"Put me back. I like it in the dark," I moan.

"It's all right. Just hold on to me." Zabriel cups the back of my head and tucks me beneath his chin. "Your bedroom has a fire and your bed has curtains around it. And lots of blankets. You'll be a lot more comfortable there."

That does sound enticing. I mumble into his neck, "How did you find me?"

"Fiala and Dusan couldn't find you all of a sudden, so they came and got me, and I followed your scent."

"My poor bodyguards. Don't punish them," I whimper.

Zabriel laughs softly. "For this? Lucky for them they're off the hook for things my naughty Omega does."

Shivers rack my body. I should have gone to my bedroom myself instead of interrupting the King of Maledin from his duties. "I'm sorry. There are more important things you should be doing than putting me to bed when I'm sick."

"No, there are not," he assures me and brushes his lips over my temple. "And you're not sick."

I feel him open a door, and a moment later he puts me down on my bed. Kneeling, he pulls my shoes from my feet, puts my legs up on the mattress, and covers me with blankets. Then he moves around the room, covering the window, stoking the fire and adding wood, then pouring a cup of water to place by my bedside.

"I can't go to bed in the middle of the day. I've got things to do," I protest, but instead of getting up, I burrow deeper into the blankets and groan in relief as some of my aches and pains are soothed. My breasts, my neck, and even between my legs is throbbing.

I feel him spread a blanket over me, then another, and another. Soon there's a delightful weight on my body and my flesh feels hot, but wonderfully so. I'm not sweating. In fact, I could do with more warmth. More layers. More blankets.

I worm a finger out of the blankets and pull a corner down and peep out. Zabriel is gazing down at me with a smile on his lips. My tall, strong, handsome Alpha. As he watches on, I stretch my legs and point my toes while arching my back, and he smiles wider.

Alpha loves seeing me cozy and safe.

For once I don't have the inclination to tell that voice to shut up. Zabriel *does* love it. He thinks I'm adorable. That voice is so right.

"Do you need more blankets, *sha'len*?" he asks, and I moan as his deep voice ripples through me.

"Yes. All of them. Do you have more?"

"Of course." One by one, Zabriel drapes more blankets over me and tucks them in around me.

Bliss. Pure bliss.

When he's finished, Zabriel sinks his teeth into his lower lip and makes an appreciative noise in the back of his throat. When he realizes I'm watching him, he smiles. His tongue plays with the sharp tooth at the corner of his mouth, and his voice is heavy with lust as he murmurs, "Beautiful, my sweet Omega."

My core blazes in response to his praise and calling me Omega. I rub my cheek against the blankets and then pull some of them between my legs so I can clench my thighs around them. "Why are you smiling?"

Zabriel is adrift in his thoughts, and it takes him a moment to answer me. "Hm? Oh, nothing. I'm pleased you're comfortable. Can I..." He hesitates and then shakes his head. With a smile bordering on suggestive, he closes the curtains around me. Another log falls into the fire, and then the door closes behind him.

I'll get up and continue my work for the Temple Mothers.

Soon.

A moment later, I fall back into a doze.

Some unknown amount of time later, I awake to a deep voice murmuring in the dark, "Do you want more blankets, *sha'len*."

"Please," I moan, dragging myself up to sit. More blankets. More weight. More heat. More cozy darkness.

When I gaze around with blurry eyes, I see that my bed is already piled high with a ridiculous number of blankets. I stroke them like they're sleeping cats, pleased with each and every one of them. But I still want more.

Why, though?

I watch Zabriel as he spreads a burgundy wool blanket across my feet. My mind feels sluggish and uncooperative, and all it can tell me is something about this is strange, but it refuses to come up with a reason why.

I tuck the blankets around me, forming them into pleasing shapes that I can cuddle my body around. Zabriel watches me fuss and fiddle with a hungry look in his eyes.

My hands stop moving. "Why are you looking at me like that?"

"No reason, little Omega." He rubs the back of his neck as he watches me and takes a ragged breath.

Alpha is pleased I'm cozy and warm.

The silly, breathy voice has commandeered my mind, but I can hear a more sensible voice muttering, *No reason? What a pile of wyvern shit. Something fishy is going on here.*

I glance down at the bed and back up at him. I'm fully clothed within a mountain of wool. This doesn't seem suggestive to me, but maybe there's something I'm not grasping. "Is there something sexy about blankets?"

He runs his tongue over his teeth and grasps one of the bed posts. "I don't know. Maybe. How do you feel?"

"Cozy. Comfortable."

"Mm. Lovely." His gaze is unfocused as he watches me, his head on one side. "Anything else?"

"Warm. Safe."

He groans a little and curses in Maledinni under his breath. "Do you want me to...come in there with you?"

"Why? Are you cold too?"

He smiles at me. "I'm fine, Omega. I thought you might like some company."

Zabriel's pupils are blown and there's the same hungry look in his eyes as when he realized my slick was all over him. Come to think of it, there's slick on my thighs now. "Wait. Is this a sex thing?"

"That depends on you. I was thinking I could find the places that are aching on your body and rub them for you. I'm always happy to touch you, *sha'len*." A heated smile slides across his face.

"There's something you're not telling me. Why am I doing this? I was suddenly overcome with the urge to hide in a hayloft, and now I'm obsessing over blankets. This isn't normal."

Zabriel steps forward and cups my chin in his large hand. For once, my skin is hotter than his. He always burns so hot, but now it's like there's a fire inside me. "Your cheeks are pink, Omega. Your eyes are dilated. There's sweat on your brow. You look so beautiful."

"Zabriel, please answer my question," I whimper. I want to tear myself away from his touch, but I'm so deliriously happy he called me Omega that I'm chanting nonsense inside my head.

Zabriel's hand drifts down my throat until he gently squeezes either side, and I moan in pleasure.

"Mm. Good girl." The man looming over me looks as flushed as I feel. "This is your false heat, Omega. Your scent is drenching the castle. It's fucking wonderful. My heart soared when I smelled how sweet your scent's become."

His thumb passes over my sensitized lips, and I take a shuddering gasp. "Why am I under all these blankets?"

Zabriel leans down and his lips ghost over mine. "Because you're nesting. You crave to build a cozy, safe place for Alpha to fuck you in. Knot you in. Breed you in. For days and days, until we're both covered in your slick and my cum. This nest keeps you safe from the outside world, and so will I." He kisses me hungrily, with teeth and tongue.

I suck in a breath at his crude, heavenly words.

"But that's months and months away," he continues. "This is just a prelude. Would you like me to come into your nest? You can have my kisses. You can have my tongue. Wherever you're aching, let me lick it better. Seeing you like this is driving me insane, and your slick smells *delicious*." There's a hungry growl on that last word and it emanates deep within his chest.

I see the dragon in his eyes, blazing red.

"Is this...sexy to you?" I ask, gazing around at all the blankets.

"It's so fucking sexy I could make a mess in my breeches just looking at you, Omega," he breathes.

Oh, my stars. So this nesting thing is the Omega equivalent of wearing a low-cut bodice or parading around in just my shift, and I'm doing it right in front of Zabriel? A vision of the High Priest rises in my mind.

Whores who invite the eyes of men are a taint upon this land.

Rip her dress open. I want to see the cuts all over her back.

More. She should remember this forever. How else will she learn?

I make a strangled noise in the back of my throat and start to push the blankets off the bed.

"Isavelle, what are you doing?"

"I'm not nesting. I was confused. Thank you for taking care of me, but you can go."

"Wait, please, it's not just a sex thing, you really do just need to be coz—"

I pull one blanket over myself, wrench the bed curtains closed so that Zabriel can't see me, and shove my head under a pillow. This isn't my false heat. I'm not ready.

I'm not ready.

I'm not *ready*.

Immediately I start to shiver, and I clench my teeth together so they don't chatter.

"Isavelle," Zabriel says pleadingly. "False heats are exhausting for an Omega. Your body knows what you need, and fighting those instincts will only make you feel worse."

My instincts tell me I want Alpha in my nest to do all those dangerous, delicious things he promised. I want his big, strong hands to rub everywhere that aches. If I'm so, so good maybe he'll use his tongue to...maybe he'll...

My Omega wails in frustration because she wants this so much.

"Isavelle, please let me help you," Zabriel says. His voice is muffled like he has his face pressed against the curtains. "It hurts so much hearing you in distress."

He must have heard me wail. I didn't know I did that out loud.

"It's not a false heat. I'm not mad at you. You're so sweet to me, and I don't deserve it." I know I'm babbling and he doesn't believe me, but I don't know what else to do.

"At least let me put all these blankets back on the bed."

"I said I don't need them. If you don't stop, I'll...I'll..." I'll what, burst into tears? I'm on the verge of dissolving into a sobbing mess. My emotions are tossing me like a ship in a storm.

"Please don't make yourself upset. I'll go."

A moment later, I hear footsteps receding and the door close.

Zabriel's voice calls through the wood, "I'm out here now, and I'm so sorry you're hurting. You're going to feel better soon, my sweet Omega. You're lovely and your Alpha adores you."

I don't feel adorable. I feel stupid and out of control. I destroyed my nest and sent Zabriel away thinking it would make me feel better, but I feel worse. Tears leak from my eyes, and I stare at the bed curtains in the darkness.

"I'm so sorry. I can never get any of this right," I cry, before stuffing a blanket into my mouth so he doesn't hear me sob.

"You're doing wonderfully, little dragon. You've done nothing wrong. Alpha's not upset with you. Alpha only wants you to feel safe."

Zabriel goes on murmuring reassurances through the wood.

"Are you comforting me with your voice?" I sniffle, dragging the blanket up to my neck and hugging it.

"If this is all you'll let me do for you, then this is what

your Alpha will do. I'm right here, Omega. You're safe in your bed and no one will hurt you."

The tears keep falling.

I can't stop shivering.

Being an Omega is completely humiliating.

22

Zabriel

I sit with my back propped against Isavelle's closed bedroom door all night. She falls in and out of dozes, sobbing quietly and tossing and turning as she desperately seeks comfort and rest. Every time I picture her shivering with her nest destroyed and pushed onto the floor, I want to crack my skull against stone.

I'm such a fucking idiot.

Showing her that it turned me on to see her like that was a selfish mistake. She was perfectly happy dozing away beneath two dozen blankets before I made it about me. What I should have done was quietly watch over her for a day and a night, then given her a cold drink of water and told her that she was such a brave, good Omega for enduring her first false heat and making a lovely nest. The first Omega in New Maledin, and she has me to rely on, but what an idiot I am.

Just before dawn, Isavelle's room falls silent, and I pray to any of the gods that might be listening that she's fallen asleep at last. My chest aches with the need to go in there and make sure she's at least warm enough not to make herself sick, but if she wakes up and sees me looming over her, she'll become distressed all over again. I reassure myself that the fire is burning in her room. The tapestries and curtains are pulled tight against any drafts. She'll be all right for a few hours.

Meanwhile, I think someone else might need some attention. I get stiffly to my feet, smothering a groan, and head for the dragongrounds with a dismal feeling that I know what I'm going to find there.

I can tell something's up before I cross the stone bridge. The Betas are all restless and milling around, trying to see what's happening at the center of the flare. I push my way through them and see Scourge trying to get his massive head beneath an overhang. From the shadows, there's a sad trill, then an indignant snarl. Something moves around in the shadows and then flops to the ground. A moment later, it's up again, and there's a flash of talons and an angry squeal, and Scourge flinches backward with a surprised grunt.

I pat his flank and duck down beneath the overhang and see Esmeral, panting, angry, and restless, squashed back against the rocks. She's coping with her first false heat about as well as her reluctant rider.

"Esmeral, I'm coming in there. Please be a good Omega and don't rip me apart."

I crawl under the overhang with her. Sitting with my back to the wall, I touch the spines on the back of her neck and gently coax her closer. She resists for a moment, snaps at me, then flops down dramatically so her head is in my lap and she's gazing up at me with anguish-filled eyes.

"I know," I murmur, stroking her snout. "You feel sore, angry, confused, and lonely. Isavelle's not doing much better, but she's finally fallen asleep. You'll feel better if you try and do the same."

Gradually, the dragon's breathing slows down. Scourge lays down protectively around the overhang, blocking out the sunlight and the cold wind so his Omega feels safe. There are caves nearby where the Omega dragons shelter during their heats with their Alphas, but Esmeral irritates Nilak so the white dragon has probably neglected to show her where they are. Dragons can be just as petty as people.

I pull Esmeral higher on my lap and cradle her head. If I can't hold my mate then at least I can hold her dragon.

This is what I should have offered Isavelle, to hold her through her first false heat, nothing more. The second one we could have tried kissing. Maybe a little touching. The third, licking her. Pushing my fingers inside her. Making her come a lot. Maybe, *maybe*, carefully penetrating her with a few inches of my cock if she really trusted me. Nothing deeper than that because fucking her properly, knot and all, is out of the question until she's had her first true heat. I could actually hurt her and then I'd have no choice but to cut my own heart out and beg for her forgiveness with my dying breaths. I could give my Omega my cock if she asked for it, but she won't because she doesn't trust me enough to let me hold her, let alone fuck her through her false heats.

Esmeral grows heavier and heavier on my thighs until her eyes close and she falls asleep. I can feel that Scourge is dozing too, relieved that his mate has found some peace at last.

I'm the only one who isn't asleep, and I sit there for hour upon hour, tormented by regret and misery.

THERE'S A CRY OF SURPRISE, and I look up from Esmeral and into a pair of beautiful green eyes. Isavelle is crouched down by the overhang, a pouch in one hand, soggy with blood.

Isavelle looks disheveled and pale, and she gazes worriedly at the turquoise dragon. "I brought Esmeral some chicken necks because I had the feeling that she might be upset as well. Is she all right?"

I lean forward and reach for her, but I'm held back by Esmeral, still fast asleep in my lap. "She's doing better now. Scourge and I have been watching over her."

Isavelle's eyes fill with tears. She gazes at the small, exhausted dragon with her head in my lap and then back to me. "Poor Esmeral. I'm so grateful that you..." Isavelle's face collapses and she starts to cry.

My heart feels like it's being sliced open. My Omega is crying and I can't reach her. "*Sha'len*, I'm so sorry about last night. I took things too far."

Isavelle shakes her head and brushes tears from her cheeks. "No, I'm sorry I panicked and threw you out. You must be so disappointed in the mate you waited so long for. I don't know what I'm doing."

Her shoulders are shaking and her cheeks are glistening.

I hold out my hand to her. "Please come here. There's

room on my lap for both of you. I need to comfort you or I'll lose my mind."

Hiccupping, Isavelle crawls beneath the overhang and into my lap, collapsing against my chest. My arms come around her, and I pull her into my lap one-handed and cradle her on my chest. My other hand is on Esmeral's head, and I comfort both Omegas at once.

Isavelle digs her fingers into my shirt and buries her face in my chest as she sobs.

"I've got you, *sha'len*. I've got you," I whisper into her hair, rocking her back and forth.

Finally, her sobs quieten, but she doesn't lift her head. In a voice thick with tears and misery, she asks, "It's really happening to me, isn't it? Becoming an Omega. I was in denial about it instead of listening to you and the Temple Crone. I'm so sorry."

I kiss the top of her head. "You have nothing to be sorry about. I'm the one who's sorry. I made it about me and what I wanted instead of comforting you."

Maybe she wouldn't find me so intimidating if our designations were emerging at the same time, but then it would be both of us out of control, not just one of us. "I'll never do anything to frighten or hurt you. I swear it."

Isavelle wipes the tears from her cheeks and takes a steadying breath. "Sometimes you look so much like a hungry dragon. What will you actually do when I'm in a heat and you're in a rut?"

"Well, I'll..."

Hold you down, fuck you insanely hard, bite you until I leave permanent scars in your flesh, and then shove my knot so deep inside you that we can't get it out of you again for an hour.

I can't say that to her.

"Dominate you," I say, and then add hastily, "in the most loving way."

Isavelle moistens her lips and holds my gaze. When I trace my finger around the curve of her cheek and stroke her hair back, her eyelashes flutter.

"Why do you want to do that?" she whispers.

"Because it's in my nature to do so, and it's in yours to submit during our heats and ruts. We can take it so, so slowly. Next time, I'll layer more blankets on your nest and then sit outside your door and talk to you. Nothing else."

"Is that dominating me?"

I smile at her. "Yes, in a way. It's protecting you. Caring for you. Those are all in the same family to an Alpha."

"And what do I do?"

"You let me do it for you, which will make me so very happy. If that's what you want."

Isavelle's face relaxes a little, and her body slowly unclenches. "All right. That actually sounds nice—if it's not boring or tedious for you," she asks anxiously.

I press a soft kiss to her brow. "It would mean everything to me. I'm learning what you want and need, and we'll go at your pace."

Isavelle plays with my shirt for a moment. "Do you remember when I was Isavelle the village girl and you were Commander Zabriel, a soldier who rides a dragon?"

I gently take her hand and stroke my thumb over her palm, murmuring, "Do you wish I was just Commander Zabriel, without the crown, without our heats and ruts, and you were Isavelle the village girl?"

Isavelle looks up at me with her lips parted, studying me

closely. "I was remembering that from the moment I saw you, I couldn't take my eyes off you."

I twine my fingers through hers, rest my cheek against the top of her head, and speak softly. "I know I'm asking a lot of a woman to be my queen and rule by my side, but I'm still just Zabriel, a soldier who rides a dragon. That's who I've been since I was fourteen years old, and it's all I'll ever be, crown and golden armor or not."

I feel Isavelle relax a little at my words and her fingers curl around mine. "You always know how to make me feel better, Zabriel."

"I've wished for you every day of my life since I suspected my own designation. I wished more fervently for you even than I wished for my own dragon."

She looks up at me in surprise. "You did? When did your designation emerge?"

"When I was seventeen. I had my first rut and got my knot. You know, the swelling—"

"I remember," she says, blushing red to the roots of her hair.

"Alphas who've had their knot for a year or so but haven't found their Omega usually give up on ever finding one. But I didn't give up. I didn't know she wouldn't be born for another five hundred years, or that my world would have to end for me to meet her."

"Did your designation emerging feel strange and uncomfortable for you?"

I nod, remembering the months when I walked around with blistering rage simmering just beneath the surface. Scourge picked fights with every Alpha in the flare, and I sparred with the other dragonriders or lost my temper over real and perceived slights and fought other Alphas hand to hand. I won just about all the fights, but I could never beat Stesha. The white-haired Alpha always had me eating dust and walking away without a fold of his pristine dragonriding clothes out of place. Stesha was always the most powerful Alpha, though in the last two years of Old Maledin, I settled down and we didn't test each other.

It's tempting to challenge him again now that I'm bigger and stronger and a better fighter, just to prove once and for all that I can beat him, but that would be churlish and immature. We're both strong for the sake of Maledin and we each have our roles.

Yet the Alpha in me still wants to prove to Stesha, once and for all, that I'm at the top. Not him.

"I didn't have my Omega to help me through my first rut, but I would like to help you through your first true heat if you want me to. It's supposed to be very sweet and loving when designations emerge at the same time, but it can still be beautiful when they're out of sync."

Isavelle hesitates, but she's overcome by curiosity. "What do other Alpha and Omega pairs do for each other?"

"Oh, this..." I murmur, running the backs of my fingers across her cheeks and down her throat. "This," I say, gathering her closer with both arms and kissing her temple.

She smiles and twines her fingers through my hair. "Is that all?"

I swallow. Hard. It's definitely not all. "Sex is the quickest way to soothe a heat. But that's not the only way," I say quickly. "You can ask the *Hratha'len* about it if you wish, and they might have some advice for you. Just don't ask another Alpha," I add with a growl.

"Why not?"

I hold Isavelle possessively to my body. "Because if my Omega says the words *sex* and *heat* and *soothe me* to another Alpha, I'll have to pummel him into the dust."

"The only other Alpha I know is Stesha, and I'm not going to ask him anything."

I growl hearing her say his name in connection to her heats. "Don't even go near him when you're burning up with your false heats. Not him, and not any other Alpha. I don't want them breathing your scent."

She opens her eyes wide in surprise. "Are you jealous?"

"Only to the point of insanity." Isavelle's neck is exposed, and I open my jaw and touch my teeth to her skin. Not a bite. A hold.

Isavelle gasps softly. "What are you doing?"

I lick her throat and then hold her again with my teeth. "Driving myself insane. My teeth ache for you, *sha'len*."

Isavelle half turns in my lap and touches my cheek, gazing up at me with concern. "Your teeth are hurting you? I'm so sorry."

Her touch is so sweet that I close my eyes for a moment to enjoy it. "Don't be sorry. The ache means that I have you, so I love the ache."

"All these lines you feed me are so smooth. How many women have they worked on?"

I open my eyes. "The things I'm saying to you? I haven't said anything like this before to anyone."

"Oh, I see. Then women just fall into your bed when you smile at them."

"Into my bed? What are you talking about?"

Isavelle's eyes open wide. "Well, um...the women before me. You've obviously had a lot of experience."

"With women? I've never had any experience. Is it usual for human men to have a lot of lovers? Betas do in our culture, but Alphas tend to obsess over their Omega even when they haven't met them." And for long after they should have given up hoping for one, in some cases.

Isavelle stares at me in astonishment. "You mean you haven't...? But that can't be right. You're so good at, um...all the ways you touch me. Everything you do feels amazing."

The reason for that is because we're meant for each other.

"You're the only girl I've ever..." I brush my thumb over her lips and murmur softly, "kissed."

Isavelle's mouth falls open. "But...but you're a grown man, and you swagger around like you've just left three women dazed and exhausted in your bed."

I burst out laughing. "What does that even look like?"

Isavelle's cheeks turn pink. "You told me to wait in your tent after you stole me from the Brethren. I assumed you were going to try and bed me right away."

"Mm, yes, I hoped I would," I murmur, brushing my lips over hers. "But only because you're my Omega. I don't go around stealing women as a habit. You were the first and only, and I knew who you were right away, remember?"

Isavelle caresses my cheek. "You didn't even know my name."

I turn my head and kiss her fingertips. "When a pair who are fated to be together find each other, all sorts of things can happen before they've even asked each other their names. I might know a few more details about Alphas and Omegas than you do, but I'm running on pure instinct."

"They're good instincts," she says shyly.

"I could say the same about you," I murmur, amused.

"You really never even kissed another woman?" she asks.

I press the tip of my nose against hers and whisper, "I already told you. I was waiting for you, Omega."

"But you're...really lovely at kissing."

A delighted smile spreads over my face. "Thank you. I have imagined kissing you a thousand times, so that's probably why. I'm listening to what my body wants. What your body wants. What feels amazing. It all feels fucking amazing to me."

Isavelle strokes her fingers over my lips, then presses her mouth to mine. Softly, sweetly.

My Omega is kissing me after her terrible night.

I close my eyes and let her control the kiss. She caresses the bow of my lip with her tongue, and then sucks briefly on my lower lip, before pressing a dozen wet kisses all over my mouth.

"What about you?" I ask, opening my eyes.

"I kissed a boy on harvest night two years ago. It wasn't very nice. Our teeth clashed."

My eyes narrow. Beyond the overhang, Scourge growls. "Who? Who kissed you?"

"Why?"

"Because if he's emerging as an Alpha, I will fight him to the death. If he's a Beta or Omega, I will make him beg for mercy. And if he's human, I'll hurl him from my dragon."

"We can't know because I have no idea where he is. He's disappeared along with the rest of my village."

I push a hand through my hair. Of course. Yet another

reason to break through that barrier. I want to look the man in the eyes who dared kiss my Omega.

Esmeral finally wakes up, snout first. Her nostrils are working hard before she's even opened her eyes, and they snap open in delight when she realizes Isavelle is here, and she's brought chicken necks. I watch with a sleepy smile on my face as Isavelle feeds them to her, one by one.

When they're all gone, Esmeral gets to her feet and leaves the overhang. Scourge accosts her immediately, sniffing her all over to reassure himself that she's all right.

I follow Isavelle out from beneath the rock and get to my feet.

My mate turns to me. "Thank you for comforting Esmeral. And...thank you for comforting me."

Isavelle turns to go, but I pull her back against my chest with one arm around her waist and my hand gently cupping her throat. Just a little domination to soothe the wild beast in my heart.

"Can I make a suggestion to my Omega?" I murmur in her ear, and Isavelle nods, hugging my forearm around her waist with both arms. "Go back to your room. Bury yourself beneath a pile of blankets, and find your slick with your fingers. Find where feels best and rub it hard. Keep going and going until you burst all over your fingers, and then cram as many of them inside you as you can. There's nothing dirty or wrong about it. You don't need it, but you have my permission. You can have it as a command if you want."

Isavelle's eyelashes flutter and she breathes in sharply. Her scent erupts around her, fragrant and sweet.

I pestered enough Alphas over the years to tell me what Omegas enjoy. What women enjoy and what gives them relief. I talked to the Temple Mothers. I listened to dirty stories. Hunted down explicit drawings. I was determined to wait for my mate to try these things myself, but I craved to *know*.

"Think of me while you do it because I'll have my length in my fist and sliding myself up and down while thinking of you. Say, *Yes, Alpha*."

"Yes, Alpha," Isavelle moans.

I put my teeth against her throat once more. My dragines drag against her flesh, and I groan with desire. "Good fucking girl. Your Alpha is so pleased with you, Omega. He always is."

I slowly let her go and Isavelle heads off in the direction of the bluff, her gaze heavy lidded.

"Other way, Isavelle," I call, grinning as she abruptly turns around and heads for the castle as if she knew where she was going all along.

When I've watched her cross the stone bridge and enter the castle, I turn and brace my forearm on Scourge's flank and bury my face in my sleeve. My other hand fumbles for my pants and I loosen them, and my hand dives down to grip my aching knot. My dragon's scales are hot against my body, and I can sense him watching Esmeral. Our Omegas are so fucking beautiful. I picture Isavelle in her nest and start to stroke myself up and down. Hidden beneath the blankets and touching herself. Dragging her slick-covered fingers over her clit, and then burying them deep inside her. A few rounds by herself and she'll be aching for me to do it for her with my stronger fingers. Thicker fingers. All the filthy words of praise I can spill into her ear while I rub her pretty clit. Her slick gushing down her thighs. Welling up around my fingers as I sink inside of her. Fuck. *Fuck*.

I think about spreading her open and tasting her slick. A tight little virgin Omega begging for her Alpha's knot, rolling onto her belly, pushing her hips and ass up into the air, and presenting herself to me. Begging me to rut her so hard we break the damn bed.

My balls tighten. Cum races up my cock and gushes in thick, white ribbons on the ground. I clamp my hand around my knot, squeezing as hard as I can, imagining it's Isavelle's pussy that has a death hold on me. Twisting. Gripping. Tugging.

I sink my teeth into my forearm and bite down until I taste blood.

Sweet fucking release.

I push myself back into my pants, do them up, and gaze at my bloodied arm. I've never bitten myself before, even in a rut. I'm going to go into a rut before Isavelle's true heat gets here, I can feel it. Fuck knows how I'm going to cope when it arrives.

23

Isavelle

Years ago, Dad had too many ciders at the May festivities and crawled out of bed to milk the goat complaining that he felt like death warmed up. Ma banged the milking buckets together and said in a ringing voice that he looked little better but it was all his own fault, and the goat wasn't going to milk itself.

I giggled into my sleeve at the time, but as I drag myself out from between the sheets with a pounding head and make my way unsteadily across the floor, I have a newfound sympathy for my father's delicate state that day. It's not a hangover that's drained the vitality from me and left a sour taste coating my dry tongue. Instead, it's a day-and-a-half false heat, but the effects seem about the same.

Water.

I need water.

I lift the ewer and drink straight from the lip and dribble water down my nightgown as I swallow it down. Between all the sweating and slicking and forgetting to eat and drink, I'm parched.

Gasping, I lower the ewer and wipe the back of my hand over my lips. They tingle, making me think of Zabriel. I can feel the ghost of his muscles against my thighs and breasts. The man watched me sweating and whimpering in a nest of blankets, and the memory makes a little flush of heat go through me.

I was so wet for Alpha because I want his knot inside me.

My cheeks color at the sound of that breathy Omega voice, and my core clenches on nothing like it's hoping to feel him there. After talking with Zabriel, I went back to bed and tried to touch myself in the ways he described. It's what Alpha asked of me, but I was told again and again you must never do that, even before I was stolen from my village. The local Brethren priest taught the children of the village all the rules we must obey. Self-gratification is the sign of a weak and senseless person. I don't think I believe that any longer, but it's hard to silence years and years of that accusatory voice in one night.

There's a knock on my door, and I open it to find a Temple Maidens standing there in her red robes with a bright smile on her face.

"The Temple Crone sends her congratulations on your first false heat, my lady. This tea will soothe your body and head if you are feeling sore. There are sachets to keep in your room for next time. Make the tea the moment you feel your false heat coming on. Ask your Alpha to remind you in case you forget. I promise he will be delighted to do so."

She gives me a knowing smile, and I thank her and close the door.

After I drink the tea, to my surprise, I do feel better. My head clears and my body feels lighter. I wash myself, dress in fresh clothes, and head out into the Great Hall in search of something to eat.

All the tables in the Great Hall have been shifted around, and people are bustling to and fro. Zabriel walks in with an enormous log on his shoulder that's almost as big as he is and drops it with a thud onto the stone flags by the fireplace. Brushing off his fingers, he sees me and heads over, a smile spreading over his lips.

"You look beautiful, *sha'len*. I think you must have slept well."

I glance shyly up at him through my lashes. Seeing him among so many people makes me wonder if they can tell I'm devouring him with my eyes.

"Thank you, Zabriel. You look lovely as well." He looks more than lovely. He looks so good I want to drag him down on top of me and beg him to squeeze me tight. "What's happening here?"

"There's a feast tonight."

Once again, I'm surprised by the fact that the king himself hauls things around when he has everyone in the country to do his bidding. He seems to have been hard at work for some time because, despite the chilly temperatures, he's dressed only in a black shirt with the laces loose down the front, and his chest is glowing with sweat. A few tendrils of his hair are clinging to his cheeks. His sleeves are rolled back, revealing his muscular, veiny forearms. There are teeth marks in his arm.

I gasp and grab his wrist. "What happened to you? Are these teeth marks? Who bit you?"

Zabriel shakes his head. "It's nothing."

"But, Zabriel, who—"

"I did it."

I gaze up at him, perplexed. "You bit yourself?"

His tongue grazes his dragines and he glances around, before pulling me through a doorway and into an empty corridor. He shuts the door behind us, traps me with his arms, and smiles. "While you were taking care of yourself, I was taking care of myself. I got a little carried away." He peers at me closely. "You did take care of yourself, didn't you?"

"Um." My face flames.

Zabriel's eyes narrow.

"I tried, I promise," I say in an anguished voice. "It's one of the things we're taught never to do. Doing...*that* means you're dirty and degenerate and will probably die from pox or winter lung because it makes your body weak and corrupted."

Zabriel glares angrily around as if he's searching for something to punch, and then he pulls me into his arms so tightly it's like he's trying to hug the dirty feelings out of me. "I remember now that you did tell me that. I hate those Brethren for filling your head with lies. None of that is true. Touching yourself is normal and healthy, and it's all you had to soothe you when I wasn't with you. For *fuck's* sake."

His fury feels like thunder crashing over my head, and I can't help but flinch. "I'm sorry. Are you angry with me?"

"Not with you, Omega. Never with you," he assures me, stroking my hair. He raises my chin so he can press a kiss to my lips. "I'm sorry for shouting and swearing. I know you did your best."

His affection and honeyed words work magic on me, sending golden warmth spiraling through my body. Everything about him feels more vivid and tastes more delicious today. I wonder if this is how it will be all the time now I've had my first false heat.

Zabriel kisses me again, with more tongue this time, and his dragines drag against my lower lip. I moan and arch into him, and he curses in Maledinni beneath his breath. I have a sudden vision of him sucking on one of my nipples and dragging his teeth over that sensitive flesh, and my knees nearly buckle.

Scooping me against his chest, Zabriel walks me into a room, slams the door behind us, and presses me up against it, all the while still kissing me.

"We're alone," he murmurs huskily. "No one can see you. Try it now."

My eyes open wide. "Try what now?"

He pulls back and gazes at me, eyes red and heavily lidded.

Oh.

"Touch myself?" I squeak. We're alone in this antechamber and Zabriel has his hand resting on the closed door. No one could get in, but it's broad daylight. I can hear people moving around in the Great Hall. And I don't do that.

I *can't* do that.

Zabriel kisses me again, coiling his tongue against mine, and heat and pleasure shoot down to my lower belly. An ache flares to life between my thighs.

Can I?

"I'll close my eyes," Zabriel murmurs between kisses. "No one will see you, not even me. Just let me hold you. Let me listen to you. I promise I won't look or touch. I'll just be here telling you that you're beautiful, and I want you to understand how wonderful your body is."

He closes his eyes and strokes his thumb over my cheek. I glance down at myself. My body is wonderful? I've always thought of my body as adequate. Useful. Just fine, thank you. I can run up a hill, milk a goat, and climb a tree. Zabriel makes it sound like feeling good is something I deserve. No one's ever said that to me before.

I lick my lips. "Are you sure I can? It's not even my false heat anymore."

A smile hooks the corner of his mouth. "Pleasure isn't just for when we're gripped by the need to mate."

I hear an echo of the High Priest's voice in my mind. The body is sinful and our thoughts should always be directed outside ourselves and away from our baser instincts. But when was the last time Brethren made anyone's life better? When have I ever believed they spoke the truth about anything at all?

With my gaze fixed on Zabriel's beautiful face, I draw my skirts up and push one hand down into my drawers. Instantly, my fingers are coated with wetness. One of the places that's aching, the part that feels like a small bump, blazes at my touch. I gasp and my back arches, pushing my breasts into Zabriel's chest.

"Tell me what you feel," he asks in a roughened voice.

"I'm...slippery. Swollen. When I touch myself, it feels like someone blowing on a hot coal."

Zabriel makes a noise in the back of his throat and the

muscle in his jaw flexes, but he keeps his eyes closed. "Good. Beautiful. *Perfect*."

I play with different ways of stroking myself, and using my middle finger to circle the nub feels intensely good. The sounds from the Great Hall fade into the background, and I'm aware of nothing but Zabriel and the pleasure that's spreading through my body.

As I draw tight circles on that bundle of nerves, I gaze into Zabriel's face. This man is breathtakingly handsome with his hard jawline, sweeping dark brows, and eyes outlined with dark lashes. The black hair that curls softly around his face seems to highlight his sculpted beauty. His expression is softened now. He braces one forearm against the door by my head, and his other arm is around my waist, holding me so carefully and securely. He promised he wouldn't open his eyes, and I know he won't unless I ask him to.

I've never seen him look like this with anyone but me.

Is this beautiful man really for me?

"Are you sure it's all right for me to do this?" I whisper. I'm past the point of no return. I just crave to hear his voice encouraging me.

"Yes, Omega. Making yourself feel good while I hold you, it's the most beautiful thing that's ever happened." Zabriel inhales deeply. "Your slick is smelling sweeter and sweeter."

Everything is feeling sweeter too. I reach up and grip his forearm, the one braced against the door that bears his teeth marks, while I breathe harder and harder. The movements of my fingers are making me blaze with fire.

"Something's happening," I pant. "It's too much."

"You need more. Don't stop, *sha'len*."

I whimper and nod, before remembering that he can't see me.

That doesn't seem to matter as Zabriel murmurs, "Good girl. I've got you."

The heat and pleasure in my core tightens and tightens until it feels like I'm going to pass out. Then suddenly everything blazes into life, and I'm gripped by pleasure. My head flies back against the door and Zabriel catches it in his palm before I can knock myself out. My fingers keep moving. The pleasure goes on and on until it finally breaks and recedes.

Zabriel plants kiss after kiss on my throat. "Good girl. Good Omega. That was the first time you've come, isn't it? That's so fucking beautiful. You're so beautiful."

His words of praise sweep over me. I pull my hand out of my drawers and let my skirts drop. That was crazy. I had no idea my body could do that.

"*Sha'len*. You can say no, but can you please touch your fingers to my lips? The ones that are covered in your slick."

My first thought is, why would anyone want that?

My second thought is, of course Alpha wants that. He can have anything he wants. He's so good to me.

I reach up and trace my fingers over his mouth. He inhales and groans and wraps both his arms around me, scooping me off the ground and turning around so his back is braced against the door.

His lips part. A wild, crazy impulse overtakes me, and I push my middle finger into his mouth. Zabriel closes his lips around it and sucks, and his warm, slippery tongue moves against me.

I stare at his mouth, panting hard. "Your tongue feels so good."

Zabriel opens his eyes, and they're blazing red. He closes his lips around my pointer finger, and then my third finger. Finally, he sucks all three into his mouth like he's trying to savor as much of me as possible.

Pulling them out again, he says huskily, "You're the most delicious thing I've ever tasted."

My hands are gripping his shirt. My breath is coming faster, and we stare into each other's eyes. I'm holding on to him. This isn't even my false heat making me do crazy things. *I'm* holding on to him. Me. Isavelle.

Zabriel sets me slowly back down on my feet. There's a bulge at the front of his breeches, and my body slides over it.

Alpha wants to fuck me.

Alpha wants to push me down onto this floor and dominate me.

A wild impulse in me wants him to do exactly that.

Zabriel kisses me, and I taste something new on his lips that must be me. "I love your kisses so much."

"Has it occurred to you what else I could do with my tongue apart from kiss your lips and suck your fingers?" Zabriel gazes meaningfully at me for a moment.

I stare up at him, frozen by realization. He would...where I just touched myself with my fingers?

With a heated smile, he moves me to one side and opens the door. As he leaves, I take a last furtive glance at his forearm, and the bite mark is so savage that it sends a shiver through me. What if he does that to me and I'm ripped in two?

What a way to go, whimpers a needy voice.

I PASS the afternoon running errands for the Temple Mothers and then return to my room with an armload of pages that are writings about Old Maledin that have been translated into the common tongue. I'm curious about the world Zabriel grew up in, and I'm sitting down to study them when there's a knock at my door.

I open it and see that Zabriel is leaning against my doorframe with a smoldering expression in his eyes and a waterfall of pale, shimmering fabric over one shoulder. There's a smile playing around his lips, and I know he's remembering what we did this morning. It's all I've been able to think about all day.

Does he look different, or am I just seeing him differently? He looks delicious. Good enough to swallow deep down inside me.

His gaze sweeps over me like I'm looking different to him as well. "Hello, little queen."

That's what he said the first time we met, and in the same amused tone. *Hello, little queen. I apologize. What's left of your bridegroom has been ground into dust.*

I knew he was trouble the moment those words were out of his mouth.

"Hello, *Ma'len*," I say with a smile. For some reason, calling him *my king* today makes his smile widen.

He draws the garment he's holding from his shoulder. "I have a present for you. You didn't like the other dresses that I had made for you. I didn't know you well at the time, but I know you better now. I thought to myself, Isavelle deserves something that's as beautiful as she is. She should put a dress on and it should look and feel like it's made just for her."

Curious, I hold out my hands and he lays the dress across

them. It's sewn from delicate silk in a luminous cream color, cut so that it sits off the shoulder, with a little seam at the waist and a simple but graceful and flowing skirt.

"I asked for it to be cut this way so I could see the long, lovely line from your shoulders up to the nape of your neck." He reaches behind me and traces up my spine with his fingertips, making me shiver in pleasure.

"It's beautiful," I tell him. It's really for me to wear?

Zabriel's eyes brighten. "Will you wear it tonight? With your hair up?"

So that he can see the nape of my neck. Touch it. Kiss it. Dress in a way that he finds alluring and that attracts his adoration. A warm flush spreads through my cheeks, and I nod again. Zabriel groans softly and presses a kiss to my lips.

I really wield this kind of power over a man, and a man like Zabriel?

"What are we celebrating?" I ask him.

"A month since we emerged from beneath the mountain." A bleak expression crosses his features and he touches my cheek. "It just occurred to me that it might be difficult for you to feel celebratory about such a thing. If you'd prefer to stay in your room, I'll understand."

I shake my head. "No, I'll come. It's not the Maledinni who are keeping my family locked away behind a barrier."

Zabriel's tense shoulders relax, and he leans down and kisses me. "I adore you. I'll be just outside when you're ready, and we'll go to the Great Hall together."

I put it on, and the dress flows like liquid over my curves. I've never worn anything as special as this, but for once the finery doesn't make me feel ridiculous like I'm dressing up in my better clothes. This dress is mine, and no one else's. I can feel how much it was made for me by someone who cares.

I rework my braid and fasten it atop my head and take a moment to pat my hair and dress down, wondering how I look.

When I open the door, I get my answer. Zabriel's eyes widen and his mouth falls open.

"*Sha'len,*" he breathes and holds out his hands to me.

I move forward and take them shyly, drinking in the delight on his face. If I look pretty to him, then it doesn't matter what I look like to anyone else.

The Great Hall is filled with people as it was on his coronation day, Maledinni and humans alike. I notice that the two peoples seem more relaxed in each other's presence this time. Some of the human lords are talking with the dragonriders. The unwed sons and daughters of each side are glancing curiously at each other. Several of the human women follow Zabriel with their eyes as we walk through the room. Some of them scowl at me. All their expressions ask, *Who even are you to catch the king's eye? A village girl. You're no one special.*

Zabriel clasps my hand tighter and pulls me closer to him, and he's smiling as we take our seats at the high table.

I stumble a little over my chair, and a feminine titter goes up from one of the lower tables. I sit with my head down and my fingers tangled in my lap. Maybe I shouldn't have put on a dress like this and drawn so much attention to myself.

"Isavelle? Are you all right?"

"Um, I'm fine."

Zabriel narrows his eyes. He glances down at his body. I realize what he's about to do the moment before he does it.

"Don't—"

Too late. Zabriel pulls me out of my seat and into his lap and wraps his arms firmly around me. My face flames as he gathers me against him, his hands cupping my behind. "Zabriel, everyone is watching."

"Fuck everyone. Listen to me." He speaks slowly and deliberately, a strong hand cupping my face. "Everyone in this room needs to understand how I feel about you. Especially you. The moment I laid eyes on you sitting in the dust with your hands tied and covered in bruises and blood, I knew I'd found my Omega. Again. And this time I could see her face. I could see her poor, half-starved, and battered body. Then, your beauty was breathtaking. Now, your beauty is breathtaking. It's got nothing to do with how you look, though I assure you, you're the most beautiful woman I've ever seen and your lips and thighs drive me to fucking distraction. *You* are beautiful. You're kind. You worry about everyone but yourself. You made yourself this way by who you are, and I'm the luckiest man who ever lived. Do you doubt me?"

I gaze up at him with lips parted, unable to find any words. Zabriel's red eyes are blazing into mine. Mutely, I shake my head.

His face relaxes into a smile. "I'm glad to hear it." He takes my hand and presses a kiss to my palm, a playful light dancing in his eyes. "And what about me? Do you think I'm handsome?"

My lips twitch. Zabriel is utterly gorgeous and he knows it. He's always so good at expressing how he feels that I have to try as well. I wrap my arms around his neck and gaze into his eyes. "It's been one month since you awoke beneath the Bodan Mountains, and the people of Maledin are freer than

I've ever known them to be. No one has spoken to me of executions or beatings, daughters being stolen, and families being punished for not going to church. The Maledinni don't wish to persecute the humans living here, drive them away, or separate them from their kind. If everyone is allowed to live peacefully in Maledin, including those who are missing, I feel hopeful about the future for the first time." I stroke Zabriel's hand that's holding on to my thigh. "And that's because of you."

I've never seen Zabriel struggle for words before, but now he's silent for a long moment. He takes my hand and presses it to his thundering heart, covering it tightly with his own. "Thank you, *sha'len*. That means everything to me. This is the part of me who burns to be the best mate and king I can be. For you. Because of you."

"Maledin is lucky to have you. I'm lucky to have you, too."

"Thank you, *sha'len*. Let's drink to that." He picks up his goblet of wine and holds it to my lips. When I try to take it from him, he shakes his head. "Let me do it."

Hesitantly, I open my lips, and as he carefully fills my mouth with wine, I swallow it down. There's a droplet of liquid on my lips and he kisses it away.

Zabriel's smile turns roguish. "So, you like me as a man and think I'm devastatingly handsome? Good to know."

"We never settled the matter about whether I think you're handsome," I tease.

Zabriel gives me a smoldering smile. "Your scent becomes so flowery when you get excited. You have no secrets from me, and when you finally catch your Alpha's scent, I'll have no secrets from you, either."

Zabriel kisses my throat and slides the blade of his nose up my cheek. Beneath the table, he wraps his large hands around my hips and thighs and squeezes. "This is what you're meant to be like, isn't it? Rounded hips and thighs and tapering little toes. I can't get enough of looking at you and touching you. Every time you let me hold you like this is a gift, *sha'len*."

I feel myself melting into him. I've never been praised so much in my life. I think I might become addicted to his voice.

He takes my chin between his thumb and forefinger and gazes at me. "That look you're giving me right now is a gift as well. So beautiful. Maybe I'm even more than handsome to you. I feel you pulling my clothes with your eyes when you think I'm not looking. You're always hunting for my knot."

"I am not!" I exclaim, though I know that's a lie. I bury my face in Zabriel's shoulder when everyone nearby turns to look at me. It's so easy to forget about everyone in the room when I'm talking to Zabriel. I can feel him laughing silently against me.

"Don't fib, little queen," he murmurs in my ear, and then he holds me tighter and presses ever so slowly up into my thighs. "It's right here whenever you want it."

I feel the bulge against my flesh, and the craving to wrap my fingers around him grows even stronger.

"We are in public," I say in a whisper without raising my head.

"It's not like I'm going to fuck you over this table," he says, in a way that tells me he's thinking about it.

Oh, stars and blood. I feel a rush of wetness at the thought of my Alpha claiming me here in front of everyone so they know who I belong to.

"If we carry on like this, everyone is going to gossip about us," I say, but I'm unable to drag my eyes away from him. I'm only theoretically aware that there are other people in the room. For me there's only Zabriel.

His mouth curves in a smirk, and he holds the goblet to my lips once more. "I know what the people in this room are thinking and saying to each other. They're saying that if the king keeps looking at Lady Isavelle like that, her belly will soon be swelling, and then there will be plenty of heirs running around the castle in the near future."

I choke a little on my wine and wipe my mouth with the back of my hand. "The people of Maledin can slow their expectations."

Zabriel slides a hand over my stomach and says in a velvety murmur, "So soft. So ready for me when I finally knot you. I can smell how fertile you are, *sha'len*. You're going to look delicious full of my knot and then full of my children, your belly big and round." He groans and sinks his teeth into his lower lip, staring at me like he's picturing it, his large fingers splayed over my stomach.

My face flames so red that I don't know where to look and can't form proper thoughts. Everything feels liquid between my thighs. "If you keep talking like this then you-know-what is going to happen all over your lap again."

Zabriel groans. "Does me talking to you like this make your slick well up? Please get it all over me. I love my Omega so wet and needy."

Oh, stars, how do I distract him? Remembering the tea that the Temple Maidens brought me this morning, I ask, "Will you remind me to drink a special tea from the Flame Temple when my false heat starts again?"

Zabriel caresses my face. "Of course, *sha'len*. I will be delighted to."

That worked. He's not saying *knot* anymore at least. I quickly think of another distraction and glance sadly at his plate. "I don't think I've been eating enough these past few days. I feel so weak since my false heat."

He reaches for a spoon so fast he nearly knocks it off the table. "Have some stew. Try these roasted vegetables."

The food is delicious, and I realize how hungry I am when I start to eat. I take grateful bites from the spoon he holds out for me.

"You have some too," I urge him when he scoops up more stew with his spoon, and he eats that mouthful.

I rip a piece of bread from the piece on his plate, dip it into a creamy dish made from ground nuts and spices, and hold it to his lips.

"You're so cute," he says, taking the bread from me and kissing my fingertips. It's pleasing holding up morsels and watching him eat them.

"What was your family like?" I ask, wondering if he misses them and if that's why he's talking about having children with me.

He sighs heavily. "My family? They were…complicated."

I chew slowly on a bite of vegetables and swallow. "I was curious about the former king and queen, but we don't have to talk about them if it's painful."

"That's all right. We can talk about them a little. What would you like to know?"

"What were your parents like?"

"My mother was a very beautiful Omega, kind and sweet and clever. She would have liked you, though you are different in many ways. She was a quintessential Omega of my time, obedient and submissive just like my father wanted. Like every Alpha expected. It's why you and I had so much trouble at first. I had all these expectations of what you would be like, and you weren't fulfilling them. Now, I'm glad you didn't. I don't want us to be anything like my parents' relationship. My father took his role as Alpha and king to the extreme."

Zabriel is suddenly frowning. I trace his lips with my fingertip. "You smile when you remember your mother, but you never do when you talk about your father."

"Alphas find it hard to get along with other Alphas."

I don't know about that. Zabriel seems to get along with everyone. He's even pleasant to Stesha. "Was he a good king?"

His expression grows even flintier, and he seethes, "We lost everything because of him. New Maledin has to do better. I have to do better. For a long time, I thought he was a good father and a good king..."

Zabriel stares at our joined fingers for a long time, his jaw tight. Then he mutters a curse. "I'm so angry with him, *sha'len*. Do you mind if we talk about this another time?"

I cup his cheek and nod. "Of course. I'm sorry if this was upsetting for you."

"My father was an arrogant, volatile, and merciless king. The people found it hard to love him, and in the end, so did his family." He presses a kiss to my lips and strokes the back of my neck. "But it's all in the past now."

It is, but that doesn't mean he doesn't feel pain. Something terrible must have happened for a country ruled by ferocious dragonriders to crumble.

Zabriel goes on stroking the nape of my neck and gazing at my throat, and he murmurs, "You're so beautiful here."

"Is this a Maledinni preference? Necks aren't something human men have a preoccupation with, as far as I know."

"Your bare neck is beautiful, but there's another reason too." He slowly strokes a finger up the back of my neck, and my whole body tingles. "That's your mating gland, where I'll bite you when we're joined. My teeth marks will remain visible in your flesh for the rest of your life, especially when you're in heat."

So that's why the teeth at the corners of his mouth are pointed like that. I touch the teeth marks on his forearm. "You'll bite me like you bit yourself here?"

He glances at his arm which is covered by his sleeve right now. "I know it sounds frightening, but it won't feel frightening when it happens, and I won't do it until you ask me to. Until then, it's going to be all I can think about. Biting you. Marking you. Claiming you. Sending a message to other Alphas that you already have a mate, and I will rip their throats out if they lay a finger on you." Zabriel grows taut with fury at the mere suggestion. "While you're unmated and unprotected, I worry that another Alpha might get his teeth into you."

"You're the King of Maledin. Another Alpha wouldn't do that. Your dragonriders respect you too much."

"I've seen it happen before," he says through his teeth. "An Alpha I knew bit another man's Omega, for no other reason than to be cruel. It destroyed all the love between the pair. She was so ashamed that she bore another Alpha's teeth marks in her flesh, and he was devastated that he couldn't protect her."

Zabriel was upset when I grazed my hands running from the Brethren. I hate to think how devastated he'd be if one of his own hurt me. "What a terrible thing to have happened."

"You want to know the worst part?" he asks, and I'm not sure that I do, but I nod. Zabriel stares at me for a long time, and I can tell he's wondering whether to tell me or not. "It was his own sister."

I suck in a breath. "This Alpha...bit his own sister?"

"He raped his sister," Zabriel says, his eyes flaming an angry red. "In a full rut, before her true heat. It was violent and bloody and cruel. One of the worst things an Alpha can do, if not the worst thing."

I'm only just starting to understand what heats and ruts are, but all the same a sick feeling spreads through my stomach. That poor woman to experience such suffering at the hands of someone who is supposed to love her.

"It's why I'm overprotective of you right now, *sha'len*. This is a vulnerable time for you."

I stroke my fingers down his forearm to comfort him, and he turns his hand palm up and spreads his fingers, inviting me to take his hand, and I do. He wraps his fingers around mine, completely engulfing me.

"What happened to that Omega?"

He gives a gusty sigh. "It's very sad, I'm sorry to say. She threw herself from dragonback and died. The pain was too much for her Alpha and he went on a suicide mission and never came back. He was my best friend," he adds bleakly.

My heart turns over in my chest. Zabriel is such a happy, vibrant person, and he must strive not to show how much he's suffered in his life. "I'm so sorry. And the Alpha who raped her?"

"He ran. I went after him. I wanted to kill him, but I never found him. Then we were all sealed between the mountain, and he perished hundreds of years ago gods know where."

Zabriel grinds the heel of his hand into his eyes. He's ashamed, I realize. He tried to punish a wrongdoer, but he wasn't able to, and even though it was hundreds of years ago, he still feels responsible.

My heart hurting for him, I take Zabriel's face between my hands. "You can check my neck as often as you want to. And I'll be careful. I won't make you worry about me."

Finally, Zabriel returns from his dark memories and gazes into my eyes. "What did I do to deserve you, *sha'len*?"

I don't know if I'm that much of a prize because I'm not a very good Omega. It doesn't sound like his father would have approved of me. "I'm the one who doesn't deserve you."

"Have you and Esmeral been bonding lately?" he asks, changing the subject.

"She follows me around sometimes. I expect she'll lose interest in me now she has Scourge."

"I promise you she won't. You're just as important to her as her mate is. What do you think about learning to fly?"

I hesitate, trying to find a way to tell Zabriel that I don't want to without hurting his feelings. "That would mean being around Stesha, seeing as he's the dragonmaster. It's better that I stay away from other Alphas."

"I trust Stesha around you, but that's fine if you don't want to associate with him. I'll teach you to ride. Your bodyguards know a great deal about flying as well, and I trust them with you. Flying is one of the greatest pleasures a Maledinni can have. I want my mate to know what it feels like to bond with her dragon and take to the skies."

Zabriel looks so hopeful that I can't find it in my heart to crush that light in his eyes.

"I'll think about it," I finally concede.

I'm supposed to want to fly, aren't I? This is yet another expectation that I'm failing to meet because every time I think about being on a dragon, my stomach feels queasy, and I want to throw up.

24

Zabriel

Vivid red and orange explosions burnish Scourge's wings and the low clouds in the night sky. He banks around the battlefield, his bulk protecting the wingrunner flying beside us. The wyvern is so close that I could reach out and touch it.

Its rider is a spellbreaker, one of only two to survive into New Maledin, specially trained by the *Hratha'len* in counter-magic. The other spellbreaker is with Stesha and Nilak, circling the battlefield across from us. The fierce women in red robes draw orbs of power into their hands and hurl them at the buildings below. The orbs explode, making the magical barrier fizzle and shudder, but it remains in place.

I remember spellbreakers being sent into battle just once in my life, when a group of Grendu outlaw necromancers raided a

Maledin town close to the border, slaughtering farmers and their families. They were caught by dragonriders and spellbreakers and sent in chains back to Grendu. The King of Grendu sent my father a dozen silver peacocks to apologize for the slaughter. The peacocks had a nasty temper and destroyed my mother's favorite flower garden at the castle, but I'm sure the king meant well.

Brethren archers attempt to pick the women off, and Scourge and Nilak send bursts of dragonfire toward the ground. It's always spectacular fighting at night. Dragonriders and wingrunners have the advantage of seeing better than most in the dark, and dragonfire terrifies our enemies. We won't be able to burn anything if the spellbreakers can't shatter that barrier.

A dozen wingrunners slash across the battlefield, ripping apart the Brethren Guard. They're protecting a shabby collection of farm buildings on Maledin soil that's filled with barrels of poison. Realizing that they're losing the war, the Brethren have resorted to cruel tactics, poisoning rivers so that people die and crops wither.

There's an almighty crack, and the magical shield over the farmhouses vanishes. Scourge roars in furious triumph.

I glance over at Stesha and nod, and he waits for the spellbreaker with him to join me before he and Nilak dive for the buildings. Nilak opens her jaws and rains down fiery death. Within the burning structures, I glimpse the barrels of poison. They explode as they burn, showering the fleeing Brethren with flames and sparks. The wingrunners swoop in to pick off the remaining enemies.

A robed archer stands by a burning wagon and takes aim at one of the spellbreakers. The archer's arrow is tipped with a gleaming greenish substance that makes the back of my neck prickle in alarm.

I'm about to shout a warning when the archer looses his arrow. The spellbreaker's wyvern screams as the arrow tears through its wing, and it buckles in midair. The spellbreaker is going down with her mount, and she's too precious to lose.

"Ashton, grab her," I shout across to the wingrunner captain.

The man swoops in on his wyvern and plucks the *Hratha'len* off her dying wyvern.

The *Hratha'len* clings onto the captain, watching in despair as her wyvern crashes to the ground. The arrowhead didn't strike a vital organ, and yet the wyvern died instantly.

The robed archer is drawing again, this time aiming at the other spellbreaker.

Oh, no you fucking don't. Scourge plunges toward the archer and snatches him up in his teeth. Clamped in my dragon's jaws, his body pierced by dozens of sharp teeth and slowly bleeding to death, the archer's face blazes with malice. Our eyes meet, and I can count the stubble on his chin. See his cracked front tooth. With the last of his strength, he draws back on his bow. I zero in on the arrow tip which is glistening with the same greenish poison that felled the wyvern.

I tug a dagger from my belt and hurl it at the archer at the same time he looses his arrow. Our projectiles pass in midair. The dagger sinks into the man's chest, killing him instantly.

The arrow rips along Scourge's flank, and he roars in pain. I feel it in my own side, the vicious burn of poisoned steel. Scourge falters in midair, dropping the man into the fire where he disappears among the flames.

Scourge.

He's laboring with every wingbeat, and the wound in his side is oozing blood.

I look quickly around. The Brethren are dead. The buildings are burning. There's no need for us to linger here any longer.

"Take the spellbreakers back to the castle," I call to Ashton, who nods. He rallies the wingrunners, and they vanish into the darkness, heading north.

I urge my dragon toward open ground and he lands with a jolt. As soon as my boots hit the dust, I hasten to his wounded flank, and my gut wrenches as I gaze in horror at a seven-foot-long greenish, bubbling wound. I've never seen anything like it before.

Behind me, there's the sound of running feet behind me. Stesha is at my side, and he places his gloved hands on either side of the wound on Scourge's side, feeling the scales and examining the torn flesh. A moment later he runs to Nilak and comes back with a bag of powder, which he begins applying to the wound.

"Ypergraf root," he mutters, working quickly. "To soak up the poison."

I grab handfuls of the powder and follow Stesha's lead, pushing it into the wound. Pain flares in my head. Pain that doesn't belong to me.

"Don't let that stuff touch your skin," he warns me.

As the powder soaks up the poison, it forms a crust and drops to the ground. A few minutes later, Stesha steps back.

"That's the worst of it. The poison didn't penetrate his hide and I can treat these burns back at the dragongrounds."

I stare in horror at my wounded dragon. No one has ever hurt my dragon in battle before. Scourge has always seemed invulnerable, and it's shaken me to my core to see him injured by an arrow.

Stesha clasps my shoulder. "He'll be all right, Zabriel."

"What the fuck is this poison?" I snarl, my chest feeling like it's being crushed in a vise.

Stesha shakes his head, worry creasing his brow. He doesn't need to tell me that a better-aimed shot could have killed Scourge. "Magical barriers. Poison that can injure dragons. The Brethren have never been capable of this."

I recall the robed archer. Decorated robes, not plain robes like the men we've been fighting. "Those weren't Brethren. They're something new. Fighters I've never seen before."

I turn toward the sound, though I can't see the barrier from this distance. Just who and what lies beyond it? Five hundred years have passed. It could be anyone. Anything. It's even more urgent that we find a way to bring it down.

I move around to Scourge's head. "Can you fly?"

Scourge growls and aggressively thrusts his crest toward the sky, offended by the suggestion that he might have been grounded by one arrow.

A few minutes later we take to the skies, Scourge leading the way, a little slower than usual, but his wingbeats are strong.

When we reach the castle dragongrounds a few hours later, a dozen Temple Mothers are waiting for us. Together with Stesha, they treat his wound while I comfort my dragon as much as he'll allow me. Scourge holds his head up proudly and never flinches, but I can feel him leaning some of his bulk against my chest.

Sometime later, his wound is cleaned and sealed with a

marseng leaf bandage so that it doesn't become infected. The Temple Mothers depart, and Stesha steps back from Scourge.

His expression is livid, as it always is when a dragon is injured.

"Poison," he spits, like it's a curse.

Esmeral has been huddled against her Alpha's side, but now she comes around toward his head, trilling and clicking her concern. Scourge presses his crest against her flank, showing her that he's fine and nibbling at her wing edges. Fussing over her so that she won't fuss over him. Scourge will not be fussed over under any circumstances.

Stesha and I stand back, watching them in silence.

"At least we killed every last one of them tonight. Your father couldn't have done any of this," Stesha says at last.

I glance around in surprise. "Done what?"

The dragonmaster is watching the dragons of the flare as they move in a tight circle around us, protecting and paying respects to their injured Alpha. "Retaken Maledin. Freed our dragons. Freed us. We fought as a unit tonight. Your father... It might make you angry to hear it, but I loathed fighting alongside him."

I glower at the wound in Scourge's side. "I just want to put right everything my father did to destroy our home."

"You will."

Despite the worry over Scourge and my post-battle come-down, I can't help but feel lighter all of a sudden. Stesha's opinion matters to me, and it always has. It doesn't surprise me that he hated riding into battle with my imperious father, who wouldn't listen to anyone's advice.

"They're changing tactics, but we'll change with them,"

Stesha says. “We won’t lose to a bunch of cultists who have joined forces with black mages and poisoners.”

I nod sharply. “Of course we won’t lose.”

A rider crosses the stone bridge toward the dragongrounds. Esmeral breaks away from Scourge and dashes hopefully forward, but her crest falls sadly when she realizes it’s not Isavelle.

I feel a stab of pain witnessing the little dragon’s distress. Isavelle would never knowingly be cruel to another creature, but Esmeral is suffering without her rider. My dragon’s Omega means almost as much to me as my own Omega.

“What are we going to do about that poor little dragon?” I say with a sigh.

Stesha gives me a sharp look. “You are going to pull your Omega in line and remind her of her duties to Maledin. If word gets out that the future queen has refused to ride, it will damage the faith the people have in dragons to protect and defend them. Especially the humans. They’ll think of her as one of their own. If she doesn’t trust dragons, neither will they.”

Stesha’s lecture slams into me and fries my already raw nerve endings. “You think I don’t know that? These are the thoughts that haunt me in the dark hours when I can’t sleep. A king of Maledin has never had to rule over so many humans before.”

“That’s only if you want the humans to remain in Maledin.”

“Of course I want them to remain in Maledin. It doesn’t matter if they settled here after Maledin fell, this is their home. Besides, there have always been humans in Maledin. We wouldn’t have witches if we didn’t interbreed.”

"Daughters of Maledinni become *Hratha'len*," Stesha points out.

"And who have the people always loved better, the witches or the *Hratha'len*?" It's a rhetorical question because Stesha knows the answer. The people love and respect the witches. Witches live among them, deliver their babies, and care for the sick. The people barely see the *Hratha'len*, who live and work in Lenhale and cloak themselves in an air of mystery.

Stesha folds his arms and gazes at me. "Speaking of witches, I've heard that the future queen is not only also refusing her dragon, but her mate as well."

I jerk my chin at the stone bridge. "I've had enough of you tonight. Be gone."

"It's an important question, Zabriel. Is your mate rejecting you? This affects all of Maledin if our Alpha can't claim his queen."

"My Omega and I are just fine. You know that when a designation emerges it's a difficult time for an Omega. Or rather you don't know, do you?" He wishes he knew, but he never will.

There's a flicker of anger in Stesha's eyes. If he doesn't like fire then he should get out of the way of my dragon.

He strides away without a word, vanishing among the dragons of the flare.

I turn back to Scourge, wondering if I shouldn't have made things quite so personal.

I stay with Scourge for several hours until I'm sure he's not sickening and he's falling asleep, and then I head back to the castle. In my rooms, I undo my gauntlets and chest piece and toss them onto a chair.

No. Fuck Stesha. It's a sensitive subject, and he should have known better than to needle me with it after battle. I don't want to play *what if* over something so devastating as my Omega rejecting me. I don't want a contingency plan. I just want Isavelle.

After battle, I usually enjoy a long soak in the bathhouse beneath the castle, so that's where I head. There's a freezing pool of water in the first room, and I strip off my clothes and leave them by a smooth, tiled seating area, moving deeper into the bathhouse to where the pools of water are hot. There are a handful of other dragonriders and wingrunners soaking up the heat and steam. I plunge into the hottest water pool and float in the water with my eyes closed.

When I open them again, I'm alone. I float for a while longer and then get out of the water, wrap a towel around my hips, and walk back to the stone bench where I left my clothes. They've all fallen onto the ground and become tangled up with several towels.

Something is moving around underneath it all.

"What the—"

A hand snakes out of the pile, seizes my wrist, and drags me down onto the ground. A petite, lush body with rounded limbs wraps around my torso and clings on for dear life. I pull my discarded shirt away from her face and see Isavelle, pupils dilated, cheeks pink, and panting.

"*Sha'len*? Are you in a false heat again already?" I press my face into her throat and breathe in. There it is, the unmistakable sweet scent of my horny, nearly fertile Omega. How the hell did this happen again so quickly? I wasn't paying attention these past three days, and I must have missed the warning signs. My poor little Omega must have been working too hard to notice as well.

Isavelle slides across my lap and straddles my thighs. She's wearing only a thin nightgown and her hair is loose down her back. "Zabriel. I missed you," she breathes.

I groan at the feel of her body against mine and the neediness in her voice. I'm about three seconds away from lavishing her with praise and kisses, but I hold it back long enough to glare at her severely and say, "Did you follow me down here? You should have sent one of your bodyguards or a maid. It's not safe for you to wander around in this state."

Isavelle hasn't heard a word I've said. There's no point scolding her when she's so far gone and she came looking for her Alpha. Smiling, I press my mouth to hers and kiss her. It seems like she's all mine for this false heat, though I had better be careful not to get carried away and scare her off.

"I'll take you back to your room. We can make a proper nest together. How does that sound?"

"I don't want to go anywhere. I like it down here." Isavelle wraps both of her legs around one of my thighs and squeezes, and she moans. That must feel good because she does it again and again until she's working herself up and down against my thigh. Her nightgown is caught between her legs and it's soaked through with her slick.

I ease slowly back on my elbows, transfixed by the sight of her. All the blood rushes to my knot. "Does that feel good? I guess you really need to climax."

"Pardon?" she asks, confusion creasing her brow and her rhythm stuttering.

I quickly change the subject before I can put her off her

stride. "You look so pretty with your legs wrapped around my thigh, Omega. Don't stop."

"I woke up and I needed you," she pants, working her sex against my thigh. Grinding her clit into my bare flesh.

My lips curve into a smile. "I can see that. What do you need from your Alpha?"

"I don't know," she moans, her head tipping back and her eyes closing.

"Does that feel good, rubbing yourself on my thigh?"

"It feels amazing," she gasps.

"Then keep doing it," I say, reaching up and holding her lightly. My hands are large, but I can't fit them around her waist. It's wonderful. Omegas are always small, and I'm big for an Alpha, but there's plenty of her to hold on to and squeeze. Her breasts are shifting beneath her nightgown as she moves back and forth. My tongue plays with my dragines while I watch her glorious body move. It's taking all my willpower not to roll her beneath me and take control of the situation, but she felt safe enough with me to come last time only because I didn't take control. This time she's letting me watch, and I'm not going to fuck it up.

Isavelle cries out. There's a gush of wetness over my thigh. Her nails dig into my chest and she works herself in short, sharp movements against me.

Isavelle opens her eyes. "Oh, my stars. Zabriel, that felt so good. I want another one. Do it again. Please, please, please."

I laugh, holding on to her. "That wasn't me. That was you."

"*Please*, Alpha."

I roll her beneath me, kissing her panting mouth, seizing her nipples through her gown with my teeth, cupping her ass, and pulling her tight against my knot. Her body is so deliciously yielding. I squeeze her, and she's so soft and sweet in my arms.

"Alpha, please."

I thrust my knot against her. "I'm here, *sha'len*. I'm here."

"Call me Omega. Please, please, please."

Fuck, she sounds so hot when she begs me. "How badly do you want it?"

"You're all I want. You can have anything. I'm yours. Please keep me forever and call me your Omega."

Fiery heat floods my veins. I rip my towel off and cast it aside. My cock is hard and heavy and my knot is aching. Her thighs are spread open and I can see her sex through her soaked nightgown.

Fuck her.

Fuck her hard until she screams.

I take myself in my hand and brace my other by her head. One thrust and I'll be inside her.

I rein myself in just in time. No, I can't do that. Not yet.

I move down her body instead. "I want to taste your slick, Omega."

I'll lick my sweet Omega until she comes over my face, and then I'll roll her onto her belly and ask her how many of my thick fingers she wants inside her. Maybe even my cock, but just a few inches. Just enough to give her a taste of me while I grasp my knot and work the rest of my length up and down in my fist until we both come. White-hot heat flashes behind my eyes as I picture her pussy full to bursting with my creamy cum. All over her thighs. Dripping down her sex.

Dragons' blood, I need that so much I can't breathe. I take a fistful of her nightgown and start to drag it up.

"Please, Alpha, please. I'm all yours. I want your knot. I want everything."

It's exactly what I want to hear, which is what makes me pause, her nightgown halfway up her thighs.

I want my mate to be reckless and a little out of control when she's in this state. To get her slick all over me. To beg me for kisses and make her come. To want things we've done together before. But her completely losing her mind like this is causing a red banner to unfurl in the back of my mind. Isavelle is starting to like me, but she wouldn't say to me, *I want your knot.* She can barely say knot under normal circumstances.

I sit up and sigh heavily, grinding the heel of my hand between my eyes. Ah, fuck. I wanted this to be real so badly. Alpha and Omega relationships are built on trust just as much as any other pairing. In fact, I've always imagined it requires even more trust because it's so easy for one or the other in the relationship to grow so drunk on their heats and ruts they make utterly stupid decisions.

"Alpha, please," Isavelle moans, reaching for my knot.

I seize her wrist and hold on tight before she can touch me, and then sit back on my heels and open my arms wide. "Come here, Omega."

My mate plasters herself against me, mewling happily as I pick her up in my arms. I press my lips to hers, and as she opens for my tongue, I enjoy one last selfish, hungry kiss.

Then I walk to the edge of the pool and throw her into the freezing water.

There's an almighty splash, a short silence, and then bursts to the surface.

"Zabriel, what—" she splutters.

I pull my clothes on, my lips pressed grimly together. A few seconds later the cold water does its work. Isavelle's expression falls as everything she said and did just now comes flooding back, and she sinks farther into the water with a moan of horror.

I hunker down on the edge of the pool and hold my hand out to her, coaxing softly, "Come on, *sha'len*. Come out of there. I won't look, and I'll get you warm and dry and take you back to your room."

Isavelle wades miserably toward me. "I'm so sorry, Zabriel. I was acting crazy. I'm so embarrassed."

I pull her out of the water, averting my gaze from the nightgown that's turned see-through and is clinging to her body, and wrap warm, fluffy towels around her. "You didn't do anything wrong, Omega. Don't apologize to your Alpha for something he should have realized was happening from the beginning."

Isavelle is hiccupping and breathing unsteadily, on the verge of tears.

I pull her into my arms and hold her, and nearly use my scent to soothe her until I remember I said I wouldn't do that. I start to ask her if she wants it, but it's too late. She starts to cry, and the sound shreds my heart as her tears roll down my chest.

I pick my mate up in my arms and carry her back to her room. She quiets into sniffles as I walk, and I feel her body start to burn. By the time I set her on her feet by the bed, she's gripped by her false heat once more. A clingy little Omega is trying to drag me into her nest, but remembering her tears from a moment ago, I remain where I am, no matter how desperate I am to follow her in there.

"Next time," I promise her. "If your false heat passes and you want me in your nest next time, I will go with you. I'll give you anything you ask for."

My words fall on deaf ears. All she hears is her Alpha telling her no, and nothing is more distressing to a needy Omega.

I tuck her beneath a dozen blankets and close the curtains.

"Why did you leave me, Alpha?" she whimpers.

I see the curtain twitch and I grasp them and hold them closed. "Just stay there, *sha'len*. I'm right here. I'm not going anywhere."

"Do you not want me, Alpha?"

Hearing her suffer is like being stabbed in the guts. "I want you. You have no idea how much."

"Then why don't you come in here and give me your knot? I'm aching so much, deep inside me. It *hurts*."

It's her false heat talking. It's her false heat talking. It's her false heat talking.

I chant this over and over again as my hands tremble on the curtains. If Isavelle welcomed the idea of sex with me when she wasn't out of her mind with lust, I'd be in there with her in a second.

"Omega," I say sharply, and she stops whimpering. "Listen to me."

"Yes, Alpha?" she sniffles.

"Are your thighs wet with your slick?"

"They are."

"Touch yourself for me. Stroke yourself with your fingers, just like you did the other day. Are you doing as I ask?"

"Yes, Alpha." This time there's a moan in her voice and her crying has stopped.

"Good girl," I breathe. "That's my good girl. Keep touching yourself and listening to my voice. I'm right here."

I listen to Isavelle's panting cries from within the curtains. Remembering that she might want something of mine to cuddle even if she's not aware of my scent yet, I thrust the shirt I wore into battle through the curtains, and she snatches it from my fingers.

"I'm so close," she moans.

"Don't stop, *sha'len*. Keep touching yourself for me."

I sit on the floor with my back against her mattress. My hand is inside my breeches and wrapped around my knot, squeezing myself as I listen to her climax again and again. The scent of her is all around me. I can practically taste her on my tongue and my mouth waters like a starving man.

Sometime around dawn, she finally falls asleep. I slip into a doze still sitting on the floor, my legs stretched out in front of me.

"ZABRIEL?"

I awaken to Isavelle bending over me, dressed in my shirt. Her cheeks are flushed but her eyes are clear. I think her false heat has passed.

Her eyes drop, and I follow her gaze, and we stare at my hand inside my pants. I'm still holding my knot.

I clear my throat and do up my breeches. "Are you feeling yourself again?"

She nods, her eyes cutting away from me as she tucks her

hair behind her ear. "I'm sorry. I think I lost my head last night."

I reach up and caress her cheek. "You have nothing to be sorry about. I'm your mate and everything you say and do is beautiful to me."

"Thank you, um, for not doing any of those things I begged you for."

I don't know what to say. *You're welcome* feels wrong when I wish more than anything that I had been able to do all those things. I'm supposed to hold my mate and make her feel amazing when she goes into heat. It's meant to strengthen our bond.

Isavelle puts her hands on my chest and beseeches me. Tears glisten on her lashes, and there's a sob in her voice. "I mean it, Zabriel. You don't know how much it means to me that you don't just take whatever you like. I didn't think there was a man like you in the whole world, except for my own father."

Taking Isavelle's hand, I draw her down into my arms and hold her on my lap, pressing my forehead to hers. "I want *you* to want me, Isavelle. All I heard was your heat talking. When you ask me for something and I'm sure it's you, I will move the earth to give you whatever you want."

I smooth the tears from her cheeks, and she gives me a soft smile. "I can't remember the last time I felt safe. Thank you, Zabriel."

With a groan, I wrap my arms around her and hold her tight. Safe? My Omega feels safe with me? The sensation that pours through my body is brighter than dragonfire. "You've given me everything I've ever wanted, *sha'len*."

I touch my shirt that she's wearing. It's huge on her, a

dress that comes down to her knees. "You look pretty cute in this."

"Thank you. I, um, had my face pressed into it the whole time because it smelled nice. I don't know if it was your scent the same way that you smell mine, but I liked having it with me."

If she's not sure, then it wasn't my scent like my Omega should smell it, but at least my shirt gave her comfort.

Isavelle strokes my face, and then tilts her chin up and kisses me. A sweet, tender kiss. Her lips are swollen from biting into them for hours.

"Was it strange to sit out here and listen to me...do that to myself?"

"I loved it," I tell her, smiling and pressing kisses to her lips, her cheeks, her throat. She's covered in the scent of her slick.

Her fingers dawdle shyly down my bare chest. "The things you were saying. I like it when you call me Omega in that tone, so stern and commanding."

Her weight is on my knot and she's so warm and delicious in my arms. "I like it when you whimper *Alpha, please* as you come."

Isavelle smiles and she pulls a handful of my hair across her face and hides in it. Fuck, she's adorable when she's horny and shy. I'm transfixed by the sight of her.

"Next time I'm in my false heat, could you, um..." she trails off in a whisper.

I wait, gently stroking her round, soft thigh with my fingertips. "If you ask me, I will absolutely do it for you."

"Will you come into my nest with me, and..." She trails off and bites her lip. "I'm not very brave, Zabriel."

She is brave. More than she knows. I reach behind us and haul one of the blankets off her bed and over us so that we're enveloped in darkness and warmth.

"Whisper it to me," I breathe in her ear.

Isavelle slides her arms around my neck and puts her lips close to my ear. "I liked what happened down in the bathhouse. Will you maybe touch me with your fingers and let me rub myself against you again?"

"Yes. Yes, of course. Anything you want, Omega," I say, pressing kisses against her throat while my heart beats wildly. "Can I see you next time? All of your beautiful body?"

Hesitantly, Isavelle nods and reaches up to touch my lips. "And that thing you said about your tongue..."

I smile against her fingers. "Did you guess what I meant? That I want to kiss you down there like I kiss your mouth?"

"Do you really want to do that?"

My knot swells in response to her question. "You have no idea how much."

"I'd like to know what that feels like," she confesses in a whisper. Her flowery scent erupts around us. My sweet girl is slicking herself just thinking about it.

"I could show you right now if you want to."

Isavelle breathes in sharply. "Are—are you sure? I'm such a mess."

"Messy from wanting me and making yourself come? That's just the kind of mess I crave."

Isavelle hesitates, then begins to tug my shirt that she's wearing up around her hips.

Oh, dragons' blood, she really wants me to lick her sex. "Do you want to stay down here on the floor, or would you like to get up on the bed?"

"I like it here in the dark," she whispers.

I wrap an arm around her and turn our bodies so she's laying back on the rug, the blanket still over us. I can just make out the curve of her cheek. Her breasts in my shirt. The tails of the shirt trailing between her legs. I kiss her lips, and then every button on the shirt as I move down her body.

When I reach her sex, the scent of her slick is irresistible. I can smell hours and hours of her frustration overlaid with fresh excitement. I draw back the shirt and I can see her pussy glistening wetly in the dark.

"You'll have to tell me what feels good. I don't know what I'm doing, remember?"

"Everything you do feels amazing," she gasps as I kiss the apex of her sex and push my tongue between her folds. "Oh, *fuck*, Zabriel."

Her thighs fall open and her fingers push into my hair.

Everything about this is so vivid. Her slippery swollen flesh against my lips. The way she cries out with every stroke of my tongue. The scent of her. The taste of her. I'm so glad I waited for my Omega.

"You feel like you know what you're doing," she breathes.

My tongue curls around her clit, and then I flick it with my tongue.

Isavelle moans my name. "Zabriel. Oh, my stars. *Alpha*."

She seemed to like that, so I do it again.

"Can I push my tongue inside you?" I murmur.

"Please, Alpha, please," she begs.

I grasp her thighs and press them upward, and then swipe across her sex. Spreading her open with my fingers, I push my tongue as deep as it can go, and Isavelle cries out. Her inner muscles ripple against me, and I nearly pass out at the thought of sliding into this tight, pink velvet with my cock. This girl was made for me. She's all mine.

I lick her all the way from the tight ring of her ass to her clit. "Omega, you're so fucking delicious," I seethe.

I stroke her clit steadily with my tongue and she cries out louder and louder. When her body tenses with her climax I go on licking and she bucks against me.

With a growl, I turn my head and sink my teeth into her soft thigh. Not hard enough to cause pain, but just enough to leave her with some indentations. I let go and run my tongue over the bite. I'm marking my Omega. She's mine. She's giving herself to me a little piece at a time, and I'm eating up every bite.

I move up her body and whisper against her lips in the dark, "When I'm in a rut, you have my permission to touch me and kiss me wherever you want. Just letting me hold you will be enough. I will probably ask you for more. I will probably pull all my clothes off and squeeze my knot and stroke my cock. I would love for you to touch me, but you don't need to do anything. You can talk to me through a door if you prefer. Or you don't need to be anywhere near me if you don't want to be."

"And if I stay and I want more than what we did just now?"

More is me fucking her with my fingers or with my cock. I groan and press my face into her throat. "Go that far the first time while I'm in a rut? Fuck, I would die from happiness."

"Would you be dangerous?"

"Absolutely not. I'll still be me, and I'll remember every word of what we said to each other just now. I'm always your Alpha, and I'm always protecting you, no matter what."

Isavelle caresses my face. "Thank you, Alpha."

I fall to one side, wrap my arms around her in the darkness, and hold her tight against my body. "I feel very close to you right now, *sha'len*."

Isavelle nuzzles against my bare chest and wraps her arms around me. "You too, Zabriel."

I groan softly. I thought her scent and her slick and her kisses were delicious, but her trust? Her trust is everything.

I remember that she's coming out of a false heat and my Omega is probably starving for praise. Sitting up, I pull the blanket from our heads, gather Isavelle into my arms, and gaze down at her in the morning light. "Your Alpha is so happy with you. You're everything I could have asked for, my sweet Omega."

I mean that. Isavelle's not what I expected.

She's better.

Isavelle whimpers and clutches my biceps. "I don't deserve that. I feel like I've been messing this up every step of the way and disappointing you. Thank you for saying that, Alpha." Then she seems to lose her head and starts to babble. "Just now all I could think about was your knot. Last night in my nest I only wanted to please you, and I thought of you the whole time I touched myself."

Isavelle claps her hand over her mouth, shocked at her own words.

Grinning, I help her off the floor and back into bed. "Sleep for a little while longer, *sha'len*. Or think about me some more. I don't mind which." I press a kiss to her mouth while she blushes furiously, and I admire my girl enveloped in soft blankets. "I'll send word to the temple that they're to bring you fresh tea."

"Thank you, Alpha," she says, burrowing beneath the blankets again.

I take one last look at my mate, then draw the curtains around her bed. Closing the door of her room behind me, I head down the corridor and toward the Flame Temple, smiling the whole way.

25

Isavelle

A whole day passes while I curl up in my nest and drift in a pink haze of warmth and my Alpha's approval. I drink so much of the temple's tea that I think I could fill a pond and go swimming in it. I'm still wearing Zabriel's shirt, and I haven't bathed since he threw me into the cold water at the bathhouse. I love the sensation of the linen against my nipples and remembering the delicious, shocking intrusion of his tongue inside me.

I need to stop thinking about Zabriel and sex, eat something, and then go and do something productive. There's a war happening, and I'm lying around in bed, dreaming of the king.

Reluctantly, I peel myself out of my nest and take off Zabriel's shirt. Standing before the fire, I use a cloth and a basin of cold water to wash myself, staring dreamily out the window wondering what to do today.

I should probably go down into the city and check for news about the people of western Maledin, and I'd like to see Odanna as well.

Twenty minutes later, I find Fiala and Dusan and we head out the castle gates. When they hear my stomach rumbling, they suggest we stop at a food cart for some breakfast. Despite Fiala's craving for something called gritty-bitty, which she swears up and down is the best breakfast I'll ever eat, all the street food in the city is human.

I wave them over to a stall where a woman is wrapping omelets in fried flatbread and slathering them with butter and honey and sprinkling them with salt.

"Eggs with honey?" Dusan asks doubtfully.

"I promise it's delicious. Salty and crispy and sweet at the same time." My mouth is watering as I pass out the rolled-up omelets and pay the stallholder.

The three of us walk along together, me munching blissfully, while the other two take tentative bites, and then larger ones.

"I bet Zabriel would love to try these," I say between mouthfuls. "He's interested in human culture, like apple fritters. The bits that aren't Brethren, anyway."

Fiala and Dusan exchange smirks.

"What's that look for?" I ask.

"You're starting to like *Ma'len*. I knew you would," Fiala says.

Dusan laughs and swallows before he can choke on his breakfast. "Of course she likes him. It's in her blood to think he's hotter than dragons' breath."

Fiala gives him a dirty look. "It's not all about what your body tells you to do. You can want to climb someone like a tree and still think they're a revolting person."

"True, true. I've done that more than once."

"I'm happy that Lady Isavelle and *Ma'len* are getting to know one another, which is something his father never bothered to do with his mate."

I feel saddened, remembering what Zabriel told me the other night at dinner. "Did they not even love one another?"

Fiala hesitates. "Zabriel's family is complicated, and I wouldn't like to speak out of turn."

"Absolutely not," Dusan says mournfully. "I can't take shoveling any more wyvern shit."

So his parents barely knew each other. I think about all the times we've talked and tried to understand each other better. The times we've shared laughter. Kisses. Sad memories. Perhaps Zabriel and I don't have the worst Alpha and Omega relationship that Maledin has ever witnessed.

We head over to the part of the city where Odanna lives, and I find her perched on the back of an unhitched cart, enjoying the sunny morning.

"Isavelle!" Her face breaks into a bright smile as she waves me over, patting the empty space next to her. "How have you been?"

I sit down and tell her the latest news about my family, which is nothing because I haven't found them, but at least I know they're not in Grendu.

Odanna fills me in on what she's been doing down in the city. Tending to travelers' horses. Mucking out stables. Helping the refugees as much as she can and speaking with the castle soldiers. It occurs to me that I don't know whether

Odanna is human or Maledinni, or both. It doesn't matter either way, but it would be nice to share designations with her. Like me, she's not very tall, so perhaps she's an Omega as well.

"Have you noticed anyone acting strangely around you because of the way you smell?"

Odanna holds her sleeve over her face and sniffs and checks the bottom of her shoe. "Do I stink? Have I stepped in something?"

"No, your scent. The natural way you smell. It's how Maledinni court each other and choose their partners."

Odanna grins at me, her lively eyes dancing. "No man has ever followed me around because of the way I smell."

My friend is beautiful, so I can imagine that plenty of men follow her around for that reason alone.

"Is your scent why the king sends his dragon after you and sits you on his lap?" She leans closer and gives me a sniff. "You smell normal to me. It's probably more because he thinks you're charming and adorable."

"Charming and adorable? I don't think so. To him, I smell like honeysuckle and other things."

"What does he smell like to you?"

I kick my legs back and forth and think about this for a moment. "Most of the time, not much. Nothing more than what a man should smell like. Cotton and leather. Sweat if he's been sparring. Smoke if he's been riding Scourge. Nice scents, but I'm sure there's something I'm missing. Every now and then it's like I can smell more, but then it slips through my fingers. Or rather, my nose." I sigh and shake my head. "Or I'm only imagining it. Sometimes I think I'm crazy."

"I'm sure you're not."

"Well, apparently I'm a witch, which is the same thing where I'm from," I grumble, and then bite my lip. I wasn't going to bring that up in case Odanna ran away screaming. Witches had a reputation for eating children and killing cows before the war, and they probably still do.

All Odanna says is, "My granny was a witch. She had to hide it, but all the family knew. She would have premonitions and the things she said would come to pass, did come to pass."

I must be staring at Odanna with an expression of shock on my face as she adds, "There's no reason I shouldn't say it. The Brethren can't hurt us anymore."

I let out a slow breath. They can't, can they? I won't be beaten for touching intimate parts of myself or for having explicit thoughts about a man. I won't be executed for seeing things I shouldn't. It's difficult to get used to this new normal.

"I think I'm like your granny. I see things that are going to happen or are happening. I'm not sure which." I explain the vision I had about Tish and Damla.

"One of those creatures were killed like that, and her rider too? That's terrible," Odanna exclaims. "Dragons still terrify me, but I feel about them like I do about storms. Powerful, frightening, but beautiful."

A dragon like Scourge is certainly all those things, but I'm starting to realize he's not as wild and dangerous as I first thought. He protected me when the Brethren attacked, and he protected Esmeral when she was suffering through her false heat.

"There's so much to understand about New Maledin," I murmur.

Odanna has to get back to her work, and she hugs me

when we say goodbye and makes me promise to come back and see her again soon.

"You're welcome to come and visit me up at the castle," I tell her. "Any of the guards will be able to find out where I am."

She hesitates and glances up at the castle. "Thank you, I'll think about it."

I have the feeling she finds the place intimidating. I can't blame her, considering how I felt about it when I arrived. The most intimidating place I'd ever been, and I was in the arms of the most commanding man I've ever known.

26

Zabriel

I'm coming down a stone staircase into a courtyard when I spot Isavelle talking and laughing with her bodyguards. She must have been down in the city, and she greets the various maids and guards she passes, and she's greeted happily in return. I smile as I watch my beloved. How easily she makes friends, and how readily the people warm to her.

A true Queen of Maledin who will be adored by all. Especially me.

From my place a few steps above, I notice Stesha striding toward Isavelle. He glances at her with disinterest and then looks away again, pretending he hasn't seen her from his towering height as he moves past my petite Omega.

Well, maybe not adored by all, but the dragonmaster will

learn to keep his disapproval to himself, or I'll have something to say about it.

A few feet past Isavelle, Stesha stops dead and stares straight ahead. I watch him idly, wondering what thought has struck the Alpha. He turns around and stares at Isavelle, an inscrutable expression on his face.

Isavelle has moved over to a stone basin for a drink of water and is working the hand pump while Fiala and Dusan stand a few feet away, chatting with each other and looking the other way.

Stesha approaches my mate until he's standing right behind her, blocking out most of my view of her with his broad back. The smile dies on my lips and unease trickles down my spine. Isavelle has no idea he's there as she washes her hands in the fresh water. Her hair is long and loose down her back. Stesha reaches out to touch it.

I grip the handrail, unwilling to believe what I'm seeing.

He lifts a tress of her hair and bends down to lift it to his nose.

With a roar, I leap over the wall and land on the flagstones. I reach the other Alpha in three steps, pull him around to face me, and bellow in his face, "What the fuck do you think you're doing?"

Stesha stares at me in shock. Everyone in the courtyard looks toward us and falls silent.

Isavelle turns around from the stone basin with water dripping from her slender fingers. "Zabriel?"

Another Alpha touched my Omega. Another Alpha is inhaling her scent. Rage like I've never known before boils up inside me.

From the dragongrounds, Scourge lets loose an earth-shattering roar.

My unmated Omega is in the sights of an Alpha who is known by all to crave an Omega of his own. An Alpha who has intense feelings about Isavelle that I believed were dislike but are apparently something more sinister.

Stesha glares at my hand gripping his wrist and his eyes narrow. He wants to throw me off and snarl at me for daring to take hold of him, but I outrank him. I'm his king, and he *touched my fucking Omega*. He's going to explain himself.

The dragonmaster looks at me—not down in submission but right at me—and in a surly tone he mutters, "Apologies."

My temper ratchets up even higher. "I asked you a question. Why were you touching my Omega?"

Isavelle turns to Stesha in astonishment. "You were doing what?"

He opens his mouth, and for an instant, he's about to correct her. *You were doing what, dragonmaster?*

I clench his arm even tighter. "Don't even fucking look at her."

Out of all the Alphas in the castle, I thought I could trust Stesha. I thought I could rely on him no matter what. He has the personality of a thorny vine, but he's a scrupulous observer of the rules that govern our designations, and I believed that he would be the first Alpha to defend my Omega if she were threatened in my absence.

It seems I've been grossly mistaken. Now that I think about it, there's been something off about Stesha since we emerged beneath the mountain. He's treated Isavelle with disrespect, calling her a brat. He's treated me with disrespect as well, but I brushed that off, telling myself that a man as stubborn as Stesha needed time to adjust to a new king. Isavelle took an instant dislike to Stesha. What if her instincts were right and mine were not? Maybe she sensed he's a threat to her, and I didn't listen.

Out of the corner of my eye, I see Fiala and Dusan hurry forward, put their hands on Isavelle's shoulders, and draw her away from us.

Though it makes his nostrils flare in disgust and fury, Stesha says, "I apologize, Zabriel. I made a mistake."

I let go of his arm but step closer to him, crowding him against the wall with my body. Intimidating him into backing down. Daring him to strike me. I don't care which he gives me, his submission or retaliation. I hope he lashes out so I can beat him to a pulp.

"I didn't ask for your apology. I asked you why you're touching my Omega."

"I said it was a mistake," he says sharply.

"It didn't look like a mistake. It looked deliberate from where I stood."

"Then perhaps you didn't see what you thought you saw. Coveting another man's Omega isn't in my bloodline."

He speaks so quietly that I'm the only one who hears him. No one has brought up Emmeric and Mirelle to my face since before Maledin fell. Emmeric, the rapist who knotted his own sister. *My* sister.

I pull back my fist and smash it across Stesha's face.

Staggering, he moves along the wall away from me, his hand over his mouth as blood drips down his arm. He moves out into open space, and onlookers back away from the Alpha as he straightens up.

The dragonmaster wipes blood from his lip and glares at

his fingers. Then he lifts his cold gaze to me. "I hope your honor is satisfied."

With a sneer of his bloody mouth, he turns his back on me and starts to walk away.

Five drops of blood for laying his hands on my Omega? My honor is not satisfied.

"Stesha. Fight me, Alpha to Alpha."

With his back to me, he shakes his head. "You don't want that."

"You still think you can best me?"

Stesha turns slowly toward me, pride burning in his icy eyes. He won't say it out loud, but he believes it in his heart that he can beat me.

He wants the crown.

He wants my Omega.

My whole life, Stesha has been like an older brother to me, or an uncle. Not a benevolent older brother or a kind uncle, because Stesha in neither benevolent nor kind, but he was what I needed. He was who I admired. Not my own father, but Stesha. The Alpha I looked up to as the epitome of everything I wanted to be. Strong. Fierce. Honorable. Courageous. The strongest Alpha in Maledin.

Stronger than my father the king.

Better than my father the king.

Now I see that all the time I was looking up to him, he was looking down on me. Resenting the boy who was becoming the man who would take his place.

"I yield to the king," he says in a flat voice.

That only makes me angrier. I didn't accept the crown because I am my father's son. I accepted it because I thought I could do better, be better, *am* better. The strongest. The smartest. The bravest. I led the invasion of Maledin, and I took our country back for us. I'm not so arrogant that I believe I can rule Maledin without the might of the dragonriders and wingrunners behind me, the dozens of soldiers as well as the *Hratha'len* who give me advice, and the love of my mate.

If another Alpha thinks he can take my Omega from me, I'm going to make him bleed.

"I'm invoking the Rule of Flame. Defend your honor, or I will banish you across the mountains and you will never see Maledin or Nilak ever again."

27

Isavelle

There are gasps all around the courtyard, and I look to Fiala and Dusan to try and understand Zabriel's words.

"Separating him from his dragon? That's a worse punishment for a dragonrider than death," Dusan whispers, and then explains to me, "The Rule of Flame means that two Alphas can duel with each other to first blood, even if one of them is the king."

"But why does Zabriel want to punish Stesha so badly?" I ask desperately.

"Stesha smelled your hair," Fiala says.

I wait for Fiala to go on, but that's all she says. It's an inappropriate thing for Stesha to have done, but was it truly so terrible that we can't all move on after Stesha's apology? "I don't understand."

"It's tantamount to forcing a kiss on you or groping as far as your Alpha is concerned," Fiala explains quietly, not looking away from the two Alphas. "In fact, it's worse. Your scent belongs to *Ma'len* and no one else."

Maybe it's more about what that gesture means. Zabriel has always adored touching my hair and smelling it. I can't fathom why Stesha would do something that's so intimate when he's always hated the sight of me. I remember what Zabriel said about another Alpha forcing his friend's Omega. The memory of that time and those losses must be excruciating for him.

Zabriel draws his sword and waits, his red eyes burning as he glares at Stesha.

Stesha puts his hand on the hilt of his sword but still hesitates.

"Fight me, or never see your dragon again."

With a snarl, Stesha draws his weapon. The two Alphas face each other at a distance of six feet, one dressed in black, the other in white. The wind catches Zabriel's loose hair and teases it around his powerful shoulders.

Neither of them are wearing armor. I don't want Zabriel to get hurt, and I don't want to see him kill a friend either, even if that friend is Stesha.

"No," I moan. I try to dash forward but Fiala and Dusan hold me back. "Let me go. They're going to kill each other."

"It's only to first blood." Dusan hesitates. "Usually. Alphas in a rage can be unpredictable."

The tension in the courtyard is stretched to breaking point.

Zabriel strikes first, raising his sword and bringing it down in a vicious blow. Stesha parries it and falls back.

After the third arm-shattering parry, Stesha has run out of room and has to strike back. I cover my face with my hands in horror as the white-haired Alpha unleashes a series of blows that have Zabriel's arms straining and his sword ringing like it might shatter. First blood could be life's blood the way these two are fighting.

Zabriel feints to the left, and Stesha is tricked into striking out. When he overbalances, he leaves his right side open to an attack. Zabriel swings and Stesha is too late leaping back. The tip of Zabriel's blade rips open his shirt and nicks his ribs. A trickle of red stains the white linen.

"First blood is yours," Stesha says, lowering his sword.

I clasp my hands together in hope. Is the fight over?

Zabriel glares at the older man. "Do you think my memory is that short? Fight me properly."

My hope dies as I realize that Stesha gave Zabriel first blood, and Zabriel could tell. Being called on his deceit makes fury blaze in Stesha's blue eyes. He spins his sword in his hand and dashes forward to attack. The fight resumes, even fiercer than it was a moment ago.

What if Zabriel loses? Will Stesha become king? Will I belong to Stesha? I watch the man who calls me his mate desperately, begging him silently to win this and get out unscathed.

Their swords cross and become locked at the hilts. Across their blades, the two Alphas are nose to nose, sparks flying from their eyes, one set blazing hot, the other bitterly cold. Both their bodies are straining. My fingernails dig into my palms as I wonder whose strength will give out first. Both Alphas are seven feet tall and muscular. Zabriel gathers his feet under him, and with a roar, he pushes the other man off, sweeping his feet from under him. Stesha lands heavily on his back, and his eyes open wide in shock. He twists to get away from Zabriel but the point of my Alpha's blade presses against his neck.

For a moment my heart is in my throat as I wonder if Zabriel will strike a killing blow. He keeps the point of his blade against the other Alpha's neck as he seethes, "Do you yield?"

Stesha's jaw flexes in rage, but a moment later he takes a breath and nods.

"I don't want your blood. I don't want your life. I want your apology to my Omega and your future queen for dishonoring her."

Stesha nods again, and Zabriel steps back, allowing the other man to get to his feet.

Speaking in a wooden voice to a spot somewhere over Zabriel's shoulder, Stesha says, "I apologize to Lady Isavelle for the offense I caused, and I ask for her Alpha's mercy."

"Do you covet her scent?" Zabriel growls.

Stesha's expression contorts with disgust. "Her scent is *nothing* to me. I thought—" Confusion flickers over his face. "I thought I could smell—"

"What? What did you think you could smell on *my mate*?"

Stesha looks wildly around the courtyard, and for a horrifying moment, I think he's hunting for me. If he even looks at me, I think Zabriel might run him through with his sword, but his eyes graze over me as he searches every corner of the square. I've never seen this aloof man look like this before. Frantic. Despairing.

Lost.

Stesha grips his head in both hands, his fingers digging into his scalp. "I think I'm losing my mind."

Zabriel watches him with narrowed eyes, clearly thinking little of Stesha's performance.

The white-haired Alpha shakes his head. "Nothing. I couldn't smell anything. It was a mistake. I apologize to you and your Omega."

"You're fucking right it was a mistake. Find yourself a Beta and get mated. Stop holding out for something that's never going to happen. Above all, stay away from my Omega, or I will rip your knot off and shove it down your fucking throat."

Zabriel sheathes his sword and strides toward me, a thunderous expression on his face. He pulls me into his embrace and his fingers find the nape of my neck, holding me tight and stoking me there. Reassuring himself that I'm unmarked. Unclaimed. Unhurt. There's so much fury in his body that he's shaking.

Everyone is staring at us, and the pressure of their eyes is too much, but my heart hurts for Zabriel, and I have to reassure him.

Taking his face between my hands, I whisper, "I'm all right. He barely touched me. You fought so bravely, Zabriel. Thank you for protecting me."

The expression in his red eyes is bleak. "I couldn't bear it if anyone hurt you, *sha'len*. I'd die if anything like what happened to Mirelle happened to you."

I plant soft kisses on his face, hoping that everyone in the courtyard has turned around and is giving us some privacy.

The next words burst angrily from his lips. "It was my brother. My brother and my sister. The Alpha and Omega I told you about. My bloodline is tainted. Stesha threw it in my face, and I saw red."

For a moment I don't know what he's talking about, and then my stomach twists in horror. The Alpha who raped his sister was Zabriel's brother?

He closes his eyes and drops his head with a groan. "I knew you would be disgusted. I didn't want you to know, but you'd hear about it eventually."

I gently stroke his cheek. "I'm disgusted with your brother. I'm anguished for your sister. And I'm heartbroken for you."

He leans into my touch. "You are too good to me, *sha'len*. I don't feel like I deserve your sweetness."

"You deserve all the sweetness in the world."

"If I ever did anything to hurt you like that, I'd never forgive myself."

I clasp his shoulders and say urgently, "You never, ever would. You could snap me like a twig with your little fingers, but from the moment you laid eyes on me, you have only wanted to keep me safe. I didn't see that at first, but now I do."

He relaxes a little beneath my touch. "Do you really trust me as much as that?"

"I do. You're so kind, and you're merciful as well. Stesha... maybe really did make a mistake."

Instantly, Zabriel tenses again, and he growls, "I saw what he did and it wasn't a mistake."

"But I don't think Stesha even likes me. He's always so cold and critical whenever I talk to him."

"It's not about him liking you or not. Omegas can make some Alphas lose their grip on reality and do crazy, dangerous things."

I nibble on my lip for a moment, remembering the frantic, lost look in Stesha's eyes. "I had the feeling Stesha was looking for someone he already knew. Or used to know. Maybe she died, and she haunts him still."

As I say the other Alpha's name, Zabriel growls. He digs his fingers into my upper arms and looks sharply over at where Stesha lay sprawled on the ground a few minutes ago as if hoping he's still there and he can charge over and finish him off.

Past Zabriel's shoulder, Dusan widens his eyes in alarm and shakes his head. I'm only making Zabriel angrier by poking his wound.

I reach up and take Zabriel's face between my hands, caressing his proud cheekbones with my thumbs. "Look at me. He doesn't matter. Thank you for protecting me, Alpha."

My words cause such a transformation in Zabriel that it's as if night has turned into day. The storm clears from his brow and his jaw unclenches. The raging dragonfire in his eyes suddenly becomes molten red gold.

He wrenches open a nearby door, pulls me inside the castle, and slams it closed behind us. I open my mouth to ask what he's doing, but before I can utter one syllable, he lifts me up in his arms and his mouth crashes into mine.

"Call me Alpha again," Zabriel commands between hungry kisses.

Heat and desire flare to life in my body. Instinct takes over, and I know what he wants to hear. "I only want you, Alpha. I'm all yours."

He kisses me again with teeth and tongue. I feel overwhelmed by his kisses. Drunk on his kisses.

"Wrap your legs around me, *sha'len*."

I do, and Zabriel pushes my back against a wall. He thrusts his hips against mine, the thick outline of his…oh, fire and blood, of his knot grinding against my sex.

"Where are we?" I ask, glancing up and down the darkened corridor. "Someone might walk along here at any moment."

"It doesn't matter. After that fight, no one in this castle will dare come near me now I'm alone with my Omega."

My face burns at the realization that everyone will know why we've disappeared and what we're doing at this very moment.

"I could feel you wanting me to win, *sha'len*."

My toes curl with pleasure, and I turn my attention back to Zabriel. He did win, and in a fierce fight against a battle-hardened Alpha.

"I did," I whimper, parting my lips so he can thrust his tongue into my mouth and moaning when he does. "I'm so proud of you."

"You wanted your Alpha to prove he was the strongest. I can smell it on you."

I twist my fingers in the silky hairs and the nape of his neck and nod rapidly. I must smell intensely fragrant right now. I'm getting more and more turned on, but I still can't smell his scent. When am I going to be able to smell his scent?

Zabriel's red eyes gleam in triumph. "Let me reward you. How would you like to come?" He flicks my lips with his tongue. "Your fingers. My fingers. My tongue. My cock."

I can't think, I can only cling to him with both arms and feel him break over me like a wave every time he thrusts his knot against my sex. He tugs my skirts out of the way so that only my thin drawers are against the bulge in his breeches.

"I want your slick all over me. I dream of your slick. I ache for your slick. Every little thing about you is precious to me, but when you show me that you want me, I lose my mind. I can't wait to rut you hard for days until we both pass out."

Zabriel kisses me deeply, both of us gasping for breath between swipes of his tongue.

"I want to fuck you like this, holding you up against a wall with your weight pulling you down onto my knot. Filling you to bursting. Lodged there so deep. Stretched to your limit around me."

His words unlock something feral inside me. My hands rip at his shirt, pushing it from his shoulders, and my nails scratch across his muscular back. "Alpha, please. *Please*."

"You want to touch me? You want to know how full you'll be of me when I mate you, my sweet Omega?"

I nod, and he grasps one of my hands and drives it down between us. Down the front of his pants. My fingers touch the broad, blunt head of his cock. It's blazing hot and slippery, wet from my slick. My fingers close around his girth. Or they try to, anyway.

Blood and stars. He's a *monster*.

Zabriel holds my wrist and draws my fingers along his cock to the base, where I feel a much larger swelling.

"Is that…?" My eyes open wide in surprise.

"That's my knot, little queen. Squeeze me," he says in a rough voice.

Tentatively, I tighten my fingers around him. His flesh barely yields, but he groans and drops his head to my shoulder. "Don't stop. Please keep touching me."

I explore his length with my fingers, feeling the fat veins, the ridge at the tip, the plush, velvety head, and then back to the hard, throbbing knot. I wrap as much of him in my hand as I can and hold him tightly.

Zabriel opens his mouth and fits his teeth around my throat. They scrape against my skin, and then he opens wider and bites the place where my neck meets my shoulder. His pointed teeth dig into my flesh, and he holds on with a growl.

Me tight around his knot. His teeth buried in my neck. This is what our mating will be like.

I bring a silky tress of his hair to my face and breathe in, hoping for an elusive whiff of his true scent, but I can only catch the faintest trace of him. I want more, and I've just remembered there's a way I can have more.

I dip my hand into my pocket and draw out the bottles that I got from the Flame Temple and from Biddy Hawthorne. I've been carrying them around ever since the day the Temple Crone gave me the second one. "The crone gave me this. It's supposed to help me smell your scent. And Biddy Hawthorne gave me this one. It will hide my scent from you."

Zabriel gazes at the bottles. "You want to try one of these?"

I nod.

"Which one?"

I stare at the bottles, which look like little glass decisions. Big ones, despite their small size. It's been easy for me to push Zabriel away and pretend he's not my mate when I couldn't smell his scent and I didn't feel anything for him. Now, I feel so much for him. This man stormed into my life, and then he stormed into my heart.

I only need one bottle because there isn't any going back after all that's happened between us. I'll dive in headfirst and figure out the rest later.

Maybe a village girl can fall in love with a king.

I let the bottle from Biddy Hawthorne slip from my fingers and hold the other one up. "This is the bottle from the Temple Crone. It will help me smell my Alpha's scent."

"And you want to use it on me?"

I nod again.

Zabriel reaches behind himself, pulls his long hair back, and angles his head to one side with his neck bared to me. He watches through heavy-lidded eyes as I twist the wax seal and cork from my bottle and pour oil over my fingers. I smooth it over his muscular neck. It drips over his collarbone, down his chest, and inside his shirt.

His eyes close in pleasure at my touch, and there's a smile on his lips.

"What if I still can't smell you?" I whisper.

Zabriel opens his eyes. "Then we'll keep trying until you do. I'm not going anywhere, Omega. And neither are you."

I lean closer to him and take a tentative sniff, and the most delicious scent I've ever smelled washes over me.

Dark cherries. Freshly split oak logs. Hot, spiced wine. Heart-pumping danger. The sky at midnight. Flashing lightning and rolling thunder. Not only is it earth-shatteringly wonderful to finally breathe in the scent that I've been straining to catch, but I recognize it. I've caught it before in tiny, tiny snatches.

I cry out in shock and tears fill my eyes. It's *him*. I can smell my Alpha's scent. I don't know why I'm crying, except that I'm so happy.

Zabriel wraps his arms around me and laughs in delight, rocking me from side to side. "It worked? Did it work, *sha'len*?"

"It worked," I say, my voice cracking in a sob. "It's you. I *know* you."

Zabriel stops moving. "You do? You know me like I know you?"

"I do," I cry, burying my face in his throat and inhaling over and over again. His scent seems to grow stronger every time I breathe in. "You're my mate. You're my Alpha. I smell it. I *know* it."

Zabriel's mouth seeks mine and he kisses me with so much feeling that my heart sings. "My Omega. My mate."

My arms are locked around him and I can't let go.

"The next time your false heat comes upon you and you dive into that nest again, I'm coming with you so I can touch you just like this. When everything aches too much, I'll soothe it for you. Your tender nipples. Your throat. Your core. Everything that aches I want to touch."

I moan and breathe in deeply, already anticipating bathing in his scent next time my false heat arrives. If I can't smell him on my own, I'll use the oil again. I'll drench him with it. "Please. I want that. I want that so much."

"Would you like to feel me now? One finger to clench on so sweetly while I make you see stars?"

"You mean inside me, Alpha?"

"Only as deep as you want me to go."

I remember the hot thrust of his tongue in my core. "Please, Alpha."

Zabriel sets me on my feet. "Put your hands against the wall."

I do as I'm told, turning around so my back is facing him with my palms pressed against stone. He picks me up again instantly, raising his knee and settling me on it, and pulling me back against his chest. We both pull up my skirts, then Zabriel undoes my drawers and slides his fingers into them and over my sensitized flesh. All four of his fingers rub over my lips and my clit, tugging gently at my flesh and spreading the wetness. My slick surges even harder. The tip of his middle finger curls and just dips inside my aching core. I lift my feet and brace them against the wall, letting my thighs fall open. I no longer care about anyone coming down this corridor. I need him inside me so badly it's all I can think about, and Zabriel won't let anyone but him see me like this.

"Fuck yes, good girl," he breathes in my ear and pushes his thick finger into me. My core lights up around him.

I arch my back and drive him deeper. "More, please," I whimper.

Zabriel reaches his other hand inside my drawers and circles it slowly over my clit as he pushes his finger in and out of me.

"I love you touching me," I whisper, my head falling back against his shoulder and closing my eyes. His scent is all around me. I reach down and slip my hand inside his breeches and close my fingers around his knot. Then I stroke his whole length, back and forth.

Zabriel groans and nips my neck with his teeth. His voice is a hot and heavy whisper in my ear. "That feels amazing, *sha'len*. Please keep stroking me. Just like that. So perfect."

I keep up an unsteady rhythm on his cock while he rubs my clit and pushes his finger into me.

"More?" he breathes.

I nod rapidly, my mouth open as I pant, and he surges deeper. By all the *stars*.

Zabriel keeps rubbing my clit while he pistons his finger in and out of me. My legs shake. The pressure building inside me is making me clamp tighter and tighter around him. There are rivers of gold inside me.

"*Sha'len*, yes. You're stroking me so beautifully. I'm going to come just from your pretty fingers."

I reach back and grip his shoulder as I cry out, "Alpha, yes," and my body rocks with a powerful orgasm that Zabriel drives higher and higher with his thrusting finger.

I feel a spasm go through him, and he fastens his teeth on my neck and bites down harder than he ever has before. His teeth are a flash of pleasure in my flesh. Liquid bursts from his cock, hot and thick, and he releases a deep and sensuous groan.

When my climax ebbs away and Zabriel stops thrusting against my hand, we're both breathing hard.

"Did that feel good for you?" I whisper.

All Zabriel can do is wrap both his arms around me and bury his face in my neck. That was the best thing I've ever felt. I forgot to wonder if I'm too heavy for him to hold me up with just one leg. I guess I'm not. My Alpha is strong.

"I could barely remember my own name. The way you clenched on my finger, *sha'len*. I've never felt anything so beautiful." He draws my chin up and slants his mouth over mine in a bruising kiss. "Good fucking Omega."

Even more pleasure rushes through me. It feels insanely good to be praised for having an orgasm.

"I loved feeling you gush in my hand," I say shyly. "I didn't think I could give you as much pleasure as you give me."

Zabriel peppers me with kisses as he lowers me slowly to the ground. "Fighting for my Omega's honor and then getting to ravish her. Feeling her touch me. Stroke me to release. Your Alpha is so pleased with you."

As I do up my drawers, I feel how soaked I am. "I'm a wet mess." But this time, I don't feel so embarrassed about it.

"A delicious mess." Zabriel grins and kisses me. "Come down to the bathhouse with me. I love a soak after a long battle."

~

We soaked for hours in the hot water, me wearing my shift and sneaking looks at his knot beneath the water because he was naked, of course. He asked me if I minded, and I didn't, though I still felt too shy to look directly at him as he got in and out of the water.

I asked if I could take his shirt soaked with oil and his scent back to my room, and he told me of course I can.

I sleep with it that night curled tight in my arms, his scent drifting around me, and a smile on my face.

I awaken in the darkness sometime later and sleepily draw his shirt up to my face and breathe in. I expect his heady fragrance to fill my head, but there's...nothing. I open my eyes with a cry of dismay. The oil must have worn off, or I hugged all the scent off his shirt already.

I try to go back to sleep, but there's a gnawing sensation in my guts. Now that I've caught his scent, I don't want to be without it.

I sit up and glance toward the door. There's no reason for me to be without it when the source is sleeping not far away.

Pushing back the blankets, I get out of bed, leave my room, and pad down the corridor. I know generally the direction of Zabriel's rooms, but a female guard in armor stationed along the corridor watches me hurry back and forth.

I go over and twist my fingers together, asking shyly, "Um, could you please tell me where King Zabriel sleeps?"

The guard's lips twitch in a small smile and she nods to her left. "Third door down and through the big red door."

"Thank you." My face erupts into a blush as I hurry away, imagining what the guard will be telling her friends over breakfast.

Lady Isavelle was hunting for Ma'len's room in the middle of the night. She must have liked her Alpha's display in the courtyard yesterday.

It wasn't the fight that got me all hot and bothered.

There's a small smile on my lips as I recall how Zabriel bested Stesha, and an answering surge of heat between my thighs.

Well, not just the fight.

Mostly it's his scent.

His scent. I breathe in with more and more purpose as I approach his rooms, hoping to catch it. At times I think I do, but I'm not sure.

My heart beats wildly as I push open the red door. Zabriel would probably be happy to find me in his rooms, but I can't shake the feeling that I'm trespassing.

There's a small antechamber and then the main room. A huge room with an enormous bed against one wall, bigger than any bed I've ever seen before. It has to be enormous because the man sleeping in it is huge. He sleeps a little diagonally in the middle of the mattress, not huddled along one edge like I do. Zabriel knows this is his bed. He's the King of Maledin by stars and fire, and he's going to fill this bed.

I tiptoe closer, my gaze sweeping over him.

Zabriel's long, dark hair is spread over the white pillows and his chest is bare, with one of his arms flung above his head. He has a sheet draped around his hips and I can see the outline of his—very thick even at rest—cock with a swelling at the base, and the ridge at the head that lays an alarming distance down his thigh. Even asleep, the man is intimidating. All that is supposed to fit inside me when just his finger felt huge. I guess there's a good reason why my slick is so excessive. I'm going to need all the help I can get.

Reminding myself to focus on why I'm here, I take a look around. Is there a worn shirt somewhere? Can I steal a blanket? A pillow? What's loose on his bed that I can slip away with?

A light blanket is tucked beneath one of his arms. If I can just get it out from beneath his elbow, I'll have it. Getting up on the bed, I crawl carefully toward him on my hands and knees, and then reach out and pull.

Suddenly, Zabriel's eyes fly open, burning red in the dark, and he grips my wrist.

In a seething voice, he accuses, "It was you."

28

Zabriel

Isavelle's eyes widen in the dark. I'm gripping her wrist so hard that I'm scaring her.

I make myself let go of her and sit up. "Sorry, *sha'len*. I was dreaming about us and..." I look around, realizing I'm in my bed and so is she. "What are you doing here?"

She touches the coverlet lying beside me. "I'm sorry. I needed something of yours and I couldn't wait."

A smile spreads over my face and I open my arms to her. "Did you miss my scent? Come here, little one."

Isavelle whimpers and throws herself into my arms. Her sweet body melts into mine as I close my arms around her.

"Can you smell me?"

Isavelle presses her nose into the hollow at the base of my throat and breathes in. "Only faintly, but you're there. Your true scent." Her arms tighten around my neck.

"Zabriel, I think that oil really helped me. It's unlocked something."

"Those *Hratha'len* are clever women," I tell her with a smile, hugging her happily.

"What were you dreaming about?"

I stroke her hair back from her face. "While I was trapped beneath the mountains, all I could do was dream. I've been having some of the same dreams again, though I can't remember them unless I'm awoken suddenly. Do you remember what Biddy said, about you trying to reach the Bodan Mountains when you were a child? I think you were trying to find me."

"Why do you think that?"

I press my forehead to hers and breathe, "Because I was trying to find you. You came to me in my dreams. The sense of you, very far away and indistinct. I never knew who it was that was brushing against my awareness and calling to me. Just now when you woke me up, I was dreaming the same dream, and when I woke up and saw you, I knew. Did something happen to you about a week before you were nearly thrown onto the pyre by the Brethren?"

Isavelle looks down at my hands and squeezes my fingers. "I got into trouble again. I talked back to the High Priest when he told me my manner was insolent, and he ordered for me to be beaten so badly that I passed out. When I woke up, everything hurt so much that I wish I hadn't awoken at all. I wanted to die. I cried for something to change. I wished for it as hard as I used to wish for the dragons to return to Maledin like they did in the stories. As I wished for it, I think I may have even thought of the dragons."

I cup her face in my hands, my heart pounding with

excitement and gratitude. "You woke me up, *sha'len*. You broke the spell on me and on my people. On all the dragons and wyverns. We're here because of you."

"Do you really think it's possible that I did it?"

I smile at her. "Who else could have done it but my mate? Scourge knew, right from the start. I felt him hunting for something the moment he took to the skies for the first time in five hundred years. I thought it was his mate he was hunting for, but it was mine."

"Whether it was me or not, I'm so thankful that you returned." Isavelle stares at my mouth, her eyes dilating. "Take something from me. Please. I'm begging you. If there's something that you crave then I want you to—"

Fire erupts in my chest hearing my Omega beg. She wants me to prove to her that I'm real and that we're together at last.

I sink my teeth into the spot between her neck and shoulder and bite down hard. I groan, and she cries out in pain. I know it hurts her, but from the way she grabs my wrists and wraps my arms even tighter around her body, I think she likes it.

"Zabriel, even the pain feels good."

I release my jaws and lick my tongue over the spot that I bit. "I don't think I should do that. Any harder and I'll break the skin."

"I'm not thinking straight, am I? I can't be if you making me bleed sounds like a good time."

"How about I just..." I choose a different spot and bite into her, faster this time.

Isavelle shrieks in pain and desire.

My mate between my teeth.

This is pleasure beyond anything I've known before.

Loosening my jaws, I press kisses to the burning red marks. "You're so perfect between my teeth, little one."

"This feels as good as the way you touched me earlier. Isn't that crazy?"

My lips whisper against her flesh as I say, "Do you trust me?"

She nods.

"Alpha and Omega relationships are built on trust. They're so intense they have to be. Show me where you want your next bite."

Isavelle arches her neck the other way and strokes her fingers along her flesh, showing me where she wants my teeth.

"Good girl. Such a perfect Omega." I bite her hard, and we both moan. Pleasure floods my body as I know it must be flooding hers. Having her to praise and sink my teeth into is everything. I release her slowly and again run my teeth over the marks. I can't wait to taste her blood bursting in my mouth.

"This is so crazy. I didn't know people could feel like this," she whispers, her neck arched blissfully.

"You're not people. You're Maledinni. You're the Queen of the Maledinni."

"Why me? I believe I'm your mate and I'm not questioning us, but it seems reckless of the universe or the gods to fate us to each other when you were asleep for five hundred years, and I was nearly thrown onto a funeral pyre."

"I believe there is a reason for everything, even Maledin falling, though it hurts to say that knowing how you and the rest of my people have suffered for all these centuries under the Brethren. If you and I are fated for each other, there must be a reason."

Isavelle muses on this for a moment, coiling a tress of my hair around her finger. "Dragon bonds, magic, witches, and visions. There are strong forces in the world, and where there is power, there must be balance, or those with all the power will run rampant. Perhaps that's what fate is, the ongoing struggle for balance."

I never thought about it that way before. My father thought he was indestructible because of all the power he wielded. If Isavelle's right, then maybe Maledin falling was to teach the dragonriders to be humble and know their place, and Isavelle and I aren't here to put things right, but we are here to rebalance this country and make it stronger.

Isavelle is sunk in thought for a moment. "Just after we met, I had a vision. I think Biddy helped me somehow. It felt like she gave me some of her power but the vision was my own."

"I'd forgotten about that. She told me that you did. Was your vision of us? Of me?" I ask hopefully.

"It was you, but you looked different to how you look now. Your eyes were blue gray. Your hair was brown."

My excitement dims. "You saw me how I was before I bonded with Scourge. My hair and eyes changed color a few years ago. Well, a few hundred years ago." I would have liked to hear that she saw us mated and happy together. My teeth in her neck. My baby inside her. That's something important that the universe should have shown her. Not how I used to be.

"You reached for me in that vision, like even your past self knew who I was. Do you ever remember seeing me? Maybe in a dream?"

I don't even need to think about it. "I never laid eyes on you until I saw you on the ground along the Proxen Road with your hands tied in front of you. If I'd been blessed with a vision, I would have remembered you. I would have known that my Omega was on her way to me and anticipated you every second that passed."

Isavelle nods. "Mistress Hawthorne didn't seem to think you should have been able to see me. Maybe another witch who understands visions better will be able to tell me one day what was happening."

"Sleep the rest of the night here with me, *sha'len*?" I ask her. "Every night if you want. You're always welcome in my bed."

Isavelle glances toward the door. "Won't there be gossip about us if I spend the night? Couples aren't supposed to spend the night together before they're married."

I laugh softly, tucking her against my body and closing my eyes. "No one cares about that in Maledin. Fated mates are meant to be together, and woe betide anyone and anything who tries to keep them apart."

29

Isavelle

There's a chilly mist hanging over the dragongrounds as I cross the stone bridge the following morning. Large bodies and angular wings move in the haze. As I am walking among the dragons, I search for a small, turquoise and gold one, or a large black one. If I find one then I've found the other, as Esmeral and Scourge are rarely apart when Scourge is not away with Zabriel.

A man emerges suddenly through the ice-laced air. He's the color of ice with his pale eyes and white hair, and his eyes widen in shock and every muscle of his body tenses as he gazes down at me. Stesha. I haven't seen him since he fought with Zabriel, and as far as I know, Zabriel hasn't talked with him either.

Someone should try and clear the air, so I say hesitantly, "Stesha, can I talk to you? I know you weren't..."

The white-haired Alpha turns on his heel and strides away without a backward glance. I sigh as I watch him go. I suppose I should have expected that. Zabriel threatened to take Nilak away from him and banish him so he'd never be among the dragons of the flare ever again. The dragons seem to be the only thing that makes Stesha happy. I don't know how things can ever be made right between the two Alphas.

I'm gazing sadly after him, thinking how hard it must be for Zabriel to lose a friend at a time like this, when something nudges against my hand. A turquoise head is butting against my palm, and when I stroke Esmeral, she trills and clicks and patters closer to me.

With both my hands cupping either side of her head, I gaze into her eyes. Beautiful eyes. Intelligent eyes. Right at this moment, they're filled with interest and hope. While I've been going through a cycle of false heats, aches, exhaustion, and intense desire for an enormous, dangerous male, so has she. While I've been hesitating, Esmeral has been hungry for each and every new thing that has come her way.

"I think you're very brave, Esmeral. You ask for what you want in a loud voice with very sharp teeth."

The dragon seems to know I'm complimenting her and she nuzzles my shoulder.

"I...I don't know if I want to fly, but maybe we can be friends if you want?"

Esmeral's head tilts to one side. Either she doesn't understand the question or she doesn't like it. Over her shoulder, Scourge is watching me, his red eyes blazing in the mist. I have the sense that he knows exactly what's going on, and he doesn't like it.

Don't you dare reject my mate. Don't you dare hurt my mate. I don't hear those words, but I feel that sentiment from him.

I take a shuddering breath. "I'm trying, Scourge. Please."

He snorts, and then swings his huge bulk around and paces away down the dragongrounds.

Turning back to Esmeral, I say, "I don't know if I can fly with you. It's frightening. It's..." I hunt deep inside myself for what I'm really afraid of.

It puts me on display.

That feels like the answer. On Esmeral, there'd be nowhere to hide. No place to run. I draw so much attention being the king's mate, but if it becomes overwhelming, I can hide my face in his shoulder and feel his arms protectively around me, or I can run to my room. It was always dangerous to be seen in Maledin. Catching the eye of the Brethren meant you were about to be punished, and I was singled out almost every single day.

"I'm still afraid of them," I say under my breath, and Esmeral trills in response.

I stroke Esmeral's scales thoughtfully, picturing myself on Esmeral's back.

"Do you think..." I begin and break off as the world wobbles.

It happens just like it did the first time.

The world turns black.

Blacker than black, without sight, taste, sound, smell, or sensation. I'm in an empty void.

I *am* the void.

I'm within it. It expands from me. The void is all places

and everything and gradually, the world reforms around me. The outline of a cottage. The sensation of cold wind brushing against my cheek. The scent of woodsmoke and apples in the air makes my stomach convulse in longing as it reminds me so much of home.

Slowly, a village appears around me from the darkness. A little square paved with uneven flagstones. A stone well with a wooden bucket hanging from a rope. A dozen cottages with thatched rooves and familiar painted front doors.

It is home. I turn slowly on the spot, marveling at every detail because Amriste looks as I haven't seen it since the day I was taken away by the Brethren. There are people here, getting off carts, hurrying up to front doors with bundles on their backs, hugging each other, and looking around with smiles on their faces as if delighted they're home. I recognize the two middle-aged Cantrell sisters, and Grandfather Ackworth, his son, and his granddaughter.

I whirl to my left and hurry forward, anxious to see one cottage in particular. The one I've known my whole life where some of the dearest people in the world to me reside, or they did until recently.

A woman is standing on the garden path up to the front door, her arms wrapped around a boy with a mop of dirty blond curls. She's smiling happily, gazing around as if she can't believe she's standing where she is.

"Ma," I whisper. Then louder in delight and with tears welling up in my eyes, "Ma."

I run toward her while calling out louder and louder, but stop when I realize she can't hear me. That's all right. She's in Amriste. She's alive and well and finally home, and so is my brother Waylen.

Through the open door to the cottage, I can see two figures moving within, and hear a bright, chattering voice and a pleasant, deeper one. Dad and my sister, Anise. They're both alive and well too. Happiness bursts through my chest, and I step forward so I can hear what they're saying, not caring they can't see or hear me.

There's a screaming overhead, and something small and black dives for me, claws first, and caws loudly. Raven feathers brush across my face. The bird wheels around and attacks me for a second time.

I fling my arms in front of my face and cry out, "Mistress Hawthorne, don't. It's me, Isavelle."

Somehow, even though no one else in the village can see me, Biddy Hawthorne's crows can. It must be a witch thing, though why she should send her messengers to attack me I have no idea.

All sight and sound snap out of existence. As I lower my arms, I come out of the vision so swiftly that I stagger. When I open my eyes, my hands are braced against turquoise scales and I'm panting hard. Two shining turquoise and gold eyes are gazing into mine, and Esmeral's head is tilted curiously to one side. She nudges me urgently as if asking what's wrong.

"They're home, Esmeral. My family is finally home. My whole village is home, and maybe even everyone else in western Maledin."

I have to go there. I need to be in Amriste as soon as possible and wrap my arms around my parents and brother and sister after all this time and let them know I'm alive, which means finding my mate and flying there together.

As if she can hear my thoughts, Esmeral trills, ducks her

body low to the ground, and nudges closer to me. She's offering for me to climb onto her back.

I take her head between my hands. "Where's Zabriel? Can you find Zabriel?"

In answer, Esmeral butts urgently against me again. I hesitate for a moment, expecting to be flooded by anxiety at the thought of riding Esmeral, but I feel only excitement. There's no reason to feel afraid of the Brethren. They can't hurt me anymore, and they can't hurt my family. I can try this and see how it feels, and at the very least, this is probably the fastest way for me to find Zabriel.

Esmeral is so delighted to feel me on her back that her hind legs stamp in the dust, and then she launches herself into the air. I feel a lurch, but it's nowhere near as stomach-juddering as it is when I've ridden Scourge. Esmeral is smaller and lighter and shoots into the mist-laden sky.

It takes me a moment to feel secure enough to get my bearings by looking toward the ground. I find we're streaking not toward the castle, but toward the west. In shock, I watch as the city slips away beneath us in mere seconds to be replaced by open fields. Esmeral is taking me to Amriste, not to Zabriel. Either she didn't understand my words, or I didn't understand how you're supposed to ask your dragon to take you somewhere. Zabriel communicates with Scourge in his mind, so maybe Esmeral heard me craving to be in Amriste with my family above all else.

I try and shout over the wind, but my voice is snatched from my lips and carried away behind me. I try thinking very loudly that I want to be taken to Zabriel, not Amriste, but it doesn't seem to work. My desire is to go home, so that's where Esmeral is taking me.

We break out of the mist and into warm sunshine, and I can't help but laugh with happiness at the thought of what's waiting for me at the end of this flight. How my family will gaze in shock and then in happiness as they see me hurrying toward the cottage. Zabriel will be angry that I left the safety of the castle without him or my bodyguards, but I know he'll forgive me when I explain that it was a mistake, and he'll be so pleased by this new turn of events and the fact that I've ridden Esmeral that he won't be able to stay angry for long.

Below, the mist has mostly lifted, but the skies overhead are now gray. I see the familiar road leading into my village and realize that it's a better place for Esmeral to land than in the main square where she might frighten the villagers. To my surprise, the dragon hears that thought loud and clear and begins to spiral toward the ground.

When Esmeral lands, I try and slide from her back as elegantly as I've seen Zabriel do it, but I misjudge it and end up in a heap on the ground. Brushing my hands off and getting to my feet, I'm grateful that no one saw my first attempt to get off a dragon by myself.

"Stay here for a moment. I'll bring my family to meet you." I pat Esmeral's neck and then hurry into the village.

As I step into the square, I'm greeted not by the delightful scents of woodsmoke and apples, but by the stench of blood and suffering. It hits me like I've been belted across the face by one of Scourge's wings.

For a moment I reel back, but as I gaze around the square my stomach convulses.

What I find in my village is so alarming that I can't make sense of what I'm seeing. Happy families unpacking their belongings from carts and donkeys are nowhere to be seen.

Thick, twisted vines have erupted through the cobbles in front of every cottage, and vicious black spikes are thrust toward the sky. They're so unnatural that they must have been conjured by magic, and what a stench this magic has. A foul, acrid scent fills my nose. Over the reek of evil is another scent. The tang of blood and misery.

On each wickedly gleaming spike is a strange shape. A head twisted to one side. An arm at a strange angle. I don't understand what I'm looking at and wonder for a moment if the thorns have grown body parts. Then I realize that the thorns are thrust through bodies, impaling them with such force they've lifted them off their feet. Blood oozes from their wounds and drips onto the cobbles.

My breath starts coming faster and faster. I don't want to see what's in front of my cottage.

Not my family. Not them as well. I saw them in my vision, and they were happy. They were *home*.

Unable to bear not knowing, convinced that my family will be fine and this is all just some horrible mistake, I keep my gaze fixed on the ground as I approach the home that I grew up in. Then I lift my eyes and see Ma, her green eyes dead and staring and her hair rippling in a faint breeze. Blood oozes from the corner of her mouth. I turn toward the other spike, and a cry so filled with pain it barely sounds human rips from my throat. Waylen. My brother's skinny, still childish body has been viciously impaled through the back and up through his fragile chest. His *face*—

I can't linger over the expression of misery and pain etched on his babyish features. I turn and fall to my knees and start to sob. This is not what I saw. This isn't my vision. This is a nightmare.

Dad and Anise were inside our cottage. I merely glimpsed them, but I heard their happy voices. I turn and look over my shoulder as tears pour down my face, but nothing moves inside past the open cottage door, and Dad and Anise wouldn't laugh while Ma and Waylen were impaled on spikes.

"Dad. Anise," I call, my voice cracking between sobs.

But they're not here. As my eyes travel around the square, I realize that everyone I saw in my vision is dead. People I merely glimpsed or heard are nowhere to be seen.

Something butts against my shoulder and gives a sad cry. Esmeral has crept closer, her body low to the ground, her head bowed in grief. There's so much sadness filling her beautiful turquoise and golden eyes, as if she's lost her family. My hands are limp and useless in my lap as I gaze at her. I can't feel anything but the pain in my heart. What has been the point of all the weeks of hope and worry only to discover that Ma and Waylen are dead? How could I have cried in the dark for them for a whole year while the Brethren beat me, only to never hug Waylen again? Feel Ma's arms around me. Listen to her voice. I'll never get to talk to her again. I'll never laugh with Waylen or chase him around the kitchen table as I threaten to tickle him.

Esmeral lifts her head and makes a loud, keening wail, as if all the pain in the world has suddenly been heaped on her back. It sounds like she's crying. Esmeral suffering with me. I wish I wasn't hurting her with the misery in my heart. I try to turn away from her, but she fastens her teeth on my sleeve and pulls me back. Esmeral unfurls her wings and wraps them around me. Holding me. Protecting me. At the same time, she enfolds her consciousness around mine. I attempt to shield her from what I'm going through, but it's too late. She's everywhere, and I'm not strong enough to push her away.

The grief rises up in a huge wave. I lean against her breastbone and sob into her neck. I cry so hard that I don't know if I'll ever stop. I cry for my family, dead and lost. I cry for Dad and Anise, who must be in the same pain as I am, or they will be if they ever learn Ma and Waylen's fate. I cry for Ma's pain, and the terror poor timid little Waylen must have felt all this time. They're gone, and I'm alone.

Only I'm not. Warm, leathery wings surround me. Turquoise and golden flames dance behind my closed eyes. I can feel Esmeral everywhere. I can't tell where I end and she begins.

I open my eyes and touch her throat. "I pushed you away as much as Zabriel. I'm so sorry. I don't deserve you."

Esmeral chitters angrily and buffets her head against my shoulder. I can feel her telling me not to be so stupid.

"You are my dragon, aren't you? And I'm your rider. You and I are like Zabriel and Scourge. Stesha and Nilak. Tish and Damla." Meant to be together. Meant to die together.

Esmeral ducks her head and rests her cheek against mine. The capricious, excitable creature I first came to know is as steady as a rock as she protects me. Comforts me. Lends me her strength.

Whole oceans of strength. I feel them coursing through me. This is what a dragon is. Pure, tempered strength.

"What are we going to do now?" I whisper.

Esmeral trills softly and wraps herself even tighter around me. Whatever we're going to do, we're going to do it together.

"Isavelle?" a tentative voice calls across the square.

Esmeral's wings unfurl a little and I peer out.

A lone figure is standing on the other side of the square, a young woman with dark brown hair and a horsey scent about her.

Surprise sweeps over me. "Odanna? What are you doing here? How did you even get here?"

Esmeral opens her jaws in a soft, warning hiss. I glance up at my dragon and see that her burning eyes are fixed on the young woman. Odanna isn't looking around at the dead villagers in horror. She's only looking at me, which is so strange that my neck prickles in alarm.

She hurries forward, her expression desperate. "Isavelle, you must go. Leave now. He'll take you. He'll *kill* you."

I curl my fingers around one of Esmeral's talons, holding on to my dragon as my heart pounds in fear. I have no intention of following anyone's orders except my own, Zabriel's, my dragon's, or Scourge's. They're the only ones that I trust.

"Who's going to kill me?" I gesture to all the dead villagers. "The Shadow King? Did he do all this?"

Odanna finally looks around her. Her fingers twist together, and she shakes her head like she's confused. "I don't know. I..."

"Odanna, what are you doing here? How did you even get here?"

"I..." she says but trails off again.

Esmeral hisses again, and there are rumblings inside her as she prepares to breathe fire.

I watch Odanna through narrowed eyes. There's no innocent reason for her to be here. She must have been following me, which is alarming, or working for the Brethren, which means she's the enemy when I thought she was a friend. "I had a vision that everyone in my village was safe and happy. I thought my visions showed me things that are happening, but instead, I found this."

Odanna clenches her fists and shouts, "*No*. It wasn't a real vision. It was a trick."

I didn't expect her to admit it. Through clenched teeth, I seethe at her, "Obviously it was a trick, but how do you know that?"

There's another confused silence, and then Odanna's anguished expression drains away until her face is blank. I say her name several times, but she doesn't seem to hear me.

Finally, she blinks, and her gaze refocuses on me. "I know you, don't I?"

Esmeral is so surprised by this strange question that her jaws snap shut.

I frown at Odanna. "Of course you know me. We've known each other for weeks. I'm Isavelle."

"But I..." Odanna's eyes widen and her hand flies to her mouth. She backs away, shaking her head. "Oh, no. No, no, *no*. I'm so sorry. This is all my fault. You must run. *Fly*. Get on your dragon and go. I didn't mean to do it. He'll never forgive me. None of them will ever forgive me." Odanna begins to sob brokenly. She's a split second from turning to flee.

"Who are you talking about? The Shadow King? Who *is* he?"

I get to my feet, but Odanna turns around and runs out of the village. I'm about to follow her when a raven caws overhead and swoops at me. Not to attack, but to get my attention.

Now what? I call out, "Mistress Hawthorne?"

There's the sound of running feet, but they're moving far too fast to belong to Biddy Hawthorne.

Esmeral shrieks in anger and alarm, baring her teeth, as Brethren Guard burst into the square on all sides. Two dozen of them. Then three dozen. Then too many to count.

There's a pitchfork lying in the weeds in front of a cottage. I grab hold of it and brandish the pointy end at my enemies. I have to keep turning because they're all around me. Is this Odanna's fault as well? Why did she have to betray me when I thought she was a friend?

"Since when did she have a dragon?" someone calls.

"Never mind the dragon. She's only small. Get the girl."

Esmeral screams in outrage, and I can feel that she's going to make them mind very much about the small but murderous dragon. Heat blazes from her scales, and she opens her jaws and lets loose a thin but vicious stream of dragonfire at three Brethren Guard. In a second, they're engulfed in flames, and they scream and fall to the ground.

Esmeral lowers her body so I can climb onto her back. Still holding on to the pitchfork, I scramble up onto her and feel Esmeral's body bunch beneath mine and her wings unfurl.

There are figures in strangely decorated robes behind the Brethren Guard, and they're chanting in low voices. We're about to leap into the sky when greenish lightning forms over Esmeral's wings and she shrieks in pain.

I yell across the square, "Leave her alone. How dare you hurt my dragon?"

While I'm distracted, two Brethren Guard grab hold of one of my ankles and pull me off Esmeral, and I land on the cobbles with a painful thud. When I open my eyes, I see the soldiers closing in around me. I'm still holding the pitchfork, and I slam it across the jaw of a man who's reaching down to grab me.

When I get to my feet, I'm surrounded by soldiers, and Esmeral has her eyes scrunched closed as she trembles beneath the green lightning flickering over her wings. She seems to be trapped in a prison of magical pain.

"No," I moan in horror, watching my dragon trying to fight the magic off.

"Get her," shouts one of the Brethren Guard.

Hands reach for me, and I brandish the pitchfork. Before I can swing, a raven shrieks and dives at a soldier, scratching at his eyes with its talons. The man reels back. Another raven attacks the soldiers, and then another and another, until the air around me is filled with black feathers, sharp little talons shining with blood, and screaming.

I push through the yelling, cringing Brethren Guard, desperate to get to the mages who are hurting Esmeral. They seem to be in some kind of trance as they chant a spell.

"Leave my dragon *alone*," I shout, swinging the pitchfork at the nearest mage's head. It connects with a satisfying clunk, and the mage's eyes roll back in his head and he falls to his knees.

The chanting stops, and the spell breaks.

Behind me, Esmeral shrieks in defiance, and a moment later, there's a rush of dragonfire followed by screaming and running Brethren Guard. Before I can swing at the mages again, they vanish into thin air.

I lower the pitchfork and turn around. Esmeral shoots a last burst of dragonfire at the fleeing men, screams, and then straightens her neck with her crest thrust proudly toward the sky.

With a clack-clack of her walking stick on the cobbles, Mistress Hawthorne shuffles into view, a raven perched on her shoulder.

"That's how you fight, girl, and don't you forget it," Mistress Hawthorne says with a sharp, approving nod. Then she gazes sadly around at all the bodies on spikes. "Why did you come here? You can do nothing for these poor souls, and you nearly got yourself taken again."

"I thought they were alive," I croak. The throb of excitement and victory is wearing off, and I start to shiver. "I thought my family were home."

The pitchfork drops from my fingers and clatters on the cobbles, and I wrap my arms around my suddenly freezing-cold body. Esmeral hurries over to me and pushes her head into my shoulder. I gaze around at the bodies on the ground and the people stuck up on spikes. So much death. When is it going to end?

Esmeral rests her jaw on my shoulder and trills softly.

I reach up and stroke her neck, whispering, "What are we going to do now?"

30

Zabriel

There's an almighty roar beyond the War Room, and every wooden piece on the map of Maledin rattles. An enormous shape blocks out all the light for a few seconds. My dragon has flown up to the castle, and he's more frantic than he has been in five hundred years.

I run out to the terrace and Scourge swoops past and bellows yet again, and I'm blasted with so much confusion and fury that it nearly knocks me off my feet.

Esmeral.

Isavelle.

Where are they?

"What do you mean, where are they?" I shout, and Scourge snarls and hurtles toward the dragongrounds. I don't wait to watch him land. I run out of the room and down the corridor.

As I cross the stone bridge and enter the dragongrounds, I see that it's shrouded in mist and Scourge is stomping up and down, hunting among the flare for his mate.

"Isavelle. Esmeral. *Isavelle,*" I bellow, but no one answers me.

Someone comes running toward us through the mist, and I see with equal parts anger and relief that it's Stesha. I hate the sight of him right now, but he has been keeping an eye on Esmeral. He wouldn't let a precious Omega dragon run loose.

"Where's my mate? Where's her dragon?" I demand.

Scourge snorts and glares at Stesha, as angry as I am with the white-haired Alpha.

Stesha glances around. "They were both right here. I thought they were still here. I was tending to a Beta at the other end of the dragongrounds."

He took himself far away from my Omega, which is what I wanted, only now I'm furious about it because my mate is gone. "For fuck's sake. They can't both be gone. Why didn't you keep a closer eye on them?"

Stesha's eyes flash. Because I threatened to strip away everything he cares about for getting too close to Isavelle.

"Where were her bodyguards?" Stesha snaps. "Where was Scourge? Where were *you*? You and he are their Alphas."

Scorn fills his cold expression. He would have kept a closer eye on his Omega. He wouldn't have let her out of his sight. His judgment makes me want to punch him twice as hard as last time.

I whirl around and press my hands against Scourge's flank. "You can find Isavelle, can't you? You always have before. Or search for Esmeral. Dragons can seek their mates."

Isavelle has been in distress before and called to Scourge. Is she calling out to him now?

The minutes stretch out, and finally, Scourge opens his jaws and roars in frustration. My heart sinks as I realize he can't hear either of them. Esmeral and Scourge aren't mated yet, so their bond isn't strong.

Stesha is searching the misty skies. "You wanted your mate to bond with her dragon, and she is impetuous. This may be their first flight, and there may be no reason for you to worry."

"There is every reason for me to worry," I snarl at him. "She could be lost. She could fall. Esmeral has never had a rider. They're both so..." Innocent. Fragile.

Gone.

I shove my fingers through my hair. This can't be happening. This is too much on top of every terrible thing that has happened in Maledin. I can't lose my mate and her dragon as well.

As little as I want to ask for Stesha's help, I say to him, "Summon the dragonriders and wingrunners. Send every—"

Scourge suddenly roars and turns his eyes skyward, and a moment later he launches into the air. The mist is finally beginning to burn off, and I watch with my heart in my throat as he flies to the western end of the dragongrounds. He's met by a smaller winged outline in the sky who greets him with a thin, high shriek.

"Isavelle," I bellow as I run forward, watching the turquoise dragon and Scourge circle toward the ground. "*Isavelle*."

Her faint voice reaches me at last. "I'm here."

They land along with Scourge. Esmeral allows my mate to

slide to the ground and immediately takes off again, streaking toward the castle. Scourge was about to greet his mate properly and gives a surprised roar and swoops after her.

Relief pours through me. They're both all right. Esmeral is unharmed, and my mate is alive. I'm preparing to ask my mate what the hell she thinks she was doing leaving the castle without telling me, when I notice her red-rimmed eyes, wild hair, and the tears streaking down her face.

I pull her into my arms and cup her face. "*Sha'len*, what's wrong? What's happened?"

Her scent is filled with grief and desperation. "They're dead. They're dead."

"Who's dead?"

Fresh tears spill down her cheeks. "It must be half of my village. They were killed in the most horrible way. It was whoever was behind the barrier to the south. The Shadow King. Some evil mage. Someone the Brethren are working for. There were strange, horrible mages there. They let half my village go, only to kill them. I had a vision—"

Isavelle is stumbling over her words between sobs, and I can barely understand her. I scoop her up in my arms and hold her face to my throat. "I'm here. Catch your breath and then tell me everything."

As she wraps her arms around my neck and cries, I try to untangle what she's just told me. She's been to her village and back on Esmeral, and there are dead people there? What the hell has been going on?

Isavelle calms down enough to take a deep breath and says, "We were attacked."

"You were *what?*" I set my mate on her feet, get down on one knee, and search her all over for blood and injuries.

She shakes her head. "I'm fine. Esmeral and Mistress Hawthorne helped me fight them off. But my mother and my brother, Zabriel. Poor little Waylen." Isavelle sobs again. "It's all my fault. I told someone I thought I could trust about my family, and they were working for the enemy the whole time."

Her words fill me with alarm, and I take her face in my hands. "Isavelle. Someone here is working for the enemy? Who is it?"

"You don't know her. She lives in the city. I met her the day I was attacked by the..." Her hand flies to her face in horror as she seems to realize something. "She lured me into the Brethren's trap. I should have realized."

Rage bursts through me. Someone Isavelle trusted has been putting her in danger. "Who is she? Tell me everything about her."

While Isavelle relates what she can remember about a young woman called Odanna, Esmeral returns. She's on foot this time and she's dragging Dusan through the dragongrounds with her teeth clamped to his arm while Fiala jogs by her side. As soon as the two bodyguards catch sight of us and see Isavelle in floods of tears, Dusan pulls himself out of Esmeral's grasp and the two wingrunners hurry toward us, their expressions horrified at seeing my mate so upset. I hold up a hand, cautioning them to remain silent while Isavelle finishes talking.

Meanwhile, Esmeral shoots off again. Scourge flies with her, unwilling to let the little dragon out of his sight.

"It was so strange," Isavelle says, wiping her eyes, lost in remembrance. "Odanna didn't seem to know where she was, or even who she was. She went blank for a moment. I saw her do that once before. Was she seeing something? Is that how I look when I'm having a vision?"

I have no idea about what this woman was seeing, and I don't care. I want her dead. This woman put my mate in danger, and she's responsible for the slaughter of half a village.

I grip Isavelle's upper arms. "Whoever she is, we'll find her and she will pay for her crimes to the full extent of my anger."

Esmeral flies back with Captain Ashton running beneath her. The Omega dragon has brought everyone I need to protect Isavelle and start giving out orders.

I stand up, wrap my arms around Isavelle, and tuck her face against my chest while I address Ashton, Fiala, Dusan, and Stesha. "Someone in the capital is working for the enemy. We have to find her right away." I describe the young woman as Isavelle described her to me.

"But how did she get from Lenhale to Amriste?" Dusan asks.

Fiala folds her arms, her expression thunderous. "Maybe she was out there waiting for Lady Isavelle."

Ashton frowns and turns to me. "*Ma'len*, a wyvern disappeared from the eyrie a short time ago. We have been hunting for it, but perhaps it didn't fly away of its own accord."

"A city girl couldn't ride a wyvern," Stesha says.

I shake my head. "We don't know who she is. Beyond the barrier, the Brethren could be training someone to fly our mounts. Ashton, be on the lookout for this missing wyvern as well as the woman Isavelle described."

My gaze locks with Stesha's, and an uneasy, angry sensation passes between us. Fury burns in my chest whenever I think about him, let alone look at him.

"I will deliver your orders to the dragonriders. We will find the culprit," he assures me.

I glower at him, before giving a short, sharp nod. I don't want him anywhere near Isavelle, so out there hunting for the woman who betrayed my mate is the best place for him.

To everyone assembled, I say, "I will stay with my mate. I'm trusting you all to find the person responsible. Fiala, Dusan, join the search. You don't need to protect Isavelle right now. I won't let her out of my sight."

"And if this betrayer has fled beyond the barrier?" Fiala asks.

"Then catch her before she can get there. *Go*," I shout, and they all disperse at a run.

I pick Isavelle up and hook an arm under her knees, carrying her against my chest as I walk up to the castle. She's still crying quietly, lost in the memory of seeing her family and the other villagers dead.

Rage mounts in my chest. She's in so much pain. Whoever hurt her will pay in blood, that I promise.

ISAVELLE IS bereft and agitated half the night, but she finally falls asleep in my bedchamber when I offer to soothe her with my scent. I hold her against my chest and she slowly quietens and falls into a slumber.

I'm too angry to sleep. Rage boils through me as I relive every painful moment from the previous day. My Omega is suffering, and I couldn't protect her. People out there have caused her suffering and they're still breathing. Inexcusable. Disgusting. *Outrageous.*

It's only as the sun begins to rise and my shoulder muscles are cramping from being tensed for hours on end that I realize that my rut is fast approaching. Down at the dragongrounds, there's a repetitive thud, thud, thud, punctuated by snarling, as an Alpha dragon paces restlessly up and down.

I glance at Isavelle, hoping that Scourge and I are days rather than hours away from erupting into obsession for our mates.

More obsession than usual.

Godric remains awake through the night to coordinate the dragonriders and wingrunners, but he has little news to tell me when he visits my bedchamber just after dawn. They've found no woman matching the description Isavelle provided, or the missing wyvern, but they're still searching. Meanwhile, a dozen Temple Mothers and Maidens have arrived at Isavelle's village.

I send Godric to his bed and stand over Isavelle's sleeping form. I should have better news for my mate. I should have fixed this by now.

Just after dawn, she awakens.

"Did they find Odanna?" she asks, rubbing sleep from her eyes.

"Not yet, but we're still searching. *Sha'len*, the people in your village..." I sit down on the edge of the bed and tell her as gently as I can that the bodies have been taken down from the spikes and have been laid out in a field.

She nods, pain filling her eyes. "I would like to see to the burials myself. They were my family. My neighbors. I loved them all, and Amriste was my home."

Was. She speaks in the past tense. Isavelle has given up on returning to her village, something I've been hoping for since I first brought her to my castle, but not under these circumstances. Never like this.

I nod and get to my feet. "Get dressed and eat something, and then we can go. There are wingrunners and *Hratha'len* protecting the village so it will be safe for you, and I'll be by your side."

Fifteen minutes later, we're down at the dragongrounds being greeted by Scourge and Esmeral. I notice how Isavelle wraps her arms around her dragon's neck and holds on tightly for a moment before drawing away and reaching out to stroke Scourge's snout. The huge black dragon half closes his eyes and allows my mate to caress him. He doesn't even let me do that.

"Would you like to fly with me on Scourge?" I ask, and he nuzzles hopefully against her thigh. If the day wasn't so wretched, I'd tease him for being so soft on my mate.

She strokes her dragon's neck and shakes her head. "I will fly on Esmeral. I feel safe with Scourge, but everything feels more natural with her."

I take off my cloak and wrap it around her shoulders, hoping that it will keep her warm and bring her comfort during the flight, and stave off any sickness that she might feel, if she even feels nauseated by riding anymore.

I watch closely as she climbs up on Esmeral's back and settles into the saddle, wondering how safe it is for Isavelle to be flying alone so soon. There's so much she doesn't know about dragonriding. "Are you sure you'll be all right on your own?"

"Don't worry. Esmeral won't let me fall."

I glance at the turquoise dragon and see how her playful, somewhat chaotic demeanor has settled into intense focus. The dragon has her rider, and nothing is going to separate them ever again.

Up on Esmeral's back, Isavelle has dark circles beneath her eyes and her color is drained, but she's straight-backed, and her chin is up. Yesterday she lost her brother and her mother. She's facing the prospect that she might lose the rest of her family, and half her village is dead. Even so, she's putting aside her fears to see to the dignity of the people who allowed her to be taken away and beaten and tortured, and there's not an ounce of bitterness in her heart.

I reach up for her hand and press a kiss to her palm. "You are breathtaking, my queen."

31

Isavelle

In a field by the village, all the bodies of my fellow villagers have been laid out under sheets, and a wingrunner gently points out which lumpy forms belong to Ma and Waylen. Some of the Temple Mothers are here, and they're arranging red blooms around the bodies and murmuring what sounds like blessings.

Forty-seven people are dead, which is more than a third of the village of Amriste. Tears sting my eyes as I gaze at them all. I wish I knew why these forty-seven people had to die. I wish I knew why any of the villagers had to die. Is this my fault? Have these people been punished because I escaped the Brethren and fell for the Flame King? Whoever this Shadow King is, whatever he is, he's cruel and unforgiving. Only the worst kind of leader kills innocent people.

As we walk among the bodies, Zabriel keeps a tight hold

of my hand, his face etched with grief. He's suffered losing soldiers and dragons, but the sight of this slaughter has shaken him. Innocent people weren't meant to die so that he could claim his crown.

Why these forty-seven? The thought keeps nagging at me. I catch a particularly strong scent from one of the largest bodies. My nose is growing more sensitive by the day, and it tells me things I never used to be able to detect before. The body must belong to Hirax Gorran, the blacksmith, for no one in the village was as big as he was. Aside from the scent of blood, I catch the whiff of ash and metal, and licorice and molasses. The sizzle of red-hot horseshoes being quenched in a tub of river water. Safety and dependability. Sweat and salt. All the things he embodies are expressed in his scent, which isn't a human characteristic at all. It's a Maledinni one.

I keep walking with Zabriel, and at the end of the row of bodies, I turn to him and ask, "Have you noticed anything strange about the scents that are coming off these bodies?"

Zabriel frowns and moves back among them, his head turning this way and that as he's deep in thought. Finally, he comes back to me, and he says, "They're all Maledinni. I can smell their designations emerging. There's not a human among them."

"That's what I thought." My heart hurts as I realize Ma and Waylen were Maledinni, and they might have been Betas or Alphas, or even Omegas like me.

"Waylen could have grown up to be a wingrunner or a dragonrider." I wipe fresh tears from my cheeks. "Why did this happen, Zabriel?"

"Whoever did this hates the Maledinni, but to do this in your village, and only yours, feels vindictive." He takes my face between his hands. "I swear to you and every single person here, every family in this village will be avenged. I swear it on my crown."

He folds me in his arms and holds me tight, and I can feel the fury and grief racing through him.

A moment later, I pull away and gaze up at him. "If these people are all Maledinni, can we give them the same last rites that we gave to Tish and Damla? Or is that just for dragonriders?"

Zabriel's eyes are red-rimmed, and he nods. "I think that's a beautiful idea, *sha'len*. Any Maledinni may have dragon rites. I wasn't in time to see that the people of Amriste were born as free Maledinni, but the very least we can do is send them off into the sky as our own."

He speaks with the Temple Mothers, and as dusk starts to fall, we all assemble on one side of the field along with a handful of wingrunners. Scourge and Esmeral are nearby, the huge black dragon standing protectively over his mate, who is grief-stricken as well, thanks to me. Her wings and neck have been drooping all day, but she straightens up now she has a duty to perform.

The Temple Mothers are singing in our ancient language, a beautiful but sad song, and Scourge and Esmeral move closer to the bodies. There's a rumbling, and then they both open their jaws and release a gentle stream of dragonfire across the bodies.

It flows like water and lights up the dusk. The wingrunners climb onto their wyverns and take to the skies, flying circles around us, their elegant, silvery bodies lighting up in shades of red and gold. Scourge and Esmeral fan the flames with their wings, sending sparks dancing up toward the stars.

I wrap my arms around Zabriel's waist and hold on tight to my mate.

"Forever flying," I whisper, and then bury my face in Zabriel's chest.

He bends down and murmurs in my hair, "I'm so sorry I wasn't in time for them, Isavelle. This never should have happened."

I shake my head emphatically, but my throat is too tight to speak. I could have found him sooner. I could have woken him up from beneath that mountain long ago if I had let my feet follow my instincts. If I'd learned to be a witch instead of swallowing all the nonsense that the Brethren told us about witches being evil.

"None of this is your fault, Zabriel. You're saving us and we need you. *I* need you. Don't..."

Don't ever let anything happen to you, Alpha, or I won't be able to bear it.

I'm filled with so much grief that I'm drowning in it, but with Zabriel's arms around me, he prevents me from sinking beneath the tide. I hold on to the man who saved me from the funeral pyre, feeling like he's saving my life all over again.

~

THREE DAYS LATER, I'm packing up the house I used to live in. Putting away my family's cups and plates that were left behind in their haste to flee. Folding up clothes and putting them in trunks. Discarding remnants of rotten food.

The dragonriders have captured the missing wyvern, and Zabriel has remained in the capital in the hope that Odanna will soon be found. The only dragon nearby is Esmeral, who is snoozing in the winter sunshine by the well, but an entire wingrunner unit is here protecting me, including Fiala and Dusan.

I meant to collect a few things from this house that were meaningful to me, but there isn't any meaning in wooden cups and bowls. Plaited rush mats and darned socks. Even Waylen's small carved horse toy. We were desperately poor people, and our belongings were scarce, but even if we were rich and this cottage was filled with gold candlesticks and velvet cushions, I don't think I'd want any keepsakes. Nothing is going to make me feel better about Ma's and Waylen's cruel deaths, though the last rites performed by Scourge and Esmeral and the Temple Mothers gave me some comfort.

I pack everything away and leave it where it is. When I step outside, I close the door behind me, feeling hollow and wrung out. Fiala and Dusan follow me at a discreet distance. Fiala shed tears during the last rites ceremony. Dusan has given me a dozen wordless but emphatic hugs, which are surprisingly comforting.

In the square, Esmeral is still asleep, so I carefully curl up next to her and leave her be. Between false heat cycles and my grief, the little Omega needs her rest. I could do with a long sleep as well, but hers is more important when she has to carry me back to Lenhale.

Stroking her beautiful scales, I wonder what the remaining people of Amriste would think of Esmeral if they all came home now. I assumed they'd be afraid of a dragon and insist that she didn't belong, but this is Maledin. Dragons belong everywhere. Esmeral belongs with me, just like Scourge belongs with Zabriel.

"I wonder what would have happened if I had called you

all out from beneath the mountain sooner," I murmur, tracing the flashes of gold over her scales. "Or if I'd never called you out at all."

"Still fretting over the past, I see," someone says with a click of her tongue. "Never called the dragons out? Yes, the people could have continued to be starved, beaten, and miserable if it wasn't for you."

Biddy Hawthorne is standing by the well with her hands clasped on her walking stick. I didn't hear her approach. The old witch can be stealthy when she wants to be.

"Your tongue is as sharp as ever," I mutter.

Biddy ignores me. "You've learned your first lesson as Queen of Maledin—there is always a price to pay. So what are you going to do? Squander these people's sacrifice, or step up and do your duty?"

What does she think I've been doing these past few days in Amriste? Since I finally caught my mate's scent? Since I accepted my dragon?

Shirking my duty?

I know my duty. There's no going back for me, but that doesn't mean I'm not reeling from everything that's happened.

"I had a vision in your cottage all those weeks ago," I tell her. "It was of Zabriel, and he was...normal. No Scourge. No burning red eyes. What if that's the future? What if he's going to lose everything?"

"Become an ordinary man? Is that what you want?"

I don't want anyone else to die horribly and violently. I'm haunted by the thought of Zabriel being killed in battle. Of Scourge and Esmeral cut open and their *riestas* ripped out like Damla's was.

"I'm so afraid for Zabriel," I confess. "He's holding the country together on his own, and that means whoever wants to take it will kill him first. Why does it have to be him?"

Do you wish I was just Commander Zabriel, and you were Isavelle the village girl?

That other life for a different Zabriel and Isavelle seems very sweet right now.

"It's a hard lot, being the Flame King," Biddy muses. "It's just as hard being the Flame King's Omega. I have one question for you."

"What's that?"

"Why are you here whining to an old woman when you could be with the man who worships the ground you walk on?"

I glare at her. "My dragon is exhausted."

"Is she?"

Esmeral has awoken and she's nibbling happily on my sleeve. Her eyes are bright, and I can feel that she's ready to fly. She gets to her feet, crouching low so I can climb up onto her back.

After a moment's hesitation, I turn back to the witch. "I never repaid you for the oil you gave me when Zabriel was hunting for me." It's not wise to be in a witch's debt. They can call it in any time they choose, and woe betide you if you refuse.

Biddy sniffs and shakes her head. "You don't owe me anything. I never intended for you to use it."

My eyes widen. "Not use it? So what was its purpose?"

The witch doesn't reply.

I frown at her, thinking. Biddy gave me one oil that would hide my mate from me, and the Temple Crone gave me another that would reveal him. The old woman is gazing at me with a crafty glint in her eyes.

"Oh, that's why," I whisper.

Biddy's gift meant I had a choice, and I chose Zabriel.

"Be off with you, chit. Sorry, *Ma'len's* mate. Come back and visit an old woman when you're ready to be a witch as well as a queen."

~

THE FLARE IS restless when Esmeral and I return, which is a telltale sign that something is up. Nilak is right up near the stone bridge, craning her neck anxiously, though there's no sign of her rider.

There are voices coming from the Great Hall, and I make my way there. It's filled with dragonriders and wingrunners, all wearing expressions of shock as I push my way through the crowd.

Zabriel is sitting on his throne, gripping the armrests, his red eyes burning and his brow tight with fury. I'm about to call out to him when I notice what he's glaring at.

Or rather, who.

A woman is kneeling before the throne, her body wrapped in chains with her arms pinned to her sides. People have moved back to give her space. Or because they're afraid to get too close to the object of the Flame King's fury.

I move around to one side to get a better look at her face. My heart is already pounding. I know who I'm going to see, but my stomach still rebounds around my abdomen as I see her blank face. Odanna.

I'm about to call out to her and demand she explain why

she pretended to be my friend and then betrayed me. There's a hand on my arm, and I turn to see Fiala with Dusan by her side. My bodyguards cast fearful glances at Zabriel and shake their heads, cautioning me to remain silent.

I close my mouth for, but I still burn for answers. Odanna once told me that her father was a priest. Did he force her to work with the Brethren? Was that even the truth?

"I will ask you again," Zabriel says with such power that his voice reverberates around the room. "Did you betray your people to the Brethren?"

Odanna takes a long time to answer. When she replies, her voice is oddly flat. "I don't...I don't know any Brethren."

"You're lying," Zabriel snarls, and beats his fist against the arm of his chair. There's a powerful scent coming off my Alpha. Anger and something else. He leans forward, eyes blazing red, and a gleam of perspiration on his brow. "You passed on information about my mate to the Brethren."

Odanna speaks in a colorless monotone and her expression is blank. "I didn't like Lady Isavelle. She told me she was having visions, and so I waited until she was alone with her dragon and gave her a happy vision of her family returning home."

Zabriel's hands tighten on the armrests. "Why?"

"I wanted Lady Isavelle to suffer."

Sadness and hurt impale me through my chest. Odanna sounds vacant as she claims to have done something so spiteful. But at the same time, what Odanna is saying makes no sense. The false vision was a trap to make me return to my village. The Brethren and those strange mages were waiting among the bodies of my fellow villagers.

"You gave her that vision? Impossible," Zabriel replies.

"You're not a witch. You have never been a witch, and you were never trained in dragon magic either."

I glance in surprise at my mate, wondering how Zabriel knows so much about Odanna.

"Nothing to say?" Zabriel growls. "So be it. You have been working with the Brethren, and you will be punished as a traitor to Maledin."

There's a cry from the back of the room and someone forces their way to the front. A dozen people are knocked aside, and a white-haired man in pale riding leathers bursts through the crowd.

His fists are clenched and his body is shaking with fury as he gazes at the young woman in chains. My heart leaps into my throat, afraid that we're about to witness the dragon-master lose his temper and beat the traitor to death.

Stesha turns toward Zabriel, but it's not anger filling his expression.

It's despair.

In a ragged voice, he says, "She doesn't know what she's saying. Please don't hurt her."

My eyebrows shoot up in surprise.

Zabriel never takes his eyes off Odanna as he seethes, "Remain silent, dragonmaster, or I'll have you dragged from the room."

Stesha gets between the young woman and Zabriel, protecting her with his body. Odanna hasn't even glanced at him. She's staring straight ahead with an empty expression. He's acting like he knows her, but the two of them couldn't possibly have met. Can they?

Or maybe they don't need to have met for Stesha to protect her. The second I met Zabriel he forgot about everything else even though he was in the midst of a battle. The day Stesha smelled my hair, I'd just been down in the city with Odanna. We were sitting close together on the back of a wagon. I could have had her scent all over me. I don't much like Stesha, but what a nightmare for him if he's finally found his Omega only for her to be a traitor to everything he believes in.

The dragonmaster sounds broken as he begs, "Spare her, I beg you. Punish me however you wish, only don't hurt Zenevieve."

I feel a jolt of surprise. Zenevieve? Stesha's ward? I thought she died five hundred years ago. I glance around, hoping to share my confusion with someone else, but Fiala's and Dusan's expressions are grim, and so are Godric's and Ashton's.

Everyone in this room knows exactly who this young woman is. Everyone but me.

32

Zabriel

Rage boils through me so rapidly that I can barely think. Zenevieve hurt my mate. She nearly gave her to the Shadow King. One of my own has been working against me all this time, and it's clear what must be done with her and anyone standing in my way.

"Move aside, Stesha."

The white-haired Alpha thinks it's wise to continue arguing with me. "Please, give her the opportunity to defend—"

"*I said, move aside.*"

What can she possibly say in her defense after admitting she wanted Isavelle to suffer? What can anyone say? If he thinks his protection is going to make me merciful, he's mistaken. I'm almost as angry with him as I am with his former ward.

I'm opening my mouth to command the wingrunners to place the dragonmaster in chains when there's movement out of the corner of my eye. Isavelle has returned, and she's gazing with shock and sadness at her former friend. I don't give a damn what the traitor has to say, but my mate deserves answers about this betrayal.

"You weren't with us under the mountain," I say to Zenevieve, but I can't see her with Stesha standing in the way. "I said *move*, dragonmaster."

Finally, Stesha steps to the side, but he stays close to Zenevieve.

"Where were you all these centuries? How did you survive? Where is Minta?"

"Who's Minta?" Zenevieve asks vacantly.

I smash my fist against the arm of my throne. "Stop playing games. A dragonrider would never forget her dragon."

Zenevieve's hair has returned to its brown color and her eyes are light brown, as they were before she bonded with Minta as a teenager. The Zenevieve we all knew for years had raven hair and forest green eyes that matched her dragon's black scales and iridescent green flourishes.

"Did you kill your dragon for your master?" I ask her. "Did he promise you power if you betrayed us all and helped him murder the future queen? Why did he slaughter dozens of villagers from Amriste?"

No matter what I ask Zenevieve, she either doesn't respond or murmurs quietly that she doesn't have a master and she did all this alone. It's not even a good lie. Only a powerful mage could have kept her alive for five hundred years, and the girl never had any magic.

My rage gathers in my chest and I bellow, "Who is your master?"

The glass rattles in the high windows. I'm sweating, and it feels like there's fire beneath my skin. I want to grab hold of Zenevieve and shake her until she gives me the truth instead of these lies. I want to fight Stesha. I want to bite my mate. My teeth are *aching*.

"If you're not going to save your own life by confessing, then you leave me no choice."

Stesha falls to his knees before me, a desolate expression on his face. "Please, *Ma'len*. This isn't Zenevieve's doing. Something's wrong. You *know* her. If you must satisfy your rage, punish me instead."

I turn to him with a snarl. "I'm *Ma'len* now that you want something for her?"

All Stesha's pride has fallen away. Before me is a man on the brink of throwing away everything he has to save his former ward from my wrath. "This isn't her fault. If Zenevieve has wronged anyone it's because I failed her."

I don't trust Stesha one inch right now. He'd do anything to protect Zenevieve and can't see what's right in front of his face. "Zenevieve came of age three years ago. Five hundred and three years ago. She was a dragonrider of Maledin and is responsible for her own decisions. You can't protect her, and you're not responsible for her."

Stesha leaps to his feet and cries out, "*Ma'len*—"

"One more word, dragonmaster, and I'll banish you from Maledin for the rest of your life."

Stesha's chest is heaving. "I will leave Maledin forever. I will release Nilak back to the flare. I will do *anything*. You may beat me. Starve me. Kill me, I don't care. Only don't hurt Zenevieve."

Beyond the castle walls, a dragon screams, shrill and distraught. Nilak's scream.

Silence reigns in the throne room.

I glance at the young woman slumped on the floor and recall all Isavelle's pain at seeing half her family so cruelly slaughtered. I couldn't save her from that pain, and Zenevieve doesn't deserve anyone to save her.

I open my mouth to condemn her.

Isavelle approaches the throne to stand at my elbow. She places her fingers lightly on my arm and says softly, "May I say something, Zabriel?"

"You may always say something, *sha'len*," I say in a tight voice, but still focused on the traitor.

"Are you thinking clearly at this moment?"

Stesha can call me *Ma'len* a thousand times but it won't change what Zenevieve did. "Sorry, what did you ask? Thinking clearly?"

Her beautiful eyes search mine. There's a glimmer of turquoise in their depths. Her dark blonde hair gleams a little more golden. In a quiet voice that doesn't carry, she says, "You told me that Alpha and Omega relationships are built on trust. That we need each other the most during our heats and our ruts. Your scent has changed, and your brow is covered in sweat. Would it be wise to delay any decision you make for a few days?"

"There is no reason for any delay. This traitor nearly got you killed. Probably worse than killed," I say around the anger that has tightened my throat.

"This is an opportunity to be merciful."

I want to quietly ask her what she means, but instead find myself bursting out with, "Why in all the fires of fucking hell should I be merciful?"

Isavelle takes my face between her hands. "Because my mate is a merciful man, and I know he wishes to be a merciful king." Her beautiful eyes are entreating me.

The Alpha instincts raging in my heart are telling me to obliterate my enemies, but the word *mercy* suddenly rings in my ears. My father wasn't a merciful man, and I hated how he ruled. None of the Brethren showed my mate any mercy.

So I should kill them all, my Alpha rages.

I take a deep breath. Isavelle has recognized the signs. I should have recognized the signs. I felt them a few days ago, but the hunt for Zenevieve drove them from my mind. I'm falling into a rut.

This is my first test as king, and how I react will set the tone for my rule.

So kill the traitor and be done with her. Kill Stesha as well. He covets my mate.

"She can't be allowed to go free," I growl through my teeth.

Isavelle glances at Stesha. "Ask your dragonmaster what he wants."

I turn to the Alpha who is standing protectively over Zenevieve and gazing desperately between me and Isavelle as we talk.

So he does care for someone after all.

I can feel him wanting to beg for her freedom, but if he does so again, my anger will burst forth afresh. "Well, dragonmaster?" I growl.

Stesha is gazing at Zenevieve with a wretched expression. She doesn't even seem to know he's there.

In a desolated voice, Stesha says, "Zenevieve should be placed somewhere until we are able—"

Imprisoning her sounds like an excellent first step. I'll deal with her after my rut. I want my mate, and everything else be damned.

"Lock Zenevieve in the dungeon," I say to Captain Ashton. The wingrunners are the best people to oversee the imprisonment of a former dragonrider. "The Temple Crone may examine her, but no one else may come near her. Including you, dragonmaster." I turn back to Stesha with narrowed eyes. "Stay away from the girl, or so help me, I will kill you both. Flee with her, and I will hunt you down and kill you both."

The white-haired Alpha's eyes are bleak as he watches several wingrunners grasp Zenevieve under her arms and drag her from the room. A moment later, she disappears from sight.

After several painful, panting breaths, Stesha strides from the room in the other direction, his hair and pale cloak streaming behind him.

Isavelle is still standing by my side, and I curl my fingers around her hand.

"I'm proud of you, Alpha," she whispers to me.

Alpha. I need to appease my Alpha or I will lose my grip on my sanity. I survey the Great Hall. "Everybody but my mate. Get. Out."

It takes less than a minute for the room to clear.

Isavelle steps between my legs, puts one knee up on my thigh and then the other until she's hugging my hips. My mate's heavenly scent washes over me, sweet and fragrant. She's not in heat or even a false heat, but she's still more delicious than anything I've ever smelled before. In my breeches, my cock stiffens painfully fast and my knot throbs. My whole jaw is aching.

My hands clench the armrests. "Fuck, I can't hold it back. I want you, but you should leave or you're going to push me over the edge into a rut right this second. Run to your bodyguards. Don't leave their sides."

She takes my hand in hers and raises it to her cheek, making me stroke her while her eyelashes flutter. In a breathy voice she asks, "Why would I go anywhere when my Alpha needs me?"

"Do you really mean that?" I ask in a strangled voice.

Isavelle arches into me, pressing her lush body into mine, and whispers, "You smell so good, Alpha."

I groan, cup the nape of her neck, and slam my mouth over hers. Her lips part for mine, and she moans as my tongue invades her mouth. The final shreds of my sanity part with a twang, and I devour her with hungry kisses.

"Do you know what your rutting Alpha's scent is going to make you feel? My pretty Omega is going to turn into a slick, wet mess who only wants to please me. Are you afraid of that, *sha'len*?"

She smiles and shakes her head, trailing my fingers down her throat and across the gland at the side of her neck. "My king is a merciful king."

I don't know about that. I'm not feeling very merciful right now. "I almost wish you were still afraid of me so Scourge and I could hunt you down. My bride who loves to flee."

Her eyes flare with interest. "That sounds exciting."

I snap my teeth together, and Isavelle jumps and gasps a little. "Then let's play a little game. Run for your dragon, *sha'len*, and Scourge and I will hunt our Omegas down. I can feel he's in a rut as well, and he's aching to get his teeth into his pretty little girl."

"Will everyone in the castle mind that we're using the place for our mating games?" she asks, her tongue playing with her upper lip, making it shiny wet.

I give a low laugh. "It's my castle. I'll play with my Omega how I choose. Let them all witness their Flame King catching his mate and dragging her to his bed. I want them to know the king has claimed his captive. Now. *Run*." I put so much dragon's growl into my command that she gasps and turns to flee.

I seize her wrist and drag her back to me. "Wait. Stay within the castle walls and the dragongrounds. If you fly farther than that, your Alpha will be furious, and I'll spend my rut taking my fury out on your ass by spanking it until it's hotter than dragonfire."

"Yes, Alpha."

A spasm seizes my knot, and I breathe in sharply through my nose. I will never not get hard hearing her say, *Yes, Alpha*.

I drag her even closer, smiling wickedly as I tell her, "Your Alpha is going to get you, then I'm going to fuck you, and I'm not going to be gentle. Is that what you want?"

Isavelle's cheeks are pink and her eyes are sparkling. "Yes, Alpha," she says again.

"Are you sure?"

Isavelle slides her fingers from my throat down to my chest. "I want Alpha to show me he's my Alpha."

My chest rises and falls with short, sharp breaths. I've never been so turned on in my life. "Then run, little dragon. The longer you evade me, the longer you'll keep my teeth from your flesh. I'll count to a thousand and then I'm coming after you. You'd better run to your dragon, because with all the blood in my knot instead of my head?" I pull her even closer and growl, "I'm not good at counting."

I let Isavelle go, and she casts one last flirty, heated look at me before running away. My fingers tighten on my throne.

Chase her.

Push her to the ground, get her beneath me, open her legs, and shove my cock deep inside her.

"One…two…three hundred and forty-eight…nine hundred and ninety-nine…one thousand."

I finish counting to one thousand in the space of five seconds, and then get to my feet and stride down the Great Hall. Isavelle can cry about it being unfair later. Who said I was going to play fair?

"I'm coming for you, Isavelle," I shout, my voice echoing around the Great Hall.

I pass Godric in the corridor and he starts to say something. I don't look at him or speak out loud, but my rutting scent must blast him in the face.

Whatever it is, not fucking now.

You deal with it.

I have an Omega to fill with cum until she's bursting.

He closes his mouth and walks away quickly.

I emerge from the castle to see Isavelle running across the stone bridge. Down at the dragongrounds, Scourge is looming over Esmeral, smoke pouring from his nostrils, his crest thrust toward the sky and his wings half unfurled. His red eyes are fixed on the little dragon and his jaws are parted. Esmeral is nuzzling against her pent-up Alpha like she's hoping to get fucked.

Isavelle runs toward them, calling her dragon's name. Esmeral sees her rider, and then me marching across the stone bridge toward them. She catches on immediately to the game and dives for her rider with a mock-terrified shriek.

Delighting in the sight of his fleeing Omega, Scourge snaps at her back legs. She swipes at him playfully with her tail and he answers with a roar that has her chittering excitedly. Isavelle jumps on Esmeral and they take to the air. Scourge watches them go, and then rounds on me with a snarl, telling me to hurry up. He wants his mate.

I want mine as well, but I'm not hurrying. Those two little dragons haven't got the first idea where to hide, but Scourge and I are experts in the hunt.

I climb up onto my dragon's back and we take to the skies. Effortlessly, we catch up to Isavelle and Esmeral and then follow them in a circle several times around the castle while the turquoise dragon and her rider dodge between turrets. As if that is going to confuse us. Isavelle hasn't had any formal training in flying, and she couldn't go into battle, but even so, her flying is impressive. I remember how ill she was on Scourge, but there's no sign of sickness or even hesitation with Esmeral. The two of them were made for each other.

We loop around the castle yet again, and Scourge is becoming impatient. Esmeral will fly to the left, and so Scourge shoots a plume of fire and smoke in that direction, forcing them to turn right and fly over the dragongrounds instead. I hear Isavelle squeal in outrage, and I grin. Below, all the dragons in the flare watch us as we swoop overhead.

Her wings working as hard as they can, Esmeral races up the bluff, her neck stretched upward until it's almost vertical. It's a tight maneuver for Scourge to reach the top with his huge size, but with his wings straining, he makes it. Esmeral and Isavelle had better not fly any farther from the castle. I warned her not to, and if they don't turn back, I am going to be furious with them.

The old, abandoned wyvern eyrie is perched atop the cliff, and that's where Isavelle and Esmeral head. They disappear inside through an open archway, and Scourge is too big to follow. In frustration, he blasts one of the towers with dragonfire before landing beside the building. It's made of wood and the fire catches, belching smoke into the sky.

I slide from my dragon's back and charge inside, bellowing, "What did I say, Isavelle? Not farther than the dragongrounds."

Isavelle is stroking her dragon's neck, breathing hard and looking so intensely beautiful I could eat her. Outside, Scourge roars, and Esmeral dances on her talons like she can't decide if she wants to run toward him or away.

"Your dragon was breathing fire," Isavelle pants, playfully backing away from me but with the same trepidation in her eyes as her dragon.

What's Alpha going to do to us? I can feel them both wondering.

"What did you expect a dragon to do when he's in a rut and he's trying to catch his mate?"

"These are still the dragongrounds, aren't they? I didn't break the rules."

At the other end of the eyrie, Esmeral is crouched before

the open doorway just out of her Alpha's reach, teasing him while he snaps his jaw at her.

I stand still and watch my mate through narrowed eyes. She bounces on her toes for a moment and then dashes to the right. I lunge forward and wrap my arms around her, pulling her full, soft body against mine.

"Got you." I push my face into her throat, breathe in, and groan, my eyes closing. Fuck me, she smells like pure pleasure.

Overhead and at the other end of the eyrie, fire crackles and pops.

"We have to go," Isavelle says, melting into me. "This building is on fire."

I shake my head. I only just got her alone. I'm not going anywhere and neither is she. "I'm the Flame King, and I love the sound of fire. I love the scent of it. I want you here, where I can taste you and the fire at once."

Firelight is flickering in her uncertain eyes.

"I won't let the fire touch you," I assure her, and finally she relents and tilts her mouth up to mine. I lean down and kiss her and groan as I taste her lips. Everything's so much more intense while I'm in a rut.

"You smell so good," she gasps, tugging at the buttons on my jacket. "You smell like danger. Black cherries. Fire and sparks. You smell like my Alpha."

I grasp the neck of my jacket and rip it open, popping a dozen buttons and sending them skittering across the floor. Scooping her against my chest, I breathe in her ear, "Does my mate like the way her Alpha smells?"

Isavelle peeps shyly up at me. In the next moment, she licks my chest, her tongue darting over my muscles. I grin wickedly down at her. Not even in a false heat and she's being so playful and brave.

I take the rest of my clothes off and lay them out on the ground so my mate doesn't feel the chill, and we sink down to the floor. Isavelle's hand trails down my body, from my throat, across my chest and stomach, and down to my knot. I watch her small fingers circling and squeezing my swollen flesh and groan. Distantly, the fire roars as hot as my desire.

"Does my Omega enjoy the way her Alpha feels?"

"You're so beautiful," she whimpers, gazing from my cock to my chest to my face. "I'm so sorry it took me so long to realize who you are."

I take her jaw in my hand. "Who am I?"

"You're my everything, Alpha."

"That's fucking right I am." I slant my mouth over hers in a bruising kiss, and then I lick slowly up the side of her throat. "Can I see you naked?"

"Please," she whispers.

I find the lacings on her dress and pull the string through the loops. The garment loosens, and I'm able to drag it down her body, revealing her thin chemise. Her nipples show through the thin fabric. Her slick has left dark, damp patches. I push my fingers against her pussy, over the wet patches, and Isavelle moans and gazes up at me with desperation.

"Your Alpha wants your beautiful body," I growl, seizing the garment and tearing it asunder. All of Isavelle is revealed to me. Her soft breasts and stomach. Her curving, fleshy hips. Her rounded thighs and dimpled knees. She is so beautiful that I wish I could bite her everywhere at once.

Isavelle's green eyes are huge and filled with desire and trust. I expected her to hand over her trust the moment we met because my scent demanded it of her. Instead, I've earned her trust, fought for it, won it, and it's all the sweeter because of that.

Her bare hips are fleshy in my hands. Her waist is warm and soft. I cup each of her heavy breasts and pluck her nipples, making her gasp. My knee is between her thighs and her slick gushes against me.

I lean over her, kissing her with my hand cupped behind her head, and then kiss hungrily down her body. I spread her pussy open and gaze at her pink flesh. The shining wet ruffles of her sex. Her swollen, tender clit.

"Do you like your Alpha looking at you?"

She lets her thighs fall open. "Yes, Alpha."

"Good girl." Her slick wells up and oozes down her pussy at my praise, and a spasm goes through my knot. "Oh, fuck. I think I might die, you're so perfect. Can I use my mouth on you?"

Isavelle makes a desperate noise, and when I glance up, her eyes are closed and she's nodding. I gently swipe my tongue up the seam of her sex, and her taste bursts in my mouth. Fire burns through me, consuming the last of my patience. I delve between her folds with my tongue and taste as much of her as I can. Isavelle is panting and clutching at my shoulders as I home in on her clit. My shoulders are butted up against her thick thighs. I've died and ascended to a higher form. She's the best thing I've ever tasted. I push my tongue inside her, and her slick channel grips me with delicious force. I thrust as deep as I can, imagining it's my cock.

Isavelle cries out, "*Zabriel.* Your tongue is so strong."

I draw my tongue out with a smile. "Thank you. I get that from my dragon." Then I push it into her again.

Fuck her. Fuck her. Push my knot right up against her. My Alpha is roaring at me to claim my Omega as much as I can claim her when she hasn't had her first heat yet. I clamber up over her body with my knot in my fist, intending to do just that.

Her beautiful, vulnerable, trusting expression sideswipes me, and I squeeze my eyes shut and shake my head. Not yet. Get a fucking grip.

With a growl, I turn her onto her side and pull her back against my chest. Her thighs are so slick that I can shove my cock between them and drag it back again.

With my lips against her ear and my arms tight around her, I hold myself still and ask, "Can I fuck you like this, *sha'len*? With my cock between your thighs, rubbing against your pussy."

Isavelle glances down at herself. Several inches of me are poking between her thighs and she wraps her hand around my slick head. She swirls her fingers over me, rubbing and squeezing, and I nearly lose my mind.

"You're teasing me, little dragon," I seethe in her ear.

"*Vru'mai desh.*"

I'm so shocked I nearly let go of her.

Vru'mai desh.

Fuck me please.

In my language.

In *our* language.

My dragines pulse with sweet agony, and I bury them in her shoulder, right by her neck, and I thrust between her thighs, right up to my knot. Isavelle cries out in pleasure as my shaft strokes against her sex, and she gushes against me. Both of her hands wrap around my cock.

"Your scent, *sha'len*. You're nearly fertile. I'm going to pump my cock into you and knot you so deep, my cum floods your womb."

"Zabriel, please," she moans.

"My teeth in your mating gland. My baby in your belly. My knot locked so deep inside you. Mine. Mine. *Mine*," I chant as I move my hips back and forth. I'm losing my mind. This sweet, precious Omega is trusting me to protect her and breed her and take care of her. "Hold me tight against your clit. Squeeze your thighs together."

She does as I command, and we both pant as the pleasure doubles. I never expected to take my Omega on the floor of the old wyvern eyrie. I thought we'd be in my enormous, soft bed, but all I need is my Omega wrapped in my arms and slicking herself all over my knot. I thrust even harder, and my knot pushes between her thighs. I give a strangled cry and wrap my arms around her thighs, pulsing with short, sharp thrusts, imagining it's her pussy tight around me as my knot swells. My cum bursts between her fingers and shoots across the floor. A great flood of it, releasing all my desire, frustration, anger, and need.

I fuck my knot between her thighs. My mate hasn't come yet. Isavelle's hair is sticking to her flushed, sweaty cheeks. "Zabriel, I'm going to—*ahh*...I'm going..."

And then she's climaxing against my cock, her pussy spasming against my length. Her slick bursts over the floor, joining my river of cum.

Isavelle opens her eyes and glances up at the ceiling, panting. Then she gasps in shock. "The roof is on fire. We have to go."

"Not yet," I rumble into the nape of her neck. There's only a small thread of fire. We still have time.

"The fire makes me nervous."

"I will protect you. Not an ember will touch your skin."

"But—"

A spark drifts down, about to burn the flesh of her cheek. Isavelle gasps, but I snatch the ember in my fist and make her meet my eyes.

"Don't imagine I'm not aware of every single ember, *sha'len*. I am the fire."

33

Isavelle

I *am the fire.*

Flames rage in the depths of Zabriel's eyes. He kisses me hard, pushing his tongue into my mouth. I can feel heat rippling under his skin as if he really is made from fire.

"I burn for you, *sha'len*."

The knot at the base of his cock has swollen even thicker after his climax. How is that supposed to fit inside me? How is any of him supposed to fit inside me?

"You will love the feel of my knot," he tells me, his mouth moving over mine as if he's read my thoughts. "You'll crave it deep inside you. Your tight pussy will stretch around me and cling on tight, not wanting to let me go, and then I'm going to fuck my seed into you while you're stuck on my knot."

Heat ripples up my body. What he's describing sounds insane. Impossible. I want it so much.

"How do your dragines feel?" I ask, noticing his tongue probing one of them.

"They hurt. They *ache*." He moves down my body and sinks his teeth into my fleshy hip. "I could fucking *eat* you."

"Again, please," I moan desperately.

He bites me over and over, leaving red teeth and fang marks in his wake until I'm covered in them.

"I shouldn't mark you up so much before we're mated, but I can't help myself. You're beautiful like this, *sha'len*."

He moves up to claim my mouth, and a droplet of his cum splashes on my aching sex, making me moan. Climaxing against his shaft was intensely wonderful, but I crave more. I ache to know what it will be like when he finally knots me.

"Alpha, please. I want you inside me."

Zabriel sucks in a ragged breath. "Are you sure?"

I smile and touch his face. Even in a rut, he's still worried about me. "I'm sure."

"How much? Show me. This much?" He wraps his middle finger and thumb around the swollen, purple head of his shaft. "This much?" He moves it down an inch.

Now that I look at his thick cock with all those beautiful veins, I'm feeling greedy. "More. As much as I can take when I'm not in heat."

Zabriel still looks uncertain. Remembering something Dusan said to me weeks ago, I roll onto my stomach, spread my knees, and raise my hips, presenting my most vulnerable parts to my mate. The Omega heat position.

The invitation is too much for my rutting Alpha. Zabriel snarls and grabs hold of my hips, moving behind me. The broad, plush head of his cock is against my tight entrance, and then he sinks into me with a guttural curse.

"Yes. *Yes*. Oh, fuck yes, Omega."

He hasn't thrust very deep, but I gasp in shock and feel like I'm being split in two. The stretch turns into a burn, and my eyes sting with tears. It feels like there's a blunt weapon inside me. He's so much. He's far more than I thought, but a moment later the pain gives way to pleasure. When he pulls back a little and surges forward, my insides light up around him, and I cry out desperately.

"Am I hurting you?" Zabriel grinds out. His teeth are grit with the effort of holding back.

If I say yes, he'll stop, and I need this so much. He needs this too. "Don't pull out. Promise?"

"*Sha'len*?"

"Promise me, Alpha."

"All right. But answer the question."

I take a shuddering breath and whimper, "It hurts."

Zabriel predictably tries to pull out, but I reach back and grab his wrist. "Don't. You promised."

"I don't want to hurt you!"

"It hurts. But I like it."

Zabriel doesn't move. It feels like he's torn between the pleasure he craves and protecting his Omega.

I walk my knees a little wider and rest my cheek on the ground. "Show me you're my Alpha. Tell me how deep you are. Make me take one more inch."

Zabriel digs his fingertips into my hips, his breathing uneven. "The sight of you stretched tight around me is making me lose my mind. I'm three inches deep. There's so much more of me. Fuck, you're so tiny."

I close my eyes as pleasure ripples through me. Three whole inches. Way past the head of his cock. "I wish I was in a heat. I know I can take more of you even though I'm not. Fuck my pussy just like you did my thighs."

He groans. "Hearing you talk like that, *sha'len*...I won't go any deeper, but it feels so good to slide in and out of you." At my whispered urgings, he starts to move again, drawing slowly back and then surging forward.

"More, please," I beg him. The burn has all faded into pleasure, but I miss the burn. The burn means the Flame King is rutting me harder and harder. Even without being in heat, it's all I crave. My Alpha's cock.

Zabriel falls into a steady, slick-inducing rhythm, and his breathing picks up. "Such a good Omega, letting me fuck your tender little cunt. Not even in heat and you're taking me so well."

His praise practically makes my eyes roll back in my head. "Are you nearly to your knot?"

He chuckles darkly. "Not even halfway. But I like your ambition."

"One really hard thrust. Just hold on to me and do it."

"I can't do that, *sha'len*. I'm already hurting you."

"But the burn feels so *good.* Please, please, please. I want to know what it feels like when you're not gentle. Please, Alpha, please."

"Don't test me while I'm in a rut," he says, practically roaring. His anger makes me tremble in desire.

"One inch. Force me to take one inch all at once. Please, Alpha."

My whimpering and pleading and wriggling against his cock have him growling and squeezing me so hard with his fingers that I'm sure he's leaving bruises. As much as I push back against him, I can't make him go any deeper. I'm stuck.

Zabriel pulls back suddenly, and I can feel it coming. A hard, hungry thrust of his cock. As he drives into me just a little deeper, I cry out with shock, pain, and delight, the sound echoing around us.

"Thank you, Alpha," I sob, tears leaking from my eyes. My clit is aching with the need to be touched. "Is that how you'll force your knot into me when I'm in heat?"

Zabriel drops his hands on either side of my head, panting raggedly, and the new angle pushes him even deeper. I already feel locked in place beneath this man. Being pinned by his knot is going to be insane.

"You're crazy for talking like this, Omega. I want to rut you so badly. I'm going to fuck you so hard and long in your next false heat that you'll be begging me to stop, just to pay you back for this torture."

I smile and bend my head back so he can kiss me. "Don't threaten me with a good time."

"You are a little brat, aren't you?" he says, sliding his hand around my throat and forcing my head back even farther so he can push his tongue into my mouth.

Knot me, Alpha. Knot me. Knot me. Knot me.

My Omega is losing her mind at the feel of Alpha lodged so deep inside me, but I can't take his knot yet, no matter how much I want to. Zabriel lets go of my throat and speeds up his shallow thrusts, the sound of our sex wet and loud as my slick drips down my thighs and onto the ground. Slicking myself stupid. That's what I've heard it called, and it sounds about right. There are no thoughts in my brain except craving to take more and more of Alpha's cock inside me.

"That's so much of me, Omega," Zabriel says in a husky whisper. "Good girl."

I groan hearing him praise me for something I so desperately hope is pleasing him. "All I want is to make you happy, Alpha."

Zabriel reaches down beneath me to my gushing pussy and drags his fingers over my clit. "Then climax hard on as much of my cock as you're able, and I'll fill you with cum."

My eyes open wide.

Yes.

Please.

I move back and forth to meet his thrusts as he rubs my clit in rapid circles. As he draws closer and closer to his climax, I can feel him growing thicker inside me.

"I wish I could see your knot," I whimper, hungry to know how big it's getting.

"As soon as I get you back to my rooms, I'm going to fuck you again. I'll put a mirror next to the bed so you can watch me thrusting into you, and you can see my knot in my fist."

"You can come again?" I ask in surprise, panting harder as his fingers and shaft work me closer and closer to my peak.

"I'm in a rut and you're winding me up, Omega. I can fuck for days. This cunt of yours is going to be well used by this time tomorrow. Maybe I will get my cock all the way up to the knot inside you," he says with relish. "I'll lick you better in between stretching you so much that Alpha can get his whole shaft inside you by morning."

I love when Zabriel calls himself Alpha. Heat flashes through me at the thought of watching him determinedly thrust his whole length into me.

He leans down and nips at my throat with his teeth. "I'll

hold my knot tight against you and bloat you with my seed. I'm dying to see your soft belly filled with cock and cum."

Those filthy words send me over the edge. My back arches with pleasure as Zabriel fucks me with short, sharp thrusts, panting, growling, and swearing under his breath until he climaxes with a shout and finally slows to a stop.

"How much of you did I take?" I ask, gasping for breath. Desperate to know. Even more desperate for praise.

"Turn over and find out," he tells me with a smile in his voice.

Feeling sore in my elbows and knees and all my joints, I ease myself onto my side and then my back, his cock twisting with some difficulty inside me, and then glance down between my thighs. I feel full to bursting, but there are still another five inches of Zabriel, plus his knot, which is the size of a prize grapefruit.

I stare at him in shock. No wonder I couldn't work him any deeper, and if he ever manages to fuck me, knot and all, he's going to puncture one of my lungs. "Are you kidding me? How is this ever going to work? I stand by what I said before. You're a *monster*."

He grins wickedly at me. "Maybe it's better that you don't look and just let me fuck you. Every Omega is a greedy Omega until she sees just how much cock she has to take before she gets to that final thrust." On the word *thrust*, he pulls back and pounds into me again. A great deal of his cum wells up around him, thick and pearly white.

I play with the liquid, scooping it from around his shaft and drawing it over my pussy lips. He could be right. But I do like the sound of that mirror.

I glance up at him with a shy smile. "Could I be pregnant?"

Zabriel puts his palm against my belly. "You will be soon. I'm going to breed you, little dragon."

Outside the eyrie, there's a roar and an answering shriek of pleasure. Sounds like another little dragon is learning what it means to be rutted by an Alpha.

I do want children, and I also want Zabriel to growl things in my ear like *flood your womb* and *bloat you with my seed.* "I want so much of you deep inside me," I confess in a whisper.

Zabriel moans in pleasure and presses his lips against mine. "You're the Omega I've always dreamed of. You hunger for me like I hunger for you. I hope I didn't hurt you too much just now."

Studying his broad chest and muscles, I realize he could have obliterated me, but of course, even in a rut, Zabriel would never do such a thing. "Will my heat make it easier to take all of you? I can already feel how I'm going to beg you to fuck me harder and harder. I think I'll cry if I can't take your knot."

He looks at me through his lashes with burning eyes. "Don't worry, Omega. Alpha's strong enough to fuck his knot into you. I told you I won't be gentle when the time comes, and you won't want me to, either. Dragons' blood, the things you were saying to me just now. *It hurts but I like it*. I thought Omegas only felt that way during their first heat."

I smile and stroke my fingers over his muscular stomach. "I started off being a very poor Omega, but I want to be the very best Omega for you from now on."

He leans down and kisses me. "You're always the best Omega. I should take you to my bed. Or I could stay right here and give you a moment's rest and then fuck another inch of my cock and even more cum into you." Zabriel's eyes gleam wickedly.

We're both covered in dust and my slick and his seed. Everything feels deliciously messy, and it's wonderful.

The shadows around Zabriel are growing brighter. Crackling fills the air.

Zabriel seizes the backs of my thighs and presses them up against my chest. I cry out in pleasure at this new angle. The heaviness of him as he rests his weight on his hands is forcing my thighs wider. His cock deeper.

As soon as he thrusts again, his breathing picks up. His eyes are locked on the sight of his cock sliding in and out of me. My slick and his cum gout up around his shaft and trickle over my ass. There's so much it forms a warm, wet flood.

With a determined expression and his fingertips bruising the backs of my thighs, Zabriel mutters, "That's my good Omega. Alpha is going to fuck himself a little deeper..."

There's an ominous crack, but Zabriel doesn't notice.

I glance up at the ceiling. While we've been lost in each other, the fire has spread and it's rapidly engulfing the building.

I gasp and clutch his shoulders. "Zabriel, the fire."

"It won't hurt you. I told you, I am the—"

There's another crack, louder this time. The roof splits open and a river of sparks cascades toward us. Panic shoots through me and I scream.

Zabriel throws himself over me, curling me into a ball beneath his chest and wrapping his arms around my head to protect me from the falling embers. I can't see what's happening, but I hear Zabriel gasp as something thuds against his back. The scent of burning and my Alpha in pain fills my nose. I can't do anything or see anything. I'm helpless as I cower beneath his broad chest.

Zabriel might be the fire, but he's not invincible.

With a roar, Zabriel scoops me into his arms and, still curled protectively around me, leaps to his feet and runs. I can't breathe. Smoke and panic sting my eyes.

We burst from the burning building into the night air and I drag deep, panicked breaths into my lungs. "Are you all right?"

"Scourge is coming," is all Zabriel says, still running in the darkness. Still carrying me despite his injuries.

He leaps off the precipice and into the abyss.

I open my mouth to scream.

There's a rushing sound and a jolt, and I realize we've landed on Scourge's back and the dragon is racing toward the ground. Scourge lands in a canyon between the sheer walls of the bluff, and I can just make out Zabriel in the moonlight as he painfully carries me to the ground. Scourge makes a panicked grunting sound.

When we're standing next to Scourge, Zabriel hunts my naked body for burns before pulling my dress over my head. He must have scooped it up off the ground along with me. "Did any spark catch you? I'm so sorry, *sha'len*. I shouldn't have let that happen. You're afraid of fire."

I was afraid of fire. In the arms of the Flame King, I'm not afraid of anything except losing him. I reach up and touch his face. "Don't worry about me. Let me see if you're hurt."

I step behind him and see that there are blisters covering his back. Angry red blisters. Even more alarming, there are charred black blisters. His flesh seems burned down to the bone, and my eyes fill with panicked tears. I've seen a child die after tripping into a basin of scalding water. Zabriel is much stronger than a child, but these are the kind of burns that can kill a grown man. He could go into shock at any moment.

"Zabriel, don't move, you're hurt."

"I'm fine," he insists, turning to face me, and the movement makes him wince. The pain is so bad that his eyelashes flutter and he has to press his hand against Scourge to steady himself.

Then he falls to his knees and sways.

I give a cry of shock and peer around in the darkness. Where even are we? "Don't move. I'll get help. The *Hratha'len* will know how to help you."

"There's no need," Zabriel gasps. Despite his assurances, his face contorts in pain and sweat covers his brow. "You shouldn't be alone in the dark. Wait—"

"Stay here. Don't move."

I get up and run along the canyon, dodging around boulders, the only thought in my mind is getting help for my mate. I should have insisted we leave the building. Zabriel is in a rut and he needed me, and he got hurt.

Some way off in the distance, I think I hear Esmeral call to me, and I follow the sound.

As I run toward the dragongrounds, I'm suddenly enveloped in darkness. It drops over me like a heavy velvet cloak. I slow to a halt, staring around me with wide eyes. I can't see a thing, and the only sound is my ragged breathing.

Another vision? Now? I don't want this when Zabriel

needs me. I blink and shake my head like I've got water stuck in my ear canal, hoping to clear my mind.

When I open my eyes, something is just visible across the ocean of darkness. A figure is walking toward me. A tall, familiar figure with long, dark hair, a strong jaw, and captivating eyes. His clothing is like nothing I've ever seen him wear before, but I'm too distracted by the strangeness of seeing him so suddenly.

My heart is in my mouth. "Zabriel? Is that you?"

The tall, muscular man stops before me and studies me with sad eyes. "Do you not know your mate?"

Fear seizes me. "Of course, but you're not dead, are you? I just left you with Scourge."

"I just wanted to see you one last time." He smiles crookedly at me, a smile filled with sadness. For a moment he holds his breath, and then lets it out in a great rush and shakes his head. "That will have to be enough. I wish..."

He sighs and turns away, and the darkness begins to fold over him.

I reach for him, a sob rising in my chest. "Wait. What do you mean one last time? Please don't die. The burns..."

"I'm not dead." He glances over his shoulder at me. "Not yet."

Those two words fill me with desolation. "You're going to be fine. I'm going to fetch the *Hratha'len*. You can't die from burns. You're the Flame King." My voice cracks and tears spill down my cheeks.

"You're right. Burns won't finish me off. I won't die today."

Fear is revolving in my chest. "Meaning you are going to die? What are you not telling me?"

He turns back to me with a soft, sad smile. "You're falling

in love with him, aren't you? That means I'm too late. I don't blame you for this, Isavelle. I blame myself. I fought my way through to you once for a few seconds and then I couldn't again until just now."

If this is Zabriel, then why is he talking about himself as another person? Why does he look like he's another person? Now that I look closer, his eyes are blue gray. His hair is dark brown.

I press my lips together and shake my head. If my other vision about my family was false, then this one might be a trick as well. "I don't believe that you're real."

The man gives a short, humorless laugh. "Well, you're right, in a way. Can you guess why I look like this?"

"This is how you looked before you bonded with Scourge. How I saw you all those weeks ago." Visions aren't supposed to look back at me or talk back to me. If this isn't a vision, then what's happening?

"I knew you were clever." His mouth quirks in a smile, but then the smile vanishes, and his expression grows bleak. "I'm not going to survive, Isavelle. Being the Flame King is a target on my back. I wanted to see you one last time with my own eyes. Not Scourge's eyes. I don't think I'll be strong enough to return to you ever again, so this is goodbye." He gives me one long, final look, and then turns away, his head bowed.

I don't understand what's happening, but seeing my mate walk away from me is the most distressing thing I've ever seen. Losing Zabriel would rip my heart out. "Don't say that. We all need you. *I* need you. You told me that you want to be the best king you can be, and I won't believe that you're just going to give up."

The man stops and glances at me over his shoulder. "I'm

not the Flame King. This is me speaking to you as Zabriel. Purely Zabriel. Only Zabriel." He hesitates and turns toward me. "Am I not enough for you like this? Is it him you really want?"

"Him who?"

"The Flame King. Scourge. The Alpha and his dragon. Look." He pulls the corner of his mouth back from his teeth and runs his tongue over them. He has no dragines.

I shake my head, confused. Zabriel is the Flame King, and he and Scourge are intertwined. I'm not choosing. Those two are meant for each other, as I am meant for Zabriel.

"Being Maledinni is a gift and a curse, and so is being the Flame King," the man explains. "You mean so much to me. The real me. I can't help but wish that I could be just a man and you could be my bride. You've wished for the same thing. I know you have."

Do you remember when I was Isavelle, the village girl, and you were Commander Zabriel, a soldier who rides a dragon?

I nibble on my lower lip, watching the man. His expression is so sad. So lost. He has the air of a man who has given up. Almost.

"Have you ever wondered why you saw me when you were fleeing from the Flame King?" the man asks softly.

Only a thousand times. It's something that's puzzled me, that I should meet Zabriel and be visited by the dragonless version of him on the same day. Is this like the oils I was given? One to hide him, and one to reveal him?

Is this another choice I must make?

The man holds out his hand. "Touch me. I'm real."

How can he be real when the real Zabriel is badly burned and waiting for me to get help? His large, strong hand has none of the calluses that Zabriel bears from dragonriding and wielding a sword. This Zabriel doesn't have to fight for his life and his people. This Zabriel isn't going to die.

I stare at his hand.

Then I look into his face.

Impatience is darkening his eyes. It's there for a fraction of a second, and then he smothers it with gentle longing.

Impatience? From Zabriel, who painstakingly waited weeks and weeks for his mate to finally realize that we belong together? Impatience from a man who continuously denied himself pleasure because he knew I wasn't ready for intimacy, even when I was lost in a false heat and begging for his knot? From a man who stood outside my door and comforted me with his voice after I panicked and threw him out? Zabriel waited five hundred years for me. Zabriel could wait five hundred more if it means that I give myself to him willingly.

This isn't Zabriel.

I step back from this impostor with a sharp cry, but it's too late. He snatches hold of my wrist and his cold, brutal fingers dig into my flesh. His longing morphs into vindictive cruelty, and panic bolts through my body.

Somewhere beyond the darkness, Esmeral screams. The sound vanishes in a split second as I'm yanked through something cold and resisting, and then stumble and open my eyes. The man is standing before me, an expression of triumph on his face as he grips my wrist.

We're in a castle room that I don't recognize, and the landscape beyond the window isn't Lenhale.

I start to tremble in fear, and ask in a shaking voice, "Where are we?"

"The veil turns the moonlight pretty colors from this side, don't you think?" the man asks in a mocking voice.

What does he mean, from this side? Sure enough, the moon is glistening green and purple in the sky instead of pure silver. Are we on the other side of the barrier? Has he transported me here somehow? I try to run for the door, but the stranger is holding tight to my wrist.

"Who are you? *Let go of me.*"

A glacial smile transforms this man's face, making him into something far more monstrous than anything I've seen before. He suddenly yanks me against his chest and seethes in my face, "Why, Isavelle. I'm hurt. My name is Emmeric. Didn't Zabriel ever tell you he has a brother?"

"You're dead. You died hundreds of years ago."

"Zabriel tried to kill me, him and that white-haired prick, Stesha, but they couldn't find me."

"You hid like a coward. You raped your sister, you monster."

Emmeric lets go of my wrist and strikes me across the face. I'm knocked to the ground, pain burning in my cheek. He glances at his own hand with distaste. "That was unpleasant. I don't like to sully myself with violence, not when someone else is so eager to do it for me." He glances toward the door to where a figure stands in the shadows. "There's someone I want to reacquaint you with, Isavelle. An old friend who's been missing you very much."

The figure steps forward, and I see he has a silver and black beard just visible beneath a familiar cowl and he's holding a birch rod in one hand. My blood turns to ice.

The loathsome, familiar voice of the High Priest intones, "There you are, girl. You have a sacred duty to perform, and this time there will be no dragons and Maledinni abominations to save you." He stands over me, his nostrils flaring. "You reek of lust and sex, you foul, disgusting girl."

I scramble to my feet and back away from him, wishing for Zabriel harder than I've wished for anything in my life. My mate has no idea where I am, and he could be dying at this very moment. Esmeral can't fly to my defense. Scourge isn't coming to save me. My breath comes faster and faster as I realize I'm all alone with two of the most cruel and violent men in Maledin, and they want nothing but suffering for me.

Emmeric's lip curls in disgust. "My brother has probably been rutting her, the animal that he is. Good Brethren girls should be ashamed to want a man to do such repulsive things to her. If she won't feel shame, then someone will have to make her feel it. Don't you think so, High Priest?"

The High Priest steps toward me, his eyes flashing with hate as he lifts the birch rod high over his head. "I do think so, Your Majesty. On your knees, girl. This time, my hand will deliver your punishment, and I won't stop until you're screaming your repentance."

Thank you for reading The Flame King's Captive. If you enjoyed this book, please consider leaving a review on Amazon and Goodreads.

ACKNOWLEDGMENTS

This book would not have been possible without the love and support of many people. Thank you to Mr. Vincent for always being so proud and encouraging. Thank you to my beta readers Aly, Darlene, Edresa, Evva, and Liz Booker, who gave me the motivation to keep going with all their excitement and encouragement. Thank you to my amazing proofreder Rumi Khan, and to my editor Heather Fox. You are everything I could hope for and more, Heather. Thank you for loving my batshit men as much as I do, from Lorenzo to Zabriel and beyond.

BOOKS BY LILITH VINCENT

Chloe Chastaine is the alter ego of Lilith Vincent, who writes steamy mafia romance with dark themes, bad men, sweet heroines, and breeding. Please always read the trigger warnings.

Steamy Reverse Harem

THE PROMISED IN BLOOD SERIES (complete)

First Comes Blood

Second Comes War

Third Comes Vengeance

THE PAGEANT DUET (complete)

Pageant

Crowned

Steamy MF Romance

THE BRUTAL HEARTS SERIES (ongoing)

Brutal Intentions

Brutal Conquest

ABOUT THE AUTHOR

Chloe Chastaine is the fantasy-loving alter ego of Lilith Vincent and an author of lush novels with OTT obsessed heroes and the strong but sweet heroines who bring them to their knees.

Printed in Great Britain
by Amazon

60323161R00288